Rhoda Broughton

Good-Bye, Sweetheart!

A novel

Rhoda Broughton

Good-Bye, Sweetheart!
A novel

ISBN/EAN: 9783337036225

Printed in Europe, USA, Canada, Australia, Japan

Cover: Foto ©Andreas Hilbeck / pixelio.de

More available books at **www.hansebooks.com**

"GOOD-BYE, SWEETHEART!"

A NOVEL.

BY

RHODA BROUGHTON,

AUTHOR OF

"COMETH UP AS A FLOWER;" "RED AS A ROSE IS SHE;" ETC., ETC.

NEW YORK:

D. APPLETON AND COMPANY,

549 & 551 BROADWAY.

1872.

"GOOD-BYE, SWEETHEART!"

A TALE IN THREE PARTS.

" Being so very wilful, you must go ! "

MORNING.

" The sleepless Hours, who watch me as I lie,
Curtained with star-enwoven canopies,
From the broad moonlight of the sky,
Fanning the busy dreams from my dim eyes,
Waken me when their mother, the gray Dawn,
Tells them that dreams and that the moon are gone ! "

CHAPTER I.

WHAT JEMIMA SAYS.

A KINGLY June day. The hay-smell drowning all other smells in every land of Christendom : battling even with the ingeniously ill odors of this little drainless Breton town. People who suffer from hay-fever are sneezing and blowing their noses ; all the world else is opening its nostrils wide. The small *salon* of a small French boarding-house—a narrow room, with a window at each end ; and, in this room, the two sisters, the two Misses Herrick.

Five minutes ago, the mistress of the establishment entered, and closed the *persiennes* of one of our windows, to hinder the sun from *abîmer*-ing the *cretonne* curtains, as she said. She was about to follow suit with the other, and only desisted on our eager and impassioned representations that not even a Breton sun can shine from all points of the compass at once. Through the one casement thus left us, Lenore is leaning out—Lenore, our youngest-born, the show one of our family. On her elbows she is leaning, looking idly into the little grass-grown *place*, on which Mdlle. Leroux's *pension* gives. Jemima—I am Jemima—is making a listless reconnoitre of the furniture—the little cheap prints on the walls, "La Religieuse défendue," "Le Guerrier pansé," "Napoléon I., Empereur des Français;" one long fern frond and a single foxglove in a wineglass on the mantel-shelf; bare parquet, cold to the feet. Jemima is twenty-eight years of age, and very good-natured; at least, so people say. I have often noticed that the eldest of many families are, physically speaking, failures. Jemima is, physically speaking, a failure.

"How one misses one's five-o'clock tea!" says Lenore, looking back half over her shoulder to throw this and the succeeding remarks at me. "From ten-o'clock breakfast to six-o'clock dinner, what a dreary waste! How do you suppose the aborigines stave off the pangs of hunger, Jemima? Do they chew a quid of tobacco, or a piece of chalk, or what?"

I reply, laconically: "Biscuits."

"Does not your heart yearn for one of those open tarts with fresh strawberries we saw yesterday at the *pâtissier's* in the Rue de St.-Malo? Mine does. I wish I had asked Frederick to bring me one."

' "And do you imagine," ask I, sardonically, "that you have reduced that poor man to such a pitch of imbecility as to induce him to carry about jam-tarts in his coat-pocket for you?"

Lenore smiles; she has that very sweet smile which is, they say, the peculiar attribute of ill-tempered people.

"I think," she answers, "that he is not far from being on a level with Miss Armstrong's lover, who allowed her to dress him up as a sheep, and lead him by a blue ribbon into a room full of company."

Lenore's face is more round than oval; it is fresh as a bunch of roses gathered at sunrise—fresh, but not ruddy; her nose, though not in the least *retroussé*, belongs rather to the family of upward than that of downward tending noses; her eyes are gray, as are the eyes of nine-tenths of the Anglo-Saxon race, large, though not with the *owlified* largeness of a "Book of Beauty," wherein each eye is double the size of the prim purse-mouth; in her two cheeks are two dimples that, when she is grave, one only suspects, but that, when she laughs or smiles, deepen into two little delicious pitfalls, to catch men's souls at unawares in.

"If Frederick were anybody but Frederick," say I, sinking into an arm-chair, and pulling out my knitting—like most failures, I'm fond of work—"it would be considered rather *risqué* of us two innocents, travelling about the Continent with a young man in our train, even though he is a clergyman."

"If Frederick," replies Lenore, contemptuously turning back to her contemplation of the *place*, and replacing her gray-gingham elbows on the sill, "were to be caught in the·most flagitious situation one can imagine, that Simon-Pure face of his would carry him triumphantly through. Who can connect the idea of immorality and spectacles? Talk of an angel, and you hear the rustle of wings; I hear Frederick's wings rustling through the Porte St.-Louis, and, oh! Jemima—Jemima, quick! come here! Who is it he has with him?"

I jump up, as bidden—I always do what Lenore bids me, though I have the advantage, or rather disadvantage, of her by ten years—and look out.

"An Englishman, evidently," I say, sagaciously, "by his beard; nobody but Englishmen and oysters wear beards nowadays."

"Is he going to bring him up here?" asks Lenore, craning her neck out to look round the balcony of the *café* next door, where, as usual, two fat men are smoking and drinking coffee. "No; I see him nodding; he is saying good-bye; how tiresome!" (with an accent of disappointment).

"You are as bad as the young lady in Nixon's 'Cheshire Prophecy,'" say I, laughing: "'Mother, mother, I have seen a man!'"

Frederick enters alone, looking very hot in the rigorous black of a priestly coat that grazes his heel, and the rigorous black of a priestly waistcoat that almost salutes his chin.

"Enter a pretty cockatoo!" cries my sister, with an insolent laugh, pointing the insult by indicating with her forefinger the curly flourish of fine fair hair that surmounts the young man's forehead and blue spectacles. "Pretty cockatoo!"

"You should not make personal remarks, Miss Leonora," answers Frederick, blushing.

"My name is not 'Leonora,'" retorts she, with a pout; "don't lengthen my two charming soft French syllables into that great long English mouthful, 'Leonora.'"

But Frederick is deeply diving into a pocket in the hinder part of his raiment. Thence he apparently draws a little *bonbonnière*.

"I have brought you some chocolate, Miss Lenore; that —that is why I called to-day. I—I think I once heard you say that you liked it."

"My dear cockatoo, I hate the sight of it!" replies she, gravely, with the utter and unconscious ingratitude of a spoiled child. "I ate it every day and at every confectioner's in Rouen last week; now, if it had been a strawberry tart—open, fresh strawberries; but it is not—give it to Jemima."

"Never mind her, Mr. West," say I, it being my pleasing life-task to mend the breaches made by Lenore in her adorer's feelings—I never having any breaches of my own to mend—"never mind her; but tell us who your new friend is; we have been on the *qui vive* ever since we saw you parting so tenderly under the arch."

"Do you mean the man that came with me to-day as far as the Porte?" asks Frederick, who has sat down upon the music-stool, and is turning slowly round and round, in order to be able to follow with his spectacles Lenore into whatever part of the little room her measured walk may take her. "But, indeed, he is no friend of mine," he adds, uneasily—"no friend at all; a mere acquaintance—a college acquaintance."

"What is his name?" inquire I, nibbling a stick of Lenore's despised chocolate, and asking the question more for the sake of something to say than from any particular interest in the subject.

"Le Mesurier."

"Hem! a good name, isn't it? And what is he doing here?"

"He is making a walking-tour through Brittany with a friend; the friend has gone for two or three days to stay at the Marquis de Roubillon's *château* near Dol, and Le Mesurier is to wait for him here."

"Where is he staying at?"

"The Hôtel de la Poste."

"And why did not you bring him up here with you, pray?" asks Lenore, joining in the conversation, and throwing herself indolently on the little hard horse-hair sofa as she speaks.

"Because he would not come," answers Frederick, quickly, and I think I detect a glance of malicious triumph in his voice.

Lenore reddens. "I dare say you never gave him the chance."

"On the contrary, I said to him, 'I am going to make a call on some ladies at Mdlle. Leroux's *pension;* will you come, too? I do not doubt that they would be very happy to make your acquaintance;' and he said—stay, let me think, I know he worded it very strongly—'Good God! No! one has enough of women in England.'"

"Interesting misogynist!" says Lenore, ironically. "What a sweet—what a holy task it would be to bring him to a healthier frame of mind!"

"I don't really think he would suit you, Miss Lenore," says Frederick, nervously, making the music-stool squeak painfully as he fidgets upon it; "he has a way of saying more coolly impertinent things to ladies, in a quiet way, than any man I ever came across."

Lenore jumps up into a sitting posture, and a mischievous, tormenting look flashes into her laughing gray eyes.

"My dear Frederick, how you excite me! After hearing nothing but how charming I am, from you and such as you, how refreshing to be told impertinent plain truths, in a quiet way, too—I like the quiet way, there's something shy and contraband about it—by a handsome woman-hater —I'm sure he must be handsome—in a reddish beard!"

"He is a man of any thing but a good character," says Frederick, lowering his voice, as if the subject he was broaching were one not fit for ladies' ears; "at least, he was not at Oxford."

Lenore springs to her feet.

"Frederick!" she says, impressively, "you have decided me; I *wish* to see him!"

"I don't quite see how, Lenore," say I, still nibbling. "Magnificently as you always affect to despise the shackles of conventionality, you can hardly force your acquaintance upon a poor man who has distinctly declined it."

Lenore's two hands are clasped behind her back, as she stands before us. Suddenly she stretches out one of them to Frederick.

"I don't care," she says, with a little emphatic stamp; "I bet you half a crown that before nightfall I have seen him!"

"You know I never bet, Miss Lenore."

"Oh no! of course not," drawing herself up very stiffly, and affecting to button a high, double-breasted waistcoat; "sacred calling—injurious example to flock, etc., etc."

"Never mind her," say I, recurring to my usual formula of soothing; "don't you know that ever since that unlucky attack of croup she had when she was a child, when the doctor said she was not to be contradicted, and was to do whatever she liked, that Lenore has never been fit to speak to?"

"If you see Le Mesurier," says Frederick, not heeding my blandishments, and getting rather pink with exasperation, "it will be against *his* will."

"Very likely, but I shall see him!"

"He is always bored by the society of respectable women; he never makes any secret of it."

"What an uncharitable remark for a clergyman to make! Every amiable trait you mention heightens my interest in him. Well, I shall see him."

"Good-bye, Miss Herrick," cries Frederick, vaulting off his stool, which at parting gives one last, worst valedictory squeak, and picking up his soft dumpling hat—"good-bye, Miss Lenore!"

"Good-bye, sweetheart, good-bye," replies Lenore, rhetorically. "If you are going to the Hôtel de la Poste—do not, however, put yourself out of the way on my account—but if you are going there, you may tell our mutual friend to expect me about four."

Two minutes later the front-door closes on Mr. West, and I hear my sister running down-stairs, and calling "Stéphanie, Stéphanie!" at the top of her fresh, gay voice. Stéphanie is the *Breton femme de chambre.*

CHAPTER II.

WHAT THE AUTHOR SAYS.

LENORE'S bed-room: over the papered walls, a design of blue pea-flowers and giant asters, straggling quaintly, yet prettily: a small bed in a little recess curtained off; a wash-hand basin as big as a broth-bowl, and a ewer as big as a cream-jug; a minute, dim looking-glass hung exactly where it is impossible to get any thing more than a suggestion of one's own face in it. Before this glass two women are standing, Lenore and Stéphanie; the first is looking at herself; the second is looking at the first. Lenore is no longer an English lady; she is a Breton peasant. Her waist is girt about with a heavy black woollen petticoat, gathered into so many great folds at the back and sides as to make her look as wide-hipped as the weather-beaten countrywomen beside her; a gay little purple shawl-handkerchief pinned over her broad chest. Lenore is a fine woman, not a chicken-breasted pretty slip of a girl; and on her head (from which the chignon has disappeared) she is struggling, with dubious success, to arrange a head-dress similar to that worn by her companion.

"Oh, que mademoiselle est adroite!" cries the latter, with the awful mendacity of a Frenchwoman, when any contest between truth and civility is concerned ; standing, with her hands on the broad hips that Nature or her petticoat-plaits have given her, looking on.

"Mademoiselle is not *adroite* at all," cries Lenore, impatiently, recklessly mingling together the Gothic and Anglo-Saxon tongues. "*Au contraire,* she is very *maladroite ; coiffezmoi,* Stéphanie, *je vous en prie,*" sitting down on a chair, and letting her handsome awkward hands fall idle into her lap.

A Breton cap off is one thing—it is merely a straight piece of well-stiffened muslin or net; on, it is quite a different matter. Stéphanie having, for a space of about two minutes, arranged, and pinned, and tied, bursts into a cascade of shrill French laughter.

"Mon Dieu ! but mademoiselle has a droll air ! Mademoiselle will pardon her; but, dame, it makes one *pâmer de rire !* "

Lenore rises, and putting her face close to the dark mirror, with its disfiguring side-lights, surveys her changed countenance with eager solemnity. A little border of nut-brown hair, emerging from the crisp white muslin ; the broad, stiff lappets, turned up and back, and secured with a pin on the crown, making a huge loop at each side of the head. Why describe what every one knows—that most piquant of head-gears that the wise Breton peasantry have not yet abandoned in favor of the mock lace and tawdry cheap flowers of our own lower orders ?

"Je suis belle, n'est ce pas ? " she asks, a little doubtfully, peeping over her own shoulder at the grave round beauty of her anxious peach-face.

"Oh, mademoiselle est belle à ravir ! Ça va à merveille ; on ne peut mieux, etc., etc."

"But my hands are too white," breaks in Lenore, stemming the torrent of encomium. "What will you sell me your nice red fingers for half an hour for ? Except on the stage, too, I suppose a peasant-woman does not wear rings " (slipping them off on the wash-hand-stand—dressing-table there is none). " Well " (with a parting glance), " I think I am unrecognizable, am I not, Stéphanie ? I should not know myself if I met myself in a shop-window."

As she passes the *salon* door, Lenore peeps in. " Do you know me, Jemima?" Jemima gives a great start, and her knitting rolls down unheeded on the parquet:

" Why, Lenore, child, what have you been doing to yourself? What a fright you look! Where are you going ? "

" To the Hôtel de la Poste," answers Lenore, shutting the door briskly, and running down-stairs very quickly to avoid questions and remonstrances.

It is but a five-minutes' walk from Mdlle. Leroux's to the Hôtel de la Poste; but in five minutes there is plenty of time for courage to ooze out at fingers' ends. Lenore's feet, which at first, despite her heavy peasant-boots, bore her along quickly enough, subside into a very lagging walk. Her bravery is considerably cooled by the time she reaches her destination. An old shabby diligence is standing in the street; on a bench, beside the hotel-door, three men in blue blouses are sitting drinking cider; in the door-way, a disengaged *garçon*, with a napkin under his arm.

" Est a que c'est ici l'Hôtel de la Poste ? " asks Lenore, almost timidly, her question being rendered rather superfluous by the fact of the hotel bearing its name in yard-long letters on its front.

" Oui, madame. Madame est Anglaise?" with a surprised glance at her dress.

" Yes, madame is English. Is there much company here now ? "

" Ça commence, madame."

" Are there any of my compatriots staying here ? "

" There are several, madame—a crowd, in fact."

" Did any of them arrive to-day ? "

" Two English messieurs arrived by the *voiture* from Caulnes. If madame wishes, she can see their *malles qu'on va monter*," pointing inward to a heap of portmanteaus and hat-boxes.

Madame enters and inspects them.

" And where is *this* monsieur ? " she asks, pointing with her finger to a small and battered portmanteau, bearing the name of " Paul le Mesurier, Esq.," in large white letters upon it.

" That monsieur is in the *salle ;* he has commanded some cognac and a siphon."

As he speaks a second garçon emerges from the unseen, bearing a small tray with the identical refreshments indicated upon it. By a sudden impulse Lenore runs forward to meet him.

" Would it be permitted," she asks, coloring furiously, " for *her* to take that into the salle ? "

" Mais oui, madame, si ça vous convient."

They both stare at her ; one laughs. If she had been by herself *now*, at this last moment, she would have set down the tray and fled ; but retreat is cut off by the first garçon politely throwing open the salle-door. With trembling knees and a galloping heart, Miss Lenore enters.

A long room and a long table laid for any number of people ; bottles of *vin ordinaire*, napkins, covered dishes full of emptiness, tooth-pick stands, pots of mangy hydrangeas and geraniums down the middle ; a little clergyman with falling shoulders that would not have disgraced a woman or a champagne-bottle—Frederick, in fact—studying an *Indicateur* in one of the windows. Another gentleman at the table, with the back of his head and a suspicion of lion-colored beard emerging from the sheets of *Gali-gnani.*

As noiselessly as her great clodhopping boots will per-mit, Miss Herrick approaches the latter and deposits his cognac at his elbow. But in so doing her hand trembles so much that she knocks down a fork and spoon, which fall with a clink on the floor. As she stoops to pick them up, and as he lifts his eyes, rather irritated at the noise, their glances meet. In Lenore's there is a mixture of expres-sions: shame, defiance, and, above all, and before all, disap-pointment; for, after all, this interesting, woman-hating *roué* is not handsome; by no one but the mother who bore him could he ever have been thought even good-looking. In the stranger's look there is nothing but extreme surprise—nay, astonishment. Glad, despite herself, to have got off so cheaply, Lenore is beating a hasty retreat, when Le Mesurier's voice overtakes her.

"I say! Marie! Julie! Marion! Hi! What the deuce is the French for *hi?* Call her back, West. I have tried all the names I know; they are generally all Maries, but she won't answer to that."

"Do you want any thing?" asks Frederick, looking up innocently from his *Indicateur* with that beamingly-be-nevolent look that spectacles always give.

But his friend, excited by the pursuit of a pretty face, has precipitated himself toward the door, which is left ajar, and, passing quickly through it, finds himself face to face with the object of his search, who, not having had presence of mind to take refuge in flight, is standing there with her empty tray—red, guilty, and beautiful.

"West, West! What's the French for 'What is your name?' Do they grow them like this here? Because, if so, we had better import a few. *Comment vous appellez-vous, ma chère?*" trying to take her hand.

"What *do* you mean?" cries the girl, in very good English, snatching it away, totally forgetting her assumed character, and looking daggers at the insolent wretch who had dared to call her "*ma chère.*"

"Are you English?" asks Le Mesurier, aghast, recoiling a step or two, and his mouth opening in horror as the thought of the admiring familiarities he has just been giving utterance to darts across his brain.

At the sound—hardly credited—of a too well-known voice, Mr. West has thrown down his *Indicateur*, and comes running to the scene of action.

"Miss Lenore!"

She looks up at him—a dare-devil light in her eyes—resolute, now that the *dénouement* has come, to brave it out.

"Did monsieur call?"

"Miss Lenore, are you *mad?*"

She stretches out her hand to him:

"Who was right? I have won my half crown; pay it me."

Le Mesurier turns from one to the other in blank astonishment:

"I say, West, what is it all about; what is the joke?"

"You had better ask this lady."

"There is no joke, none," says the girl, looking at him archly, but growing crimson. "I came here to see you. I put on this dress to avoid being recognized; I have failed, that is all."

"To see *me!* I am sure I am immensely flattered" (looking excessively surprised, and biting his lips hard to repress a broad smile); "but are you sure that you are not mistaking me for some one else?"

"It was not that I cared in the least to see you," she says, frowning, and tears of shame rushing to her eyes.

"Of course not ; of course not ! " bowing.

" But when I say that I will do a thing, however foolish, I always do it."

" An excellent rule to go through life with," replies he, gravely, still fighting with a laugh; "but there are difficulties sometimes in the way of putting it into practice, are there not ? "

" Miss Lenore, Miss Lenore," says Frederick, the veins in his forehead swelling, and all his little pink features working with nervous vexation, " will you allow me to see you home ? If we walk very fast—it is not an hour when there are many people about—perhaps you will not be recognized."

"I don't in the least care if I am recognized," answers Lenore, stoutly.   " I have done nothing to be ashamed of."

As she passes out, Le Mesurier holds open the door and bows formally and solemnly; and through the Place Duguesclin and the Fossé Miss Herrick carries the recollection of a rather ugly tanned face, in which she conjectures the contempt that does not appear—carries away with her also the pleasant consciousness of having made an utter and unladylike fool of herself, without the poor consolation of having done it amusingly.

" ' Girl of the Period ! ' " says Paul to himself, thrusting his hands into his coat-pockets as he watches her departure through the lowered Venetian blinds ; " after all, the *Saturday* does not overcolor; from all such, ' Good Lord deliver us ! ' "

CHAPTER III.

AT our *pension* we dine at six; it is a small and select establishment; at present it contains only two families: *la famille Lange*, and *la famille Erreeck*. We are *la famille Erreeck*. *La famille Lange* is French, as may be imagined from its name. It consists of a mother, son, and daughter. The mother is a handsome, black-haired widow, mourning jovially for the four-months'-dead M. Lange, in uncovered head and huge jet rosary. Mdlle. Péroline deplores her papa, in white muslin, lilac ribbons, and a wonderful mop of little frizzled curls and rolls. M. César is a youth with an eye-glass, which is forever dropping out of his right eye—a youth tall of stature, and spotted like the pard. We are all dining together as sociably as their total ignorance of our tongue, and our very partial acquaintance with theirs, will permit. Through the open window, in the still yellow evening, we hear plainly the clump of *sabots* in the *place;* the voices, as often as not English or Irish—for Dinan, as is well known, swarms with both—of the passers-by.

There are but few disadvantageous circumstances in this world that have not also their advantageous side; and the fact of our being the only people in the house that understand the English tongue, enables my sister and me to impart our opinions concerning the company and the viands to each other with a freedom which, to a stranger entering unacquainted with the posture of affairs, would seem startlingly candid.

" I wish they would let us have our potatoes *with* our *bifteck*, as they call it, instead of afterward and separate, as a side-dish," say I, grumblingly, being hopelessly John-Bullish in my culinary tastes.

"Look at this nasty fellow!" rejoins Lenore, with a disgusted intonation, directing my attention to her neighbor, M. César, who, with his napkin tucked under his chin, is holding the bone of his mutton-cutlet in his hand, and gnawing it. "Do you suppose, Mima, that French *gentlemen* worry their food in such a cannibalish fashion, or is it a manner and custom confined to *bourgeois* like these?"

My reply is strangled in its birth by the unconscious Madame Lange, who, interrupting for a moment her succulent employment of chasing the gravy round her tilted plate with a crust, inquires, with some volubility, whether mademoiselle has made a promenade to-day? Doubtlessly mademoiselle has already visited Fontaine des Eaux, and Lehon, and the Saint-Esprit—an object, in fact, truly remarkable?

My French never was my strong point, even in schooldays; and the waste of many immense years that have elapsed since my education was completed, has not tended to make it stronger. I answer, stoutly:

" Non — pas — aujourdhui — très — chaud;" and look piteously across to my junior for succor. But Lenore is still disdainfully eying the innocent M. César and his mutton-bone.

"Mademoiselle is right; there has been a *chaleur épouvantable ;* in truth, she herself has been *très souffrante* all day; she has had *mal au cœur.* My children, however, César and Péroline, have been to play at the croquet, with the Demoiselles Smeet and the Demoiselles Ammeelton; César loves the croquet; is it not so, my friend?"

" Mais oui, maman!"

I try to say in French that croquet is the best game that ever was invented for bringing the two sexes together

—a trite and pedantic remark at best—and, failing to make myself understood, relapse into silence, feeling rather small, and resolving henceforth for evermore to cleave to the vulgar tongue. Lenore laughs malignantly, but does not help me. M. César, having eaten a huge strawberry-mash, and more white-heart cherries than the rest of the company put together, pushes back his chair, and requests to be permitted to retire to make his toilet for a promenade *à cheval.*

On the occasion of M. César's making a promenade *à cheval,* we are all expected to group ourselves at the salon windows to watch him, as, in lavender gloves and cream-colored trousers, he caracoles a little, a very little—for M. César knows that discretion is the better part of valor—under our admiring eyes. His mamma, meanwhile, is wont to retire into a corner of the room, cover her face with her handkerchief, and cry.

As he passes by her now, she catches his hand: "Great Heaven! César, take care that that wicked animal does not overturn thee!"

"Fear not, mamma," replies César, doughtily. "I will be careful."

"Imagine an Englishman contemplating the possibility of parting company with his horse, while ambling along the king's highway!" says Lenore, scornfully. "Hush!" (with heightened color and brightened eyes)—"is not that the hall-door bell?"

She runs to the window and looks out.

"It is Frederick, of course, isn't it?" I ask, finishing my last cherry.

"Yes."

"Anybody with him?"

"*Anybody with him!* of course not! Who should there be?" replies my sister tartly, from which, being a person of very superior intelligence, I concluded that Lenore expected somebody. We go up to the salon to receive our guest, and Lenore, contrary to her usual custom, runs to meet him with outstretched hand, and without any of her usual insults to his hair, his gait, or his physique generally.

"Well, Frederick!" she cries, eagerly, and, as it seems to me, expectantly.

"Well, Miss Lenore!" replies Frederick, growing purple to the ears, as he always does, when his idol flings him a brace of careless words.

"Don't say 'Well, Miss Lenore!'" retorts my sister, angrily; "it does irritate one so. Have you nothing to say?—nothing to tell me?"

"Nothing to tell you?" echoes Frederick, bewildered, and again lapsing into his former offence. "Why, it is such a very short time since we parted, that it is not likely I can have very much to relate."

Lenore turns away with an ill-tempered movement of head and shoulder, and, walking to the window, looks out. M. César is kissing his lavender gloves repeatedly. Madame Lange is screaming out shrill cautions to her son not to be too audacious. Mdlle. Leroux—an adorable old creature, in yellow cap and luxuriant gray beard—is waving her pocket-handkerchief, and crying, "Au revoir! M. César, au revoir!" Lenore does not appear to perceive any of them.

"I suppose," says Mr. West, addressing me, but glancing timidly toward the window, "that you have heard of Miss Lenore's—*adventure?* I am really in hopes that we shall be able to keep it quite quiet—*quite* quiet. Le Mesurier fortunately knows no one here, and we luckily met no one but Mr. Stevens on our way home, and I don't think he saw us."

"If he did see us," says my sister, turning round her face again, ornamented with a rather grim smile, "I would not give much for your character in Dinan by to-morrow, Frederick. You will be *affiché* all over the town as having been parading about, in broad daylight, arm-in-arm with a *bonne*. I asked you to give me your arm on purpose; do you know, Mima" (beginning to laugh), "we came toddling along so affectionately, like a pair of cits out on a Sunday afternoon?"

"You forget that I saw you coming through the Porte," reply I, with severity; "and indeed, Lenore, when next you take it into your head to play a practical joke, I sincerely hope that it may be a more amusing and less unladylike one."

"Why did you tell us your friend was handsome?" asks Lenore, abruptly, without paying the slightest attention to me.

"I did not say so, Miss Leonora; you said so yourself!"

"*I said so myself!* Why, how could I? I had seen nothing but the back of his neck."

"You said you were sure he must be handsome."

"Well, the wisest of us are liable to error," replies my sister, leaning her folded arms on the back of my chair, and gazing calmly over my head at Mr. West. "In that case I certainly erred egregiously; he is *hideous*, 'laid à faire peur,' as Mdlle. Péroline humorously remarked of you the other day."

"In that case, Miss Leonora," replies Frederick, worked up into something like spirit, as I am glad to perceive, by her rudeness, "there does not seem to be very much love lost between you!"

Lenore blushes angrily. "Has he been expressing his disapprobation of me to you?" she asks quickly; "is it the last new thing in manners to abuse people to their

most intimate friends?   If so, commend me to the manner-
less *sans-culottes*."

"I wish you would not get into the habit, Lenore, of
loading your conversation with French phrases ; it reminds
me so much of the *Journal des Demoiselles*."

This I say in the weak effort to turn the conversation
into a new channel ; meanwhile I endeavor to signal " danger ! " to Mr. West, cough, and wave the white flag ; but,
as he is not looking at or thinking of me, it is all in vain.

"I don't think he had any idea that I was so much
atta—, so intimate, I mean, with you and Miss Jemima, as
I am," replies Frederick, earnestly.   "Indeed, Miss Lenore,
I must do him that justice."   -

"Who cares whether he has justice done him or not ? "
cries Lenore, impatiently ; " what did he say ? what did he
say ?"

"It really would not at all amuse you, Miss Lenore "
(nervously kneading his soft hat) ; " on the contrary, I am
afraid it would make you very angry."

"You may as well tell me at once," says my sister,
composedly sitting down on an arm-chair and folding her
hands in her lap, " because you shall never leave this room
alive, if you don't ! "

"Well, since you insist upon it—please, Miss Jemima "
(turning piteously to me), " please, Miss Jemima, bear witness that it is not my fault—that Miss Lenore has brought
it on herself—he said—I dare say he did not mean it—that
—that—he could not have believed that any English lady
could have lowered herself to such an extent as to do such
a thing ! "

The blush on Lenore's face grows painful—spreads even
to her soft, creamy throat.

"Oh, indeed ! Any thing more ? "

"He said," pursues Frederick, deceived by the apparent quietness with which his hearer takes the unflattering comments made upon her, " that if he had ever caught his sister playing such a trick he would never have spoken to her again as long as he lived."

" Oh, indeed! what a loss for her! Any thing more?"

" He said he did not doubt that you were very good fun, if one went in for that sort of thing, but that you were not his style."

" Not his style! am I not?" cries Lenore, rising suddenly from her chair, quivering from head to foot with passion; "and what is his style, pray? Whatever it is, thank Heaven that I am not like it! Frederick, I wonder that you are not ashamed to insult me by repeating such speeches.— Jemima" (turning eagerly to me), "you can have no conception how ugly he is; I only wish you could see him. Little eyes like a pig's, and a huge nose, and such a villanous expression! What a fool I am to care what he says! I don't care—it amuses me immensely— ha, ha! Wretch! I wish he was dead!"

And to prove how little she cares, she bursts into a tempest of tears, rushes out of the room, and bangs the guiltless door behind her.

" There, Mr. West," say I, not without a certain sombre triumph, "perhaps you will pay some attention to me next time." And I rise with dignity, and, shaking out my brown-holland dress, prepare to follow and comfort my afflicted relative. As I reach the door I canon against Madame Lange.

" Péroline, Péroline! where art thou, dear friend? come and try thy new body.—Pardon, mademoiselle, a thousand pardons!"

CHAPTER IV.

WHAT LENORE SAYS.

"To the day of my death I shall always hate Stéphanie," says Lenore, lamentably, sitting leaning her elbows on the little round table in the middle of her bedroom, having broken off suddenly in the writing of a letter, to thrust her hands in among her crisp, untidy hair, and give way to a fit of angry despondence; "if I had not seen her going clacking about the house in that linsey petticoat and that vile cap" (nodding her head to where the unlucky garments are lying on her bed), "it never would have entered my head to make a mountebank of myself."

"If I were you," I replied severely, in answer to this jeremiad, "I should buy the whole suit from her, lay it up by me, and look at it whenever I next felt inclined to make a fool of myself."

"It would not do badly for a fancy ball," says Lenore, with a sudden change of tone, from the lachrymose to the lively, rising briskly from her chair, and walking toward the bed; "much more piquant than the everlasting Fires and Waters, Nights and Days, Louis Quartorzes, and Marie Stuarts, that one is so sick of; I never yet knew a very ugly woman go to a fancy ball that she did not go as Mary Queen of Scots." An austere silence on my part. "I have a good mind to try" (with considerable cheerfulness of tone). "I must get Stéphanie to give me lessons in the art of arranging the cap. Let me see; how did it go? It looked quite simple." Still, silence on my part. "One thing is certain, one would be quite unique; one would not run the risk of meeting one's double."

"I should not have thought," say I, stiffly, unwilling

that the wholesome lesson my sister has learned should so soon be forgotten; "I should not have thought that your associations with that costume were so pleasant that you would be in any hurry to put it on again."

She covers her face with her hands: "How brutal of you to remind me of it, just when I had succeeded in directing my thoughts from it for a moment!" I say nothing. "You know, Jemima, I had meant it to be just a spirited little freak; and it all fell so flat, so tame. Pah! it is a thing that one could not think of without blushing, if one were in a dark room by one's self, with the shutters shut."

"I should think not."

"Shall I ever forget," cried Lenore, drawing away her hands from her crimson face, and clasping them together— "shall I ever forget my feelings, as Frederick and I sneaked out together, and *he* held open the door so ceremoniously for us? If he had had any good feeling he would have laughed, would not he, Mima? If he had not been a monster, he would have tried to look as if he thought it a good joke, but he did not; he was as grave— as grave as I am now, which is putting it as strongly as I possibly can."

"Frederick told you that he hated respectable women," say I, gravely; "so that his want of cordiality was, at least, an indirect compliment." She stands with her eyes moodily downcast, but does not answer. "He evidently thought you respectable," I said, cheerfully—"*evidently;* that, at least, is a comfort, is not it? I don't see how he found it out; it must have been intuition."

Neither does this thrust move her to speech. I begin a fresh sentence. "Frederick said—"

"Frederick?" interrupts Lenore, impatiently stamping, and relieved at having found another object besides herself

2

to vent her rage on. "Little thought! If he had never been born, or if he had not been there, or if he had had sense enough to hold his tongue, it would have all gone off well enough, as I meant it: I should have seen Mr. Le Mesurier—not, Heaven knows" (with great contempt), "that he is the least worth seeing—and *he*—" She pauses.

"Well, what about *him* ?"

She draws in her breath, and her eyes flash spitefully: "If a wish could have killed him at that moment, as he stood there bowing and sneering, and saying that he was afraid there must be some mistake—he knew as well as I do that there was no mistake—he would have been as dead as a door-nail now!" She stops, breathes hard, and clinches, and again unclinches, her hand. "'I'm sure I'm immensely flattered. What is the joke next? An excellent plan, no doubt.'"

I hear her muttering over to herself these, as I conjecture, fragmentary speeches of her new acquaintance, while her cheeks grow ever more and more hotly red.

"Console yourself," I say, with vicarious philosophy. "I imagine that he did not hear your name; you were so thoroughly disguised by your dress that he probably would not recognize you if he met you; and the world is wide— we shall hardly be so unlucky as to happen upon him again."

"Do you think not?" answers Lenore, with hardly so much exhilaration of tone as might have been expected. "I don't know about that. Brittany is not so very large, and everybody goes to see the same places. His route will be pretty sure to be the same as ours—Morlaix, Quimper, Avray."

"We must hope to be either a few days before or a few days behind him at each place. There is no use in anticipating evils." A rather demurring silence. "Our great difficulty," I continue, cheerfully, " will be to avoid him as long as he remains here; but we must find out from Frederick every day in which direction he means to walk or drive, and take care to walk or drive in the opposite one."

" I shall do nothing of the kind!" cries Lenore, quickly. " You may please yourself. One's life would not be worth having if it were spent in dodging a person about a tiny place like this. As to meeting or not meeting, we must trust to chance; and, for my part, I should rather enjoy it than otherwise."

" In that case," reply I, sarcastically, " I would call again at the Hôtel de la Poste. Next time I would go as a garçon; it would be still more spirited."

" He could not have looked more scandalized than he did even if I had," replies Lenore, bursting into a short vexed laugh. " After all "—brightening up a little— " when I think of the things I might have done, and did not, the enormity of the thing I did dwindles surprisingly." I shake my head dissentingly. " I only wish I could have the chance of letting him know how direly disappointed I was in him," says Lenore, viciously. " I wonder shall I ever ? "

" I sincerely hope not."

" If I do, you may be sure I will not lose it," she says, with an angry emphasis. " I know nothing that would give me such pure, such lively pleasure."

This is on the day following Lenore's escapade. In the evening, old Mdlle. Leroux gives a little party, according to her lights. When we enter the salon, about half-past seven, we find most of the company already assembled. The piano is open (it is generally locked), and Mdlle. Péroline, with her hair newly frizzed, and her muslin flounces mightily goffered, is executing a surprising fantasia, wherein the air loses itself perpetually in variations that seem to have nothing to say to it, and reappears anon, when least expected, like a train out of the Box Tunnel. Mdlle. Leroux, in a fresh burst of yellow ribbons, is in the act of shutting the one open window. A youth with an unearthly-deep voice, in bright purple kid gloves, and a vivid-green tie, is turning over the leaves for Péroline. Round the table are sitting five young girls, sisters—English, certainly; insolvent, probably. They are of the usual type of British dowdy—red cheeks, hearty laughs, big flat waists. Among them—Jack among the Maids—sits M. César; his eye-glass is in his eye, and a piece of tapestry-work in his hand. An English couple, and a French gentleman in drab thread gloves, whose name never transpires, complete the gathering. Lenore, whom I have had great difficulty in inducing to appear at all—Lenore, who, if she is in a company not congenial to her, or if she has nothing to say, maintains that absolute silence which is unluckily tabooed in society—throws herself, after the first salutations and presentations have been gone through, into a corner of the sofa, and keeps her head bent directly over her work. I draw a chair next to M. César and the moderator lamp, and ask him halting and ungrammatical French questions about his Berlin wools. The fantasia comes to an end.

"Are you fond of music, M. César?" I ask, having exhausted the subject of the wools.

"Yes, mademoiselle; I love it passionately."

"Do you play or sing yourself?"

"No, mademoiselle; I draw."

"César sketches from the Nature," says his mother, coming up, laying her fat white hands on her son's shoulders, and smiling in her plump *débonnaire* widowhood over his head.—"My child, show to Mdlle. Erreech that pretty

little drawing that thou madest yesterday when thou went-
est on horseback with thy uncle to Corseul."

"But, mamma, it is but a bagatelle," replies César, with
proud humility. His modesty being overcome, the sketch-
book is produced.

"Is it not of a surprising resemblance?" asks his parent, proudly smiling, and leaning forward in order to feast
her eyes.

"Monsieur has not yet perhaps quite finished it," I say,
hardly able to contain my laughter, as I examine, with admiring gravity, the rolling trees, little wriggling black
shades, and houses utterly out of the perpendicular. M.
César's mode of treating foliage is singularly *wormy.* Then,
seeing that I have not said what was expected of me, I
added, "A thousand thanks, monsieur! It is, indeed, a
charming talent!"

"But it is nothing!" rejoins César, with a bow and
deprecatory wave of the hand.

At this moment Stéphanie enters, bearing a tray, and
thereon weak tea and sponge-cakes, supposed to be *à
l'Anglaise.* As she hands these delicacies to me, she stoops
over me, and says, in a confidential half-whisper:

"There are two messieurs down stairs, come to make a
visit to mademoiselle."

"Two messieurs!" cry I, surprised; while the five
Misses Brown prick the attentive ear—rarer than green
peas in January are resident men at Dinan—"and who are
they, Stéphanie?"

"One, mademoiselle, is the little gentleman who comes
nearly every day—the little *ministre Anglais* with the
spectacles—and the other, never, mademoiselle, have I seen
him before; he is a tall, a very tall gentleman, with a great
red beard."

I look involuntarily across at my sister; her head is raised, her work is dropped—she is listening.

"Very well," I say, with a sigh of impatience; "if Mdlle. Leroux will have the goodness to permit it, ask them to walk up here."

As I speak I lay down the chip I am plaiting on the table, and cross over to Lenore.

"Stéphanie tells me— " I begin.

"I know," she answers, briefly; "I heard."

"And don't you think," continue I, with doubtful suggestion, "that it would be better for you to be out of the way while they are here—they cannot stay long—and it can hardly be pleasant for you to meet that man?"

"It is neither pleasant nor unpleasant," she answers, doggedly. "I shall not stir; not for the world would I give him the satisfaction of thinking that I was ashamed to face him."

In two minutes more they have entered—Frederick first, shyly smiling, small, and priestly; and behind him, a large, grave, and unpriestly stranger. When first the brightness of the lit room smites his eyes, when first the smell of hot tea and cakes assails his nose, when first the clack of the many women's tongues—French and English—attacks his ears, he shows an involuntary inclination to turn and flee, but, overcoming the temptation, advances, with the air of a martyr, to where we are sitting. Glad of the opportunity of gratifying my curiosity afforded by Frederick's tremulous and deprecatory presentation, I look up at him. So this is Le Mesurier! Surely, surely, I should never have known him, from my sister's angry description. His eyes are not large certainly, but I have very frequently seen smaller. His nose, on the contrary, is certainly not small, but I have very often seen larger. As for the villanous expression she mentioned, if it is any-

where it must be about his mouth, which is lying perchance
under great plenty of tawny hair. He looks at me with
the cursory, superficial glance with which men always regard me; looks at me because I am standing opposite to
him—because he has just been introduced to me—not in
the least because he thinks me worth looking at, which indeed I am not. Lenore bows also, and, but for her utter
unsmilingness and her extreme rudeness, there would be
nothing differing in this from any ordinary introduction.

"In what country is it the mode to pay morning-calls
by moon-light?" I hear her brusquely ask in a low voice
of Mr. West, who has seated himself on the sofa beside her.

"Indeed, Miss Lenore" (leaning his two hands on the
top of his green umbrella, and beaming wistfully at her
through the blue haze of his spectacles), "we did not mean
to have come in at all. I sent up a message to ask
whether your sister would be good enough to come down
and speak to me for a minute; but you know I am not a
great adept in French, and I suppose the maid must have
mistaken my meaning."

"You might easily have corrected the blunder without
coming up," retorts my sister, ungraciously.

"Do you think so?" asks Frederick, humbly. "Perhaps; but, indeed, it would have been difficult, you see:
old Mdlle. Leroux overheard something of it, and she came
down herself—and—I am sure she meant it most hospit-
ably—but she, I may say, almost *drove* us up before her."

"And *he!*" (glancing irefully in Mr. Le Mesurier's direction, who, in bitter misery, and looking unspeakably
cross, is trying to make Madame Lange understand that he
does not comprehend one word of what she is saying to
him)—"and *he!* What brings *him* here? It is execrable
taste, and I have a good mind to tell him so."

"Pray, *pray* don't!" cries Frederick, eagerly; "if

anybody were to blame, it was I.   I asked him whether he
would mind walking with me as far as the Porte St. Louis,
and he said, 'Oh, no, not in the least.'   He wanted to
have a cigar, and it was the same to him to walk in this
direction as in any other; all he stipulated for was *that he
should not have to go in.*"   Lenore is still working; she
gives her thread a vicious tug, which snaps it.   "Indeed,
Miss Lenore, he had no more thought of seeking your acquaintance than you of seeking his."

This mode of expression is unlucky, as he feels as soon
as it is out of his mouth; but Lenore, fortunately, does not
seem to perceive it.

"He had no intention, then, of paying us the honor of
a visit?" cries Lenore, looking not much·appeased by the
information, but, on the contrary, rather more exasperated
than before.

"Not the least," replies Frederick, earnestly; "you
may reassure yourself on that head—nothing was farther
from his thoughts."

"He has, then, a *second* time been forced into our company against his will," retorts the girl, with angry eyes.

"He is not fond of society," replies Frederick, evasively; "he says himself that he is totally unfit for it."

"There, at least, I have the happiness entirely to agree
with him," cries she, dryly.

Mr. Le Mesurier has at length succeeded in making
Madame Lange understand that hers are to him dark
sayings.

"Monsieur does not comprehend?   A thousand pardons; it is unfortunate, but I talk not the English.—Péroline, my friend, thou hast learned the English when thou
wast at school; come hither and talk to monsieur."

But Péroline shakes all her *crêpéd* head.

"But no, mamma; monsieur would but laugh at me!"

"Have you given your message, West?" asks Le Mesurier, abruptly, joining his friend, and looking nearly as much goaded to madness by the women's shrill clatter as a mad bull by red cloth, "because, if so, I should say we had better not intrude on these ladies any longer."

Thus reminded, Frederick comes over to impart his errand to me, and Le Mesurier, having parried by dumb show all old Mdlle. Leroux's offers of chair, sponge-cakes, *eau sucré*, remains standing silently by Lenore.

"What is this message?" she presently asks, abruptly, not raising her eyes from her work, and seeming to address her question rather to the air than to her neighbor.

"Something about a boat, I believe," replies he, formally, his careless glance wandering away from her to West, and his foot beginning to tap an impatient tattoo on the floor.

"What about it?" still more brusquely.

"Some fellow here of the name of Panache, or something like that, has lent him one, and he invites you and your sister to have a row up the river to Lehon in it, to-morrow."

"Oh! I should have thought that errand might have kept till the morning."

"So should I," he answers, dryly; "so I told him."

A little silence.

"Does he want you to go, too?" she asks, moved by some sudden impulse, lifting her eyes and looking at him hardily, yet shamefacedly.

"Me!" (with surprise), "not that I am aware of."

"Oh!" dropping her eyes again.

"Why do you ask?"

"I had no particular motive" (nonchalantly). "I never have a motive for any of my actions."

"Take a tea-kettle. Light our own fire; there must

be plenty of sticks in those great chestnut-woods—have tea. What do you say, Lenore?" cry I, anxious to interrupt a *tête-à-tête* that must be so distressing to my sister.

"Charming!" answers Lenore, ironically. "A fire that one lights one's self never lights; the kettle invariably topples over, and water of the river tastes of old iron; but what are such trifling drawbacks? Let us go, by all means!"

CHAPTER V.

WHAT JEMIMA SAYS.

A STEEP path, and steps cut on the hill's rough face, from the blinding white high-road to the water's edge. A beautiful brown river washing the feet of the granite height, on which Dinan sits like a queen; Dinan's walls, and towers, and spires, looking down upon its lonely Rance. The Rance, that a little lower down will go stealing under the worn stone arches of the old bridge, and a little higher up came flowing beneath the great viaduct, that, with its ten giant arches, strides across the valley. At the landing-place, a little narrow four-oar, with a sharp nose, is lying, and around it four people talking.

"Of course, if you wish it, Lenore, we must go," I say, resigned, but gloomy, as I stand beneath a huge buff sunshade, which casts a becoming yellow light on my interesting face, clad in a dust-colored gown, and girt about the waist with a leathern bag—the impersonation of travelling Englishwomen. "But, if we *all* get in, we shall inevitably swamp it."

"It is only intended for three, *really*—two to row and one to steer," says Frederick, setting down a very large basket, under which he has been staggering along all the way from Mdlle. Leroux's. "But I thought that, perhaps, if Miss Jemima did not mind, one of us—the one that is lightest—Miss Jemima, for instance, might sit at the bottom of the boat, on shawls, and cloaks, and so forth, in the bows."

"It reminds one rather of Raphael's cartoon of 'The Miraculous Draught of Fishes,' does not it?" says Le Meurier (for he is the fourth person), laughing, as he jumps into the little skiff, and deposits in it an immense stone jug of claret-cup. "The proportion in size between the Apostles and their boat is something like the present case.—Miss Herrick, if you are to sit in the bows, I'm afraid it will have to be upon the claret-cup."

"Frederick!" cries Lenore, from the lowest step, on which she is sitting, lifting up calmly-commanding eyes, and a little round cleft chin toward him; "suppose you solve the difficulty! Suppose *you* walk; it is charming along the towing-path; no wind, no flies, no nothing!"

"Of course, if you wish, Miss Lenore," looking rather blank, and still panting from the effects of his wrestle with the basket; "but—"

"You can add some more butterflies to your collection," continues my sister, in a wheedling voice. "I dare say you have got your green gauze scissors in your pocket.—Do you know" (bringing the whole battery of her dimples to bear upon Mr. Le Mesurier), "he catches butterflies with a pair of green gauze scissors, and sticks pins in their poor fat bodies; how he reconciles it to his conscience and his bishop I don't know, but I suppose, like fishing, it is a form of cruelty purely clerical."

"It is rather hard to turn poor West out of his own boat, isn't it?" replies Le Mesurier, looking down on my sister more collectedly than men are in the habit of looking; nor, indeed, am I able to detect one grain of admiration or approbation in his cold blue eyes. He looks at her much as he looked at me. "I say, West, you weigh, I regret to say, at least five stone less than I do; *you* take my place. *I really and truly don't care a straw about it.*"

This last sentence, emphatically spoken, is intended for an aside; but I, who have a happy knack of overhearing things that I am not meant to overhear, catch it. Frederick's piece of information about his friend, "the society of respectable women always bores him—he makes no secret of it," recurs to my mind. He is doing his best to shirk two eminently respectable women at the present moment.

"Lenore!" cry I, reddening, as I feel, under my yellow umbrella; "let us row ourselves; we have, at all events, got the mainstay of the entertainment—the tea-kettle and the claret-cup."

But Lenore frowns, and turns away.

"Perhaps, after all, I had better walk," says Frederick, uncertainly, glancing with uneasiness toward my sister's averted head. "Perhaps, after all, it is the best arrangement."

"Just as you please, of course," replies Le Mesurier, looking rather disappointed, while a little smile of contempt plays about his mouth, and the half-inch of tanned cheek that his beard leaves visible. Lenore rises.

"As soon as this amiable contention as to who should show most alacrity in trying to avoid us is ended, perhaps some one will help me in," she says, rather sharply, and with a certain elevation in air of nose and chin. Le Mesurier gives her his hand; he does not rush forward to do so, as most men would in her case; does not tumble over his own legs in his precipitancy, like poor Frederick; only he is standing nearest her, and therefore he gives it her.

"Put your foot exactly in the middle; walk steadily;

go to the stern; you had better steer!" he says shortly, and rather austerely.

Half an hour afterward, Frederick and his green umbrella are tramping disconsolately along the towing-path, and we are being sculled up-stream by an unwilling gentleman, upon whom we have forced ourselves, and who is longing to be rid of us. The sun pours down in broad golden rain upon the blinding bright river. Through the viaduct's great arches, towering up against the June sky, we see heaven's sapphire eyes looking. The air is astir with the winged families that live only a day, but whose one day is all joy. The sombre chestnut woods that darkly clothe the steep slopes, run down to the river's side, as if hastening to drink; white-capped women are kneeling by the edge, washing linen and beating it viciously on stones with wooden shovels; no wonder that there are jagged holes in one's cotton gowns when they come home from the laundress. Long blue dragon-flies sail slow and kingly among the flags and flowering rushes that grow along the river—that grow again, the same, only wrong way up, in the vivid, clear reflections. We are each of us rather silent, partly because we are hot, partly because we are none of us in a very good temper. Lenore leans over the side, and drags her bare right hand through the water, making our little cockle-shell lurch unpleasantly.

"You had better sit straight, Miss Herrick; it takes very little to destroy the equilibrium of this sort of boat," says Mr. Le Mesurier, rather dryly. Lenore does not appear to hear; she only leans a little farther over, and admires her own slim fingers, that look unnaturally, lucidly white, seen through the watery veil.

"For Heaven's sake, sit straight!" cries he, a second time, but much more energetically, as the gunwale of the boat comes almost on a level with the water. Lenore draws herself slowly up.

"Were you speaking to me?" she asks, with provoking coolness; "how could I tell? You said, 'Sit straight, Miss Herrick.' I am not Miss Herrick!"

"Miss Lenore, then. I will call you what you please, only for Heaven's sake sit still."

"I wonder you ever go in a boat, if you are so nervous," says my sister, tartly.

"I am not *nervous*, as you call it, when I am with people who behave rationally," replies he, coldly; "but I know that a mere touch will upset a boat of this kind, and I also know that, if it did upset, one of you two would infallibly drown, for I could not possibly save you both."

"*One* of us? *Which* of us?" cries my sister, and I see a mischievous devil come into her eyes as she begins to laugh, and to rock violently from side to side, "I *must* see which."

"Lenore! Lenore!" cry I, in an agony, clutching the sides of the boat, "stop, for Heaven's sake! I beg, I implore. Lenore! Lenore!"

But all in vain. Lenore only laughs and rocks the more. Mr. Le Mesurier says nothing, nor can I see the expression of his face, as I am sitting behind him; he only turns the boat's head toward shore, and half a dozen vigorous strokes of the oar bring us swish through a great company of stiff bulrushes to land. Mr. Le Mesurier jumps out.

"Miss Herrick," he says, gravely, "I shall be delighted to row you home this evening, but as I cannot answer for your life for five minutes, as long as your sister is in the boat, I should be very much obliged if you would get out now."

"Perhaps I was foolish," reply I, grasping my umbrella, and scrambling out on the oxeyed bank, "but I have such a horror of drowning."

CHAPTER VI.

WHAT THE AUTHOR SAYS.

"Now, Miss Lenore, I am quite at your service," says Le Mesurier, resuming his seat, taking the oars again, and pushing out into mid-stream. Lenore hangs her head, and dries her fingers with her pocket-handkerchief, but does not answer. "It was no doubt very spirited of you, trying to upset the boat, because your sister asked you not," continues he, sarcastically; "but as she did not seem to see it in the same light, I thought that the kindest thing I could do was to land her."

"Jemima is a coward," replies Lenore, pouting; "the only kind of boat she likes is a great broad-bottomed tub, that one might play leap-frog in without upsetting."

"I should think it would be the pleasantest kind of craft to go out boating with you in," rejoins he, with rather a grim smile; "but now, as I said before, I am quite at your service; upset me as soon as ever the spirit moves you."

"You give me *carte blanche?* "

"*Carte blanche!* "

"But if I *did* upset the boat," says Lenore, half laughing, half vexed—"I don't say that I *am* going—but if I *did*, your first care ought to be to pull me out."

"Ought it?"

"*Oughtn't* it?"

"I don't know what it ought to be," replies Paul, pulling leisurely along through the shining flood; "I know what it *would* be."

"What?"

"To pull myself out."

" You are like a man I heard of, who said one day to another man out hunting, ' Don't look behind, there are two women in the ditch; and if you look you'll have to stop and pick them out.' "

"*I* was the man."

Lenore laughs.   " You would let me drown, then ? "

" Undoubtedly."

" Well, you are the only man in the world who could sit there and tell me so to my face," cries the girl, angry scintillations flashing from her superb eyes, and the ever-ready color rushing headlong to her checks.

" If you were to upset the boat," replies Paul, calmly, looking with intense disapprobation at his beautiful companion, " I should know that it was your deliberate intention to commit suicide, and I hope I have better manners than to run counter to any lady's plainly-expressed wishes."

" I have a great mind to try," answers Lenore, looking down into the clear brown depth, where her own image lies, tremulous and shimmering, and then into Le Mesurier's impassive face.

" Do, by all means; only let me pull you a hundred yards farther on.   It is five or six feet deeper under those poplars."

" After all, I think I won't," says Lenore, naïvely, her anger subsiding, as soon as she sees that it neither alarms nor awes, nor even very much amuses him.   " I don't know how it is with other people, but, with me, the mere fact of being given leave to do a thing, takes away all desire to do it."

" From the little I know of your character, I should imagine that you did not often wait to be given leave."

" Not very often," replies the girl, gravely, looking away beyond him, to where, on the Rance's right bank, Lehon

Abbey lifts its roofless walls and gray arches to the sky. "Once, long ago, when I was little, I was very, *very* ill—I'm not over-strong now, though you would not think it to look at me—and the doctor said I was to have whatever I asked for, for fear of bringing on a fit of coughing if I screamed; the consequence was that, if ever I wanted any thing, I always threatened to break a blood-vessel, and straightway got it."

"I should think that that threat had lost its efficacy now," says Paul, looking incredulously at the girl's full, womanly figure, and at the plump though slender dimpled hand, that droops over the boat-side—at the round cream-white column of her proud throat.

"No, it has not," she answers, shaking her head; "the prestige of my delicacy still remains, though the *fact* no longer exists, and I, of course, am careful to keep up a tradition which tends so much to my own interest, as it enables me to have my own way in every thing."

"What a very bad thing for you!" says Le Mesurier, brusquely. "If I were your sister, I should set up a rival blood-vessel."

"It would be no use," answers Lenore, laughing, and swinging her broad straw hat to and fro. "Jemima is one of those hopelessly healthy people who will live on, without an ache or a pain, to a hundred, and then tumble down-stairs or get run over by an omnibus, natural means having proved utterly inadequate to kill her."

They are slowly sliding past Lehon, past the ivied bridge, past the steps down to the waters, wherein the Lehon monks used to bathe their holy, sleek bodies in the by-gone summers, in the quick stream. Pious Sybarites, who reconciled God and Mammon as never any one has done since then!

"It would have been very different if papa had lived,"

continues Lenore, beginning to dabble again, unremon-
strated with this time. "He used to make us get up at
five o'clock on winter mornings to go out walking by star-
light with him; used to make us stand in a row before
him, with our hands behind our backs, to repeat the Catechism; and if we stumbled in our 'Duty to our Neighbor,'
or 'I desire'—Jemima always stuck fast in 'I desire'—
made us hold our hands to be caned."

"What a thousand pities that he died!" says Paul,
almost involuntarily, resting on his oars, and staring
straight from under his tilted hat at his *vis-à-vis's* face, his
keen eyes undazzled by all the pretty tints and harmonious
hues that feast them.

"Do you think so?" cries Lenore, looking up from the
contemplation of her own face in the water. "Now, on
the contrary, I think it was such a mercy that he did. I
never feel tempted to question the wisdom of Providence's
decrees in that particular instance."

"What a truly filial sentiment!"

"Don't look so shocked," answers the girl, beginning
to laugh again. "I was but five years old when he died,
and the only very clearly-defined association that I have
with him is the biting his hand one day, and being shut up
in the black-hole because I would not say I was sorry. I
was not sorry; I *never* was sorry; I am not sorry now."

"All the same, I still regret that he died."

"Why?"

"Every woman needs some one to keep her in order,"
replies he, gravely, as if giving utterance to a sentiment
against which there can be no appeal. "Until she has got
a husband—her natural and legitimate master—she ought
to have a father."

"Natural and legitimate master!" repeats Lenore,
scornfully, drawing up her long throat. "Did I hear

aright ? That *would* be the subjection of mind to matter, instead of matter to mind."

" I can't say that I agree with you " (very dryly).

"There is not that man living that could keep me in order ; I would break his heart, and his spirit, and every thing breakable about him, first ! "

"I have no doubt that you would try."

"I should succeed. I have got papa's temper; they all tell me so—Jemima—my other sister—everybody " (speaking very triumphantly).

"You say it as if it were matter for pride. It is astonishing what things people pride themselves on. I believe there was once a family which piqued itself on having two thumbs on each of its hands."

" I *should* pity the poor man who undertook to keep me in order," says Lenore, folding her hands in her lap, while delicious ripples of laughter play about her lips and cheeks at the thought of the sufferings that await her future owner.

"*Of course*, you never mean to marry ? "

"*Of course*, I do, though ! " (getting rather angry, and coloring faintly). "Do you think I mean to be an old maid ? "

" I think," replies Paul, bluntly, " that considering the utter docility which with you would be a *sine quâ non* in a husband, you run a very good chance of being one."

Silence for a few moments ; no sound but the " swish " of the oars—the cool wash of the water against the keel ; then Lenore, resolute, womanlike, to have the last word, recommences :

"Confess," she says, leaning forward toward him a little, and emphasizing her remarks with her forefinger ; " confess that there is not a more laughable, degrading sight on the face of the earth than a woman in a state of abject subjection to her husband!"

"Confess," replies Paul, leaning forward a little also, and also speaking with emphasis, "that there is not a more contemptible, degrading sight on the face of the earth than a man in a state of abject submission to his wife!"

"You may laugh!" cries Lenore, loftily, carrying her head very high, and looking defiantly at him; "but I maintain that there is not a more contemptible creature in creation than a patient Grizzel!"

"And I maintain," retorts Paul, looking back with equal defiance, "that there is not a more pitiable reptile in creation then a hen-pecked husband, if such a being ever existed, which I have some difficulty in bringing myself to believe."

They have both raised their voices a little in their eagerness. Three Englishwomen riding by on donkeys, their draperies extending from head to tail over those ill-used animals, turn their heads. M. Dunois, the barber's son, taking his afternoon canter, on a big bay horse along the towing-path, turns his also.

"The aborigines are astonished at our vehemence," says Paul, recollecting himself; "and really," with a careless laugh, "as we neither of us have at present a victim to test our theories and wreak our cruelties upon, we need not excite ourselves over it, need we?"

Lenore's sole answer is a vivid blush, of whose birth she herself could give no account.

"What on earth has come to the girl?" Le Mesurier says to himself, staring at her with the open, unconscious stare of utter surprise; "alternately making very silly remarks, and getting as red as a turkey-cock over them. I wonder does she smoke? As likely as not. Shall I ask her? At all events, I wish she would let me."

"How long are you going to stay at Dinan?" inquires Miss Lenore, presently, with an abrupt change of subject.

Paul shrugs his shoulders.

"God knows!"

"What an unnecessarily forcible expression!"

"Do you think so? It is what the shopkeepers in one part of Spain answer if you ask them whether they have such and such wares in their shops; they are too lazy to look, so they say, 'God knows!'"

"Long, do you think?" pursues the girl, perseveringly, not heeding his apocryphal little anecdote.

"Until *my* friend gets tired of *his* friend, M. de Roubillon's *château*, with all its absurd little turrets and weathercocks, I suppose," replies Paul, being not entirely free from an old-fashioned insular contempt for every thing Gallic.

"What is your friend's name?"

"Scrope."

"What is he like?"

"Oh, I don't know;" looking vaguely round at the water—the chestnut-trees—the flags, for inspiration. "I'm a very bad hand at describing; he is much like everybody else, I suppose."

"Like *you*, for instance," rather maliciously.

"Good Heavens! no;" breaking into a short laugh; "he *would* be flattered at the suggestion!"

"You mean that he is good-looking?"

"Oh! yes; he is all very well" (rather impatiently).

"And how soon do you imagine that he will be here?"

"Oh! in two or three days, I should hope."

"You should *hope!*"—with a little accent of pique—"you don't like Dinan, then?"

"It is all very well for France," replies Paul, magnificently; "but it is rather like a penny bun—a little of it goes a long way."

Lenore bends down her small head, heavily laden with great twists and curious plaits of crisp brown hair, and ceases from her questionings. It is Le Mesurier's turn to catechise.

"Are you so very proud of Dinan, then, Miss Herrick?"

"We are fond of any place that is cheap," replies Lenore, shortly. "Any place where mutton is sevenpence a pound seems to us prettier and pleasanter than one where it is tenpence."

"Oh, really!" looking and feeling rather awkward, and not exactly knowing how to take this manifestation of unnecessary candor.

"We are real Bohemians, Jemima and I," pursues the girl, resting on her hand her small downy face—downy with the wonderful bloom of life's beautiful red morning; a bloom as transient and unreplaceable as the faint gray dust on just-gathered grapes. "We pay our debts, but otherwise we are quite Bohemians. We go and stay at places out of the proper season; we drive all over London in omnibuses, and go down the Thames in penny steamboats, and do a hundred other uncivilized things. One summer we spent at Boulogne; I liked that, Jemima hated it."

"I dare say."

"Oh! that *établissement!*" cries Lenore, clasping her hands together in childish glee at the recollection, while her speech trickles off into pretty low laughter. "What fun it was! and how happy all the wicked people looked! Everybody walking about with somebody that did not belong to them."

"No wonder you enjoyed yourself," replies Paul, sarcastically, rather disgusted; not, as I need hardly say, at the fact related, but at the narrator.

"Look at Jemima gesticulating from the bank," cries Lenore, happily ignorant of the emotion she has produced; nor, indeed, is the idea that any one can be disgusted with her very much prone to present itself to her mind. "How eloquent an umbrella can be when wielded by a cunning hand! What a great deal Jemima's is saying!"

"It is saying, 'Land!' I imagine, isn't it? Let us land," replies Paul, with some alacrity, his thoughts turning more affectionately toward claret-cup than toward a prolonged *tête-à-tête* with Lenore.

"Let us land," echoes the girl, with the slightest possible unintentional sigh.

CHAPTER VII.

WHAT JEMIMA SAYS.

THE flags and the thick green rushes make way for the little boat; on either side they part, and through them and over them she slides, smooth and slow, to shore.

"What have you done with my cockatoo?" cries Lenore, putting one little high-heeled shoe on the prow and springing lightly to my side. "Have you mislaid him on the way, or has a lily-white duck come and gobbled him up?"

"Neither," reply I, rather morose at having been defrauded of my water-party, "he is up in the wood picking sticks; he has been gathering you a nosegay as big as a coachman's on a drawing-room day, as we came along."

"I wish I could break him of that habit," cries Lenore, petulantly ; "it is a bore having to carry them, and a still greater bore having to say 'Thank you' for a great posy of dandelions and buttercups."

"Poor West!" says Le Mesurier, with a half-contemptuous laugh; "he shall give them to me; *I* like dandelions."

"Oh, so do I," replies Lenore, quickly. "I'm wild about flowers ; they are the only things that do not deceive us— as I once overheard a girl saying to her partner at a ball."

"We had better keep in sight of the boat," I say, with my usual excellent common-sense, "or the Dinan *gamins* will be sure to steal it."

"Have you been here long enough," asks Lenore, addressing Mr. Le Mesurier over the top of my head, "to discover how cordially these interesting natives hate us English ? Even abandoned infants of three and four throw stones and ugly words at us, only luckily one does not understand Breton Billingsgate."

"We spend a good deal of money in making ourselves hated in every quarter of the globe ; it is a little way we have," replies Le Mesurier, with languid interest, as he stalks along, a martyr to circumstances, with a great stone jug in one hand and a kettle in the other.

"It is *too* hard upon us poor out-at-elbows English—you must know we are all out-at-elbows here," continues Lenore—"wasting our substance in clothing these Bretons and giving them better food than their wretched *galette*, and then getting pelted for our pains."

"One always gets pelted, literally or metaphorically, when one tries to do one's neighbors good," replies Le Mesurier, misanthropically; "better leave it alone."

We have turned off from the towing-path, and into the chestnut-wood. There is no undergrowth, nor do the trees stand so close together but that there is pleasant space for walking shadily beneath them. A little way ahead of us we see a small gray smoke and little shoots of fire rising straight upward through the windless air, and beside it, Frederick on his knees, with his cheeks puffed out like a trumpet-player or a wind-god's, blowing the flame.

"Here's devotion for you," cries Le Mesurier, laughing, and indicating Mr. West with his kettle. "Poor West! making himself into an improvised pair of bellows!"

"*Dame!* as they say here, how ugly he is!" cries Lenore, bursting out laughing.

"What base ingratitude!" says Le Mesurier, casting up his eyes theatrically to the chestnut-boughs; "a man ruins his trousers kneeling on damp grass, puts himself into a ridiculous attitude, and runs the risk of getting congestion of the lungs for you, and all you say is—what was it? did I hear aright?—'Damn! how ugly he is.'"

"I said French *Dame*, not English," retorts Lenore, still laughing; "there is a very great difference in force between the two."

"*Dame* is about equivalent to our 'Lor,'" I say, sententiously, "and I should imagine nearly as vulgar."

"One can use it with a pleasant *arrière pensée* of swearing, you know," says my sister, "without the wickedness."

"I think that will do now," cries Frederick, looking up at us with bland triumph from his kneeling posture, his cheeks reddened with the exertion of inflating them, and his eyes watering from the smoke; "the sticks were rather green."

"You looked an impersonation of Zephyr, as we came along," answers Lenore, banteringly—"didn't he? Didn't we say so, Mr. Le Mesurier?"

"We did, all of us; there was not a dissentient voice,"

3

replies Le Mesurier, inattentively, fighting with an immense
yawn, and his eyes fixed upon the stone jug.

"Will you run and fill the kettle? Frederick must
make a nice flat place for it to sit upon," continues my
sister; "you know" (looking up at him with a sort of
sleepy coquetry from under her eyes) "that it was only on
the condition that you were useful that we allowed you to
come at all."

It may be my imagination, but I cannot help fancying
that our new acquaintance elevates his eyebrows almost
imperceptibly at this speech.

"I don't think that Mr. Le Mesurier would have broken
his heart if we had not let him come," I say tartly, in irritated surprise at Lenore's want of perception. So speaking, I kneel down, and with a chafed spirit begin to unpack
the basket and cut bread-and-butter. Lenore flings herself
down on the grass, and lying all along among the wood-
flowers, watches with a malicious smile Frederick, who has
begun again to blow his flagging fire. The three English
ladies on donkeys pass along the towing-path; they turn
their blue-veiled heads toward our little encampment, and
stare. The youth, whose pleasing task it is to goad their
jackasses into fitful and momentary gallops, stands stock-
still, with wide hungry eyes fastened on the bread and
marmalade.

"Frederick has overblown himself," says Lenore, laughing; "he has blown all his fire away.—Mima, dear, you
must go and pick up some more sticks for him."

I am preparing to rise and obey with my usual tame
docility, when Mr. Le Mesurier, who has just returned
with his full, dripping kettle from the Rance, interposes:

"Miss Lenore—your name is Lenore, not Leonora, is
not it?—may I ask you one question?"

"So as it is not how old I am, or whether my chignon

is all my own hair," replies Lenore, with a sort of uneasy smartness.

"It is neither; I don't want to know either," he answers, gravely.

"What is it, then? Say on," throwing her head back a little, to be able to get a good look at him.

"Why do not you go and pick up sticks yourself, instead of sending your elder sister?"

"Elder sister!" cry I, with a mirthless laugh. "Please don't challenge respect for me on that head; I had rather be treated with contumely for evermore, than reverenced for such a *triste* superiority."

"I do not go myself," replies Lenore, not listening to me, but still looking steadily up at him, "because I make it a rule never to do any thing for myself that I can get any one else to do for me."

"Oh, indeed! Thanks," turning away.

"I set no manner of store by those little every-day virtues," continues Lenore, disdainfully thrusting out her red under-lip; "running on other people's errands, carrying their parcels, ordering dinner, sitting with your back to the horses—any one can do them; they are a great deal of trouble, and there is no credit to be got out of them.

"Anybody cannot sit with his back to the horses, for it makes some people sick," replies Le Mesurier, laughing.

He has thrown himself forward, full length on the ground, in one of those carelessly-graceful attitudes that the British gentleman affects; his hat is on the back of his head, and his feet are kicking about among the catchflys and ragged-robins.

"Now if it were some *big* thing," continues my sister, flushing, as she, having raised herself from the grass, leans her back against a chestnut-trunk, "I could do it—I know

I could; that is, if I had the chance, and if there were
plenty of people to look on."

"And cry 'Hooray!' like the little boys on Guy-Fawkes
day.—Would you ladies mind my smoking *one* cigar?"

"I could have driven in the cart to the Place de la Ré-
volution, like Madame Roland," continues Lenore, beginning to march up and down, with her head up, and her
hands behind her back; "standing up all the way, in a
white gown, with little red carnations on it, and my long
black hair hanging down my back; I could have smiled
back at the yelling *sans-culottes*—"

"I'm afraid you could not get guillotined nowadays if
you were to be shot for it," returns he, coolly, holding his
cigar suspended between his fore and middle fingers; "it is
next door to impossible to get hanged."

"I could have stabbed Marat in his bath," pursues Lenore, clinching her hand upon an imaginary knife. "Yes,
stabbed him as he sat there, unshorn, sick, with a dirty cloth
about his head—"

"I'm afraid if you stick Beales or Bradlaugh in their
tubs, you will only get ten years for it, commuted to two,
if you make love to the chaplain," replies Le Mesurier,
resolutely prosaic.

"I could have—"

"You could have hammered Sisera's temples to the floor
or sawn off poor tipsy Holofernes's head," interrupts Mr.
Le Mesurier, rather impatiently cutting short my sister's
heroics. "I know what you are going to say; perhaps you
could; for my part, of all the characters known in history
or fiction, I dislike those two strong-minded females about
the most."

"I know exactly the kind of woman you like," says Lenore, stopping suddenly in her tramp, tramp, and looking
down with contemptuous pink face on her prostrate and
sprawling adversary.

"I don't well see how you can," replies he, throwing away the end of his cigar, and burying one hand in the tawny beard. "You have never seen my womankind; you have never seen me with any woman."

"I did not even know that you had any womankind," she answers, a little inquisitively.

He does not gratify her curiosity.

"What is exactly the kind of woman I like?" he asks, raising his cold, quick eyes to hers.

"Amelia in 'Vanity Fair,'" she answers, promptly, with a pretty air of triumph.

"I knew you were going to say that," he says, calmly.

"But it is true, is not it?" inquires she, eagerly.

"Not in the least; you never made a worse hit in your life."

"She was dollishly pretty; she cried on every possible occasion; she allowed everybody who came near to bully her; she had not two ideas in her head. With all these qualifications, how could she fail to be charming?" inquires my sister, with withering sarcasm.

"I like her better than Jael," says Le Mesurier, doggedly.

"So do I," cry I, tired of keeping silence, and clattering the teacups.

"What is your opinion, West?" asks Le Mesurier, trying to extract the cork from the claret-jug with his fingers. "I say, is there a corkscrew anywhere about? Which is your *beau idéal* of feminine excellence—Heber the Kenite's amiable wife or Amelia Osborne?"

"Frederick has no *beau idéal* of feminine excellence," answers Lenore for him, with an ironical smile; "he hardly knows a woman when he sees one; his bride is the Church. Let us come to tea; the steam is beginning to lift the kettle's hat off at last."

As I have before remarked, the dinner-hour at Mdlle. Leroux's *pension* is six o'clock; so it is at the Hôtel de la Poste; indeed, the great event of the day happens throughout Dinan at the same hour. To avoid, therefore, losing our daily portion of ragged beef, raw artichokes, and tripe (as half-past five has already come chiming through the chestnut-boughs from the town-clock), we are compelled rather to hurry up the conclusion of our *al-fresco* feast. We give the rest of our French roll-and-butter, and the remainder of our tea (which, thanks to the Rance and Frederick, has an agreeably mixed medicinal flavor of old iron, alluvial deposit, and smoke), to the donkey-boy aforementioned, who, careless of his fair charges, and leaving them to the wild will of their asses, has been haunting us as a young vulture haunts a battle-field. We stand on the flowered bank, prepared to reëmbark. The boat lies so still, so still on the windless tide, like a young child asleep in the sun; near the other bank a man, naked to the waist, is standing up to his middle in water, pulling bundles of rotten, ill-odorous flax out of the river.

"I shall take an oar going home," says Lenore, with decision. "I can row."

"Please don't," cry I, nervously; "you know you always catch crabs, and the last time that we went out boating on the Seine, at Rouen, you caught such a big one that you tumbled backward over the seat and all but upset us."

"The oars were too short," she answers, looking displeased at this allusion; "it might have happened to any one."

"One crab will be fatal to us to-day," says Le Mesurier, laconically, as he stands holding the boat's head steady for us to get in.

"If people *will* make boats no wider than knife-blades or paper-cutters they cannot blame me if they upset," returns she, carelessly, giving him her hand and preparing to step in. To my surprise—I might almost say *alarm*—by the very hand she gives him he detains her.

"Miss Lenore, if you get in will you promise to sit still?"

"I never promise," she answers, lightly, leaving her hand peaceably in his. "When I was a child I never would promise to be a good girl, because I knew I never should be."

"If you will not promise, you really must not get in."

"*Must not!*" cries she, giving her head an angry toss. "Who says *must not?* *Must not* is an ugly word."

"Not so ugly as *must* in a woman's mouth," getting rather angry, too.

"May I ask whose boat this is?" loftily.

"I think you said M. Panache was the name of the fellow; but I am not a good hand at French surnames."

"If it is M. Panache's boat, what right or authority have you over it, may I ask?"

"None whatever," he answers, quietly, "except possession, and that is nine points of the law."

"Did he lend it to *you?*"

"On the other hand, did he lend it to *you?*"

"Mr. Le Mesurier, I'm not joking."

"Miss Lenore, *I'm* not joking."

"What business can it be of yours?"

"I do not wish to see *your sister* drowned," with an invidiously-perceptible accent on the two words.

"You do not care whether *I* drown or not?" snatching away her hand, and flashing annihilating looks at him. They do not seem to do him much harm.

"We discussed that question *fully* before," he answers, rather bored.

"*Please* promise, like a dear child," cry I, coaxingly,

from the bows, where I am seated uneasily under my yellow umbrella.

"Be rational," says Le Mesurier, looking at her gravely, yet with a suspicion of laughter about the eyes. "I promised to row your sister home; is not it only natural and Christian that I should wish to spare her the abject terror she suffered this afternoon?"

"I will not promise," says Lenore, doggedly, and breathing hard. "I will not be dictated to by a stranger. I will walk home."

So saying, she turns sharply away, and begins to walk quickly down the glaring, sun-baked towing-path.

"Mr. Le Mesurier, Mr. Le Mesurier!" cry I, jumping up, and almost bringing on the catastrophe about which we have been squabbling; "let her have her own way. She has never been thwarted in her life; we have always let her have her own will from a child!"

"For fear that she would break a blood-vessel if she had not," replies he, smiling. "She told me so as we came along.— Miss Lenore," rising his voice a little. "Miss Lenore! we throw ourselves on your mercy."

"Come back, come back," cry I, excitedly, shaking my umbrella; "you will get a sunstroke!"

But Lenore is too indignant to answer.

CHAPTER VIII.

WHAT THE AUTHOR SAYS.

THE blandness born of after-dinnerhood is upon all Dinan; everybody is as *suave* as fed lions; a child might play with them. The moon is holding her great yellow candle above the town, and ugly black night skulks away in corners. On the other side of the Place St. Louis, the old priest is sitting at the bottom of his garden, reading his breviary by moonlight. His white house's green shutters, that have been closed all day to keep out the dust and glare, are just opened to let in the evening cool. The mysterious family in the large yellow house a little lower down, who always go out driving in a ramshackle, old, close carriage, with all the windows up, about sundown, are setting off on their nightly expedition. The immense shadows of their horses are running up the face of the Pension Leroux; the heads and ears reach to the salon windows. Madame Lange, César, and Péroline, are out. They have gone *faire de la musique chez M. le Capitaine O'Flannigan*, a broken-down Irishman, who tells the credulous natives that he has been in the Guards, and who, with his numerous progeny, lives in the graceful retirement of an *entresol* in the Rue de St.-Malo. The Herricks are therefore in undisputed possession of the salon. The piano belongs to Madame Lange, and she mostly locks it when she goes out. She has forgotten to do so to-day, and Frederick is committing piracies upon it. Like most little men with small, puny voices, he is fond of ferociously warlike and rollicking Bacchanalian songs, on the same principle, I suppose, which often induces a Hercules or a Samson to express in music his wish to be a butterfly—

"In his love's bosom for to lie "—

or a daisy, or a swallow. Frederick has just been giving faint utterance to heathenish *berserker* sentiments, such as that to fight all day and drink all night are the only occupations really worthy a Christian gentlemen's attention; and now, leaning forward on the music-stool, and peering near-sightedly through his spectacles at the score, he is piping—

"Soho! soho! said the bold Marco!"

Mr. Le Mesurier—he is here, too; it is a few days after the tea-picnic—is leaning out of the window, smiling to himself, and whistling inaudible accompaniments to the singer. He is not gigantic enough to wish to be a butterfly, and too big to insist upon being a buccaneer. So he does not sing at all. Jemima is smiling, too, and beating time with head and foot, as she knits. Lenore is not in the room at all; she is sitting on the front-door step, rather to the disgust of Stéphanie, whose favorite seat it is, where she sits and chatters rough guttural Breton to her neighbors, in a clean stiff-winged cap, when her hard day's work is done. Lenore is chatting to nobody; she is only staring at the moon.

"Does your sister sing?" asked Le Mesurier, turning away from the window.

"Yes; rather well—*when she chooses,*" replies Jemima, rhythmically, still nodding time.

"Would she sing now, if one asked her?" ·

"Probably not; but I can but try.—Lenore! Lenore!" (going to the window and looking down). "Come in out of the damp, child; you'll catch your death of cold."

"Never did such a thing in my life, my dear."

"What are you doing?"

"Only baying at the moon, as Mademoiselle Leroux's poodle did last night."

"Come up here and sing."

"Could not think of superseding the present able performers."

"He has stopped," puts in Paul, leaning his arms on the sill, and craning his brown neck out. "He is exhausted. The bold Marco takes a great deal out of a fellow—does not he, West?"

As he speaks, he turns away again, laughing, and, so laughing, forgets the request, about which he had never been much in earnest. A quarter of an hour passes. Frederick is still singing ; the billiard-balls' gentle click from the café next door mixes with his voice.

"Lenore! Lenore!" cries Jemima, rising, knitting in hand, and leaning a second time out of the wide casement.

> "'Onora! Onora! her mother is calling.
> She sits at the lattice and hears the dew falling,
> Drop after drop from the sycamores, laden
> With dew as with blossom, and calls home the maiden.
> Night cometh, Onora'"—

says Le Mesurier, spouting. "Onora, *alias* Miss Lenore, went down the *place* toward the *fossé* five minutes ago."

"Alone ?"

"Alone."

"In that *demi-toilette* gown ?" (with a horrified accent).

"*Was* it a *demi-toilette* gown?" asks Paul, with the crass ignorance of mankind.

"I mean without any shawl, or wrap, or cloak of any kind ?"

"She went just as she was when she was sitting on the door-step."

"Let me run and bring her back !" cries West, eagerly, jumping up and snatching his hat, prepared to rush forth on his quest with devouter haste than ever Sir Galahad showed in the pursuit of the Holy Grail.

"Oh, you know she never pays the slightest attention to you," answers Jemima, a little impatiently, forgetting her politeness in agitation, "nor to me either, for the matter of that—Mr. Le Mesurier, I think she minds you more than most people—I don't know why—would you mind trying to persuade her to come in out of the dew?"

"Delighted!" says Le Mesurier, with a ready lie, walking toward the door; "and, if fair means fail, am I to employ foul?"

Lenore is not in the *fossé*. The gray towers of Duchesse Anne's castle rise beside it like a faint, dark dream, black as Erebus, quiet as death; the tree-boughs spread above him; beneath them, on a black-and-silver path, he walks along—walks along slowly, enjoying his cigarette, and in no particular hurry to overtake his Holy Grail. On and on to the Place du Guesclin, and there, a long way from him, he sees the white glimmer of a woman's dress. He walks up to the glimmer: he has found his Holy Grail.

"Your sister sent me to ask you to come in out of the dew," he says, rather stiffly, and delivering his message with the exactitude of an Homeric messenger. He has come up rather behind her; she did not perceive his approach.

"Tell my sister to mind her own business!" she cries, startled and angry.

"I suppose she thinks that *you* are her own business," he answers, coldly.

"At all events, I am not *yours*," she says, rudely, yet laughing.

Without another word, he turns to go.

"Let her catch her death of cold! No great loss if she does!" he says to himself, beginning to light a second cigarette. He has not gone three yards, when he hears a step behind him. A charming face, with little waves of moonlight rippling over it, smiles up at him.

"Why are you going?" she asks, in a low voice, as if saying something she was half ashamed of.

"I am not a spaniel, or *a Frederick West*."

"I was rude, I suppose" (hanging her head).

No answer.

"I often am, I fancy."

" *Very* often " (emphatically).

"It is my way."

"It is a very bad way."

"I do not think it is *quite* all my fault either," she says, almost humbly; "it is partly *theirs*—I mean Mima's and Frederick's, and my other sister's. When I was a child, if I said any thing rude, they only laughed, and thought it clever. I wish they had not, now."

"So do I."

"It makes people hate one a good deal," says the girl, naïvely. "This year we went to a ball that the Fifth Dragoon Guards gave, and several of them did not ask me to dance *once*, because I had said things about them. I told one that he was like a pig set up on his hind-legs. So he was; but he never came near me all the evening in consequence."

"Poor fellow!" says Le Mesurier, laughing. "You could hardly blame him."

"You are not angry now—you are laughing!" cries Lenore, joyously. "Tell me "—coming confidentially close to him—"is the bold Marco still saying 'Soho?'"

"He was when I left."

"Do not let us go home, then; let us sit on this bench and talk."

So they sit on a bench with a back to it, in the deep shade cast by a double row of young lime-trees. The heavy, sweet lime-flowers sway above their heads—sway so low as almost to touch their lips and cheeks. The lights from the café and the Hôtel de la Poste opposite make little red reflections on their clothes and faces. Three Englishmen are coming back from fishing, with rod and basket in their hands—two very tall Englishmen, and a very little

one. At something that the little one says, they all laugh
uproariously. It seems a sin to speak above one's breath
in this holy moonshine. Two Frenchmen and three women
saunter by in the deep shade; it takes a little effort to
count how many there are. Whether they are old or
young, pretty or ugly, who but a bat can tell in this fragrant gloom?

"What are you thinking of, Miss Lenore?" asks Paul,
presently, peering a little inquisitively into his companion's
face, as she gazes at the stars that are trembling like heavenly shining fruits between the dusk tree-boughs.

"I am thinking," she answers, a little dreamily, "of
how the Rance is looking *now*, *at this minute*, down at
Lehon, as it laps against those ivied steps where the monks
used to bathe."

"Shall I row you down there to see?" he asks, banteringly. She springs to her feet in a moment.

"*Will* you? Do you mean *really?*" she cries, eagerly.
"Ah, no!" (her voice falling with a disappointed cadence).
"I see by your eyes that you did not mean it—that you
were only tantalizing me."

He feels her thin draperies wafted against his knees in
the slow night-wind, as she stands before him; the breath
of the lime-flowers comes passing sweet to his nostrils. It
is all but dark.

"I did not mean to tantalize you," he answers, simply.
"I will take you, and welcome, if you wish; only what
will your sister say?"

"She will say, 'Lenore, are you mad?' She always
says that. Perhaps I am mad; I sometimes think so."

"But what time of night is it, do you suppose? Is not
it nearly bedtime?" he asks, taking out his watch, and
trying to decipher the hour by the little crimson gleams
from the café.

"Bedtime!" she cries, impatiently. "I feel as if I shall like *never* to go to bed again as long as I live."

"'What has night to do with sleep?'"

"All right, then—come along," says he, recklessly, seeing that he is in for it, and that it is not his business to find his companion in prudish scruples, which do not seem inclined to occur to her. A quarter of an hour more, and no woman's dress glimmers white from the shaded bench in the Place du Guesclin; it is glimmering, instead, in M. Panache's little cockboat on the broad, bright, Rance. Death's lovely brother, Sleep, is ruling over every thing; even the river sleeps, and no passing breeze breaks its slumber. The moon comes up behind the chestnut-woods, and the water lies smooth as glass; while the trees, and the tremulous grasses, and the great squadron of broad ox-eyes—yellow sun-disks with white rays round them—live again in the black depths, where the moon also lies drowned, like a pale, bright maiden. They are floating along so stilly, so stilly, on the opaline flood! The little boat hardly moves. Lenore is sitting in the stern. The red cloak Paul brought her is drooping from her shoulders; pearly lights are playing about her hair, and her grave, fair face, and her wonderful eyes.

"If one were fond of her, one would be in the seventh heaven, I suppose," says Paul, cynically to himself. But even though one is *not* fond of her—even though one disapproves of her—even though she is not one's style—yet flesh is weak, and blood is blood; and in cool manhood, as in hot youth, blood still tingles, and pulses throb, with the seductive enervation of night, proximity, and great fairness.

"Shall I sing?" asks the girl, almost in a whisper—

"'Sing! sing! what will I sing?
The cat ran away with the pudding-bag string.'"

" By all means, if you like."

" What shall I sing, *really?*—English, French, German, Italian—"

" Whatever you please.   The smallest contribution thankfully received."

She leans her round white elbow on her lap for a moment or two, and her head on her hand, in reflection; then the pensive look fades out of her face, and a dare-devil smile flashes over it.

" You are a civilian, are not you ? " she asks abruptly.

" I am *now.*   Why ? "

" You cannot take my song personally, that is all.   Listen ; I am beginning."

This is Lenore's song, as it rings gayly out over the dumb woods and waters.   Most of you, my young friends, know it well enough :

> " Oh que j'aime les militaires !
>   J'aime les militaires ;
>   J'aime leur uniforme coquet,
>   Leur moustache et leur plumet.
>   Je sais—ce que je voudrais.
>   Je voudrais être cantinière.
>   Avec eux toujours je serais,
>   Et je les griserais.
>   Près d'eux, vaillante et légère
>   Aux combats je m'élancerais—"

She breaks off abruptly.

" Do you like it ? "

" Immensely."

" That means, not at all."

" It is a song that I was always particularly fond of, and I think the line in which you express your intention of making your friends drunk peculiarly happy," he answers, ironically.

She looks down, half-ashamed.

"The ideal woman would not have sung such a song, I suppose?"

"Probably not."

"Tell me," she cries, impulsively, "is the ideal woman clothed with flesh?"

"What do you mean?"

"Is she some living, breathing woman, that you have in your mind's eye?"

He hesitates a little, and also reddens—unless the moon belies him—a very little.

"Since you ask me point-blank—well, she is."

The girl turns her fair head aside, and droops it over the stream, through which she draws her hand listlessly.

"Tell me what she is like; I wish to know," she says presently, very softly.

Silence for a few minutes; then Paul begins:

"She is not at all clever—of the two, I think, she is rather dull. She does not say much, but she always thinks before she speaks."

"What an intolerable prig she must be!"

"She talks about things, not people. She is very loving—"

"Pooh!" interrupts Lenore, contemptuously. "What woman is not? It is our besetting sin. What a list of attractions! But tell me—tell me, is she handsome—as handsome as—as—as *I* am?" she ends, laughing confusedly, and growing scarlet.

The water falls drip, drip, in long, lazy drops, from the idle oars.

"*Are* you handsome?" he asks, gravely—not with impertinence, but as though wishing for information—and, so asking, looks at her long and steadily in the moonlight—a familiarity of which she cannot complain, as she has brought it on herself. "Well, yes" (drawing his breath rather hard), "I suppose you are."

She laughs again, but constrainedly.

"But waiving the question of *my* beauty—is she handsome—pretty?"

"I do not know," he answered, slowly. "Some one asked me that question the other day, and I said I did not know. I do not."

Lenore leans back in the stern, with the rudder-string in her hand.

"Describe her to me. I will tell you in a moment whether she is or not."

He stares absently over her head, at the viaduct, striding gigantic across the valley—at the town, with its house-roofs white as silver sheets in the moonshine.

"She is small," he begins, slowly, "*very* small! not more than ·five foot one, and thin—rather *too* thin, perhaps," his eyes resting, as he speaks, for an instant, with reluctant admiration on the superbly-developed figure of his *vis-à-vis*. "Her eyes are—" he stops short, in want of an epithet.

"Bright!" suggests Lenore.

"Bright! No!" cries he, energetically repelling her suggestion with scorn. "I hate your bright eyes. They always look *metallic;* hers look at you as if they were looking through a mist, and they have a dark, shady hue under them."

"Belladonna!" suggests Lenore again, with supercilious brevity.

"Some one said to me the other day that they were like the eyes of a shot partridge," he continued, not heeding her; "so they are."

"What a lackadaisical, dying-duck sort of idea!"

"She is pale—as pale as—as—as—a lily!" he continued, unable to find a new white simile. "That clear yet opaque look—"

"Like a hard-boiled egg !" interrupts Lenore, scornfully.

"Not in the least like a hard-boiled egg !" retorts he, nettled, and the river of his eloquence suddenly dried.

"I do not know whether you are aware of it," says the girl, with a heightened color, "but you have described a person in every respect the exact opposite of me."

He gives a half smile.

"Have I? I apologize. I really was not aware of it. I only did as you bade me."

He pulls a few yards further on ; no sound but the oars turning in the rowlocks—the plash, plash, of the smitten water. Lehon Abbey lifts roofless gables to the mighty sky, and Lehon Castle its round dim towers, whence never a knight will look again. The water-fairies have been supping on the river to-night : they have left their rare white water-lily cups and broad green platters behind them.

"Stop rowing," cries Lenore, imperiously, "I want to gather some of those lilies."

He obeys. Motionless they lie among the great round leaves and white chalices. She leans back over the stern, and pulls with her strong, white hands at the tough, long stalks.

"What will you do with them ?" asks Le Mesurier, indolently, his unwilling eyes taking in the lazy grace of the half-recumbent form, of the large, white, outstretched arm, at which a happy moonbean is catching; "they have not at all a nice smell in water—faint and sickly—they will only die."

No answer.

"What do you want with them ?" he asks, rising, he does not know why, and stepping over the little seat that intervenes between them.

" You will see," she answers, briefly.

They are so wet—so wet, as they lie in her lap. He watches her as she dries one dripping bud with her pocket-handkerchief, and then, with quick, deft fingers, places it closed and sleepy in her hair.

" Do you like it?" she asks, in a half whisper, raising her eyes to his, with a slow, bright smile.

How still it is! Not a sound; every thing is asleep; only the wakeful moon sees his cold, quick eyes flash. He would have laughed this morning, if you had told him that Lenore Herrick could make his heart beat as it is beating now.

" What would you have me say?" he answers, in the same key in which she spoke. " If I did not like it, would you have me tell you so? "

" Yes."

" I do like it," he says, half angrily; " you know I do; you knew I did before you asked me."

" Take it then," she says, with a low laugh, holding it out to him. " Keep it as a memento of the fast girl who *would* go out boating with you, against your will, at ten o'clock at night—of the girl who *may be very good fun, if one goes in for that sort of thing, but is not your style!* "

He reddens.

" What do you mean? "

" You will not have it? Well, then, here it goes! "

As she speaks she flings the blossom away, far out into the river. It fall with a little flop, and a little gleam of broken silver, into the water, and so floats down to Dinan.

" What do you mean?" he cries, eagerly. " How impatient you are! I *did* want it; I held out my hand for it. I will have it yet! "

So saying he snatches up one of the oars, and makes

frantic lunges with it at the little valueless prize. It is exactly three inches too far off for him to reach. Paul's arms are long, and he hates being beaten. Unmindful of the tiltuppy nature of little cockboats, he leans farther and farther over the side. It is *almost* within his reach—it is *quite* within his reach; he has got it—has he, though?

"Take care! take care!" cries Lenore, wildly; but it is too late. In another moment M. Panache's boat is floating away, bottom upward, after the water-lily, and two people are struggling and splashing in the moonlit Rance.

CHAPTER IX.

WHAT THE AUTHOR SAYS.

WHEN Paul rises to the surface, sputtering and blowing unintentional bubbles, his first thought naturally is, "Where is Lenore?" At about three yards' distance from him he sees something white. He swims toward it, and catches at it; it is Lenore. Feeling his grasp, she flings out her two arms wildly, and clutches him spasmodically round the neck.

"Loose me!" he cries, breathlessly, still sputtering. "Lenore, Lenore! you will drown us both!"

But Lenore is too much blinded and deafened by the water to pay any heed to his remonstrances. She only clasps him the more convulsively. With a strong effort he manages to unlock her arms, and, grasping her firmly with one hand, with the other strikes out for shore.

Swimming in one's clothes is never pleasant, but swimming in one's clothes with only one hand at one's disposal —the other being occupied in supporting a perfectly help-

less, inert woman—is more unpleasant still. Happily it
does not last long; the adventure is not of heroic dimen-
sions.   Not half a dozen yards from the fatal lilies the bulrushes have advanced their thick green standards, and,
where the bulrushes are, water is shallow and footing
easily gained.   The flags and the rushes swish against his
face and buffet it rudely as he scrambles through them,
half dragging, half carrying his companion through the
deep river-mud and the chilly midnight waters.   Having
deposited her in a living bundle on the bank, he sits down
beside her and pants.   As for her, she is a little stunned
by the shock of the plunging water; that is all.   She is
not wont to faint, and has not fainted now.   Presently she
sits up, and, pushing her dripping hair out of her bewildered eyes, says, gaspingly :

"Don't scold me; it was you that did it."

"I know it was," he answers, as distinctly as the chattering of his teeth will let him.

"Well, you did not let me drown after all, you see," she
says, with a smile that, though forlorn and drenched, is still
half malicious.

"Well, no; not this time."

They look at one another for a minute, then both burst
into a simultaneous fit of violent laughter.

"What a ridiculous drowned rat you do look!" cries
she, politely.

"The same to you," he answers, grimly, as he sits dripping dismally on the dry June grass.

"What have you done with your hat ?"

"The same as you have done with yours, I fancy."

"And Mima's Connemara cloak ?"

"Half-way back to Connemara by now."

"I have lost one of my shoes," says the girl, half crying,
"and the other is full of mud."

She looks up at him piteously, as innocently as a baby might do. The Rance has washed all the coquetry out of her eyes, on whose long lashes the river-drops are hanging.

"How shall I ever get home? I shall have to hop all the way."

"Perhaps I might carry you," he says, not unkindly, leaning forward to examine the unlucky shoe; while his nose, and his beard, and his short hair, water the buttercups and refresh them.

"Carry me!" she cries, derisively. "Why, I weigh nine stone eight! I might as well talk of carrying you!"

He is not particularly anxious to carry her, and does not repeat his offer.

"How cold I am!" she says, shuddering. "How it runs down one's back, does not it? I wish one's clothes would not stick to one like court-plaster. I am sure it will be the death of me."

"By-the-by," cries he, a brilliant idea striking him, and beginning to search frantically in his coat-pockets (we, in Dinan, never dress for dinner, therefore he is still in his shooting-jacket), "if it is not gone—no, thank God! here it is!"—drawing out a little silver flask—"take a pull at it, it will keep the life in you."

"What is it?"

"Brandy."

"Will it make me *drunk!*" she asks, gravely holding it in her hand, and trembling all over like a smooth-haired terrier on a frosty day.

He laughs. "No such luck. It would be the best thing that could possibly happen to you if it did; but it will not, I am afraid. Go on."

She obeys, and drinks. It burns her throat, but her teeth become a shade less vocal. He follows her example; and then, jumping to his feet, gives himself a prodigious shake, like a Newfoundland who has just deposited the re-covered stick at his master's feet.

"Come on," he says; "we had better be getting home as quick as we can. Let us pray that we may meet no one! I feel uncommonly small, do not you?"

"Uncommonly!" replies Lenore, with assenting emphasis.

"Give me your hand, and let me help you up."

She does as he bids her, and as she rises to her feet a fresh deluge rustles, drips, pours down from her.

"How heavy water is!" she says, staggering. "I have half the Rance about me. I feel like the woman who was killed by the weight of her jewels."

"Stay; let me wring out your clothes a little for you."

He kneels before her on the grass, and with both hands twists and strains, and wrings her thin flabby gown and her soaked petticoats, as a laundress might.

"There, is that better?"

"Yes, thanks. I think so—a little," replies she, doubtfully.

"Come on, then,"—employing the invariable phrase with which a Briton embarks upon any undertaking, from a walk with his sweetheart upward to a Balaklava charge. Without more speech, they begin to tramp along the towing-path, leaving behind them a track as of a thunder-shower or a leaky water-cart. On to the landing-stage, up the steep steps to the highway. At the corner of the silent, shining road, a great rock abutting casts a sharp, black shadow; and out of this shadow, and into the light, come two people, running in disorderly haste.

"Your sister and West to the rescue," says Le Mesurier, speaking for the first time since they set off homeward.

"My long-lost Frederick!" says Lenore, with grim

merriment; "flying to the riverside to poke about for my dead body with drags and a boat-hook. How I wish we could avoid them! How small and thin, and drowned I feel!"

"Lenore, is that you? where *have* you been? how wet you are! what *has* happened?" cries Jemina, incoherently, scorning punctuation, and precipitating herself upon her sister.

"Jemima, my sin has found me out," replies Lenore, solemnly. "I *made* Mr. Le Mesurier take me out on the water; and, in order to pay off all old scores, he upset me."

"And himself into the bargain," says Le Mesurier, laughing.

"Jemima, your Connemara cloak is just about arriving at St.-Malo; so is my hat, so is Mr. Le Mesurier's."

"And you are not hurt, only drenched?" cried West, tremulously; and, forgetting his shyness, lays an audacious hand upon one of the shoulders that are glimmering, so wet and shining, through her transparent gown.

"Not hurt, only drenched," she echoes, laughing cheerily, and eluding him, while her face smiles out, pale and pretty and altered, from the thick frame of heavy damp hair that cleaves so closely and lovingly to cheeks and throat. "See, Jemima!" exhibiting a small, muddy foot, "my right shoe has gone the way of all shoes."

.   .   .   .

"A very blessed upset!" says Paul to himself, half an hour later, oracularly shaking his head, as he scrambles into dry clothes at the Hôtel de la Poste. "She was doing her best to make a fool of me, and she had all but succeeded.

4

CHAPTER X.

WHAT THE AUTHOR SAYS.

A WEEK has gone by. Lenore's teeth no longer chatter. She is quite dry again, and has bought a new hat seven times more coquettish than the drowned one. She keeps, however, a tender memento of her adventure with Paul in the shape of a sore throat and trifling cough, which not even the unwonted dose of cognac has kept off. Breakfast at the Hôtel de la Poste is over. The twenty or thirty commercial travellers and clerks, who, according to the wont of French hotels, share that feast with the visitors and tourists, have disappeared again into private life. Paul is sitting in the little dark salon, writing a letter to his sister, with a sputtering pen. Paul's caligraphy is rather like that of John Ball of the Chancery bar, who wrote three several hands: one that no one but himself could read, one that his clerk could read and he could not, and one that *nobody* could read. Paul is just staring hard at his production, and wondering what on earth was the mystic remark that he had made at the top of the second page—searching his mind for the history of the past week, in order to be able to give a guess as to what it was likely to have been, when the door opens, and admits Mr. West.

" Le Mesurier ! "

" Well " (not looking up).

West enters, and walks over to the window.

" Well," says Paul again, abandoning the idea of reading over his letter, and beginning to fold it.

West advances to the table, and lays a small, tremulous hand on his friend's broad shoulder.

" Le Mesurier, I—I—have a favor to ask of you."

"My dear fellow, do not say that it is to lend you five pounds," cries Le Mesurier, in affected alarm. "I have had severe losses myself lately; I have a heavy engagement to meet to-morrow—"

"Oh, pooh! it is not that, of course; but—but—I have something to say to you."

"Say on."

"Not *here*" (glancing round uneasily); "we might be overheard."

"By whom? The noble army of shop-boys dispersed itself half an hour ago, and the landlord informed me yesterday that the only English word he knew was, 'Snap, snap, snorum, a cockolorum!'"

"Would you mind coming outside for a moment?" says Frederick, pertinaciously.

"All right. Give us a light."

He leisurely folds and directs his letter, and then takes out and lights a cigar, while West stands beside him, shifting feverishly from leg to leg, and rolling up his dumpling hat into a hundred weird shapes. They emerge from the hotel door; the *voiture* is just starting for Caulnes, drawn by a pony and a huge white horse, both in the worst possible spirits. A man, all clad in white flannel, is stepping into the interior; a fat priest, with his limp cassock clinging about his legs, climbing up into the dusty *banquette;* the blue-bloused driver mending a rift in the rotten rope-harness; and, over all, the broad sun laughing down, and the lime-flowers from the Place du Guesclin shaking out their lovely scent on the morning air. The two men cross the street, enter the place, and sit down on a bench—the very one on which Paul and Lenore sat in the dark a week ago.

"Well," says Le Mesurier, expectantly, after they have sat three minutes without speaking.

"I am going home—to England," says Frederick, abruptly.

"Have you brought me out here to tell me that?" asks Paul, banteringly.

Silence!

"So you are going now, are you, eh?" pursues Paul, carelessly. "So will I, I think. Let us toss who shall pay —heads or tails," throwing up a napoleon into the air and catching it.

But Frederick's thoughts are far enough away from heads or tails. The *diligence* is just moving off.

"Allez! allez!" cries the driver, flicking with his long whip the old white horse's sharp back. The bells give a cracked jingle; off they go!

"I am naturally particularly loath to leave this place just now," says West, his spectacles mournfully fixed on the lessening vehicle.

"Are you?" says Le Mesurier, staring at him obtusely. "Why? and why *naturally?*"

Frederick pulls a supple lime-leaf that is fluttering just above his nose, and tears it into thin green strips.

"I thought," he says, blushing and stammering, "that you must have seen that there was—was something between me and—and—and Miss Lenore."

Paul shakes his head.

"Indeed I cannot say that I ever noticed any thing of the kind," he answers, bluntly, feeling rather angry, he cannot imagine why.

"Did not you?" (pushing his spectacles down on the bridge of his nose, and gazing over them with meek surprise at his friend). "I fancied that my attachment—my— my *devotion*—must have been patent to the most superficial observer."

"My dear fellow, of course they were," says Paul, laughing, not ill-naturedly. "But you said something *between* you and Miss Lenore. Now, the word *between* implies that there are *two* to the bargain."

"And you think that there is only one to this bargain?" says Frederick, despondently, looking down, while the blush fades out of his face, and the gay motes run up and down about his hair.

"Good Lord! West" (a little impatiently), "how can I tell? Does the girl confide in me, do you suppose?"

"No doubt you think," says Frederick, turning toward his companion again, while his sensitive mouth twitches painfully, "that I am not the sort of man to take a handsome, spirited girl's fancy?"

"How can I tell?" repeats Le Mesurier, embarrassed by the exactitude with which his friend has hit his thought.

"'Different men are of different opinions;
Some like apples, some like inions—'

and I dare say women are the same."

How drowsily the bees are humming high up among the faint, thick blooms! It is enough to send one to sleep.

"After all," says Frederick, brightening a little under the influence of his companion's homely saw, "I am not altogether sure that the mere fact of her treating me cavalierly—chaffing me, calling me names, and so forth, tells entirely against me. It is the way of some girls, I believe. Even if Lenore *did* like a fellow, she would die sooner than show it."

"Would she?" says Le Mesurier, with a half-absent smile, throwing his head back, and staring up into the flickering, tremulous leafage above him, while his thoughts travel back over the past week, to the silver wash of a midnight stream—to a lady, with pearly lights playing about her, holding out a water-lily to him, and saying, with a slow, soft smile, "Take it, then." He is woke out of his trance by two Breton housewives, chattering past in those shrill, screechy voices that God has given to Frenchwomen alone, as they step out stoutly in their short, heavy, and trim black-stuff stockings.

"Now I have told you the state of things with me," says Frederick, with a nervous laugh, "perhaps you can guess what is the favor I am going to ask of you."

"I?" says Le Mesurier, giving a great start, and looking thoroughly puzzled.

"Guess."

"Not I. Perhaps" (with a brilliant flash of intuition) "it is to ask me to be best man: only that is no great favor, and it is rather premature—is not it?"

Frederick jumps up suddenly.

"If you are going to make a jest—" he says, with a hurt intonation.

"My good fellow," cries Paul, energetically, laying his hand upon his shoulder, "I give you my word of honor that I know no more than the dead what you are driving at. I never *was* good at guessing. I never found out a riddle in all my life. I give it up."

West looks at him distrustfully; but, seeing no mirth, only boundless bewilderment, in his friend's ugly face, he continues, speaking with difficulty, looking down, and kicking about some stray cherry-stones that a former occupant of the bench has left strewed on the ground:

"I do not know why it is, I am sure—cannot make out —but you have certainly more influence with Miss Lenore than any one else."

"Have I?" says Paul, shortly, turning away his head.

"She will do for you what she will not do for either her sister or me."

"Will she?" still more shortly, while a slight flattered

flush rises to his forehead. " I really have not discovered it."

" And, such being the case," continues West, with increasing hesitation, stammering, floundering, and reddening ever more and more, "I thought that perhaps you might—"

" I might *what?* " asks Paul, still staring stupidly at his friend.

" I thought," says West, plunging desperately *in medias res*, seeing that he is not likely to get much help from his companion's intelligence, " that you might perhaps— say something about me to her—sound her feelings with regard to me, to a certain extent."

" I ! ! ! " says Paul, turning sharp round, the mystified expression of his face giving place to one of enormous astonishment. " I ! my dear West ? Are you *quite* cracked ? "

" She would, at all events, give you a hearing," says Frederick, downcast, but pertinacious.

" Would she ? " cries the other, laughing violently. " I very much doubt it. She would be more likely to bang the door in my face, and tear out my few remaining hairs, and quite right, too."

" Perhaps it is because you saved her life," pursues West, ruefully, keeping on his own track.

" Saved her life ! " breaks in Paul, now really angry. " My good fellow, for God's sake, do not talk like a fool, whatever you do ! To upset a woman into a ditch, and then pull her out, can hardly be termed ' saving her life,' even in these days, when every little thing is called by some big name."

Silence. The little yellow lights glancing and flashing up and down about their hats and coats.

" West," says Paul, abruptly, rising from his seat,

thrusting his hands down to the very bottom of his pockets, in his favorite attitude, and looking full and keenly into his companion's downcast face, "suppose you got Miss Lenore, what on earth would you do with her?"

"Do with her?" repeats West, staring. "What do you mean?"

"Can you fancy that girl a parson's wife?" says Le Mesurier, beginning to laugh, while with inner vision he sees again that dare-devil smile, those lovely half-lowered eyes, that had kindled such unwilling fire in his own cold veins. "Do not be angry with me, West; I could not stop laughing now if you were to kill me. I think I see her holding forth at a mothers' meeting, or teaching at a Sunday-school! Poor little wretches! would not she cuff them!"

"She is so young," says Frederick, deprecatingly. "I should hope that one might be able to *mould* her—"

"*Mould* her?" echoes Paul, derisively. "My dear boy, it would take you all your time. She would comb your hair with a three-legged stool."

A pause.

"I am to understand, then," says Frederick, trying to speak stiffly, but with a suspicion of tears in his voice, "that you decline to help me?"

"Decline to propose to Miss Lenore for you? I do, distinctly," replies Paul, stoutly.

"Perhaps," says Frederick, with the easy, baseless jealousy of unlucky love, "you would have no such objection to speak to her on your own account?"

A dark, unbecoming flush rushes over Le Mesurier's face.

"I?" he says, angrily. "What are you talking about, West? Must everybody be in love with her because *you* are? Did not I tell you, the very first day I saw her—the day that she took it into her head to play that unaccountable prank—very bad form it was, too—that she was not my style ? No more she is. I must say that she improves upon acquaintance ; but no, no—not my line at all."

Frederick sits down upon the bench again, in a stooped, shapeless attitude of utter despondency.

"Why cannot you ask her yourself ? " inquires Le Mesurier, with a mixed feeling of compassion for the sufferer's misery and raging contempt for his poverty of spirit. " If a thing is worth having, it is surely worth asking for."

" It would be no use," replies West, dejectedly ; " she would not listen to me—she never does ; she would only laugh, and turn every thing I said into ridicule."

" Why on earth do not you go in for the old one instead ? " asks Paul, impatiently. " She would suit you down to the ground. *She* would listen to you fast enough, and *she* would not *need* any moulding."

"I dare say it would have been happier for me if I could have fancied her," replies West, with the admirable conceit of man, in whose vocabulary " ask " and " have " are supposed to be interchangeable terms. " She is a dear, good girl, and really fond of parish work. But no, no " (with a heavy sigh), " *that* is impossible now."

He covers his face with both hands, and relapses into silence. Paul eyes him doubtfully for a few minutes ; then, laying his hand on his shoulder, says, not unkindly :

" Cheer up, old man ! It is a long lane that has no turning. I would do any thing *in reason* I could for you, for old acquaintance' sake ; but what you ask is *not* in reason—come, now, is it ? "

" Perhaps not " (in a stifled voice).

" She would box my ears, or order me out of the house, as likely as not ; she is quite capable of either," says Paul, trying to steel himself in his resolution in proportion as he finds it melting under the fire of his compassion.

"No doubt—I ought not to have asked you," West says, lifting his face from his hands, which fall nervelessly on his knees. "I should not have thought of doing so if I had not known what an opinion she had of you."

"Has she?" says Paul, coloring again slightly, while a warm glow of self-satisfaction steals pleasantly over him. "But now, my dear fellow, do think what a fool I should look. How should I begin? How should I go on? How should I finish?"

"I would leave all that to you, of course."

"No, no," says Le Mesurier, rising hastily; "*upon my soul, I cannot;* it is impossible. I have no opinion of go-betweens. Ask for yourself, and take your answer, whatever it is, like a man."

CHAPTER XI.

WHAT THE AUTHOR SAYS.

BRAG is a good dog, but Holdfast is a better. Mr. Le Mesurier, however, shows himself incapable of being the latter; incapable of keeping to the wise and rational resolution expressed at the close of the last chapter. On the morning of the day following that on which Frederick preferred his request, Paul might have been seen, walking slowly and with a hang-dog air, in the direction of the Pension Leroux. He is smoking like a chimney; his eyes are fixed on the ground, and his hands are buried deeper than ever in the pockets of his old gray shooting-jacket.

"I would give any one twenty pounds to stand in my shoes for the next half hour," he says to himself, as he drags his feet one after another through the calf-market, between the miserable calves, flung down roughly, with legs tied together, and heads moving wistfully from side to side, to lie for hours together, baking, helpless, and un-pitied, in the mid-day sun. Paul need not have gone near the calf-market at all; it is quite out of his way; but then it takes a little longer. He stands for a quarter of an hour staring in at the clever little terra-cotta models of men and beasts, in M. Noel le Quillec's small shop-window, close to the Porte St.-Louis; but, however ingenious two clay-pigs, set up on their hind-legs and walking arm-in-arm, or a donkey playing the concertina, may be, it is impossible to stare at them forever.

"Please God she is out!" he says, piously, turning with a sigh through the shady *porte.*

But she is not out. As he comes in sight of the salon-window he sees two arms resting on the sill; a woman in a bright-blue gown, and with bright-brown hair, leaning out. It is not Jemima, Jemima is not addicted to gay colors, save in the matter of that Connemara cloak that Providence has sent sailing down the Rance to St.-Malo. The cherry-market is held in the Place St.-Louis. Groups of snowy-headed women, with great-eared caps, are trudging about the little square, with huge baskets of piled-up cher-ries, shaded by great cotton umbrellas; little luscious black cherries, juicy red ones, pale, fleshy white-hearts. Lenore is in treaty for some of the latter.

"Tenez!" she cries, sending her clear English voice, fresh as the voice of a water-fall or of a blackbird on a green April evening, down through the singsong French screams below, and pointing with her fore-finger to a tempt-ing heap. "Combien?"

"Quat' sous la livre," replies a weather-beaten little housewife, briskly.

The girl's eyes wander round the baskets to see whether any other saleswoman has bigger cherries than those under her notice, and, so wandering, they fall on Paul's upturned face. Instantly she forgets that such fruit as cherries exists.

"Anybody at home?" asks Paul, shading his face with his hand, and smiling up.

"It depends upon who 'anybody' is," she answers, gravely. "If *anybody* means Madame Lange, *she* is out; if *anybody* means Jemima, *she* is out; if *anybody* means me, I am not out."

"I may come up, then?"

"If you are sure that you can find your way," retorts she, laughing.

He turns, and enters the house. Old Mdlle. Leroux puts her head out from the door of the dining-room, where she is sitting, mending table-linen, waggles her gray curls and yellow ribbons, and cries, "*Bonjour, monsieur!*" cheerily.

"Oh, for a brandy-and-soda!" sighs Paul to himself, as he reaches the landing.

Screwing up his fast-oozing courage, he marches in. Lenore has turned away from the window to greet him; she looks as if she were a piece of the summer sky, all blue and smiling.

"You must not stay long," she says, stretching out a ready hand to him; "it is Wednesday, and on Wednesday we are obliged to evacuate this salon, because it is Madame Lange's day for *receiving*. Fancy receiving *here!*" (looking round contemptuously).

"Well, are not you *receiving* here yourself now?" says Paul, trying to speak with airy nonchalance, and feeling as if he were looking extremely sheepish. "Are not you receiving *me?*"

"Oh, yes; but, then, you are nobody," she says, with a gay little laugh.

"Thanks."

"I mean, you are only one—not a party" (laughing again, and standing before him, straight, and fresh, and beautiful).

"She is meat for his masters," is Le Mesurier's involuntary thought, and, so thinking, looks at her (unknowing it) with grave, critical intentness. Under that look, her great frank eyes pale suddenly, and her color comes and goes—comes and goes—in tremulous carnation.

"I am so glad you have come!" she says, beginning to talk very fast. "Mina is gone out sketching with Mdlle. Péroline, and I have been so hard up for something to do that I have been reduced to trying to educate Monsieur Charles. Look at him! He is rather wobbly, perhaps, but not so bad for a beginner—is he?"

So speaking she points to where, on a small stool, Mdlle. Leroux's unhappy poodle sits dismally upright, on tottering, shorn hind-quarters, *with his arm in a sling*—that is to say, with one poor little paw unmercifully tied, with a bit of blue ribbon, round his neck.

"*Faites mendiant, Monsieur Charles!*" cries the young girl, flinging herself on her knees on the floor before him. "Up! up! Unfortunately, he does not understand English!"

"Does not he?"

"He has been going through a regular course of exercises," says Lenore, gravely. "Just before you came in, I put one of M. César's hats on his head, and a pair of old Mdlle. Leroux's spectacles on his nose, and you can have no conception how like Frederick he looked."

As she kneels there, with all her blue draperies spread about the floor, and the dimples appearing and disappearing in her cheeks, a spasm of unwilling admiration contracts his heart.

"Frederick is going," he says, brusquely, turning his head away, and looking out of window—"going home, to England, to-morrow."

"Is he?" says the girl, carelessly. "Why does not he come and say good-bye to us, then? or are his feelings too many for him?"

"He is talking of coming this afternoon."

"I hope he will not cry, or have a great access of emotion; he generally has at this sort of crisis. It always makes me laugh—don't you know?—and that looks so unfeeling?" she says, glancing appealingly up at him.

"You *are* unfeeling!" he blurts out, unjustifiably, with a mistaken feeling of loyalty toward his friend.

She looks at him quickly, to see whether he is joking, but, perceiving that he is serious, says, quietly and without anger:

"Am I? What makes you think so?"

"I gather it from your own words."

"About Frederick?" she asks, composedly. "Poor dear little gentleman! We shall miss him very much—getting tickets and claiming luggage; but you would hardly expect me to go into hysterics over *him*—would you?"

He is silent, meditating on the utter bootlessness of his errand.

"Would you?" she repeats, pertinaciously.

She has sunk down in a sitting attitude on the floor; her idle hands lie, white as milk, in her lap. Monsieur Charles has availed himself of the diversion effected in his favor to abandon his upright posture, hobble off on three legs to a corner under the piano, where he spends himself in vain efforts to bite off his blue ribbon.

"It would be much better for you if you *had* some one to go into hysterics about," says Paul, drawing a small cane chair near Lenore, and resolving to attack the fortress indirectly.

She blushes vividly. Some girls blush at *a nothing;* other girls blush at nothing.

"Would it?" she says.

"You will not be angry with me for speaking plainly to you? We have seen a good deal of each other, considering how short a time it is since we first met—have not we?" says he, with a benevolent sense of fatherly enjoyment in lecturing this fair delinquent, this embodied storm, whom only he can calm; "but you are one of those women who would be much better and happier *married* than *single.*"

"Am I?" (in a very low voice).

"You ought to marry either a tyrant or a slave," continues he, surprised at his own eloquence; "either a fellow who would knock under completely to you, or a fellow who would make *you* knock under completely."

"And which would you recommend, may I ask?" she says, lifting her eyes archly, yet with difficulty, to his face.

"In *your* case, I think, the slave."

She looks slightly disappointed, but makes no rejoinder.

"I do you the justice to think," pursues Paul, warmed by the fire of his own rhetoric, "that a man's *looks* would not influence you much—that he would not be damned in your eyes, even if he had the misfortune not to be good-looking."

She looks at him again, bravely and firmly this time.

"You are right; I hate your beauty-men; they trespass on *our* preserves" (laughing).

"If a fellow had been fond of you, ever since he had known you, then," continues Paul, drawing his chair three inches nearer, and half wishing that he were not a proxy, "if he had never cared two straws for any other woman—if he were a real good fellow at bottom, even though he might not have much to recommend him in the eyes of the world, you would not send him away *quite* without hope, even though you do turn him into ridicule now and then."

"Into ridicule?" she says, stammering. "What do you mean?"

"Well, we will not say any thing about that—but, you would not send him away *quite* without hope, would you?"

Her lips tremble and form some word, but it is inaudible.

"You will at least listen to him when he comes this afternoon?" says Le Mesurier, with a sigh at his own magnanimity.

"Listen to him? To whom?" she asks, lifting her head in bewilderment, while the color dies out of her cheeks.

"Whom? Why, of whom have we been talking all along? Frederick, of course," replies Paul, a little blankly.

There is a painful pause; the girl's face has grown ghastly, and her eyes are dilated in a horrible surprise.

"I am to understand, then," she says, in a husky, choked voice, "that you are his messenger—that you have been good enough to take the trouble of making love to me off his hands?"

They have both risen, and are confronting one another. It would be hard to say which of the two, considering their different complexions, was the paler.

"Tell him," she says, making a strong effort over herself, and speaking each slow syllable with painful distinctness, "to do his own errand next time."

As she speaks, she points to the door. Half of Paul's vision is fulfilled. She has not boxed his ears—he wishes to Heaven that she would—but she has turned him out of the house. He is down-stairs and in the little hall before he perceives that he has left his hat behind him. He runs up-stairs, three steps at a time, in his hurry to fetch it and be out of the house. He enters the salon hurriedly, and is half-way toward the table, when he stops short with an expression of shocked astonishment; for, on the little stiff sofa, Lenore is lying, long and limp, her face hidden in her hands, her body, and all her smart blue gown, shaken with great, violent sobs. ·

"Good God? what is the matter?" he cries, hastily; "what has happened? are you ill?"

Hearing his voice, she starts, and buries her face deeper than ever in the little hard bolster, as if trying to hide it forever from the light.

"Lenore! Lenore!" cries the young man, in high excitement, flinging himself on his knees beside her, entirely forgetting his proxy character, and speaking now altogether on his own account. "What have I done? Tell me! Have I said any thing to vex you? If I thought I had, I would cut out my own tongue."

She does not stir; but through her fingers he sees the hot tears trickling, and, stooping over her, hears her murmur, almost unintelligibly, in a voice of choked rage and shame:

"Leave me alone! Why have you come back? Go away!"

"I will *never* go, until you tell me what I have done!" cries Paul, quite forgetting himself, and, so saying, with his two hands, by main force draws hers away from her face. "Tell me—Lenore! Tell me—*darling!*" ·

Her lovely eyes are drowned in tears; her cheeks are

crimsoned with shameful weeping—weeping for *him*—as, with a throb of irrepressible, passionate exultation, he feels. Whether divining the exultation or not, she wrenches herself away from him.

"What do you mean?" she cries, flashing at him through her tears. "I told you to go! I hate you! *Go!*"

So he goes.

.   .   .   .

Evening again, and bedtime. The market-women have sold all their wares, and gone home again. The old priest in the white house has just opened his door, and let out two dogs, in a whirlwind of excitement; but for them, the place is empty and silent. The two Misses Herrick are in the elder one's bedroom. Lenore is sitting on the edge of the low bed; her cheeks are as white as privet-flowers, and there are red rims round her eyes. Jemima is devoured with curiosity as to the cause of these phenomena; but she does not ask.

"Jemima," says her sister, brusquely, "let us leave this place! Let us move on somewhere else!"

"Leave Dinan! leave *Mr. Le Mesurier!*" cries Jemima, archly, raising her eyebrows, as she stands before the glass, screwing up her pale, thin hair into a little lump at the top of her head, and drawing a white crochet-net over it, in preparation for her virgin slumbers.

"I am sick of Dinan and Mr. Le Mesurier," rejoins Lenore, petulantly.

"Sick of Dinan! sick of Mr. Le Mesurier!" exclaims the other, now thoroughly astonished, turning round with her mouth open. "Since when?"

"Since five-and-twenty minutes past eleven this morning, if you wish to be exact," replies Lenore, with candid bitterness. "There, do not tease, but let us go!"

" Go where ? "

" ' Anywhere, anywhere out of the world ! ' " answers the young girl, falling back wearily on the bed, and dishevelling the cool trim pillow on which her sister's chaste head is to repose. " To Guingamp, to see the *pardon*."

" And what is a *pardon*, pray ? for I have not the remotest idea," answers the elder, coming toward the bed, having finished her night-toilet, in the severe simplicity of which she looks at least twenty years older than in her day one.

" If you had read novels less, and your Murray more, you would not have needed to ask that question," replies Lenore, rolling her head about. " A *pardon* is a sort of religious *fête ;* very dull, I do not doubt, but "—with a tired sigh—" it all comes in the day's work ; let us go ! "

CHAPTER XII.

WHAT JEMIMA SAYS.

WE are at Guingamp. We have been here two hours. Two hours ago we arrived hot and hungry ; hustled by thronging groups of peasants, that are pressing into the little town to receive the annual pardon of their sins, and open a fresh account with God. The Hôtel de France brims over with guests ; insomuch that we have been relegated to a stuffy little chamber *au quatrième* into which the afternoon sun beats full ; hotter than ten thousand Christmas fires. Just now we asked for hot water, to wash our dirty faces ; and a woman in a huge starched white collar, and clear cap, brought in some in a tiny *teapot*. This has put the culminating point to our despair.

It is one of those days when one's very *soul* is hot, and longs to throw off the heavy cloak of the body; a day when one would fain take off one's flesh, and sit in one's bones, according to Sydney Smith's time-honored waggery. It is not windless; on the contrary, there is a very perceptible air; but it is such air as meets you at the mouth of a furnace. Lenore has abandoned the struggle with circumstances. She has acknowledged herself beaten, and lies all along, in extremest dishabille, on the narrow bit of parquet between the two beds, where the hard oak communicates a little coolness to the back. Her head rests on a pillow that she has pulled down; a white dressing-gown is loosely wrapped about her, and her small bare feet wander about impatiently in the vain search for a cool spot on the hot boards. Now and again, odd, sluggish, beetleish animals, with slate-colored bodies, crawl over her outflung arms. She has just energy enough to shake them off, and call piteously to me to come and kill them with my shoe-heel. Our two windows and our door are open; we are trying to believe that we are in a draught. A regiment is passing through Guingamp; the officers are billetted on our hotel. Every now and then one hears the clink of a sabre, and the sound of heavy feet coming down our corridor.

"Heavens, Jemima! shut the door!" cries my sister, unwilling to be exposed in her present sketchy toilet to the gaze of the French army. I spring forward and close it; and as soon as the large-busted, small-waisted hero, in his hot red trousers and tight epauletted frock-coat, has passed, fling it wide again. I have been unpacking, my head buried in my small canvas-covered box; it is more than woman born of woman can bear. I rise and lean out of the window. Outside a lugubrious horn is playing "Partant pour la Syrie," *very* slowly; the omnibus is just driving into the court-yard.

"Poor omnibus! poor horses.!" cry I, compassionately, "how many times have they been down to the station to-day? What a heap of luggage!"

"Jemima, my head is not high enough yet; give me your pillow too!" calls out Lenore, lamentably, from the floor. I comply, and then return to the window, and look again at the omnibus, which is just beginning to empty its load.

"Good Heavens!" ejaculate I, with animation. "Why, Lenore, there is Mr. Le Mesurier getting out! He has a puggry round his hat; how odd he looks!"

Lenore is disposing two pillows and a bolster to her mind; she gives a great start, but her head is turned from me.

"I wish he would get a new portmanteau," pursue I, soliloquizing, "the P. Le M. on his is getting nearly effaced with age."

The omnibus still disgorges: an old priest in a broad felt hat, and limp sash round his huge waist, with a yellow face and black teeth, yawning prodigiously. A peasant-woman with a queer baby in a tight calico skull-cap; then another gentleman in a puggry.

"The plot thickens," cry I, with a sprightly air. "Lenore, I think the friend has turned up at last. I began to fancy that he was a sort of Mrs. Harris; but seeing is believing, and here he is!"

Silence.

"*How* good-looking!" say I, under my breath, as the second gentleman joins the first, and indicates his worldly goods to the garçon. I hear a scrambling noise behind me. Lenore is at my side; her face is white, and she peeps obliquely behind the curtain, as the hot breeze blows back her loose bright hair.

"How ugly your friend Paul looks beside him!" say I, spitefully.

" When does not he look ugly ? " rejoins my junior, with bitterness.

" They are parleying with the landlady," say I, leaning out. " No doubt she is civiller to them than she was to us ; I suppose two maidless, courierless, husbandless women must resign themselves to being snubbed ? Ah, poor dear Frederick ! How one does miss him ! "

" Under which head did he come ? " asks Lenore, dryly ; " maid, courier, or husband ? "

The luggage is carried into the house ;. the pageant fades. I return to my packing, and ten minutes pass.

" Lenore, dear, you had better be beginning to dress," I say, hortatively ; " the clock struck the quarter five minutes ago."

" I am not thinking of dressing," replies Lenore, looking enormously long, as she lies stretched straight out.

" You are going down to dinner as you are, in fact— bare legs and a dressing-gown ? " say I, humorously.

" I am not going down to dinner at all," replies she, clasping her hands underneath her head.

" Not going down to dinner ! What *do* you mean ? " exclaim I, in high astonishment.

" Jemima, do French people *ever* open their windows ? Do not they hate fresh air ? Would it be possible to eat steaming ragouts in a close room with fifty commercial travellers to-day of all days ? "

" Before the omnibus came from the station, you thought it quite possible," reply I, dryly.

Silence.

" Come, now, did not you ? "

" Well, yes " (looking rather sheepish).

" It is on account of Mr. Le Mesurier that you are going to forego your dinner ? "

" Well, yes " (much more sheepishly).

"Lenore! Lenore! what has he done?" cry I, kneeling down beside her, in a frenzy of curiosity; "tell me."

"He has done nothing," turning her face away, and plucking at the pillow with her fingers.

"What has he said?"

"He has said nothing."

"Did he tell you that you were not good form, according to his pet expression?" (laughing).

"No."

"Did he make love to you?" suggest I, growing wild in my conjectures. ·

"No, no."

"Did he propose to you?"

"*No!* no! NO!"

I can ·only see her ear, which has grown suddenly scarlet.

"What *did* he do?" ask I, at my wit's end.

"Jemima," says Lenore, sitting up on the floor facing me, and looking very serious, "if I live to be a hundred and fifty, I will *never* tell you."

"I shall have to ask *him*, then; *he* will tell me quickly enough," answer I, nettled, and rising to my feet again.

"Perhaps; very likely," rejoins she, curtly.

"But you will come down to dinner, like a good child," say I, coaxingly, as I wrestle with a white muslin Garibaldi, which has shrunk in the washing, and is too small to contain my charms.

"I will not."

"But you have had no luncheon?"

"No."

"Nor afternoon tea?"

"No."

"You would probably be at a distance of half a mile

from him," say I, encouragingly; " the table is as long as from here to England; I saw it."

" Jemima," replies Lenore, gravely, looking at me with her large, solemn eyes, " I might sit exactly opposite to him, and that would kill me on the spot."

I shrug my shoulders.

"He is ugly enough, certainly," I say, severely; " but he is hardly such a Medusa's head that it is death to look at him.

But Lenore is obdurate.

"I had rather *die* than go down," she says, with the tragic exaggeration of youth, shaking her head, and all the shining tangles of hair that ripple about her throat.

The bell rings, tingling and jangling through the open doors and narrow passages. I am obliged to go down alone, in my shrunk muslin Garibaldi and shabby old black-silk skirt, into a crowd of bearded English and shorn French, who are gathered to raven like wolves in the *salle à manger*. I leave Lenore lying prone on the parquet, hungry and frowning, and slaying an occasional beetle with her slipper. At dinner I sit between the landlord and a close-shaved little Breton, with a vast and greasy appetite. In silence and loneliness I raven like my neighbors. Mr. Le Mesurier fulfils my prophecy; he is half a mile off. Now and again I have a vision of his leonine beard between the thirteen or fourteen intervening guests, and of a handsome blond head beyond him. On remounting to our garret I find that Lenore has resumed her clothes, and is sitting on the window-sill, pelting a stray dog in the court-yard with cherry-stones. Her eyes turn with a sort of anxiety to me as I enter.

" Well, well," say I, spitefully, " there was an excellent dinner; I have brought you a ' *menu*,' to show you what you have lost:

'POTAGE.—Vermicelli.

'POISSONS.—Soles, fines herbes.

'ENTRÉES.—Jambon Madère. Poulets sautés. Champignons—'"

"Pooh!" interrupts my sister, impatiently. "What do I care? Well, did you—did you see him?"

"I caught a glimpse now and then of his chestnut curls," reply I, banteringly; "only a glimpse, though, as he was at least a kilometre off."

"Did he see you?"

"Probably not; the dear fellow did not seem to have eyes for any thing but his dinner."

"He did not miss me, then?" with an accent of chagrin.

"If he did, he disguised it admirably."

"I might have gone down, after all."

"Perfectly."

She picks up the *menu.* "'Jambon Madère'—how good it sounds! Why did you not ask it to walk up-stairs? Jemima, are there any biscuits left in your bag?"

I investigate, and find half a one, and a great many dusty crumbs, upon which my sister pounces, as a kitten upon a ball of worsted.

"I could not, conscientiously, say the children's grace, 'Thank God for my good dinner,'" she says, shaking her head. "Jemima, let us go out."

"It is only eight o'clock, and the *pardon* does not begin till nine."

"Never mind; there is, at all events, more to see in the town than there is here, and I shall be more likely to forget that fifteen hours must elapse before I see food again."

So we go and pass through the court-yard, and out into the cheerful, swarming streets. The prospect of having a year's sins wiped off seems pleasant, for all faces look gay.

5

The town is thronged with exquisitely-starched, clean
lace caps, sticking out half a mile behind their owners'
heads—thronged with broad felt hats, and loose embroidered waistcoats, trimmed with chains of silver buttons.
They are like peasants in a melodrama—real benighted
peasants—who have not yet begun to tell themselves that
they are quite as good as their betters, and that there is no
reason why they should not wear hats and bonnets of exactly the same shape and fabric.   But even here Innovation
is laying her ugly hand.   Even Brittany is setting forth on
the road that leads to chimneypot-hats and shooting-coats;
even here the ancient Breton costume, in all its purity, is
the exception; the old world trunk-hose of yesterday is
ceding to the new-world trousers of to-day.

We stroll slowly up through the chattering crowd,
among long-haired, lank men, and laughing, weather-beaten
women.   On most Breton faces is written, " Life to us is
arduous."   No one is drunk, and no one was swearing.
" How *can* they be happy, then ?" would be the thought
of an English working-man ; but they are, or, at least, they
look so.

The church is already lit, though it is yet day—little
points of yellow light, flickering feebly in the broad, white
light of the summer evening.   We mount the steps—
mount them gingerly, lest we should tread on the outspread
legs of the crowded worshippers, crowded as swarmed bees,
upon the steps, and in the porch, before an image there.
We enter the church; censers are swinging slowly ; the
fragrant hush of a holy gloom is spread between the dim,
high arches—gloom that the thousand little yellow lights
are fighting against.   Grown men, with swart heads bent,
and doffed hats in their rough hands; women ; little, prim
children in caps like their mothers', and petticoats down to
their little heels, all—all are prostrate before each gaudy

shrine, sending up their simple souls in prayer to God's great mother.

Not to her alone, however. As thickly as about the crowned and sceptred virgin the people press around a brass head, with a glass window in its chest, and its nose blackened by the salutations of many past years and generations. Standing a few paces off, I am watching a tall youth who, with long, thick hair hanging straight and black about his harsh, melancholy face, is stooping to kiss the uncouth, brazen feature, when an English voice sounds low and laughing in my ear :

" Worse than the pope's toe, is not it ? " I give an angry start. Devotion is as catching as mumps. Without any feeling of the ridiculous, I could have followed the Breton boy's example, and kissed the blackened nose. Paul Le Mesurier is beside me, and, beyond him, heedless of the praying Bretons, staring with all his blue eyes at Lenore, stands a fair, handsome youth, leaning against a pillar.

" Is it wicked to introduce people in church ? " asks Paul, *sotto voce.* " I cannot help it if it is ; I have had no peace since.—Scrope, let me introduce you to Miss Herrick."

CHAPTER XIII.

WHAT THE AUTHOR SAYS.

" I hope you are better, Miss Lenore," says Paul, leaving his friend and his acquaintance together, and treading his way between the kneeling country-people to where the young girl stands with her back resolutely turned to him, and her eyes as resolutely fixed upon the high altar, aflame with lights and laden with flowers.

"Better of what?" she asks, brusquely, not turning toward him.

"I always think there must be something radically wrong with a person who foregoes her dinner in a land where luncheon is unknown," he answers, trying to get a peep round the corner into her averted face.

"How do you know that I forewent my dinner?" she inquires, sharply, glancing at him for an instant, and then looking away again as quickly."

"I saw your sister, and I did not see you."

"I dined up-stairs," she answers, shortly. He looks at her doubtfully.

"Did you, really?. Why?"

"I hate talking in church," she says, flashing round impatiently at him; "it is irreverent."

"So do I; the incense gets into my head. Let us go outside."

"You may go, if you choose," she says, setting her back against a pillar, and resolutely ignoring his presence. "I prefer to stay here."

A little child kneeling at her feet in a close calico cap, with a rosary between its little fingers, stares up wonderingly, with wide eyes, at the monsieur and the madame, standing so erect and chattering so irreverently in the great solemn church.

"Your sister and Scrope are going down the steps now," he says, stooping a little to whisper to her in deference to the sacred place, while an amused gleam flashes in his eyes. "The procession will begin in a quarter of an hour. Come!"

She makes a half movement of compliance.

"Mind," she says, looking at him, defiantly, "I am coming, not in the least because you ask me, but because I do not want to miss this fine sight."

The street is fuller than ever. The dusk is drawing on. Gendarmes in cocked hats and tail-coats; tight-belted, red-legged soldiers, leavening the mass of the peasants. A woman at a stall selling candles—candles as thick as your waist; candles as thick as your wrist; candles no thicker than your finger. Every one is buying, each person laying down his francs or centimes, and walking proudly off with a hollow taper as tall as himself.

"You have not forgiven me yet, then?" says Le Mesurier, as he elbows a way for his companion between the woollen-shawled women and embroidered-jacketed men.

"Forgiven you for what?" she asks, resolutely obtuse, while her cheeks show a sudden rivalship with the poppy-bunch in her hat.

"For my—my unlucky embassy," he answers, with a rather awkward laugh.

She looks away from him to the illuminated church, at once bright and dark against the warm gloom of the June twilight.

"I thought it was very officious of you," she answers, coldly.

"*Officious!*" echoes he, quickly, while his own tanned cheeks catch the pretty angry poppy hue. "Do you suppose I did it for my own pleasure? Do you suppose that I ever, in all my life, had a job that I hated more?"

"Why did you undertake it, then?" asks the girl, dryly.

"Because I was living in the same house with him; because I had no peace day or night; because I was sick of the sound of your name; because—poor little beggar!— he *cried*—yes, actually *cried!* If I said 'No' once, I said it a hundred times."

" It was a pity that you did not say it a hundred and one times."

" I not only," continues Paul, becoming exasperated, and consequently spiteful, while his usually quiet eyes give a cold flash, " I not only declined the office for myself, but I did all I could to dissuade him from asking you himself."

" Thank you."

"I told him that, if he *did* induce you to marry him, you would make him rue the day."

" Thank you."

" I told him how utterly unsuited you were for a parson's wife."

" Thank you."

" How much more suited to him your sister was."

"Thank you; *two* 'thank yous,' indeed—one for myself, and one for Jemima."

" He had some fatuous idea in his head of being able to *mould* you into the proper clerical shape; but I flatter myself I, at all events, succeeded in weeding *that* grotesque notion out of his mind."

" In short," says Lenore, turning sharply upon him a lovely crimson face, like a blown rose, and proud eyes trying to wink away the mortified tears, " in short, not satisfied with hating me yourself, you have been doing your best to make one of my few friends hate me too."

" Well, at all events," retorts he, smiling, and recovering his good-humor at the same moment as she loses hers, "at all events, I did not succeed; for, despite all my dissuasions, you see, he still wished to gain you."

The crowd grows thicker and thicker. In five minutes the procession will begin. Leaning over a little balcony above them, some English ladies and gentlemen are laughing real English laughs, unlike the high cascades of shrill French laughter.

"We shall be hustled to death down here," says Paul, lifting his high head to look over the press. "We ought to have secured a window, like those Britishers up there. It is not too late now. Let us ask the candle-woman."

The candle-woman turns from the diminished heap of her tapers to listen politely to Paul's slow, laborious English-French.

"Monsieur and madame desire a *croisée*, in order to see the procession? *Mais oui, certainement.* If monsieur and madame will have the goodness to follow her, she will conduct them."

So saying, she leads them under an archway, through an empty workshop, and up a perfectly dark and filthy flight of stone stairs. The room to which they at length attain belongs to a *blanchisseuse*. It is low and poor, but very clean. Neatly-starched caps are hanging on a line across the room; two tidy little beds are in the small recesses; a crucifix hangs over the chimney-piece; and an excruciating smell from the gutter below rises up to their offended nostrils. The owner of the apartment, having expressed an obliging hope that madame will not be "*trop gênée par l'odeur*," and, having placed a hassock on the low sill for Lenore to lean her arms upon, leaves her visitors in peace. Paul stands upright and silent, with an expression of face as if he were trying entirely to repress the faculty of smell. Lenore lets her eyes wander round, and gives the reins to her imagination.

Supposing that this garret were her home—hers and Paul's; supposing that she spent her life in ironing caps, and hanging them on lines. Supposing that Paul spent his in digging in the fields, and came back at night to *galette* and cider, in a broad Breton hat and trunk hose. Good Heavens! how ugly he would look! She breaks off her suppositions to smile involuntarily at the idea.

"What are you smiling at?" asks Paul, stooping over her, and swallowing a large mouthful of *bouquet de gutter* as he speaks.

"Must I tell you, *really?*" she asks, lifting her face— every dimple full of mischievous laughter—to his.

"Yes."

"I was thinking, then—mind, you *made* me tell you— how ugly you would look in a flapping felt hat and trunk hose."

"Is that all?" he answers, carelessly. "I can assure you that I am nothing to what I was when I was a boy. In my old regiment we used to pique ourselves upon being the ugliest corps in the service; we had not a decent-look- ing fellow among us."

There is a little pause. Everybody is lighting his or her candle; one or two unlucky mortals have broken theirs off in the middle.

"Did you *really* think I should marry Frederick?" asks Lenore presently, with abruptness.

"How could I tell?"

"But did you think it *probable?*"

"If I were a woman, I do not think I should care about undertaking him," he answers, laughing. "But you might have done worse."

She looks away, vexed; she could hardly have said why.

"He is exactly five feet two inches high," she says, scornfully, drawing up her long, white throat, and looking insultingly tall.

"Do you mete out your love to a man according to his inches?" he asks, leaning his arms on the back of his chair, and laughing again.

"He has a nose like a piece of putty."

"He has."

"He wears barnacles."

"He does."

" And goloshes."

"Yes."

" He plays the concertina at tea-parties."

" Does he ? "

" And sings, ' I'm a nervous man.' "

" So he is."

" He turns up his trousers at the bottom when it rains."

" Well, why should he not ? "

" It would be impossible," says the young girl, with trenchant emphasis, " to marry a man who did *any one* of those things; it is a thousand times more impossible to marry a man who does them *all.*"

" He would let you have your own way in everything, big or little; he would let you ride rough-shod over him. It would be very bad for you, but I suppose it would please you," answers Paul, half cynically, taking in, with an uncomfortable, unwilling glance, the poppy-crowned hat; the eyes, dew-soft yet spirited; the fine nostrils, and blood-red lips, half parted, as if for some sweet speech of his young companion.

" Perhaps it would, perhaps it would not," she answers, gently. " I have never loved anybody *yet*—never; at least, not for long—not for more than two days; but, of course, I shall some day; and then, I suppose—I fancy—I imagine " (stammering) " that what he likes, I shall like."

Is it some reflection from the lights outside, or are her cheeks a shade more deeply colored than usual, as she lifts her eyes, with a sort of tender trouble in their shady depths, to his?

He shakes his head.

" May I be there to see ! " he says, with a light laugh; but there is no laugh in his eyes—instead, an eager gravity, touched with the stirrings of a restless passion. When an

uncivil woman is to *you* alone civil, when a cold woman is
for *you* alone warm, when a high-spirited woman is for *you*
alone meek, the flattery is trebled in value. It is difficult
to feel sentimental in a very bad smell; but I think, if you
asked him, Paul Le Mesurier would tell you that he accomplished that feat in the little Guingamp garret. The procession is really beginning, at last; out of the lit church-
doors it streams, and the surging sea of heads parts and
cleaves asunder to make way for it. Gilt and colored lamps
lead the way, carried by Breton peasants; then the relics
of a saint in a gilt case; then a troop of young girls in
white, clear and clean as St. Agnes; then a troop of sail-
ors, also in white, with red sashes—two carrying a little
model of a ship, two carrying a gilt anchor between them;
then a wax figure in a red-silk petticoat, carried on a bier.

"It is *le petit* Saint-Vincent!" cries the good woman
of the house, in high excitement, clasping her hands, "carried by Basse-Bretagne peasants, clad in soutanes for the
occasion, an honor for which they will have to pay high.
Has madame observed him? How pretty he is! how
fresh! how white! as white as a little chicken."

"And who is le petit Saint-Vincent when he is at
home?" asks Paul, in crass ignorance of the Roman Catho-
lic calendar.

"He was martyrized at fourteen years," explains the
woman; and so falls into fresh raptures.

"O! qu'il est gentil, le petit Saint-Vincent! Il est si
frais! si rose!"

"If she is so much struck with le petit Saint-Vincent,
what would not she be with Madame Tussaud's establishment?" says Paul, laughing and leaning on the sill.

He is past now—he and his red petticoat. *La bonne
Dame des hommes* follows close on his heels, borne on de-
vout shoulders; then the brass head with the blackened

nose waggles along; then gray-haired priests, in glorious, flowered damask robes, holding high the effigy, in ivory and gold, of the slaughtered Christ; then two bishops in mitres; then a great flood of snowy caps and broad-brimmed beavers; everybody with a candle—some big, some little, but everybody with one. It is the greatest wonder how they managed to avoid setting fire to each other. All together, singing loudly yet sweetly, they float away slowly into the distance.

Half caught by the infection of their devotion, Lenore throws herself forward half through the rusty casement to look down the street—one sea of waving light, an undulating river of light, rather, flowing between the two dark banks of the houses on either side. The soft glamour of the summer moonrise makes glorious each little detail of the queer pretty show. The colored lamps sparkle like real great jewels—rubies, sapphires, amethysts—through the cool night. The young girls' dresses shine dazzlingly, candescently white; even the brass head with the black nose is transmuted to gold.

"What a pleasant, easy way of getting to heaven!" says Lenore, withdrawing her head. "I wish I could believe that a big candle and a kiss to little Saint-Vincent would take me there!"

"Do not you think we have had almost enough of this?" asks Le Mesurier, rather indistinctly, from between the folds of his pocket-handkerchief, in which he has now completely enveloped his nose and mouth. "O libelled Cologne! If Coleridge had but smelt Guingamp!"

So they descend into the street. The procession is to circle round the town, chanting always, and reënter the church by another door. It will be some time before this is accomplished. Meanwhile, people still swarm in the space before the church—women in close, stiff, black bonnets or hats, and big black collars to match, taking one back to the reign of Edward VI.; dark, sad-faced, lean men. These are from the very, *very* Basse Bretagne. They are so poor, so poor! They have come on foot many a weary mile, to have their sins forgiven; they will sleep in the street to-night, and at cock-crow to-morrow set forth on the trudge back to their far, lone homes. Others, with almost low-necked dresses, and wide, loose muslin collars. They are all tramping hither and thither, talking very merrily, hustling Paul and Lenore with their stout Breton elbows, threatening them with their heavy sabots, which at any moment may come pounding down on their feet.

" You had better take my arm," says Paul, with a protecting air, as they move slowly along. " I might easily mislay you in this crush, and, if I did, it would be like looking for a needle in a bottle of hay to try and find you again."

" It would be no great harm if you *did* mislay me," she answers, with a pretty air of independence. " I, who have travelled all over England, Scotland, and Ireland, quite by myself, am hardly afraid of coming to harm in the half-dozen safe yards that intervene between here and the Hôtel de France."

" What business had you to travel all over England, Scotland, and Ireland, by yourself?" he asks, brusquely. " It was very wrong of your people to let you."

" Of course," she answers, with irony, " of course, I ought to have had a maid to carry my dressing-case, and a footman to take my ticket and look after my luggage. So I will, some day, when I marry the Marquis of Carrabas, or —or *Frederick!*"

" You will *never* marry Frederick!" he says vehemently, involuntarily pressing the small hand that lies on his arm close to his side. " *Never!* NEVER!!" (looking down at her face, on which the flaring candles are throwing capricious little crimson flushes).

"Shall not I?" she says, lifting her limpid innocent gaze to his. "I do not know." He is silent, at least as far as speech goes. He has forgotten the *pardon*, the white caps, the thronging peasants. His reason is drowning fast—*fast*—in the unfathomed wells of a woman's slate-blue eyes. "You told me just now that I might do worse," she says, under her breath.

"So you might," he says, with some excitement. "So you might. I said true: you might" (with a rather reckless laugh)—"you might marry—*me!* who am the younger son of a younger son—have not a sixpence to bless myself with, and have the devil's own temper to boot."

At his words her head droops forward, like a snow-drop's, weighed down with a heavy shame; her hand falls from his arm. It is past eleven o'clock; the people are hurrying into church again for the midnight mass. At the door every one gives up his or her candle to men stationed to receive them. There is a great heap, as high as your shoulder, already in the porch. A throng of peasants—lean, long men; stout, square women; big lads—come pushing by, nearly hoisting Lenore off her legs. As they pass she utters a little sharp cry of pain.

"What is it? Are you hurt?" asks Paul, vigorously shouldering aside the peasants, who are beginning to crowd again as thickly as ever, and digging his elbows viciously into the plump ribs of a matron behind him.

"It is nothing," she says, a little faintly; "one of them trod on me, I think, and a *sabot* is not the lightest—there!" (beginning to laugh a little), "do not look as if you were bent on knocking *somebody* down; it would be sure to be the wrong somebody."

"You *are* hurt," he says, with vague indignation, gazing down solicitously at the cheeks that the little sudden pain has drained of their sweet, red blood; "I know you are, only you are too spirited to own it."

"You are wrong," she says, smiling; "from a child I have always cried out *before* I was hurt."

"Lean on me; lean all your weight on me," says Paul, obligingly, drawing her away out of the press, and into a little side street.

"Ah! here is a door step—let us sit down and rest."

The little street is quite dark, at least on the side where Paul and Lenore are; as dark as the Place du Guesclin under the limes. Only on the faces of the houses opposite the moonbeams are sliding pearl-white.

"I never *could* bear pain," says the girl, languidly, leaning her back against the closed door of the unseen house. "I never *could* understand that line of Long-fellow's—

'To suffer and be strong.'

'To suffer and *scream*,' is my version."

There is a momentary pause between them. They are beginning to feel as if they need not be talking all the while. In the deep shade where they are sitting they can hardly see each other's face: they only feel one another's pleasant proximity. The tramp, tramp of wooden shoes, the distant chant, bandied about, tossed this way and that by the frolic airs, come, now loud, now low, to their ears.

"I wonder what time it is?" says Lenore, presently, reluctantly breaking the happy silence; "ten? eleven? twelve?"

"What does it matter?" replies Paul, indolently, clasping his hands behind his head. She is the exact opposite of every thing he has hitherto thought good and fair in woman. Her very beauty—large and noble—is the reverse of the small, meek prettiness that has hitherto been his

ideal, and yet—and yet it is pleasant to him to sit in the
dry, warm gloom beside her, while the night winds, fresh
from the tanned haycocks, fondle his hair with lightest,
gentlest hands. The church-clock strikes midnight: each
slow stroke falling on the air like a rebuke.

"I must go," replies the girl, half-frightened, springing
to her feet.

"Go!" repeats Paul, impatiently, rising too. "Why
must you? Shall we be better off in two stuffy garrets in
the Hôtel de France, *apart*, than here *together?*"

They are standing in the middle of the street: a tall,
ugly man, a tall, beautiful woman (men always have the
best of the bargains in this world). She has taken off her
hat: it hangs with its coquettish poppies and black ribbons
in her drooped right hand; the moon is throwing little jets
of silver on the waveless sweep of her hair.

"We shall at least be less likely to take cold," she answers, demurely.

But Paul is losing his head. Lenore and the moonshine are too much for him.

"Cold?" he repeats, crossly. "You never thought
about cold that happy night when we went on the Rance
together."

"*That happy night*, when you tried so hard to get out
of going, and said it was time to go to bed," she answers,
mockingly, while her eyes for the moment lose their love-
light, and glitter maliciously. He laughs rather consciously.
"That happy night when you soaked all the color out of
my blue ribbons, and drowned my best hat for me," continues she, gayly. "No, no! we will have no more happy
nights. My wardrobe would not stand it! Come, let
us go!"

CHAPTER XIV.

WHAT JEMIMA SAYS.

"IT is too late now," says Lenore, with a sulky pout, leaning her arms on the top of the wrought-iron rails of the balcony; "l'Américaine is at the door."

We are no longer at Guingamp. We have moved on to Morlaix, and are lodged in a certain hostelry, that is scented through and through with the ill odor arising from the very unclean stable over which it is built:

> "I do not wish to tell its name,
> Because it is so much to blame."

No one dislikes the smell of a *clean* stable. The warm, pungent odor that greets you, when you go to see your friend's hunters, need offend no well-educated nostrils; but the terrific reek that ascends from the lodgings of the Breton beasts of hire, that you swallow, *nolens volens*, in bed, in your bath, with your tea, with your cider—which enters not only your nose and mouth, but even your very eyes and ears—is trying to the least sensitive organs. We two are seated—by-the-by, Lenore is standing—in a little salon whose balcony overlooks the street, and whence we may spy the passers below, keep a lookout on Lozach, *Débitant de boissons*, opposite, and refresh ourselves with a slightly-varied version of essence of manure. A great bow-pot, full of immense roses, stands at my elbow: each several rose smells mightily of tobacco: a phenomenon accounted for by the fact that the salon is daily resorted to for smoking and coffee-drinking purposes by the noble army of commercial travellers who breakfast and dine at the *table d'hôte*. When "*ces messieurs*," as the landlord, with innocent irony, calls them, have retired, we are permitted to enter, and work our own wild will among the tobaccoed roses and the jingling old spinet in the corner.

"It is too late," says Lenore, from the balcony; "l'Américaine is at the door."

"It would be very easy to send it away again, I suppose."

"I suppose it would."

"I do not believe that there is any thing to see at Huelgoat," say I, skeptically, turning over the leaves of my familiar spirit, "Murray," and hunting among the H's in the index.

"I dare say not."

"Nothing but lead-mines and a reading-desk," say I, having found the place.

"Oh, indeed!"

"It is, then, merely for the pleasure of a *tête-à-tête* with Mr. Le Mesurier that you are going?" cry I, raising my voice a little, for fear that the lazy wind, that is ruffling the smoky roses and swaying the muslin curtains, may disperse my gibe.

"Merely for the pleasure of the *tête-à-tête* with Mr. Le Mesurier, as you felicitously observe," replies my sister, with baffling candor, leaving the balcony, and coming to stand defiantly before me, with her chin a little raised, and her hands folded behind her back, in her favorite attitude, like a child saying its lesson. Some people's clothes look as if they were *thrown* on; some as if they were put on; some as if they *grew* on. Lenore's is the latter case.

"I should have thought that you must have had a surfeit of those delights by now," say I, disdainfully, with all an outsider's intolerance for the insipid repetitions of love-making.

"I have had exactly nine," answers Lenore, growing grave, while a happy absorption fills her eyes; "I think" (smiling) "I must make it a dozen; and then, perhaps, if Mr. Scrope is very good, I may give him a turn."

I feel vexed, and, unable and unwilling to explain why, rise, and, walking over to a little *étagère* in the corner, begin to fiddle with some deplorable spar-boxes with "A Present from Brighton" on them; traces, even here, of the indefatigable Briton, who has inscribed his name and that of his blacking on the pyramid top. Lenore sits down at the old piano, and opens it.

"You might be *man and wife*, from the way in which you travel about together," say I, fuming.

"Perhaps we are," answers Lenore, with a laugh, her low, rippling laughter mixing pleasantly with the crash she is making among the bass notes; "to the prophetic eye, present and future are one."

"Heaven forbid!" say I, devoutly. "I cannot fancy calling that man 'Paul,' and kissing him, as I suppose one would have to if he were one's brother-in-law; one would lose one's self in the intricacies of that scarlet beard."

"It is *not* scarlet!" cries Lenore, in a fury, wheeling round on the music-stool; "it is not even red."

"It is like Graham's hair in 'Villette,'" reply I, gravely; "whose color his friends did not dare to specify, except when the sun shone on it, and then they called it golden."

A little pause.

"I do not think that two young women in our position *can* be too careful," say I, primly; "and really, Lenore, it is hardly advisable."

"Advisable!" interrupts my sister, jumping off her stool and giving a little stamp, while her pretty pink nostrils dilate with angry wilfulness. "I hate the word; it is a mean, sneaking, time-serving word. Either a thing is right, or it is wrong; if it is not right, it is wrong: and, if it is not wrong, it is right. If it is not wrong to take a drive on a summer day with a man whose society—"

She stops as if she had been shot. The door has opened, and the man whose society—is looking in and saying—

"Miss Lenore, are you ready?"

There is a flushed confusion on his honest, ugly face, as if he had overheard Lenore's last speech; and, indeed, as she has always a singularly pure, clear enunciation, and declaimed this last sentence in a high key, and with a distinct and trenchant emphasis, I do not see how the poor man could well help it.

"*Am I ready?*" says Lenore, with an awkward laugh, turning away to hide her discomfiture. "That is amusing! A man keeps one waiting an hour and a half, and then comes and asks innocently, 'Are you ready?'"

At the door stands the "Américaine," so called because more *un*like an Américaine than any other conceivable vehicle; a little, heavy, jingling rattletrap, with a hood in the last stage of shabbiness. A little old mare in her dotage, and a tall colt, hardly come to years of discretion, compose the team. One has bells, the other has none; both are smothered under immense sheepskin collars, like leviathan door-mats; the flies are teasing them sadly. A noble army of beggars—

"—— Men and boys,
The matron and the maid,"

press round with obliging *empressement;* old, blear-eyed men beggars; capped and long-frocked little girl beggars— lame boy beggars—beggars with ingeniously-horrible malformations of Nature, well brought forward into notice.

"So this is a walking-tour through Brittany, is it Paul?"

asks Mr. Scrope, pensively, as we emerge from the door.
He is leaning against the door-post, looking very handsome,
very lazy, and half asleep, as he mostly does. "So *this* is
the pedestrian exercise that was to make you two stone
lighter by next season!—O Miss Herrick!" shaking his
head at Lenore, and smiling reproachfully with his indolent
blue eyes, "how much you have to answer for!"

They get in. I think they feel rather foolish, sitting
perched up on high, side by side. There is something absurdly nuptial about this departure.

"Go on! what are you stopping for?" cries Paul, in
the worst possible French. The driver says "*Sapr—r—r,*"
the poor beasts stretch to their work; the old rope traces
strain; the grin of expectation vanishes from the beggars'
faces.

"Do not you feel as if we ought to throw old shoes after them?" asks Mr. Scrope, turning languidly to me, as
the bells go tinkle tinkle down the street. I smile.
"Would a sabot do as well? I might borrow one." The
jingling has ceased. They are fairly gone.

"What shall *we* do, Miss Herrick, now that our natural
protectors have left us?" says my companion, appealing
piteously to me, as I stand on the broiled and broiling
steps under the umbrella with which I have judiciously
furnished myself; while the sun catches his yellow hair
and the young, soft mustache that rather directs attention
to than hides his handsome mouth—the feature that is sel-
domer than any other in the human face good. "What
shall we do? Shall we hire a couple of jackasses, and go
out riding?"

"Rather too hot, I think."

"It *is* hot, now you speak of it. Phew!"

CHAPTER XV.

WHAT THE AUTHOR SAYS.

CERTAINLY it is sleepy work, driving to Huelgoat. The day is one of those that remind one of a bad painting or of the landscape on a papier-mâché tea-tray: garish, staring, inartistic. The sky is all dead blue, and the trees are all dead green. Jingle, jingle, jingle, tingle, sound the bells; jig, jog, with their noses down to their knees, go the horses along the road—that is white as flour, and quite as powdery. Up long-backed hills, down long-backed hills; up, down, up, down; there is no end to it. The driver forgets to flick his whip, and cry " *Allez! allez!* " He sits swaying to and fro in the sunshine, fast asleep. He looks old and starveling, as if he never had enough to eat in all his life. Great sweeps of fern and gorse spread around, only broken by little miserable patches of oats and *blé noir;* endless reaches of desolate moorland—gray, barren, silent. It makes one shiver, even in this broiling noon, to think how the north wind must rush and rage over these eerie wolds, these awful *landes*, on a January night. Jig jog, jig jog. The road still twists, twists always, like a white snake writhing its endless folds about the hills.

"I wonder how they are getting on?" says Lenore, after a twenty minutes' silence, blinking in the sun, and trying to believe that she is enjoying herself.

" *They!* Who?" asks Paul, with an absent start.

"Jemima and Mr. Scrope, to be sure."

"I do not know about your sister, I'm sure," replies Paul, leaning back, and resting his head against the stained and discolored leather of the old hood; "I have not known her long enough to say; but, as I knew Scrope when he was in round jackets, and have seen a good deal of him, off and on, ever since, I can tell you to a nicety what he is doing, if you wish."

"What?"

"He is lying on his back, in the coolest place he can find, and drinking claret-cup, if he can ask for it in French, which I doubt; but if not, brandy and seltzer, cider and siphon, any thing—certainly *drinking;* and as certainly making love to some one—the landlady, the *femme de chambre,* your sister, perhaps, if she does not snub him as resolutely as she does me."

"Poor dear Mima!" says Lenore, laughing. "She will be sorely puzzled to know how to take it if he does."

"If it is not your sister, it is somebody else," says Paul, tilting his hat over his nose, and closing his eyes; "he is the sort of fellow that one could not trust alone in the room with his own grandmother for five minutes."

"Indeed!"

"Generally," pursues Paul, in a sleepy voice, "after a two days' acquaintance, he proposes to every woman he sees; if she refuses him, he asks her to be a sister, or mother, or aunt, or something of the sort, to him: if she accepts him, he is off by the next train, and never heard of (by *her,* at least) again."

"He must remind one of the saying that the best way to be rid of a troublesome friend is to lend him a five-pound note."

Their talk flags; the dust seems to have got into it; there is no juice in it. A little public-house stands by the roadside, a bunch of box over the door, to show that they sell cider there. Inside, a woman with a distaff, an old, old woman, all grin and wrinkles, every wrinkle filled up with dirt. Immensely tall pigs, with finely-arched backs, noses like greyhounds, and legs like antelopes, throng about the door. Now and again a primitive cart passes ; the shaggy, unkempt horses prick their ears and rear and plunge, as if they had never seen a civilized being before. With hardly less astonishment do their wild-eyed drivers stare. It is three o'clock and past by the time that Paul and Lenore reach Huelgoat—Huelgoat, sitting in the sunshine, at the *very* end of the world, beside her still gray tarn.

"I am ravenous," says Lenore, gayly, as they jingle up the dead gray street. "I ate no breakfast, did you ? One cannot eat in that smell. What shall we have ? Cutlets, trout ? There ought to be trout in that lake."

"Do not be too sanguine," answers Paul, shaking his head ; "it is uncharitable to judge by appearances, but, from a bird's-eye view of Huelgoat, I should say that whitebait was hardly less unlikely than trout *or* cutlets."

No one, it seems, at first sight, lives at the Hôtel de Bretagne, at least no one appears. They descend from the Américaine, and enter a flagged passage, with two doors exactly opposite each other, one on each side. That on the left is open, and gives admittance into a bright and fireless kitchen—innocent of the very faintest odor of cooking. A woman, in a cap that is a cross between a nightcap and a chimney-pot of the hooded kind, comes to meet them, with an immense white collar and a clean sour face.

"What did monsieur and madame wish ? "

"Monsieur and madame wish for something to eat, *now, immediately, à l'instant.*"

"Monsieur and madame can have some bread and butter—some cheese ; there is unhappily nothing else in the house *au moment.*"

"*Nothing else in the house !* " repeats Lenore, with angry volubility. " Why, there is a *chicken !* I saw it. I see it now, *there !* " pointing with her finger to where a long, lean cock lies, lank and plucked, in a meat-safe in the passage.

" There is, as madame has observed, a chicken, a superb chicken, but he is for the *table d'hôte*."

" But we are dying, perishing, *affamés !* " cries Lenore, eking out her uncertain talk with plentiful gesticulation.

" Monsieur and madame can have some bread and but-ter—some excellent cheese—an omelette."

It takes ten minutes of entreaties, expostulations, prayers, before she can be over-persuaded to the sacrifice of the "*superb*" chicken. On being asked how soon it will be dressed, she answers, " Half an hour ; " and, being earnestly besought to abridge that time, repeats, inexora-bly, "*Une demi-heure, à peu près.*"

" Let us go into the *salle à manger* and shut the door," says Lenore, despondently. " It will drive me mad to see her pottering and dawdling about ; and, if we watched her, she would only potter and dawdle the more, to spite us."

A quarter of an hour passes. They devour huge slices of the loaf, and make a clearance of three miserable little dry sardines, brought in on a plate. They look out of win-dow at the silent street, call it Welsh, Irish—every ugly name they can think of. Lenore could not coquet with Paul now, were she to be shot for it ; neither could Paul say any thing affectionate, even if under the same penalty. They are both far too hungry.

" Look if it has gone out of the meat-safe yet," says Lenore, presently.

" If it has not," replies Paul, gravely, " I am aware that it will be unmanly—but I shall *cry*."

He opens the door, and peeps out into the passage.

" It is there still ! "

Despair for a few moments—then rage ; then a rush

into the bright kitchen opposite, bright with pewters and coarsely-painted pottery plates ; bitter reproaches, quickly sunk in hopeless silence.

" Madame is unreasonable ; madame must have patience ; the fire is not yet lit ! "

They return to the *salle à manger*, and Lenore sits down ȯn the flagged floor, while her pretty blue gown makes what children call " a cheese " all around her. Paul stands over her in gloomy silence.

" How well I can understand now how shipwrecked mariners eat one another," she says, looking up at him, pathetically.

After a while a few coals of charcoal make a feeble glimmer in the open hearth. The enemy with the chimney-pot cap takes the fowl—his sex plainly declared by the comb which still adheres to his head—and runs him once or twice through the flame to singe him ; then, taking a few warm (not hot) coals, places them in a sort of tin box, and lays the carcass in the box at some distance from them.

" As if those wretched, half-dead embers could ever cook any thing ! " cries Lenore, indignantly. They sit stupidly gazing through the two open doors.

" How does he look ? "

" There is not a sign of cooking upon him," answers Le Mesurier, morosely. " He is as white as when he went in."

" He will be done only on one side," says Lenore, half crying ; " is not she going to turn him at all ? "

She comes in presently, and turns him over deliberately ; then goes, with unfeeling calmness, about her other occupations.

" Well ! *Now ?* " (eyes sparkling, and her long neck stretched to look into the kitchen).

" There is a slight shade of brown coming over him,"

6

says Paul, with a smile. Ten minutes more and he appears ; his legs and arms are all straggling wildly about, his skin is burnt blacker than any coal, and his flesh is as pink as a bit of catchfly ; but he is—oh, how delicious !

By-and-by, after he is eaten, and nothing but memory is left of his charms, they stroll out together down the dumb stone street, where tiny old-world children, in tight, white skull-caps, not showing a curl of their baby hair, are playing gravely in the gutter, with their long petticoats flapping about their heels and entirely hiding their little fat legs—where, just inside the doors, women in the home-*dishabille* of filthy-white chimney-pots sit at their spinning-wheels.

Coming to Huelgoat is synonymous with putting back the clock two hundred years. Down by a mill, along a narrow path, across a ferny slope, to see the *pierre tremblante.* Great rounded bowlders lie about like couchant elephants ; dusky fir-woods clothe the hills, that rise so close and stern, and on their barren breasts great gray granite masses heave huge shoulders out of the heathy ground. Below, a little brawling stream slides coyly under the great rocks, then bubbles coldly out again, talking to itself all the way and to the small marsh-flowers that grow about its low brim ; a little mountain-beck, like a flashing smile on the valley's lips, like a silver chain about the hill's cool feet.

Paul and Lenore have been climbing the hills, have been straying among the piny odors, have been pushing and fighting their way through the thick bilberry-bushes, and now they are hot and tired. Lenore is kneeling on a flat gray stone, and, stooping low down, lays her mouth to the clear water and drinks.

"I am too old and stiff to be so supple," says Paul, with a smile of admiring envy. "Make me a cup of your hands; I have no letter in my pocket to make a leaky *cornucopia* of."

She complies, gravely. Joining her white hands together, she dips them into the water, and then holds them up for him to drink. He has to drink very fast, as the water runs out nearly as quick as it came in. Then she stoops again, and bathes her head in the stream. The water rolls in diamond beads from her hair, and on to her turquoise-blue gown, as she kneels on the broad gray stone; long-legged flies are walking about on the stream; little blue butterflies hover round, like flying flowers that have grown tired of their stalks, and are gone visiting their kinsfolk. Paul is stretched on the short, fine grass on the other side of the brook, but yet not a span off. His elbows rest on the ground, and his hands are buried in his bronze beard. It is all so pretty, so lorn, so silent, as if, long ago, God had made this fair spot, and then forgotten it.

"Mr. Le Mesurier," says Lenore, suddenly, "do you think it was wrong of me to come with you here to-day? I would not ask any other man, because I know I should only get some silly, civil speech; but I know that *you* will tell me the truth, however disagreeable—perhaps" (laughing) "with all the more alacrity, the more unflattering it may be."

Paul lifts his head, and stares at her in some surprise at the demand made upon his veracity.

"Since when has your conscience grown so tender!" he asks, evasively. "Who has been putting such an idea into your head?—for I am sure it never grew there of itself."

"Jemima," she answers, dabbling her hand and her pocket-handkerchief in the bright water, with more than a child's delight. "When you came in this morning, she was in the middle of telling me how improper it was. I

do not mind *her;* she is an old maid—or, at least, in her,
coming events cast their shadows before.   But I want *you*
to tell me.   Is it wrong, incorrect—*hazardé*, as the French
say ? "

"Not one of the three, in the very least," he answers,
warmly.   "The worst that any one can say of it is, that it
is a little, a very little, unconventional."

"The woman with the eyes like a shot partridge would
not have done it, I suppose ?"

"Probably not."   Then, seeing her look mortified:
"If the woman with the eyes like a shot partridge has a
fault, it is being in the slightest degree in *too* great bond-
age to Mrs. Grundy.   She would hardly dare to go along
the road to heaven, unless she knew that many very respectable people had gone there before her."

Silence, save for the low, small noise that the glossy
bees make in visiting from heather-bloom to heather-bloom.
The high sun is already sloping westward ; in two or three
hours one will be able to look him in the face.

"If I had but Joshua's gift!" says Paul, sighing, as he
lies gazing up at the flawless sapphire above him.   "If I
could but say, with any hope of being obeyed, ' Sun, stand
thou still ! ' "

"Why *should* you say so ? " asks Lenore, opening her
eyes, as she busily wrings out her pocket-handkerchief, and
lays it on the grass to dry.   "Why should you *wish* to
stop him ?   He will last quite long enough to light us
home, and that is all we want him for to-day."

"*To-day !*   Yes," answers Le Mesurier, sighing again ;
"but, when one thinks that, in all human probability, he
will shine upon us two together at Huelgoat never
again ! "

"He will shine upon us two together at Morlaix," says
Lenore, playfully, " which will be much the same, will not

it? Probably he will not only shine upon us, but will freckle us a good deal."

"He will not shine upon us *together* anywhere long," says Paul, rather crossly, as if vexed by her gayety.

"What do you mean?"

"I mean that I am going back to England the day after to-morrow; that is all."

"Going!" she repeats, while a cowardly, treacherous white spreads over cheeks and lips; and her wet hands drop forgotten into her lap.

"Yes; I am going," answers Paul, his vain man's heart all astir at sight of her change of countenance, and his face gaining all the color hers has lost. "My people, who have never hitherto shown much propensity for my society, have suddenly found that I am indispensable to them."

She turns her head aside, and looks away toward the piny hills.

"So you are going away?" she says, almost under her breath. "Well" (forcing a smile), "considering how in-auspiciously our acquaintance began, we have got on very well together, have not we?"

"*Very* well," answers Paul, emphatically.

"We have managed to agree pretty well, although I am *not your style*" (with a perceptible accent on the last three words).

"*Not my style?* What *do* you mean?" he asks, red-dening consciously.

"Although you *did* think it such a hardship coming on that tea-picnic with us down the Rance, although you *did* look at your watch so often and sigh so heavily! I thought once or twice" (laughing a little) "that you would have blown out Frederick's new-lit fire."

"Is it possible?" cries Paul, tragically; not in the

least struck by the ridiculousness of the offence imputed to him, but rather by the state of mind in himself that such an offence evidenced.

Lenore bends her eyes on the ground; her fingers, ignorant of what they are doing, pluck at the fine blades of grass, and dwarf yellow flowers about her; her figure has a drooped air of languor.

> "There was a pretty redness in her lip
> A little riper and more lusty red
> Than that mixed in her cheek; 'twas just the difference
> Betwixt the constant red and mingled damask."

"Yes, we have got on very well," she says, in a tone that is half a whisper and half a sigh.

Paul has risen to his feet, and now steps across the narrow barrier of the brook that parts them, and stands over her, with his hands in his pockets, and a strong emotion agitating his plain, burnt face.

"Lenore," he says, impetuously, "do not you think that we should get on very well together *always?*"

If only premeditated proposals came to pass, every parish-register would be the poorer by two-thirds of its marriages. When he set off this morning from Morlaix, Paul had as much idea of offering himself to Jemima as to Lenore; only he would not believe it now if you were to tell him so. At his words, she springs to her feet, and a slight quiver passes over her features.

"I think," she says, trying to laugh, "that we should quarrel a good deal."

"Lenore," says Paul, earnestly, "I do not know why I am asking you. You are not in the least the sort of woman that I ever pictured to myself as my wife, and I have no earthly business to ask *any* woman. My face" (with a rather grim laugh) "is my fortune, and you see what a handsome one that is; and yet—and yet—tell me, Lenore, am I worth living in a garret on cold mutton with?"

She gives him no speech in answer; only she stretches out her arms, and her eyes flash softly through her happy tears. He must read his answer there.

The beck tinkles at their feet; the butterflies hover about their heads; the sun gives them his broad, warm smile; and three little Breton girls, going a-bilberrying, with tin mugs in their hands, stand on a neighboring slope, aghast at the manners and customs of the British. She is lying in his arms, and he is kissing the beautiful lips that have kissed none but him, that (as he confidently thinks) will kiss none but him ever again.

"Are you sure," asks Lenore, presently, lifting her ruffled head from his breast, and smiling through her tears, "are you sure that you are asking me for yourself *this* time?"

"*Quite* sure."

"That it is not for Frederick?"

"No."

"Nor for Mr. Scrope?"

"No."

"Are you quite, *quite* sure that you like me?" she asks, drawing a little away from him, and reading earnestly his gray eyes, as if with more confidence in *their* truth than in that of his mouth.

"I am not at all sure of it," he answers, laughing. "You are not the sort of person that any one *could like*, but I am very sure that I *love* you, if that will do as well."

"Better than the shot-partridge woman?" she asks, smiling, half ashamed of her question, and yet with solicitude.

"*Immeasurably* better!" answers he, devoutly.

At that she seems satisfied, but in a very little while her restless doubts return.

"Paul," she says, withdrawing herself from his arms, "you have not yet asked me whether I like you."

"I suppose," he answers, gayly; "that I thought actions spoke louder than words."

"You did not think it worth while asking me," she says, reddening painfully, "because you were so sure of what the answer would be; you *knew* I was fond of you; you have known it all along! Oh, why did not I hide it better?" clasping her hands together, and flinging herself down, disconsolately, on the grass.

"I knew nothing of the kind," answers Paul, pulling his mustache, and looking very much embarrassed; "if, indeed, you had been any other woman, I might have been conceited enough to fancy from your manner that you did not dislike me, but, as you are not in the least like any woman I ever saw in my life, I could not possibly argue from their manners and customs to yours."

"You are very kind," she answers, shaking her head, "trying to put me in good-humor with myself, but you cannot: I have been a lame hare—a lame hare!"

"Do not call my wife ugly names!" cries Paul, playfully, yet distressed, sitting down beside her; "it is very bad manners."

"If you had been less sure of me, you would have valued me a hundred times more," says the girl, with bitter mortification, fixing her solemn tragic eyes on his face.

"Do not get into the habit of talking such nonsense!" retorts he, brusquely; all the more brusquely perhaps from a latent consciousness that there is a grain of truth in her self-accusation. "How many times must I tell you that I was *not* sure of you; that I did not know but that you might give me my *coup de grâce* with as little remorse as you did Mr. West ? "

How Mr. Le Mesurier reconciles this astounding fib to his conscience, I must leave the reader to determine.

Another little silence; the bilberry children have disappeared in the wood; the long-legged flies are still promenading on the stream; the sleepy mellowness of afternoon is upon every thing.

"Paul," says Lenore, again presently, not in the least convinced by her lover's perjuries, and lifting a charming, quivering face to his—"can you *swear* to me that you did not ask me because I looked grieved at the news of your going ? Can you swear to me that you like me *always ?* Not only *now, here,* but *always,* all day and all night— even when you are away from me."

"Even when I am away from you, strange to say," he replies, heartily, drawing her fondly toward him.

"I know," she continues, not yielding to his caresses, but rather resisting them, " that while I am with you, I please you, as any man is pleased with the company of a young, good-looking woman, who has evident delight in his society; but when you are away from me—alone in your own room at night, quietly thinking over things—do you like me *then ?* do you approve of me *then ?* "

He looks a little pained at first by this puzzling catechism; then putting an arm of fond and resolute ownership round her, answers gravely, but without hesitation :

"Lenore, since you are bent on tormenting yourself and me with these ridiculous doubts and questionings, I will tell you the *very* truth : I would not have loved you if I could have helped it; for the last three weeks I have been trying *honestly* to dislike you. I have told myself over and over again—yes, I have even told West too, that I did not admire you; I have pretended to hold you cheap;

I have said that you were *fast*—that I could see you had a
temper—that you were bad form—that you were not even
pretty—God forgive me for such a lie!" breaking off suddenly, to smooth her ruffled hair.

"Well; go on," she says, curtly, impatient of the inter-
ruption, while her cheeks wear as deep a dye as the strewn
petals of a red rose.

"I felt—well, to tell the truth, I feel now" (laughing),
"that you were not a woman that a man would have an
easy time with. Lenore, I shall be frantically jealous of
you; I shall very often fly into a rage with you—"

"There," cries Lenore with spirit, "we shall be
quits; for I never stayed in the house with any one for a
fortnight in my life, without quarrelling *à outrance* with
them."

"You are," continues Paul, still smiling, "as unlike as
it is possible to be to the patient Grizzel, the amiable fond
drudge, that I have always imagined trudging humbly
through life beside me; I cannot fancy *you* trudging
humbly beside any one; you would be more likely to stalk
on *in front* of them, with your head up—but yet—but yet
Lenore—look me in the face for as long as you please—the
longer the better—I defy even *you* to find any falsehood
there—I would not change you now for all the Grizzels in
Christendom."

"Would not you?" she says, softly laying her head
caressingly down on his shoulder, "I am glad!"

"Poor darling!" he says, with a passionate pang of
self-reproach, "I wish I was better worth being glad of."

Neither speaks for a few moments, and both are happy.
Lenore, womanlike, is the first to break silence.

"Paul," she says, lifting her head from its new resting-
place, laying a hand with innocent familiarity upon each
of his shoulders, and scanning closely his face, which looks

even less handsome under this minute inspection than when
viewed from the respectful distance at which his acquaintance are wont to regard it, "do you know that I am not
at all nice? Not at all; quite the contrary. I would not
have told you, only that I am sure that you would very
soon have found it out for yourself: hitherto, I have not
cared whether I was or no; but I am not a nice person, certainly. As yet you have seen only the best of
me."

"The best of you!" cries Le Mesurier, raising his
brows in feigned dismay, "if what I have seen be the *best*
of *you*, what *must* the worst be?"

She smiles. "You remind me of the man, who, when
his lady-love refused him, saying that she wondered how
he could have the presumption to propose to her, as she
had never shown him any thing but her coldest manner,
answered that if such were her coldest manners, he shud-
dered to think what her warmest must be." The laugh
becomes a duet. "Do not you remember," continues Lenore, gravely, "what Miss Richland says in Goldsmith's
'Good-natured Man?' 'Our sex are like poor tradesmen
that put all their best goods to be seen in the windows.'
All *my* best goods are in *my* windows."

"Why do not you leave me to make these discoveries
for myself?" asks Paul, half-vexed, half-playfully. "Why
do you tell me? it is like telling me the end of a novel."

"Do not you see," she says, eagerly, "that I want you
to know the worst of me at once?"

"And about how bad *is* the worst?" asks Paul, jest-
ingly, as he takes her two hands, and puts them about his
own neck, while he gazes at his leisure into the shady
depths of her deep-fringed eyes, "is it that you have a
will of your own?—I know that already—I knew it from
the day when you first burst upon my dazzled sight in

Stéphanie's cap and petticoat—is it that you snub your sister? I know that too—is it—"

"Oh, do not joke," she says, earnestly, "it is no joking matter, but I will try to be nicer for the future; I *will*, indeed, for your sake! I will begin directly—to-morrow."

"Why not to-day?" (smiling).

"I shall have no temptation to resist to-day," she answers, simply. "To-day I am too happy to be wicked."

Again he presses her to his heart, with a feeling of remorse, as one that has been given a good gift, and prizes it not according to its worth.

"O poor child!" he cries, with emotion, "why are you happy? Is it because you have made the worst and most losing bargain ever woman made since first this cheating world began?"

"I have been so lucky all my life," she says, with a pensive smile. "From a little child, I have always succeeded in getting what I wanted! You are the first person whose love I ever wished for, and—is it forward of me to tell you so?—I wished for it from almost the first day I saw you, rude and surly as you were to me—and now, so you tell me, do not you? Against your will I have got even that."

"There is not much doubt of it," answers Paul, with more emphasis than eloquence. "Oh, perverse, pretty darling! What blessed contrariety ever induced you to take a fancy to such an ugly, ill-conditioned devil as I? Most women hate the sight of me."

"And you return the compliment with interest," rejoins Lenore, smiling, "so Frederick told us. That was what first made me think of you. O Paul!" (her gravity returning, and the unbidden tears rising to her eyes), "was there ever an instance of any one being always happy? or shall I have to pay for my good luck by-and-by?"

"Do not talk like that," says the young man, hastily, with a pained look; "it makes me feel as if I had been misleading you, and yet God knows I have not done so consciously. O love!" (with an accent of bitterness) "you will find soon enough that there is nothing alarmingly fortunate in the lot you have drawn."

"If you think," she answers, with a spirited smile, "that I am deceiving myself in my estimate of you, you are mistaken; I am not elevating your excellences at the expense of my own; if I am not remarkably amiable, neither I am sure are you; we shall probably lead a cat-and-dog life, to the edification of all our neighbors—but yet, try as you may to persuade me to the contrary, it still seems—it will *always* seem to me—good luck to belong to you. Come, let us go!"

As she speaks, she rises, and stands beside the little quarrelsome stream, tall, and straight, and beautiful, with a grave, fond smile on her shut lips, and a bulrush wand in her small white hand; his own, his very own, and not another man's.

CHAPTER XVI.

WHAT JEMIMA SAYS.

It is half-past eight, but still broad daylight. Paul and Lenore have not yet returned. I wish they would. "Good-night," say I, closing the old spinet at which I have been warbling in the little *salon* that overhangs the street.

"Are you going to bed?" asks Mr. Scrope, dissuasively; "do not." He is lying on three chairs, meditating, like Mr. Pickwick, with his eyes closed.

"I have a headache," I answer, rather crossly; "can *no one* keep awake in my society?" is my reflection.

"Please sing 'Good-night, good-night, Beloved,' before you go," says he, lifting his blue eyes with lazy entreaty to my face, "*do.*"

I laugh.

"You are like the man in 'Sam Slick,' who said to the girl, '*Thing* me that little *thong*,' when she had already sung it twice. I sang 'Good-night, good-night, Beloved,' ten minutes ago."

He first looks confused, and then laughs with boyish heartiness.

"Did you? You see it was a better lullaby than you had any idea of."

"Good-night," say I tendering my hand for the second time.

"Do not go," he says again, drawing himself languidly up; "it is only half-past eight."

"Is it not as well to sleep comfortably and peacefully in bed as uncomfortably and spasmodically on three hard-bottomed chairs?"

"I think not" (rising and yawning). "In order to get to bed we have the trouble of going up-stairs. Now, if one had some one to *carry* one up it would be different."

"I wish they would come back," say I, uneasily stepping out into the little balcony. "It is a great shame of Mr. Le Mesurier keeping Lenore out so late."

"How do you know that it is not she that is keeping *him* out?"

I drew myself up with dignity.

"What *do* you mean?"

"I meant no offence," he answers, good-humoredly; "only, from the very little I know of your sister, I should say that she was not the sort of person to let any one make her come in or go out against her own will."

"You do not like Lenore," say I, leaning my arms on the rails and gazing down the street.

"To tell you the truth," he answers, confidentially, "she frightens me out of my wits! *You* do not in the least; but, when I see her come into the room, my first impulse is to take to my heels and hide in dens and caves."

"Is it?" say I, surprised. "Why?"

"Her eyes go through one like *gimlets*," he says, his handsome young cheeks flushing; "and she has a way of looking over, and under, and through, and on each side of one, without affecting to perceive one."

"Has she," I say, wonderingly; "I never observed it."

"Perhaps it is only *I* who am invisible to the naked eye," rejoins he, with an indolent smile. "She perceives *Paul*, no doubt; we can all see that, of course."

"There is no accounting for taste," I answer, tritely; "Bottom and Titania are of very frequent occurrence nowadays."

"I did not mean *that* exactly," says Mr. Scrope, too loyal to his friend to relish the ingenious comparison that I have instituted between him and the ass-headed weaver of Athens. "I am not in the least surprised at Miss Lenore's preferring Paul to me, for he is the very best fellow in the world, and consequently I *can* only be the second best."

"*Very best!*" cry I, carping at such unlimited praise bestowed upon a person whose merits I have as yet been unable to discover. "How *very best?* Most religious, do you mean?"

He looks down.

"No, not that, I suppose."

"Steadiest?"

He smiles significantly.

"Hardly.   Poor old Paul! they used to call him Lincoln and Bennett in his old regiment, because he was as mad as two hatters."

"Most amiable?"

"Well, no, I think not.   Paul is a queer-tempered fellow; he can be very nasty when he likes."

"In what, then," inquire I, astonished, "may I ask, does his supereminent merits consist?"

"It knocks one up so much this hot weather explaining things," answers he, stretching.   "All the same, he *is* the very best fellow in the world."

"That is the Italian mode of argument," say I, smiling; "which consists in repeating the disputed assertion over, a certain number of times, in exactly the same words as at first."

With this parting thrust, I take my leave.

Early as is the hour, many of the commercial travellers have already retired to bed; at least many boots stand outside many doors.   As I walk slowly up the stairs, the problem that engages my mind is : "Wherein can Mr. Le Mesurier's charm lie?   Ugly, irreligious, dissipated, ill-tempered!"   I fall asleep without having solved it.   I am awoke, or half-awoke, by a sensation of being violently called upon and shaken by some one.   I sit up and blink: "I have sung it *twice* already," I say, irrelevantly, imagining that Mr. Scrope is still pressing me to sing "Goodnight, good-night, Beloved," and is shaking me to enforce compliance.

"Sing what?   Who wants you to sing?   Wake up, you foolish old person!" cries my sister's laughing voice.   I obey.   Broad awake, I look round.   The moonlight is lying in silver bars on the floor, having shone through the Venetian blind.   A candle glares uncomfortably into my eyes, and on my bed Lenore is sitting, still dressed in her hat and jacket, her clothes wet with the night-dews, and the steady shining of a great new happiness in her eyes. " Jemima," she says, with an excited smile, snatching my hand, " are you awake ? Wide ? Can you understand things ? "

" It is not your fault if I cannot," I answer, drowsily, rubbing my eyes.

" Stop blinking ! " she cries, impatiently, " and look at me. Do you know that you are looking at the very happiest woman in all France ? "

" And you at the sleepiest," reply I, lying down again.

" Do not go to sleep," she says, laying her sweet, fresh face, cool with the kisses of the night-wind, beside mine on the pillow. " You do not know what interesting things I have to tell you. Do you know ?" (in a confidential, emphatic whisper), " I dare say you will hardly believe it at first—I can hardly believe it myself yet—but Paul likes— me—*very—much !* "

" Much ? " say I, crossly, half at my interrupted slumbers, half at the unwelcome though expected news ; " there is nothing very wonderful in that ; for the last three weeks you have been doing your very best to make him like you, and your efforts in that line are not generally unblessed with success."

Her countenance falls ; her tone of gay triumph changes.

" Doing my very best ! " she repeats, slowly. " Ah, that was what I was afraid of ! So I have—so I have."

" Your friend Paul had no need to see farther through a stone-wall than other people, in order to perceive that it was a case of ' Oh, whistle and I'll come to you, my lad ! ' " pursue I, with clumsy badinage.

She covers her face with her hands ; then, lifting it, looks with wistful anxiety at me.

"Did I do any thing to make a person *despise* me, do you think?" she asks, in a low voice. "Was I unlady-like? Did I run after him?"

"Run after him! Pooh, nonsense!" reply I, carelessly; then, after a pause, meditatively: "Paul, Paul! it is an ugly, abrupt little name. Paul Pry! Paul Ferroll, who killed his wife! Are there any more Pauls? You really must have him rechristened, Lenore."

"Paul and Virginia," says Lenore, assisting my memory, having recovered her smiles; "I do not think I am much like Virginia."

"And do you mean seriously to tell me," continue I, becoming grave, "that it was with the deliberate intention of asking you to share his exceedingly indifferent fortunes, that he took you out on this expedition to-day, in that little, dusty, tumbled-down pony-gig, in the roasting sun?"

"I do not know whether it was deliberate intention or accident," replies my sister, looking down, and plucking at the clothes. "I rather think it was accident; but whichever it was, he *did* ask me."

"And you said 'Yes,' and 'Thank you kindly,' I suppose?" cry I, reddening with indignation.

She nods assent: "If I did not *say* it, I *felt* it."

A little silence: "You will at least have an excellent *foil*, on all occasions, ready to your hand," I say, spitefully, in bitter vexation that Damocles's sword has fallen— that the catastrophe which I have been vaguely dreading for the last three weeks has happened.

"What do you mean?" (with an absent look). "Oh!" (with a smile), "I see; you think him so ugly."

"Extremely!" reply I, dryly.

"So do I," rejoins she, calmly; "I like ugliness."

> " ' Come, sit thee down upon this flowery bed,
>   While I thy amiable cheeks do coy,
>   And stick musk-roses in thy sleek, smooth head,
>   And kiss thy fair large ears, my gentle joy,' "

say I, maliciously, quoting Titania's apostrophe to Bottom.

Lenore reddens. " You are rude, Jemima, and not at all witty."

" He is poor, too," say I, with rising exasperation— " unjustifiably poor : I suppose he goes upon the principle that what is not enough for one is enough for two ? "

" I suppose he does," she answers, quietly. " I like poverty."

" He is ill-tempered, too," pursue I, eagerly. " Ah ! you remember what a fury he flew into at Guingamp, with that poor *garçon* who could not understand his bad French when he asked for the time-table ? "

" I remember—I like ill-temper."

" And he is also a gourmand," continue I, relentlessly. " Did you notice how thoroughly put out he looked, yesterday, at dinner, because the gelatine was finished before it reached him ? "

" Did he ? I dare say—I like greediness."

I shake my head, silenced and baffled by this hopeless agreement with all my objections."

" You see," cries Lenore, with a triumphant smile, " that, try as you may, you cannot put me out of conceit with him."

" The point I am trying to arrive at," say I, with a sigh, " is, what could have ever put you *into* conceit with him first ? Do not look so angry, my dear child ! I am not so wedded to my own opinion, but that I am quite ready to change it, if you show me good reason why I should. But—I really do not mean it offensively—but what good qualities of mind or body has Mr. Le Mesurier ? "

Lenore springs off the bed, and begins to walk rapidly up and down the room: her little high heels tap-tapping against the carpetless boards. "How you talk!" she cries, angrily. "Do you think that when a person loves they pick out this quality and that, and say, 'This is lovable,' and 'That is lovable,' and, therefore, I will be fond of the person who owns them all? One loves because one loves—because one cannot help it, and because one would not, if they could."

"Talk High Dutch or Coptic, you will be quite as intelligible to me," I say, indignantly.

She returns to the bed, and fixes her large, bright eyes on my face. "Is it possible, Jemima," she asks, "that in all the many years you have been about the world" (I wince), "you have never had a lover that you cared about with all your heart and soul for no particularly good reason that you could give either yourself or anybody else?"

"Never," reply I, with a rather grim laugh. "Humiliating as the confession is, I should have thought, Lenore, that you might have known by this time that I never have had a lover, either that I cared about, or that I did not care about, and I do not think that there are many women of eight-and-twenty that can make that proud boast."

"Poor Jemima!" cries my sister, in a tone of the sincerest compassion, taking my hand; at this moment she feels ten years older in experience and emotion than I.

"Do not pity me!" say I, with asperity; "*l'appétit vient en mangeant:* if I had *one* lover, I might wish for more; but, as things stand, the more I look around me, the more inclined I am to think that 'ignorance is bliss.'"

"Good-night, Jemima!" says Lenore, stalking to the door, with as much dignity as a water-proof down to the heels and a brass candlestick in her hand will permit; "I am sorry I woke you; next time that I come to you for sympathy—"

"Stay—stay!" cry I, vexed at the effect of my words, and yet puzzled how to mend them. Sitting up in bed, and stretching out my arms to her: "Remember, I was only half awake; I did not quite take it in; I—I—dare say he is very nice when you come to know him." (Lenore pauses with the open door in her hand.) "He looks quite like a gentleman, and—and has the usual younger son's portion.— Very good teeth," continue I, laughing awkwardly, and floundering about in search of a possible excellence in mind or body, on which to be able conscientiously to compliment my sister's lover. "I am sure—at least I think—that he will improve on acquaintance."

"It is not of the least consequence what you think!" says Lenore, in a fury, banging the door.

CHAPTER XVII.

WHAT THE AUTHOR SAYS.

"The Lord of Naun and his lady fair
    In early youth united were,
    In early youth divided were."

"Do not you think that we are rather like the Lord and Lady of Naun, engaged yesterday, to be separated the day after to-morrow?"

It is Lenore who says all this: she is strolling along beside her lover down one of the lovely old streets of Morlaix, that the malignant mania for smart new quays, oroad, bright new thoroughfares, has not yet swept away. They have been prying into the dim interiors; climbing unforbidden the dusty, beautiful wrecks of carven stairs, up and down which the stately nobles used to pace, in the gone centuries; and where now only dirty *gamins* roll and tumble, and the clump of *sabots* comes. Life seems easier here than in England. In the ancient, timber-fronted houses people are leaning on the heavy window-sills miles up in air; below, in the street, they seem to have naught to do but to *jaser* with their neighbors, sitting in old carved door-ways; while bright blankets and rugs hung out in the front make a brilliant bit of color. At almost every house, birds, hung in wicker cages—parrots, canaries. A little child is trotting about in the gutter with a bunch of cherries in its little hand. The sun is beating, blinding hot, on the fine, bare, new streets, but here the tall friendly houses lean over, story above story, so close to gossip together that they intercept his rays.

Lenore has furled her umbrella.

" I do not think that my worst enemy could accuse me of being in early youth," Paul says, with a smile.

" About how old are you ? " asked Lenore, peering up inquisitively at him. " You are one of those baffling sort of people who might be any age, from twenty-five to forty-five inclusive."

" I am half-way between the two ; I am thirty-five."

" You look more, I think," says Lenore, with charming candor ; " I suppose it is that horrid beard."

Le Mesurier does not answer, but he does not look particularly pleased.

" You know I have never yet seen your *real* face," continues she, slipping her hand through his arm. " I have the vaguest idea of what sort of features I am undertaking ; I shall be like the lady who was so short-sighted that she said she never knew her husband by sight until they married : this appendage must come off before we meet again."

She speaks playfully, but in the imperative mood which has been habitual to her through life.

Paul thinks the imperative mood very good *in a man*, but utterly inadmissible in a woman.

"Must it?" he answers, very shortly; then, with a rather awkward attempt to recover his good-humor: "Do not you know what the early Christians said?—that shaving was a lie against one's own face, and an impious attempt to improve the works of the Creator?"

Lenore thrusts out her fresh lips in a mutinous pout.

"I can quote, too; did you ever hear this distich?" she says, saucily:

> "'John P. Robinson, he
> Said they did not know every thing down in Judee.'"

Paul looks grave. He has not read the "Biglow Papers," and he particularly dislikes flippancy in a woman. *Men* may be allowed to be a little wicked; but all *women* should be religious. They have emerged from the old street; have left behind them the tall slate-fronted houses, nodding to each other over the way; have left also the gables, the dormer-windows, the strange saint-faces, deftly wrought in wood. They are sauntering slowly back to their hotel through the more modern part of the town. Morlaix lies so prettily—viaduct, river, churches, peaked houses, all hobnobbing in the hollow between green hills.

"What will you be doing this time three days hence?" asks Lenore presently, with a half-pensive smile, abandoning the obnoxious subject of beards.

"Undergoing, probably, a catechism at the hands of my people, as to your merits and demerits," answers Paul, laughing.

"What will they ask you first about me?" inquires she, with anxious curiosity.

"How can I tell?"

"What points are they likely to lay most stress upon?"

"They will, probably," begins Paul, with some reluctance, "wish to know first whether you are of a good family. By-the-by, do not be angry with me for not knowing; but, you see, I should like to be ready with my answer. Are you?"

"Of course," replies the girl, dryly, tossing her head away with a jerk. "Came over with the Conqueror."

"Really?" cries Paul, with an eagerness which shows that, whatever other weaknesses he may be superior to, he is not above that of a sincere *penchant* toward pedigree.

"How do I know?" cries Lenore, impatiently. "Who cares? What does it matter? Grandfathers do not make a man, or a woman either."

"They are rather apt, however, to make a gentleman," answers Paul, somewhat stiffly.

"I always tell everybody," continues she, with an arch-smile, "that we are lineally descended from the poet. I shall not mind being great-great-great-granddaughter to 'Fair Daffodils.'"

"And are you?" asks her lover, resigning himself to come down six centuries in his expectations.

"I have not the slightest reason for supposing so," answers she, with a careless laugh.

Paul heaves an involuntary sigh.

"What will the next article be, as shop-keepers say?" asks Lenore presently, giving her head an uneasy toss, and with a sort of *swagger* in her voice, which is quite as much the result of nervousness as of pride. "Whether I have any money, I suppose?"

"Possibly," answers he, uncomfortably.

"And you will reply, ' Not a sou!'" (Raising her two

hands, and letting them fall again with a gesture expressive of utter destitution.)

"Exactly."

She laughs maliciously.

"How I should like to see their faces! Grandfather
doubtful, and pennilessness certain! You would, however,
not be *quite* correct; I have several sous—an immense
number, in fact. How many sous are there in four thousand pounds in the three per cents?"

"As many as in four thousand pounds *out* of the three
per cents," he answers, laughing.

"A base evasion of a difficult arithmetical problem!
Well, sous or no sous, I really have four thousand pounds."

"I am delighted to hear it."

"Could not you put it into *francs* when you mention it
to your family? It sounds so immense, then."

"I am afraid they would detect the imposture."

"Jemima has more—a good deal more," says Lenore,
communicatively; "still, we only make up five hundred
pounds a year between us—a fact, however, which we carefully conceal from our acquaintance, having learned by experience the entire truth of Solomon's epigram, that 'the
poor, even his neighbor hateth him!'"

They reach the hotel, the empty salon.

"It *is* a contemptible *dot!*" cries Lenore, indignantly,
flinging down her hat on the floor, and herself on the sofa.
"One ought to be superhumanly handsome to induce people to overlook it."

"It is better than nothing," replies Paul, with a philo-
sophical if lugubrious attempt to look at his beloved's minute portion from a cheerful point of view.

"Four thousand pounds!" repeats Lenore, scornfully.
"Not four thousand pounds *a year!* That would be all
very well; but four thousand pounds for the whole main-

7

tenance and support of a reasonable educated being, with a fine feeling for lace, and a just abhorrence of country boots and thread gloves!"

"And gingham umbrellas!" supplements Le Mesurier, laughing.

"You must know that we are not *all* church-mice. However," says Lenore, presently, "for the credit of the family I must tell you that we have *some* rich people among us—my sister Sylvia, for instance."

"Your sister Sylvia!" cries Paul, rather aghast. "I had no idea that you had a sister Sylvia, or a sister any thing else, except Jemima. I suppose Thezia, and Therese, and a few more, will transpire by-and-by."

"Some years ago, she married," continues the girl, biographically. "She is a pretty little cat, with eyes as big as teacups; and he—well, he was old enough to be *everybody's* grandfather" (stretching out both arms comprehensively). "He was as bald as my hand" (opening one pretty pink palm), "as fat as Falstaff, as ignorant as a carp, and he had made his money by that yellow grease that they put on railway-wheels."

"Good Heavens! how awful! Is he alive still?" asks Paul, nervously.

"That is what I am coming to," continues she, gravely. "In poetic justice he ought to have had creeping paralysis, softening of the brain—any thing that would have kept her tied to the leg of his bath-chair for the next twenty or thirty years, as a judgment on her for marrying him—instead of which, what happens?" (Standing before him, and gesticulating.) "Within four years he is carried off by an attack of apoplexy! Bah! What luck some people have!"

"So that is your idea of *luck?*" rejoins Paul, leaning his chin on the back of the chair on which he is sitting astride, and staring curiously up at her—"to marry a commercial porpoise, and survive it !"

"It is to be hoped," resumes Lenore, after a thoughtful pause, marching up and down the little room, " that your people will ask whether I am good-looking. That is the one question to which you could give a really satisfactory answer." She speaks, not with the blushing *naïveté* of a *jeune ingénue*, but with the matter-of-fact calmness of a woman whose early contact with the world has taught the value of the one great gift she has been given.

" If they do not ask, I must volunteer the information."

" You might also," pursues Lenore, beginning coolly to check off her accomplishments on her fingers, " hint to them that I dance extremely well, that—"

" My father does not approve of dancing," interrupts Paul, tilting the hind-legs of his chair till he nearly topples over.

Her hands drop to her sides, and her great eyes open wide like large blue flowers in the sun. " Not approve of dancing ! What a dreadful old man ! What can he be made of ? "

" If you asked my eldest brother, he would answer, ' Cast-iron,' judging from his duration," replies he, with a lazy chuckle of amusement.

" And does he not allow your sister to dance ? " asks Lenore, looking thoroughly *dashed* by the insight just afforded her into her future father-in-law's character.

" They may walk through a quadrille, or romp through the ' Lancers,' if they choose," replies Le Mesurier, still laughing at the expression of his betrothed's face. " I would not be they if they were to be caught indulging in any wilder mode of progression."

" Poor dears ! " ejaculates Lenore, with a sigh of heartfelt compassion ; " no doubt, however, they dance like dervishes as soon as his back is turned."

"Is that the course *you* mean to pursue when I forbid you to do any thing?" asks Paul, in jest, but almost most heartily in earnest.

"Undoubtedly," replies she, coolly, looking back at him with defiant gravity. "From the time I could walk alone I can safely say that I have never yet been forbidden to do any thing that I did not instantly strain every nerve to do it."

If Miss Herrick expects her lover to show either pleasure or amusement at this proof of her spirit, she is disappointed. He only says "Oh!" and coughs rather dryly.

"Parents and guardians, tutors and governors, *forbid*," continues Lenore, incisively; "one does not hear such an ugly, hectoring word mentioned between man and wife."

"I have an idea, however," retorts Paul, quietly, "that one can find such ugly, hectoring words as 'honor' and 'obey' in the Prayer-book. I will show you the place, if you like."

"One cannot always take the Prayer-book *au pied de la lettre*," says Lenore, lightly. "After all, I dare say I shall be quite as likely to 'honor and obey' you as you to 'worship' me!"

"I do not know that" (rising), "when you have that blue gown on, and a blue ribbon in your hair, and look *meek*, I am not far off it now." As he speaks he takes her two hands in his, and the look that for the moment makes the wise man half-brother to the idiot—that no doubt made even Solomon himself seem but a foolish fellow among his seven hundred charmers—invades his usually shrewd eyes.

"I had that identical blue gown on, the day that you so good-naturedly acted as Frederick's proxy," replies Lenore, demurely.

"Lenore!" says Paul, neither heeding nor hearing her allusion, loosing her hands, and clasping his own round her waist, " I have told you what I shall be doing when I am gone ; tell me now what *you* will ! I do not want you to promise to look at the moon, or say your prayers, or drink your cup of tea at the very moment I do, or any such folly, but (with an impatient sigh) I—I suppose in these sort of cases we are all pretty much alike, and—do not laugh at me, I hate being laughed at—I should like to be able to say to myself at such-and-such an hour, Lenore is doing such-and-such a harmless thing ; if not, I shall be sure to imagine that you are up to some mischief."

" Thank you."

" Come, Lenore, what will you be doing the first day ? "

" The first day," says the girl, feeling a vile inclination to be sentimental and tearful, and resolving not to be conquered by it ; " the first day I shall be in bed all day with the window-curtains drawn ; I shall refuse all food, however hungry I may be ; hitherto I have not found that love takes away the appetite, and I shall cry noisily, obtrusively, and without intermission."

" And the second day ? "

" Half of the second day I shall spend in gazing at your photograph, that one of Disderi's, in which you are sitting with your back to Mont Blanc, looking like a murderer ; and the other half in wrangling with Jemima about your attractions ; we have already had one or two passages-of-arms as to the shape of your nose, and the color of your eyes."

" And the third day ? "

" The *third day !* " flinging down her head on his shoulder ; " the third ugly, empty, immense day ! How *shall* I get through it ? Well " (recovering herself, and feeling rather ashamed of her ebullition), " the third day I may, perhaps, pluck up my spirits enough to enable me to try and while that handsome, sulky, sleepy Scrope boy into the mazes of a gentle flirtation."

Paul unclasps his hands from about her suddenly, and walks toward the balcony.

"What is the matter now?" cries the girl, half bewildered, half offended; then, breaking into a laugh, as she catches a glimpse of his face; "Good Heavens, Paul, how ill-tempered you *can* look when you try; I thought I was a pretty good hand at it, but I'm nothing to you."

"I detest that sort of jokes," replies Paul, tersely, turning upon her a thoroughly cross, jealous face; "they are not ladylike!"

"But I am not ladylike, either," retorts Lenore, flinging up her head and growing scarlet; "did I ever say I was? we *did not* come over with the Conqueror; we have no more to say to the poet than you have; it is my belief that we are *roturier* to the back-bone!"

She was standing beside him, very upright, with her hands behind her; her voice is not *shrill*, it is not its *way* to be so; but it is undoubtedly raised two or three tones above its usual low key; little sparks of fire are darting from her eyes, and her cheeks are redder than the red rose in her belt.

Delightfully handsome as a *picture*, certainly; but as a future wife? "Is it possible that she can have told me the truth when she said that hitherto I had seen only the best of her?" thinks Paul, with a cold qualm.

CHAPTER XVIII.

WHAT THE AUTHOR SAYS.

"GOOD-BYE" is an ugly word: written or spoken, it has an ill look—a down-looking, sighing, weeping word. There is something faintly disagreeable even in the limp hand-shake with which one parts from a disrelished, tedious guest, as one thinks, with slight remorse, that perhaps he was not so bad after all. But of all delusions and all snares, seeing people off is the worst. It is bad enough to take indifferent acquaintance to the train—to stand with your hand on the carriage-door—the last civil regret uttered, the last friendly hope for a speedy meeting again expressed; the smile of farewell stereotyped on your lips, while your ears thirst for the engine's parting whistle, which will not come for five minutes yet. But how far worse to see one that is really dear to you off on a long voyage! To stand on a cold, dirty quay on some dull November morning, while the huge, drab-gray sea heaves and booms before you, suggestive of shipwreck, while the harbor is robed in mist, and through it the tall ship's masts and rigging show indistinctly great; while all about you unfeeling men roll barrels and carry bales, and under your veil your tears drip miserably, to the great annoyance of the dear one, who, if he be equally grieved, yet, manlike, feels angry with you for adding to his sufferings; and if (as is most probable) he is *not* equally grieved, yet is constrained, out of sympathy, to pull a long face, while his manly soul yearns for the consolation of a pipe and cognac! Even if you are absolutely certain never to see a beloved one again, yet abstain from "seeing him off."

But Lenore thinks differently; she is bent on seeing

the last of Paul. The voyage from St.-Malo to Southampton is certainly not a long one, but in this case it is not the actual breadth of the seas which lie between the lovers that constitutes the bitterness of the parting. Paul is going on a doubtful errand—to break to two doting sisters and a gouty Calvinistic father the news that he has at length found a woman to his mind; a woman (as he himself uncomfortably feels) of the very kind most antipathetic to his people.

Lenore, meanwhile, has resolved to pass the time of suspense that must ensue at Dinan. She has wisely made up her mind to go over each sacred spot where they first met and squabbled, and to weep plentifully at each. She will be in no whit behind Marianne Dashwood in "Sense and Sensibility," who "would have thought herself very inexcusable had she been able to sleep at all the first night after parting from Willoughby."

Meanwhile, they have made up their little differences. Paul has eaten his words—has assured his betrothed that he habitually values people for their own merits, not for those of their forbears; that, in fact, he looks upon ancestors as rather a disadvantage than otherwise. And she, on the other hand, not to be behindhand in magnanimity, has been racking her brains to recollect an authentic great-grandfather.

Le Mesurier has done his best to dissuade his beloved from coming to wave her pocket-handkerchief after him as he sails away from St.-Malo, but in vain.

"It will be too much for you; it will upset you!" he has said, tenderly, but she has answered with a wilful smile and shake of the head.

"Nothing ever upsets me, except not getting my own way; *that* has always injured my health from my youth up."

So he is silenced, and has perforce to submit, with what grace he can, to the prospect of what he most dreads on the earth's face—a scene, and being publicly cried over.

Still he makes one struggle more against his fate.

"I hate saying 'good-bye'—do not you, Scrope?" he says, that night, to his friend, as they sit on the hotel-steps smoking, under the yellow moon, which in her third quarter looks odd and three-cornered.

"I hate saying any thing this weather," replies Scrope, languidly. "I should like to keep a little boy to make remarks for me, and they would chiefly be requests for iced drinks."

"Suppose," continues Paul, "that we give *them*" (indicating, with a motion of his head, the direction where he supposes Jemima and Lenore to be) "the slip, and start by the early train to-morrow morning; I have been looking, and there is one at 6.40."

"Start!" echoes Scrope, with more energy than he had any idea that the hot weather had left him, holding his cigar between two fingers, and looking reproachfully at his friend. "Your sole ideas of the pleasures of travelling are 'starting' and 'arriving;' the sole enjoyment you have in a landscape is tracing where the railway runs. My dear fellow, I have already an indigestion of trains, boats, diligences; I have as much idea of starting by the early train as the late train, and the late train as the early train. I mean, D. V., *never* to start again."

"No more would I, if I could help it," replies Paul, gloomily. "I have naturally more cause to wish to stay than you, but when one has a father, and that father has the gout—"

"Gout *is* apt to make parents insubordinate," says Scrope, coolly; "but, you see" (in a tone rather self-gratulatory than regretful), "I have no father, and there is no reason why I should get up in the middle of the night because *you* have one."

" You do not mean to come home yet, then ? " exclaims Paul, in a tone in which surprise and suspicion contend for mastery.

Scrope turns his head half away.

" Why, no—I think not ; I expect to be a sadder and a wiser man by the time I next see the chalk-cliffs of Albion."

A few moments of silence.

Scope picks up a pebble, and aims it at the landlord's poodle, which, at once dirty and ridiculous, and happily unconscious of being either, is trotting bravely along, with his shorn tail borne gallantly aloft.

" Which route do you mean to follow ? " asks Le Mesurier, presently, with hardly so much of confidential friendship in his voice as there was when the conversation first began. " Strike across country from here to Napoleonville, or go round by Auray and Carnac ? "

Scrope does not seem in any hurry to answer.

" I do not think I shall follow any route at all," he says, at length, slowly, and looking rather guilty. " Walkingtours " (beginning to laugh) " wear out boots in a way that I cannot justify to myself."

" What are you thinking of doing with yourself, then ? " rather austerely.

" How do I know ? " says Scrope, wearily, and yawning ; " do I ever know ? I shall probably go wherever the wind blows me, like a dead leaf."

" A most apt simile," says Paul, with a dry look at the healthy solidity of his companion's tall figure, and of the legs, at which he is at the present moment pensively gazing. " Cannot you give a guess as to the direction in which your attenuated person is likely to be wafted ? "

" Not the slightest," replies Scrope, nonchalantly; then, with a boyish blush : " To Dinan, perhaps."

" To Dinan !" cries Paul, sharply, looking thoroughly and unaffectedly and most angrily jealous. " What on earth should take you back there ? "

" Did I not tell you just now—the wind ? " replies the other.

Paul rises, unable to conceal his ill-temper, and, not willing to indulge it, begins to walk hastily up and down before the hotel-door. Scrope draws himself lazily up from the sitting posture, and languidly walks to join his friend.

" My dear Paul," he says, coldly, and yet smiling, " if you had not been so completely taken up with your own little game—so brutally selfish and self-absorbed as lovers always are, you might have perceived that I too have a little game.

" What *are* you talking about ? "

" My good fellow, do not look as if you were going to run your nose through my body," says Scrope, with a rather unkind allusion to the saliency of *one* feature of his friend's face. " What I mean is this : while you have been amusing yourself making love to the *young* Miss Herrick, *I* have been laying siege to the *old* one. It has been rather up-hill work, as she did not seem to understand the situation ; but I hope, by God's grace, to make her see my drift in time."

" My dear boy," taking his arm, but still looking half unbelieving, " she is old enough to be your grandmother ! "

" I know she is ; that is why I like her. You know you have often accused me of a depraved taste for old women. I own it ; I like them *mellow*."

Paul laughed, but not merrily.

" So you see," continues Scrope, " so far from *my* helping you to evade your 'good-byes,' you have a harrowing parting with *me too* to look forward to."

"I wish to Heaven it was over!" says Paul, devoutly. "I would give any one ten pounds to get me clear off, without saying 'good-bye' to any one. But," with a sigh, "you see, Lenore," the name does not come very glibly yet, "seems to have set her heart on seeing me off."

"You ungrateful dog!" cries Scrope, with an indignation none the less real because affected to be feigned. "Why *will* the gods always cast their pearls before swine? Would to Heaven that any handsome woman would set her heart upon seeing *me* off! I should be the last to oppose her."

"It would show how little you cared about her, then," replies the other, briefly; and then, ashamed and afraid of having been demonstrative, walks away into the hotel.

CHAPTER XIX.

WHAT THE AUTHOR SAYS.

So Lenore has her wish; and together they all retrace their steps, and journey back to St.-Malo. And now the heavy parting day has come—the day that is to interpose the cold, gray sea between him and her. There are but three hours now till the moment when Paul will set forth on his return to old associations, to the strong influences of use and wont, leaving Brittany and new love behind him. All the morning they have been strolling about the old town and the ramparts, two-and-two—the lovers and the playing-at-lovers. Judging by appearances, the latter seem to be enjoying themselves the most.

By-and-by Lenore and her betrothed stray away from the others, across the sands, that twice a day the tide's long wash covers, and twice a day again uncovers; across the sands to the little bare island, where Châteaubriand—in no graveyard, hustled by no dead kin—has wished to sleep out his last sleep. They have climbed through the sands and the sand-colored bents to the little eminence, where, with no name graved upon them, no date, no valedictory text, stand the simple white cross and slab that mark the spot were the restless Réné lies. On the very edge of the precipice he is sleeping, and beneath him the rocks slant sheer down, and at their base come the stealing summer waves with a slow, soft lapping. Lenore leans on the railing that Châteaubriand begged his fellow-townsmen to place round his tomb, "*pour empêcher les animaux à me déterrer*," and stands looking seaward, parted-lipped, tasting the salt wind.

"Jemima will be very clever if she gets Scrope up here," says Paul, with a determination to say something very commonplace, in the hope of ridding himself of the sense of sad solemnity that the place, the sighing wind, and his own approaching parting, combined to produce.

"She will not try," answers Lenore, not changing her attitude. "Jemima *hates* 'Atala,' and she *loves* limpets, and little crabs, and all sorts of noisome monsters of the deep. If Mr. Scrope were not with her, she would take off her shoes and stockings, and *paddle*."

"Scrope would *paddle*, too, on the smallest encouragement," says Paul, laughing; "just the sort of thing that would suit him—cool, and no trouble; and besides, he tells me that he is very much smitten with Jemima."

Lenore turns away her large eyes from her abstracted contemplation of the purple waves and the glancing sea-gulls; turns them on Paul, full of a sort of careless surprise. " Unhappy young man," she says, calmly ; " what could have induced him to tell such a shocking story ? "

" Why might not it be true ? "

" It might," says Lenore, indifferently ; " but it is not. Mr. Scrope—Charlie Scrope, is not he ? he looks like Charlie—is no more smitten with Jemima than he is with—— Who shall I say ? "

" Than with *you !* "

" Well, than with *me*, if you like."

" You do not seem to think that that is putting it very strongly," says Paul, suspiciously.

" What does it matter whom he is smitten with, or whom he is not ? " cries Lenore, with evasive vehemence. " What does it matter whether he is alive or dead ? We have only two hours left, and we are wasting our time talking about *him*."

" I am, naturally, rather interested in my successor in walks, and talks, and moonlight strolls," says Paul, with a bitter jest.

" Is not he going to set off to-morrow on that ever-talked-about, and never-walked, walking-tour ? " asks Lenore, surprised. " I thought he was, but I suppose ' the wish was father to the thought.' "

" Walking-tour, indeed ! " says Paul, scornfully. " I know what *that* means : lying at your feet under the chestnuts at Mont Parnasse, and reading Byron and Shelley to you ! "

" Being read aloud to always sends me to sleep."

" Promise me " (looking very eager), " asleep or awake, not to flirt with him."

" I will promise nothing so ridiculous," answers she, contemptuously. " *Flirt* with an *infant* that gets red all over when I speak to it !—that trembles and stammers when I remark to it that ' it is a hot day ! ' Bah ! "

"It is a singular fact," says Paul, dryly, " that it is only in *your* society that *it* blushes, and trembles, and stammers; most people find it a brazen-faced and fluent infant enough."

"Do they ? "

" You will, at all events, promise not to let *it* " (laughing) " read poetry to you?—for it is a handsome fellow, and a sentimental."

" *Can* it read ? " (with an air of surprise). " I should have thought it had not got beyond B—a, ba, B—e, be, B—i, bi, B—o, bo, B—u, bu—"

"Lenore," says Paul, very gravely, " however you may choose to ignore the fact, you know, as well as I do, that Scrope is a grown man, and a disgustingly good-looking one. Swear to me to be as little alone with him as possible—swear to me not to flirt with him ! "

" Make me swear not to give him a pop-gun, or play 'tip-cat' with him ! It would be much more rational," answers Lenore, derisively. (Paul turns away.) " Do not be vexed," she cries, very gravely, laying her hand on his arm. " If it will give you the least grain of pleasure, I will promise to cut him out-and-out, henceforth and forever. I will not even say ' Good-morning ' and ' Good-evening ' to him. Do you think it would be any privation to me ? Set me some *harder* task—something difficult and disagreeable to do—against you come back, for your sake ! Perhaps it will make the enormous days go a little quicker." Her eyes fill with tears as she speaks; the sea-gulls scream, and Paul sighs heavily. " I hope it is not a bad omen," she says, winking away the drops from her curled lashes; " but you are the first person or thing that ever succeeded in making me cry. I never *could* cry over books, or at plays, or when people died; I did not know that I had any tears about me, till I met you."

"Lenore!" (half indignantly, half hurt), "what a more than doubtful compliment!"

"I will never pay it you again," she says, with confident hopefulness. "Henceforth, my life will be all plain-sailing: I see it as clearly as that shining wake of yellow light behind the steamer out there. You must tell your father" (speaking between joke and earnest) "that no one has ever thwarted or contradicted me all my life, and that he must please to follow suit."

Paul smiles rather sadly, and shakes his head: "I am afraid he would answer that neither has any one ever thwarted or contradicted him all his life, and that *you* must please to follow suit."

A pause.

"What is there so obnoxious about me?" cries Lenore, suddenly turning away from the grave, and facing her lover with a flushed, proud face. "Why should he object to me so strongly, as I see you think he will?"

"God knows! Perhaps he will not! Who can answer for the freaks of a man possessed by the twin devils of gout and Calvin?"

"I have no money, certainly; but neither have nine-tenths of the women that men marry, and no one thinks of getting up to forbid the banns."

"Quite true."

"I come of a good and a healthy stock; we never run away with our neighbors' wives, or have D. T., or go mad!"

"That is more than I can say for us! At least, we do not go cracked; but we occasionally indulge in the other two pastimes you mentioned."

"I am not a flirt."

"No?" (more interrogatively than assentingly).

"Nor fast."

"No—o" (rather slowly and doubtfully).

"I am *not* fast," she repeats, stoutly; "how *can* I be? I do not hunt; I do not drink hock and seltzer for breakfast; I do not *smoke*."

"Good Heavens, I should hope not!"

"Make me out as nice as you can to your people, even at the expense of strict veracity," says Lenore, coaxingly. "Indeed" (with a little air of complacency), "by softening a shadow here and striking out a light there, I really describe very well."

"Even without that process," says Paul, with a proud smile.

"For instance," continues she, with a deepened color, and a shamed, though defiant laugh, "you need not enter into detail with regard to the peculiar circumstances that attended our first meeting."

"*I should think not!*" (very much accentuated).

"I do not see what necessity there is for so much emphasis," rejoins Lenore, rather offended; "it was a bad joke, because, thanks to Frederick's imbecility and your straightlacedness, it failed. If you had been a different kind of man, and it had succeeded, it would have been a good one."

"Good or bad," says Paul, with a promising forestalling of marital authority in his voice, "I shall be very much obliged if you will not repeat it while I am away, Lenore."

For a moment she looks mutinous; then, at the sight of the green sea, the steamers, and the thoughts that both suggest, melts utterly. "I will not—I will not!" she cries, eagerly. "Do you think I shall have time for jokes? I shall spend all my days and all my nights in trying to be a really nice girl by the time you come back. A really nice girl," she repeats, dreamily. "I have been called a tall girl, and an odious girl, and a sharp girl, and now and then a deuced handsome girl; but never to my recollection, in all my life, have I been called a nice girl."

"Poor Lenore!" (stroking her bright hair), "strange to say, you have at last found some one to think you nice."

"Have I?" (looking quite at sea). "Who?"

"Who?" Why *I*, to be sure."

"*You!*" (shaking her head). "Oh no, you do not."

It is a flat contradiction; but it does not sound rude. He does not asseverate. Bewitching, charming, maddening—she is all these; but "*nice?*" The epithet has a domestic, home-keeping, quiet sound, that does not seem to fit her.

"I must practise being lady-like, and gentle, and sweet, against I see your people, or these virtues will sit as uneasily on me as an ill-made cloak," she says, with a rather anxious laugh.

"Do not be in any hurry to see my people," cries Paul, hastily. "I am not. I had far rather keep you to myself."

"Would you? Do you know" (taking his hand, and smiling softly), "I have been vexing myself with the thought that, try as I may, I *never* can give you *all* my life? There must always remain eighteen years in which you have had neither part nor lot, and in which other men have. I cannot, indeed" (laughing a little), "accuse myself of having ever been *over*-civil to your sex; but once I gave a man a bunch of violets, and once I got up at five o'clock in the morning to see another man off to India. I dare say you have done many worse things, but I do not believe they can weigh on your mind half so much?"

"For Heaven's sake, do not let us compare notes!" says Paul, with a hasty flush, while his mental eye flashes back over the occupations of his grown-up years. "I do not want to make you believe that I have been worse than other men, and I have not Lawrence's idea, that, by being superlatively immoral, one is more likely to win a good woman's love; but still (sighing), beside your sweet white life, mine looks black enough. Let us cry quits, Lenore, and make a fresh start. If you stick to me, I swear to you that, for the future, mine shall be as white as yours."

"We shall be like two lilies on one stalk," says Lenore, with levity; but her eyes are wet.

After all, it is Paul that sees Lenore off, and not Lenore Paul. The Dinan boat starts several hours before the Southampton one. The bitter "good-bye" has really come. The passengers are stepping on board, and seating themselves in the bows. and on the rickety camp-stools on the hatchways. Three old Frenchwomen are chattering together, asking each other whether they are not *"fatigué par le vent?"* Black smoke is pouring out of the little black funnel; the paddle-boxes, black and white like magpies—bird hateful to the French soul—contrast the green water that they rest on. A devoted Breton *père de famille* is returning to his home with three red-and-yellow paper twirligigs in his hand; evidently his offspring number three.

"For God's sake, do not forget me, Paul!" Lenore is saying, in a low, broken voice. She has one of her lover's hands tight held in both hers; her face is as white as death, and the tears are pouring down it. She has never much regard for appearances, and she is entirely reckless of them now; in a water-proof, quite down to her heels, she looks like a young grenadier—only, surely, never had grenadier so wet and woe-begone a face. "Think of me *every* minute, even if you think something disagreeable. Oh, if I had but some one to talk of me to you! But I have not —no one; you will never hear my name, or, if any one does mention it, he will say no good of me: nobody ever does!"

"My dearest child, do not talk such nonsense!" says

Paul, hastily, casting a furtive glance round to see whether any one is laughing. He is very miserable himself, but he is not quite so much swallowed up by his grief as not to retain an uneasy curiosity as to whether their pretty pose does not afford mirth-matter to their fellow-voyagers. He catches the stoker, who has just come up, streaming with perspiration, and black as night, from the lower regions, *flagrante delicto.* He is smiling, and nudging a neighbor. Mr. Le Mesurier relieves his mind by scowling at him.

"I cannot stand this much longer," says Scrope, in a suppressed voice, to Jemima. Mr. Scrope is unable to keep quiet; he is turning red and pale, and biting his lips. "It really is too sickening. These ceremonies ought to be strictly private, or altogether omitted. Do not you think so, Miss Herrick?"

"Do not look that way," said Jemima, drily.

"I cannot help it; there is a sort of horrible fascination. Thank God, there's the bell! Miss Jemima, why the—why, I mean, does no one ever cry over *me?*"

"You are not going away?"

"But if I were, who would? I never caused any one's tears to flow in my life, except my small brother's, when I licked him at school."

"Be a good girl, Lenore, and *do not flirt with Scrope!* These are my last words to you. God bless you, my darling!"

Paul has at last forgotten the rest of the company; the stoker may laugh his fill; he sees nothing but Lenore's drowned blue eyes, and his own are not far from matching them.

And in this fashion they part.

N O O N.

"And in the eye of noon, my love
   Shall lead me from my mother's door,
Sweet boys and girls, all clothed in white,
   Strewing flowers before.

But first the nodding minstrels go,
   With music meet for lordly bowers;
The children next, in snow-white vests,
   Strewing buds and flowers.

"And then my love and I shall pace,
   My jet-black hair in pearly braids,
Between our comely bachelors
   And blushing bridal-maids."

CHAPTER I.

WHAT THE AUTHOR SAYS.

ARE you of those who hate Winter, or of those who love him? Do you shrink from his strong ice-clasp; or do you hold out your right hand to him heartily, saying, "You are welcome?" Do you love the enjoyments that are to be fought for (so to speak) by effort and exertion, with quick blood and high pulses; or those that come lazily and warmly, without your seeking? To whichever class you belong, you must come with me into Winter's innermost stronghold. I bid you; and, shiver and shake as you may, you must not say, "No." Forget June—forget its hot, faint airs and thronged red roses; remember only Decem-ber, with all his cold, white train. It is Christmas: a season which, if one took one's idea of it from Dickens's books, would seem to be a season of universal jollity, of widely-diffused sausages and mince-pies, of great crackling fires and hard, bright frost; when every one is gladder than his wont; when each man greets his neighbor lovingly, and godly charity and pious mirth shine out of each happy eye; a season which, if one judge it by one's own experience, is for the most part mildly drizzling—a season of bills and influenza triumphant; when one reckons up the empty chairs by the fireside, and, counting over one's losses in love and joy, finds smiling—much more, broad laughter —but difficult. Into an English country-house you must come: till to-morrow you must wait to see whether it is Gothic, Tudor, Ionic, Inigo Jones-ish, or a happy medley of these styles; for now the black night-winds are feeling blindly round it, and the harsh rains are lashing its front. It is dressing-time; but who can bear to tear themselves away from this hall-fire—hall that is the liveablest room in the house, with its floor spread with warm beasts'-skins, its low, wide hearth, its thick-draped windows, its round table groaning under new novels—novels proper and novels improper—novels ritualistic and novels evangelical; novels that are milk for babes, and novels that are almost too strong meat for men. There are no gone faces to sadden this hearth; the only face that is gone would cause considerable consternation were it to come back again. On the deep, woolly hearth-rug Jemima is sitting, with a book in her hand; she is reading a pretty love-story by the firelight. Opposite to her, in a low chair, sits (or rather *lies*) her sister Sylvia, the widowed house-mistress. Her little chin is buried in her chest; the large jet-beetles in her ears bob gently to and fro as she nods, nods; on her lap rests a pug-dog. His face is blacker than the raven's wing; his nose turns mightily upward; his tail curls tightly twice to the left; his toes turn out, and his tongue protrudes, like a pink rose-leaf; if he squinted, he would be perfect; but, alas! life is made up of "ifs." A little farther off,

two young people are playing at *bézique*—Lenore and
Scrope. Yes, though it is neither Brittany nor June,
Scrope is here. Twining round his legs, scaling Jemima's
back, playfully trying to poke their fingers into their
mother's shut eyes, running heavily on their heels, plunging, wrangling, with all the innocent vivacity of childhood,
are two *enfants terribles*—terrible as only the healthy
male young of the human species can be—little red-faced
scourges to society. If parents, when they give their
children smart names, would but reflect on the number of
ugly-named men whom they may possibly, nay probably,
espouse! Why did not Sylvia's parents? Sylvia Prodgers!

"Is these children's bedtime *never* coming?" cries Lenore, impatiently, as she begins a fresh deal. "It seems
to me that that blessed epoch moves farther and farther on
every night.—Tommy, dear, are not you sleepy? I will
give you sixpence if you will say you are."

"Mother said we might stay up to see Uncle Paul—did
not she, Bobby?" replies Tommy, triumphantly.

He has just succeeded in tying himself in a true-love
knot round Mr. Scrope's neck; his feet are beating a playful
yet painful tattoo on that young gentleman's ribs.

"*Uncle* Paul, indeed!" cries Scrope, indignantly. "Who
taught you to give people brevet rank? I say, young man,
fair play is a jewel. Let *me* get on *your* back, and hammer *your* ribs a bit now."

"Stay up to see Uncle Paul!" echoes Bobby, who, not
being very rich in ideas himself, draws chiefly on his elder
brother's stock.

"How pleased he'll be!" says Scrope, laughing. "I
think I see the benignant smile with which he will greet
you when you run at his legs and kick his shins, as you are
in the pleasant habit of doing mine."

"He will not mind," says Lenore, feeling impelled to
stand up for her lover's amiability. "I hate children, myself, as you know—*loathe* them, in fact. They seem to me
to combine all the worst qualities of both sexes, with *no*
redeeming points of their own—egotism more than man's,
garrulity more than woman's. But I always like a man to
be fond of them; there is always some good about a man
that is."

"I wish they were not quite so fond of me," says Scrope,
groaning, as he takes Tommy by the scruff of the neck, and
deposits him in a vociferous heap on the floor.

"Uncle Paul is going to be Aunty Lenore's 'usband—
Morris says so" (Morris is the butler), remarks Bobby, from
the background, with that utter contempt for the letter *h*
that one often notices in little children.

"Quite right, Bobby," answers Lenore, gayly; "Morris
never said a truer word in all his life."

Scrope makes no comment; he only throws your kings
viciously on the table, and announces, in a sulky voice, the
unanswerable proposition that eighty and seventy make one
hundred and fifty.

"I wish Aunty Lenore's 'usband would come," says Lenore, laughing, but rather anxiously. "I *feel* as if it were
getting very late.—Jemima, you can see the clock; what
time is it?"

Jemima starts, drops her book, and stretches her neck.

"Five minutes past seven."

"He *ought* to be here, ought not he?" says the girl,
wistfully, playing a queen of trumps that she has been carefully hoarding for the last ten minutes, and looking inquir-
ingly across at her antagonist.

"Perhaps he has thought better of it," suggests Scrope,
in his slow, lazy way. "Perhaps his pretty cousin has per-
suaded him to stay and eat his plum-pudding with her."

"He has *not* a pretty cousin," answers Lenore, quickly, and quite unaware that she has double *bézique* in her hand.

"He has, though," replied Scrope, carelessly, looking doubtfully over his cards, to see which he can best spare. "He may have kept it dark; but he has. I saw her last month, when I went down there for covert-shooting. She had on a gray cloak down to her heels, and a long poke-bonnet, like a tunnel; but I looked down the tunnel, and saw a pretty little prim face at the end of it."

"She was a Sister of Mercy, no doubt."

"Only a lay one."

"I *wish* he would come," repeats poor Lenore, feverish-ly.—"Children, run to the window, and listen if you can hear a carriage."

"You must remember it is Christmas-Eve," says Je-mima, reassuringly; "the trains are often three hours late."

"Everybody drunk, and collisions imminently prob-able," remarks Scrope, pleasantly.

Lenore flings down her cards on the table, and, running to the window, disappears behind the heavy red curtains with the children.

"My word, Bobby, is not it raining?"

"He is *not* to get up upon the window-seat, is he, Aunty Lenore?"

"Yes, I may; mayn't I?"

"Aunty Lenore, is not he a naughty boy?"

"You *shall not* get up here; I won't have you!"

A sound of hustling—a yah—a howl. Scrope to the rescue.

Unmindful of her nephews, Lenore is standing with her nose flattened against the pane, staring out into the rough night. The clouds are breaking, and, from underneath one heavy black one, the moon is pushing and pouring wet silver; it streams on Lenore's eager face, making it look extra pale. The children tumble back, over one another, again into the warm room: in the dark recess behind the curtain the young man and the young woman stand alone.

"Do you think there has been an *accident?*" asks the girl, in a low voice, turning to him her pretty tragic face. "Do you think any thing has happened to him?"

"I am *certain* nothing has," answers the young fellow, bitterly, turning on his heel.

In ten minutes more, doubt as to Mr. Le'Mesurier's fate is at an end, and Lenore's nose may recover from the pressure it has suffered against the window-pane as soon as it can. Through the bellowing wind and the fighting rain carriage-wheels are plainly heard, and a bell's sharp "Ting, ting" vibrates through the house.

"How about the pretty cousin and the poke-bonnet?" cries the girl, her face all alight, flying triumphantly past Scrope into the outer hall.

"Wait a bit; perhaps he has brought her with him."

But Lenore is out of hearing.

"Why could not she stay here?" says the young man, advancing, grumbling and shivering, to the fire. "It would not have robbed her of two seconds of his precious society. Why do not they come in?" (walking impatiently to and fro). "I suppose they are falling into each other's arms under the chaperonage of Morris. Bah! I hate lovers! Do not you, Miss Herrick?"

"I never had one, so I cannot say."

The bell has awaked both Sylvia and her dog. The latter tumbles down, in a fat, fawn-colored ball, from his mistress's lap. The former stands sleepily up, and mechanically puts her hand to her head, to feel for her plaits.

"Is he come?" she says, in a little plaintive voice. "I wish people would not come so suddenly—they make one's heart beat so. Jemima" (standing on tiptoe, and trying to get a glimpse of her little head, and of the mountainous hair-erection that makes it look top-heavy, in the looking-glass over the high old chimney-piece)—"Jemima, does my *frisette* show? Do I look a great object? What will he think of me?"

"It does show a good deal," answers Jemima, candidly. "But do not be uneasy; he will not *see* you—he never. sees anybody when Lenore is by; ten to one he will forget to say 'How do you do?' to you!"

"What—to the mistress of the house!" cries Scrope, with his eyes eagerly fixed on the door.

"I hope he will not expect one to be very affectionate," continues Sylvia, simpering; too entirely taken up with herself to hear or heed Jemima's remark, and carefully putting down the little Gainsborough fringe of hair on her forehead. "I suppose I am peculiar, but I always feel so *reserved* with strangers; if he is hurt by my coldness, you must explain to him that it is *my way.*"

"I do not think there will be any need," replies Jemima, dryly.

As she speaks, the door opens, and the betrothed pair make their triumphal entry. To Lenore, at least, it is such: her two hands are clasped on her lover's arm, and her glad, proud eyes are fixed on his face. It is not much of a face to be proud of, after all; but, such as it is, sisters, nephews, friend, butler, footmen, are quite welcome to see her radiant happiness in again looking upon it. Paul is happy, too—inly, heartfeltly happy; but, coming in straight from a long December railway journey, only just delivered from the wind's cuffs and the rain's stings, shivering and shy, it is difficult to look radiant. Paul's shyness, like that of many other men's, takes the form of a peculiar ferocity of aspect. Sylvia has arranged herself in a pretty *pose;*

she has disposed all her neat little features symmetrically into a smile of welcome: Bobby and Tommy, awed into momentary silence and stillness by the stranger's advent, are filially grouped around her.

"So happy to make your acquaintance!" she murmurs, extending her hand, and then dropping her eyes bashfully. —"Darlings, give Mr. Le Mesurier a nice kiss!"

But the darlings—whose *mauvaise honte*, on first introduction, is only to be exceeded by their painful intimacy at a later stage of acquaintance—burrow their coy heads in their mother's skirts and decline. As kissing is with them a damp and open-mouthed process, perhaps their future uncle has the less reason to deplore their refusal. He shakes hands with them all—unknown sister-in-law, known sister-in-law, nephews-in-law, friend (with the last, perhaps, with less warmth than the rest); and then they stand round the fire, and say clever things about the rain and the wind, and the train and the dog-cart. These do not last long, however, and when they are finished a rather constrained silence falls.

"So some one has been playing *bézique*, I see?" remarks Paul, with an effort to break through the silence and his own shyness at the same time.

"Yes," answers Lenore, laconically, not thinking it necessary to explain who the players were.

"It is Mr. Scrope and Aunty Lenore," cries Tommy, officiously; "they play every night, and one night Bobby spilt the cards all over the floor. My word! did not Aunty Lenore smack him!"

"Play *every* night!" echoes Paul, glancing quickly from his love to Mr. Scrope, and back again; "I had no idea that you had been here any time, Scrope?"

"About the inside of a week, I suppose," answers Scrope, nonchalantly.

"Why, you *knew* he had!" cries Lenore, reproachfully. "I told you so, ages ago.—It shows" (turning to the company, with a rather nervous laugh) "how attentively he reads my letters, does not it?"

"Her hand *is* difficult, is not it?" says Sylvia, sweetly. "We all write illegible hands; I am shockingly scolded about mine."

Mr. Le Mesurier does not seem very much interested as to whether his hostess's hand is decipherable or not; he walks to the card-table, and begins to fiddle with the *bézique* markers.

"I do not know what any one else thinks," says Jemima, depositing her novel on the table; "but *I* think that it is quite time to prepare for the great event of the day.—Mr. Scrope, will you light my candle?"

They all troop off up the lit stairs—women, children, man; Lenore and Paul are left for the first time alone. In a moment they are together, standing on the hearth-rug: her face is between his two cold hands, and he is looking down on it, with an expression a little troubled, perhaps, but as truly, heartily loving, as even she could desire.

"Lenore, have you been a good girl?"

"Paul, have you been a good man?"

"Middling, for that" (sighing), "but I think I have tried."

"And I think *I* have tried to be a good girl, but I am not at all sure that I have succeeded."

"And Scrope?"

"Has *he* been a good man, do you mean? I really cannot say."

"You know I do not mean that, Lenore; but what about him?"

"*Nothing* about him."

"Do you think him as much of a child as you did that day at St.-Malo?"

" No, I do not; I think he is rather precocious."

 . . . . . .

Soup is apt to make the nose red, but after a long winter journey it is certainly solacing. It does not matter whether Paul has a red nose or no, as he has no beauty to spoil; nor (owing, I suppose, to the deeper-coloredness of their whole faces) is a red nose as absolutely fatal to men's loveliness as to women's. Sylvia's sherry is good; it is her champagne. Paul does not feel half so shy, or half so cold, as he did an hour ago. Why should he be, either, sitting near this kingly Christmas fire, that one sees, without feeling it oppressively, through the glass screen, and among all these kindly, smiling faces? Sylvia smiles on principle, because her teeth are white and even. Jemima smiles from habit: in this world it is politer to smile than to look grave. Scrope smiles, because dinner is involuntarily cheering, even when one's heart is sick, and angry to the pitch of longing to knock *anybody* down. And Lenore—neither soup nor sherry has power to add to her perfect well-being. Indeed, she cannot eat. She has had plenty of time to eat and sleep, and go through all the dull necessities of life, during the last void six months. Lenore is *absolutely* happy! It is something to have been able once to say that; but why do not peole know *when* to die? Why does life insist on staying on:

> " Like some poor, nigh-related guest,
> That may not rudely be dismissed ;
> But hath outstayed his welcome while,
> And tells the jest without the smile ? "

" So your father has been having the gout ? " says the girl, considerately waiting till her lover has swallowed his last mouthful of soup, and not " starving her man," as the *Saturday*, in the long-gone days when it used to write pleasant articles, once happily worded it.

" Yes."

" Quite *safely* and *long-livedly*, I suppose ? "

Paul looks rather shocked; he has not yet had time to get acclimatized to Lenore's startling candors of expression.

" I hope so."

" Is he very cross ? "

" Very."

" Gout is apt to sour the sweetest temper, as no one has better reason to know than I," said Sylvia, with a sigh, and a downward glance at her dress.

Sylvia's grief has passed out of the capped and craped stage; it has declined into the more supportable phase of colored silks and white tuckers.

" Would he like me to go and nurse him ? " asks Lenore, laughing, yet eagerly awaiting the answer.

" I do not know about that," says Paul, laughing too; " he has already *three* lone spirits for his ministers. I do not think even *he* could find work for a fourth."

" Three ! " cries the girl, growing pink, with a faint suspicion. " Why, Paul, I thought you had only *two* sisters ! "

" Suppose I have a cousin ? "

Lenore involuntarily glances across at Scrope; he is smiling malevolently, and reciting half under his breath:

> " I have brothers and sisters by the dozen, Tom ;
> But a *cousin* is a different thing."

Nothing has happened; the fire still radiates warmth from its deep, red heart. The footmen are carrying round sweetbreads, and *fricandeaus*, and timbales, and all manner of nice things. Sylvia and Jemima are still smiling; but yet—but yet—Lenore has made one step, a very little step indeed; but still a step, down from her pinnacle of heaven-like bliss.

. . . .

"I *quite* like him, Lenore—I do, really. I am not joking," says Sylvia, that evening, patronizingly, as the three
ladies stand round the drawing-room fire ; "and you know
I am not one to say what I do not mean. If I have a fault
in that way, it is being too sincere. I had my misgivings,
but he really is *quite* nice ; but—but—what an odd way
he has of *staring* at one ! "

"I never remarked it."

"I thought he looked rather queer when I called Charley Scrope 'Charlie,' at dinner," continues Sylvia, sinking
down upon the fender-stool, and carefully disposing her
skirts about her. "You must explain to him that poor,
dear Charlie is one of my *oldest* friends. I hate people to
get that sort of idea about one into their heads, don't you
know ? "

CHAPTER II.

WHAT THE AUTHOR SAYS.

"Babe Jesus lay on Mary's lap,
    The sun shone in His hair ;
And so it was she saw, mayhap,
    The crown already there.

"For she sang, 'Sleep on, my little King,
    Bad Herod dares not come ;
Before Thee sleeping, holy thing,
    Wild winds would soon be dumb.

"'I kiss Thy hands, I kiss Thy feet,
    My King, so long desired ;
Thy hands shall ne'er be soiled, my sweet,
    Thy feet shall ne'er be tired.

" ' For Thou art King of Men, my Son!
    Thy crown, I see it plain;
And men shall worship Thee, every one,
    And cry Glory! Amen!'

"Babe Jesus opened His eyes so wide,
    At Mary looked her Lord;
And Mary stinted her song and sighed,
    Babe Jesus said never a word."

NOBODY sings those old carols nowadays; but to me they have a heartier, truer ring than any of the new-fangled Christmas psalmodies. Yes—it is Christmas-Day, though there is neither snow, nor frost, nor ice; only stripped trees, a chilly little sun, and mild west-wind. Everybody has been to church, has prayed, has crossed his arms, and yawned; has stared at the hollied font and the ivied pillars, at the blue and red and gold texts, that tell us the old, old news, that " Christ is born; " has thought of his earthly accounts, and of his account with High God, as the bent of his mind inclines him. Tommy has dropped his mother's smart prayer-book into a puddle on his way to church; has been hoisted up on the seat, on his arrival there; has made faces at a little girl in the next pew; has broken into audible laughter, during the Second Lesson, at something that tickled his fancy in one of the footmen's appearance; has been privately admonished that expulsion from church, and deprivation of pudding, will be the consequence of continued mirth; has therefore lapsed into tearful gravity, and finally into sleep. Now they are all at home again; Lenore and Paul have succeeded in the object—always a primary one with lovers—of eluding every one else, and are dawdling about in the conservatory till the luncheon-gong shall summon them back into the control of the public eye. The proud camellias, the Roman matrons—Cornelias and Lucretias—of the flower nation, hide no ears under their sleek, dark leaves; the jonquils, whose gold throats are so full of sweets, tell no tales.

"I never saw you in a frock-coat and tall hat before," says Lenore, playfully surveying her lover from head to heel; "turn slowly round, that I may judge of the *tout ensemble.*"

"Nor I you in a bonnet." ,

"You have seen me, however, in a *cap*," returns Lenore, with a mischievous smile.

Paul looks a little grave.

"Do not abuse it!" cries the girl, laughing. "With all its misdemeanors, it was a *blessed* cap, and I have a good mind to be married in it."

"Lenore, I *hate* that episode!"

"Do you? Well, then, we will dig a hole and bury it; all the same" (sighing a little), "though I am a great deal *gooder* than I was, I am not yet good enough to regret it."

"*Are* you 'gooder' than you were?" (with a fond, but rather incredulous smile).

"Do not you think so?" she asks, eagerly. "Have not you remarked it? Do not you think I am improved?"

Paul is a little puzzled; he has not been here four-and-twenty hours yet; but, as far as he sees, she is the very identical Lenore that he left sobbing on the deck of the St.-Malo steamer. She is not sobbing now, and, instead of a water-proof, she is clad in a smart winter-gown and a bonnet with a feather; but, for the rest, he sees no change.

"Have you heard me say any thing fast?" asks Lenore, growing serious.

"No."

"Or slang?"

"No."

"Or seen me get into one of my rages?"

"No," answers Paul, half laughing at the idea of the

self-control implied by keeping out of a rage during eight-
teen hours, of which seven were spent in sleep, and the
rest in the company of a favored and adoring lover.

"Have you heard me snub Jemima?"

"No."

"Or seen me box Tommy's ears?"

"No."

"Well, then, I *must* be improved," cries Lenore, triumphantly; "for I can tell you, you could not have spent
an hour in my society this time last year without seeing
me go through some of those manœuvres."

"Well, then, you *are* improved," answers Paul, smiling,
and smoothing her shining hair; "and we all know there
was room for it, do not we?"

"Plenty," replies Lenore, briefly.

"All the same, I did not think you needed much mending that last day at St.-Malo," says Paul, indulging himself
in looking as thoroughly sentimental as even Scrope could
have done, now that he is sure that nobody is by.

"You prefer me with my nose swollen and my eyes
bunged up, do you?" asks Lenore, gayly. "Good Heavens!" (growing quite grave), "how I hated everybody
and every thing that day—Châteaubriand and his tomb,
and the ramparts, and the old houses, and the steamer, and
the stoker, and Jemima! Do you know, I cried *all* the
way back to Dinan; I do not think I stopped for one
minute, and Jemima and Mr. Scrope sat on two camp-
stools opposite to me. They did not look at the view, and
they did not look at the other people; they kept staring
at me the whole way. What possessed them I cannot
think."

"I wish I had been there," says Mr. Le Mesurier, looking rather vicious; "I would have turned Jemima's camp-
stool straight round, and kicked Scrope overboard."

"And what would he have been doing meanwhile?" asks Lenore, archly. "Poor Mr. Scrope! *how* bored I was by him those first few days after you went!"

"The *first* days!" echoes Paul, suspiciously. "You were not bored by him *afterward*, then?"

She does not answer immediately, and he has to repeat his question. Then she speaks with perhaps a shade of unwillingness:

"Well, no; I do not think I was. One gets used to things, you know, and he is not a bad boy, after all, and—and—and he was almost as useful as Frederick himself in running errands."

"And expected the same reward, I suppose?" says Paul, with a sneer.

"I have not a notion what he expected," retorts Lenore. beginning to look rather rebellious, and to hum a tune.

"Lenore! Lenore!" (the sneer disappearing as he snatches her hands, and gazes with anxious, grieved love into her face), "what were the *very last words* I said to you at St.-Malo?—do you remember?"

"Perfectly; they were, ' God bless you, darling!" she answers, speaking softly, her lips framing the words lovingly, as if they were dear to them.

"Ay, but the words just before them?"

"They were ugly, stupid, unnecessary, jealous words! I do not remember them," says she, impatiently, snatching away her hands, and not perceiving that the first half of her sentence contradicted the last.

"Ugly, stupid, and jealous, they may have been," says Paul, with forced calmness, "as many of my words, I dare say, are; but *were* they *unnecessary?*"

"What were they?" (very impatiently). "Let us hear them, and have done with them!"

"They were, ' *Do not flirt with Scrope!*'"

" Well ? "

" Whatever else you do, I know you do not tell lies: *did* you flirt with him ? "

" Upon my soul, I do not know ! " answers Lenore, ingenuously.

" I would have given you *carte blanche* to bully Jemima and maltreat your nephews," says Paul, magnanimously. " What do little flaws in the temper matter compared to— O Lenore ! to lower yourself and me by flirting with *that boy*, my own friend, whom I myself had introduced to you, and after all I had said to you?—Why do not you turn your face this way? Good God ! is it possible that you are *blushing* about him ? "

" I am blushing with *rage* at being put through such a degrading catechism ! " answers Lenore, coloring scarlet, and flashing indignantly at her lover.

" *Did* you flirt with him ? " repeats Paul, sternly ; his lips look thin and sulky, and his eyes also sparkle coldly.

" Is sitting by the hour in a person's company, wondering when he means to go, and yawning till the tears come into your eyes, flirting with him ? " asks the girl excitedly, her mouth beginning to twitch, and the tears to gather in her eyes.

" Certainly not."

" Is thinking a man very good-looking, and wishing that he would fall in love with your elder sister, and being sure that he will not, flirting with him ? "

" Certainly not."

" Is going endless expeditions to places that you have not the heart to look at, in a man's company, letting him spread his overcoat on the grass for you to sit upon, and carry your prayer-book to church and forgetting to say, ' Thank you '—flirting with him ? "

" No—o."

"Is" (this last query comes much less trippingly and more reluctantly from her tongue than the former one)— "is seeing that a man is going to make a fool of himself about you, and being so shamefully fond of admiration as not to do *every thing* in your power to stop him—is *that* flirting with him?"

"Of course it is," replies Paul, roughly, all his brown face turning white in his deep anger.

"Then I *did* flirt with him!" cries Lenore, bursting into a passion of penitent tears, and throwing herself into her lover's arms, which neither expect nor are willing to receive her.

"You did—did you?" says Paul, cuttingly, not making any attempt to press her to his heart, or otherwise caress her, but, on the contrary, endeavoring to restore her to the perpendicular, which she has abandoned in his favor. "And you can stand there smiling, and tell me so?"

"Not much *smiling* about it, I think," replies the girl, ruefully, wiping her eyes; then, more tartly: "Why did you go on asking me, if you did not want to be answered? O Paul!—Paul!" catching his hand and holding it, "I am not much of a person; long ago I told you that, and you would not believe me. Ah! you see it now—but don't—*don't* be too hard upon me! I have not been, like your sisters, pent all my life in a good, steady, stagnant English home, where never a man dare look over the park-palings. All my life I have been a Bohemian, as I told you almost the first time that we met—up and down the world, here, there, and everywhere, and I have always had some man dangling after me. I did not care for them, Heaven knows, and I dare say they did not care for me; but they were useful, and pleasant, and made the time pass—"

"As Scrope no doubt did! I dare say," (looking very ugly and sardonic, for a sneer deforms the beautifullest face, much more an unhandsome one) " that you did not find the days between June and December so *endless* as you expected; perhaps you did not buy that *pop-gun*, after all ? "

" No, I did not," says Lenore, her wrath bursting out into a blaze. " Paul, I warn you that you are going the very best way to hinder me from being sorry for what I did. What am I saying ? What *did* I do ? I cared too little about his comings and goings to shut the house-door in the face of a boy, who had got into a stupid habit of staring at me, and who—I own to you—would have loved me if I had let him, without my running after him, and per-secuting him in the way I did you "—throwing herself into a rustic chair, and sobbing violently at the reopening of the old wound caused by the reluctant origin of Paul's affec-tion.

Paul hates a scene with all his strength. He kneels down beside her, but even then he is too angry to be able to bring himself to say any thing fond. "Good God ! Lenore, stop crying; they will hear you in the drawing-room."

" If I *had* turned him out of the house," she says, from the depths of her pocket-handkerchief, " I should have met him fifty times a day in the street."

" Why could not you leave Dinan ? "

" We had taken the lodgings for six months."

" *Lenore !* " (very impatiently), " what are you *going* on crying about ? What more have I said ? It is five min-utes to luncheon-time."

" Hundreds and hundreds of times I have told him, honestly, what a bore I thought him ! " continues she, dry-ing her eyes, having successfully stained and disfigured her face almost past recognition.

" It implies a considerable amount of intimacy with a

man to be able to tell him, to his face, that you think him
a bore," retorts Paul, dryly.

"I *was* intimate with him," replies Lenore, boldly.
"Who says I was not?—not I, certainly. He was kind
and manly and gentlemanlike, which not one of the half-
dozen broken-down Irishmen who form the manhood of
Dinan was: he was a sort of tame cat about the house,
and so near my own age, and altogether—"

Paul winces; he himself was verging on eighteen,
full of man's impulses and thoughts, when this his betrothed was born.

"When I gave myself to you at Huelgoat," continues
the girl, more calmly, but with profound earnestness in her
swimming eyes, "and you took me—more, I think, out of
compassion and gratitude than any thing else, but still you
took me—did I keep back one smallest fraction to be able
to give it to another man? Not a shred! *Myself*, with
all my badness and my goodness—not much of the latter,
perhaps—I gave you, and you have it."

"I have—have I?" says Paul, whose harsh face has
been gradually softening throughout the last sentence, and
at the end looks almost mollified. "Well, then, with your
permission, I will keep you, and not hand you over to Mr.
Scrope, manly and gentlemanlike as he no doubt is, and
also so much more suitable to you in age, as you kindly reminded me just now. Lenore, I have been counting: I
was eighteen the day you were born."

"And I am sure you were an ugly, gawky, hobblede-
hoy, all arms and legs! I am very glad I did not know
you in those days," says Lenore, laughing; then, quite
gravely: "Paul, never pretend to be jealous of me again!
It is patent to everybody that I love you a hundred times
better than you do me; you know it yourself, and I—I am
not blind to it."

" Bosh ! " says Paul, turning away uneasily, not feeling exactly guilty ; for he does love her heartily, yet with an uncomfortable lurking sensation that there is a grain of truth in what she asserts.

" It is the way of the world, I suppose," says the girl, sighing. "One gives, and the other takes; it would be superfluous for *both* to give, would not it ? Perhaps some day—some far-off day—the balance will be changed, and we shall love each other equally; till then—"

" Till then," says Paul, gayly, mimicking her tone— " till then, Lenore, let us go to luncheon, and eat so many mince-pies as to incapacitate us for afternoon church."

CHAPTER III.

WHAT THE AUTHOR SAYS.

It is afternoon tea-time, and that high festival is always held in the hall. Scrope knows that there is no hope of *bézique* to-night, and Paul sees that a *tête-à-tête* is unlikely. They have therefore retired to the smoking-room, and, with their enmity temporarily smothered, and their friendship as temporarily reborn, are smoking the pipe of peace together. Only the three sisters lounge round the fire in easy-chairs; the fire, in burning, makes the low, quiet noise that is fire's talk.

" How I ever shall bring myself to call him ' Paul,' I am sure I do not know," says Sylvia, gently moving to and fro the hand-screen with which she is shading her face. " If it were a three or even a two-syllabled name—Augustus, or Reginald, or Henry—it would not sound half so familiar ; but ' *Paul!* ' there is something so abrupt and uncompromising about it; however, I managed to bring it out at luncheon. I said, ' *Paul*, will you cut me some partridge?' Did you hear? He looked so pleased."

"I do not think he heard," says Jemima, maliciously. "I always tell Lenore that he is like Dr. Johnson—*deaf* while he is eating."

"Oh, but he did, though!" retorts Sylvia, quickly, getting rather pink. "I knew it by his face; one can always tell by a man's face when he is rubbed the right way."

Jemima looks across skeptically at Lenore, who smiles lazily back.

"Do you remark that he never calls me any thing but ' Mrs. Prodgers?'" continues Sylvia, complacently; "many a man would have taken advantage of his situation to ' Sylvia' me at once. I think it so particularly gentlemanlike of him, and I shall tell him so as soon as we get on a little more easy terms; you might give him a hint, Lenore, that he need not be so ceremonious for the future."

"I do not think it has any thing to do with gentleman-likeness," replies Jemima, who has retained all her old aversion for hearing Mr. Le Mesurier complimented. "He does not remember your Christian name."

"Impossible!" cries Sylvia, now thoroughly nettled. "How can he help knowing it when he hears Charlie Scrope calling me by it fifty times in the course of the day? By-the-by, I must tell that boy that it will not do for him to be Christian-naming me before all those people at the Websters' to-night. Poor fellow! he means no harm; but I suppose it is one of the penalties of being left so early alone in the world, that one sets people's tongues wagging more easily than others do."

"What a trial the Websters are!" says Jemima, groaning. "To dine out on Christmas-day! It would be hardly greater heathenism to give a ball on Good Friday!"

"And such a regiment of us going, too!" says Lenore, sitting up in her chair, and pushing back the restive hair-pins that her reclining attitude has displaced. "One, two, three, four, five—like a flock of ducks *waddling* into the room one after another."

"I do not see why we need *waddle!*" says Sylvia, with dignity.

"I do hate visiting in a patriarchal manner with all my tribe!" returns Lenore, energetically.

Her betrothed is quite of her mind; suavity of manner is never his *forte;* but he has difficulty in manifesting even his usual amount of complaisance, when he discovers what his fate is to be.

"O Mrs. Prodgers, could not you leave Lenore and me at home? We should never be missed out of such a multitude," he says, vainly hoping for a reprieve at the last moment. "There is something so appalling in being trotted out as two people who are going to commit matrimony; an engaged couple are always everybody's legitimate butt."

"I do not think you need be afraid of that," says Sylvia, speaking with the happy mixture of sisterliness and coquetry, with which she always addresses her future connection. "You see you have never been seen with us before, and Char—, I mean Mr. Scrope, has always been *en évidence.* I think he is generally looked upon as the happy man.—Lenore, would not Paul have laughed the other night to see the way in which the Ansons manœuvred to let you have the morning-room to yourselves? If they are there to-night, we may have quite a pleasant little mystification."

At the conclusion of this speech, Scrope smiles oddly, Jemima reddens, Lenore rushes headlong into a remark that has neither head, tail, nor middle, and Paul—Paul is

putting on his overcoat; his face is turned away—one cannot see it.

.   .   .   .

They look to themselves—or rather to some of themselves—an inordinately long string, as they file into the
Websters' drawing-room : three long-tailed ladies, two
swallow-tailed men.   The light is very subdued, even more
so than people usually have it in the five minutes before
dinner.   Paul gives up the idea of making out the Webster
family in detail till dinner; then Lenore will explain them to
him sufficiently to prevent his descanting on the ugliness of
a wife to a husband, or making disparaging remarks about
a child to a parent.   As he stands near the fire, *furnishing*
the room, in company with half a dozen other men—whom
he regards with the innate distrust and thinly-veiled suspicion with which every Englishman regards every other Englishman who has the misfortune to be unknown to him—
his spirit soothes itself.   The drive was the worst part, and
that is over : not allowed to decline into comfortable
silence and semi-sleep by Sylvia, next whom he sat, and
obliged by the noise the omnibus made to say "What?"
and "I beg your pardon, I did not catch what you said,"
in answer to all her low-murmured prettinesses.

He will be very kind to Lenore to-night.   Hitherto he
has made her Christmas-Day rather tearful, poor child!
Well, she shall have a thoroughly happy evening, if he can
compass it; after all, perhaps, he will have better chances
of private commune with her, of sweet, grave talk, and
sweeter looks into her lovely, loving eyes, than he would
have had in the small home party, with Jemima and Sylvia
staring at him.

These thoughts are interrupted by the approach of an
old lady in a yellow gown (to whom he has a dim idea of
having been introduced as hostess), who leads him up to a

plain girl in blue, presents him, and leaves him beside her, with a whispered request that he will take her into dinner.

In a moment afterward that festival is announced. Paul sees men and women, all equally unknown to him, paired together, marching solemnly off. Presently a couple, of whom neither man nor woman is unknown to him, sweep by—Lenore and Scrope.

"This is part of the pleasant little mystification, I suppose," he thinks, setting his teeth. "Who knows if Lenore were not a party to it?" But the ungenerous thought is no sooner formed, than he is disabused of it by the expression of the beautiful face, that, unhappily for itself, can never keep its own secrets. She looks at him over her shoulder with a look of unaffected angry disappointment, shrugs her shoulders almost imperceptibly, while her lips frame words which he rather *feels* than hears to be, "Too bad!"

On the very smallest encouragement, she would outrage propriety by dropping Scrope's arm and running to him. Perhaps, after all, he may be able to sit on the other side of her. He catches up his ugly blue fate in a hurry, and hastens off with her in pursuit; but it is too late—another couple have struck in and occupied the coveted place; he has to content himself with being nearly opposite.

There is a great deal of holly and mistletoe about the room. Most of the women have holly in their hair; it does not look particularly pretty, and scratches their heads and necks. Altogether, there is a great affectation of Christmas cheer and jollity. But the *entrées* are cold, the champagne is all froth and sweetness, and the sherry is not to be named in the same breath with Mrs. Prodgers's.

Scrope has no idea of allowing his neighbor to lapse into sentimental silence, and wistful gazes across the table. He has got her now to himself for a full hour and a half;

except under pretext of a bleeding nose, or improbably sudden indisposition, she cannot get away from him.

"Miss Lenore, the expression of your face reminds me of a scene in 'The Taming of the Shrew:' 'Enter Horatio, with his head broken.'"

Lenore declines to smile.

"It is not my fault that Mrs. Webster has not entered with her head broken," she answers, with perfect gravity.

"Why so?—for giving us such a drink as this? Well, it *is* filthy stuff!"

"For making such a stupid mistake as to send me out to dinner with *you*."

He bows his blond, curled head ceremoniously. "Thanks."

"Engaged people *always* go in to dinner together," says Lenore, trenchantly.

"On what principle, I never could divine. With a whole lifetime to get sick of each other in, why they should be crammed down each other's throats before there is any legal necessity, I never could see."

"That is *their* affair."

"Mrs. Webster was aware of the barbaric custom," says Scrope, growing as red as any girl. "She was good enough to imagine that it was *I* that was engaged to you."

Lenore reddens, and turns down the corners of her mouth.

"What could have put so *grotesque* an idea into her head?"

"There is nothing grotesque about it," replies the young man, coolly. "Internally, we may be conscious of how distasteful to, and dissimilar from, each other we are; but *outwardly*, we are rather suitable."

"I do not see it" (very icily).

"Miss Lenore" (turning round and bending over her,

to speak low and eagerly), " why do you thrust your happiness so obtrusively under my nose? Do I deny your bliss? Do I pretend to be as happy as you?" She is silent. "We cannot *all* be Paul Le Mesuriers, you know," says Scrope, with a rather jarring laugh. "Of course, we would if we could; but, as we cannot, you must bear with us."

Lenore glances across apprehensively at her lover, to see whether he has caught his own name; but no—he is not looking at her. With grave interest, he and his blue neighbor are together consulting the mystic French secrets of the *carte*. Bah! how greedy the best of men are!

"Was it good manners," continues Scrope, growing more excited at each word, "to shrug your shoulders so perceptibly, and exclaim so audibly, 'Too bad!' because your hand had to rest on my coat-sleeve for the tenth part of a minute?"

"I never pretend to good manners," replies Lenore, shortly.

"He will sit into your pocket all this evening; he will sit into your pocket," says the young man (making use of an audacious figure), "all the rest of your life. Need you have grudged me my miserable half-hour's innings?"

Again Lenore glances hurriedly across; still he is not thinking of her. She looks at Scrope: his blue eyes are always bright, but the champagne, bad as it is, has made them sparkle more brightly than ever. With his straight nose, and soft, gold mustache, most women would have thought him distractingly handsome. An innocent, cherubic, yet stalwart beauty, such as some men manage to preserve through half a dozen seasons, Scrope looks as if he had said his prayers and gone to bed at eight o'clock every night of his life.

"For one half-hour forget that there is such a person,"

says the young man, entreatingly. "At cheese-time I will give you leave to remember him again."

"You are very good. Till then—"

"Till then—bah!" cries he, with a reckless laugh; "let us eat and drink, for to-morrow we die, or—*marry, which is worse.*"

"The one is at least optional, which the other is not," says Lenore, with a demure but rather wicked look at him from under her eyes.

Paul has abandoned the *carte;* he has discovered what the word that puzzled him was. "It is ' *Topinenbourgs,*'" he says to his neighbor; and then he leans wearily back, and thinks that he will refresh himself with a look at his beautiful sweetheart. He does so just in time to witness the glance that she is bestowing on his rival: it is the only look with the slightest tendency to coquetry in it that she has given him during dinner, and it is the only one that Paul intercepts. Pouf! is not that ill-luck for you?

CHAPTER IV.

WHAT THE AUTHOR SAYS.

THE men are left to themselves—left to work their wicked will upon the walnuts, and to raven among the candied fruits, of whose existence, as long as the women were in the room, they pretended to be unaware. And the women, meanwhile, stand, gently rustling, softly chattering, about the drawing-room fire; sipping coffee, holding gossamer handkerchiefs between their pretty pink faces and the flame, and mentally pricing and depreciating each other's gowns. Sylvia is very happy; she has, indisputably, a longer trail and a thicker silk than any one else present; her toilet, happily, hits the golden mean between the mournful and the magnificent, and she is almost sure that, as she left the dining-room, she heard some man ask who she was. Presently every one sinks into chairs, and upon ottomans and sofas; breaking up into groups of twos and threes, as similarity of tastes in point-lace, dressmakers, and children, prompts. Lenore forms part of no group—takes part in no chat. The night is cold, and the room not particularly well warmed; yet she chooses an easy-chair apart from the rest of the company, and unsocially sitting by itself in a little recess. Lenore deposits herself upon it, and bides her time. When the walnuts, candied fruits, and ungodly after-dinner stories are done, that time comes.

Paul is determined not to be checkmated a second time; he may dislike to be pointed out as an engaged man, but he dislikes still more to have Mr. Scrope pointed at as such. He walks straight up to Lenore.

"Do you know what I have got hidden here?" asks the girl, looking up at him, while her whole face laughs— not only mouth, but eyes, dimples, cheeks—as she points to the wide spread of her gown. "Guess!"

"I have not an idea."

She sweeps away her skirts, and discloses a tiny, light cane-chair.

"Sit down! You are an unfortunately big person; but, I think, judiciously sat upon, it *may* bear you."

He had meant to scold her—well, the scolding will keep; it may be carried over, and added to the next account. He sits down, and his jealousy goes to sleep.

"I was determined to have no more *malentendus* tonight," says the girl, gravely. "If any one had come this way, I meant to have looked at him with my own scowl—

9

the one you used to admire so much—and say, ' This is Mr.
Le Mesurier's chair.' "

"Lenore " (looking round with a sense of lazy well-
being), " is there *any one* in the room that is not a Webster ? "

" Hardly anybody; they are all directs or collaterals.
That tall old woman whose forehead has good-naturedly
gone round to look for the back of her head, who is *ambling*
about saying indistinct civilities to everybody, is Mrs. Webster, the head and fount for all the others ; she always reminds me of *Agag*—she ' goes so delicately.' "

"I know her, the old cat!" says Paul, resentfully.
" Serve her right if she were drowned in a butt of her own
gooseberry, and I cannot wish her a worse fate."

" The old young woman who never stops smiling is Miss
Webster; we call her ' the savory omelette,' because she is
so green and yellow ! *Does not she* smile ?—it makes one's
face ache to look at her." Paul laughs. " Paul, if you
jilt me, and no one else takes compassion on me, do you
think I shall ever get to the pitch of smiling like that ? If
I thought so, I would have the corners of my mouth sewn
up."

"Prevention is better than cure—I would."

"The man with the red beard is Major Webster; do
you see how short and broad he is ? His brother officers
say that he has *swallowed a box ;* is not it a delicious idea ?
—it quite invigorates me."

Paul laughs again; after dinner, it is pleasanter to be
amused than to be amusing.

"Apropos of beards," says Lenore, turning from the
company to a subject that interests her more, " yours has
not disappeared yet, Paul ? "

" Why, did you think it would ? Did you suppose I
moulted, like the birds ? "

"I thought, perhaps, you might have *moulted volun-tarily*, to please me," replies she, with a slight pout.

"When my beard moults," retorts he, gayly, with an expressive glance at the sleek but unnaturally luxuriant twists that bind her head, "I shall expect your (or rather the *unknown dead person's*) plaits to moult, too."

Lenore shrugs.

"*Que voulez-vous ?* Look at Sylvia. She has at least five pounds' worth on her head; I have certainly not more than two pounds ten shillings on mine. Nowadays, without a chignon of some sort, one's head looks mutilated and indecent."

"Then I like mutilation and indecency."

"Do you know, Paul" (with a pretty air of candor), "without my plaits, I hardly look handsome at all ?"

"I do not believe it," replies Paul, with warmth; "I would stake my existence that you look infinitely hand-somer, sweeter, modester! Why cannot you be content to wear your hair as Nature meant it—*flat* to your head, and *low down* on your ears and cheeks ?"

"Merciful Heavens!" cries Lenore, expressively cast-ing up hands and eyes to heaven. "Paul" (with a sudden suspicion), "have you been seeing any one lately with her hair dressed like that ?"

To her searching eyes, he seemed to redden ever so slightly.

"No—o, nobody particular."

She is not satisfied, but does not pursue the subject.

"Well" (with a sigh), "to return to your beard— Bah! what does the old woman want with us now ? Apro-pos of beards, look at hers! Has not she a 'menton d'une fertilité désolante,' as Gustave Droz says ?"

"So sorry to disturb you, but we are going to play Dumb Scrambo."

This is Mrs. Webster's errand.

"And what *is* Dumb Scrambo?" asks Paul, with a disgusted intonation, when, hunted out of their cold and quiet alcove, and the hostess having moved on to collect fresh recruits, he and Lenore advance to join the rest of the company.

"It is not bad fun," answers the girl—"a sort of silent charade, you know. Did you never see it? Oh, you *must* have done!"

"But I have not."

"Oh, you know, the audience think of a word. You will be audience, will not you? I am sure that you can no more act than a tom-cat."

"Well?"

"And then, do not you know—they give the actors another word that rhymes with it; and then they—the actors, I mean—have to act in dumb-show all the other words that rhyme with it, till they hit upon the right one."

At this lucid explanation, given with surprising rapidity, Paul looks a good deal mystified. Mrs. Webster has some difficulty in collecting a troupe. Sylvia is among those who positively decline.

"Oh, no, indeed—thanks, Mrs. Webster—I really could not; I am so childishly nervous that the feeling that everybody's eyes were fixed upon me, would make every word I had to say go out of my head."

"But you have *no* words to say; it is all *dumb-show*."

"Oh, thanks! but that really would not make any difference; I should have the same dreadful feeling that everybody was looking at me."

It being useless to try and convince her that some of the other actors might divert a portion of the dreaded public notice from her, Mrs. Webster desists.

Paul declines, too, with that decisive brevity which forbids pressing. He is angry with Lenore for not having done likewise; but she is firm.

"Impossible, my dear boy," she says, in a smiling aside. "If they were to ask me to walk on my head to-night, I should have to try and do it. Have not they given us a huge family teapot, and is not this part payment?

He is the more displeased when he sees Mr. Scrope march off, with the best of the performers, into the dining-room, which opens out of the hall, and is converted into a temporary greenroom.

It is a pretty old house, oak-floored; a step here, a step there, in and out of the rooms. The audience have disposed themselves about the hall-fire in chairs set a-row for them. The leading spirits among them have fixed upon a word, a very little one indeed, but which they hope will prove puzzling: it is *jet*. The word that rhymes with it, which they have given to the performers, is *net*. In the interval of waiting, until these latter shall be prepared to be dumbly funny, they beguile the time with talk.

"I always envy people who have *aplomb* enough to act, and do all that sort of thing that makes one conspic-uous," says Sylvia, leaning back in her chair, biting the top of her black fan, and looking pensively over it at Paul, who happens to be her neighbor. "I am afraid I am not *quite like other people*, but I should feel ready to *sink in-to the earth*, don't you know! Now, Lenore has none of that feeling."

"Evidently not," replies Paul, dryly.

His eyes are fixed on the dining-room door; it is a little ajar, and, through the chink left, he sees a dim vision of green. Lenore has a green dress; he is straining his eyes to see whose are the legs that are in juxtaposition with that green gown.

"Last time we were here," continued Sylvia, "they

acted the word ' tail ; ' and all the ladies fastened long boas
to their dresses behind, and walked about the stage wagging them. You can have no conception how droll it
looked."

Further talked is stopped by the opening of the dining-
room door, and appearance of the performers. Mr.
Scrope makes his entry on his hands and knees, crawling
awkwardly along. It is plain that he is meant to represent a horse ; his gait much more nearly resembles a cross
between that of a bear and a monkey, but the equine *intention* is evident ; it is rendered the more so by the fact
of Major Webster being seated astride on his back, with
a tall hat on his head and a dog-whip in his hand ; with
this latter he pleasantly flogs him round the stage. Then
another Webster enters—a heavy fellow, who has been dis-
tinguishing himself by making stupid and impossible sug-
gestions—comes up, and *feels his legs.* Mr. Scrope lashes
mostly out at him, and then continues his victorious
course, kicking and plunging round the room. It entails
fearful exertion, and feelings verging on apoplexy ; but he
is rewarded by the plaudits of his fellows. Having un-
horsed Major Webster, and sent that gallant officer rolling
on the oak-floor, to the great benefit of his dress-clothes,
the *cortége* retires, amid laughter and well-deserved
hisses.

" How good for the knees of his trousers ! " says Paul,
who, with a mind relieved from the apprehension of seeing Lenore in some grotesquely affectionate or affectionately grotesque attitude with Scrope, is able to laugh as
heartily as the others.

" Poor man ! did not he look as if all the blood in his
body had rushed to his head ? " says a young lady, compassionately.

" That was a good *bona-fide* kick he gave Webster,"

says a man—" no mistake about it. I wonder how his shins feel ? "

Meanwhile the actors are talking over their late performance, and planning the next.

" It was not obvious enough," says Major Webster, who, being manager, is responsible for the *éclat* of the proceedings.

" It had no more to say to *bet* than I have," said Lenore, bluntly. " I cannot imagine how they ever guessed it ; I do not believe they have."

" Well—no, perhaps not (looking rather mortified). " You see " (gnawing his mustache reflectively), " we were supposed to be betting about *him* " (nodding at Scrope). " It is rather difficult to be explicit when one does not say any thing."

" Phew ! " cries Scrope, wiping his face, and stroking down his tossed curly locks. " I had no idea that being a horse was such apoplectic work.—Miss Lenore " (turning eagerly to her), " did you see me ? Was not I a very free goer ? "

" I did not look at you," replies Lenore, indifferently. " I was thinking what we could have next. What on earth rhymes with net ? Set ? pet ? fret ? "

" Fret ! " cries Paul's blue dinner-neighbor, determined not to be behind the rest, though in her the dramatic gift is, to say the least, latent. " Might not we all go in, and sit in a row with our handkerchiefs up to our eyes, crying, ' Don't you know ? ' "

" I do not think it would be very amusing," replies Lenore, dryly. " Let ? set ? pet ? "

" *Pet !* " suggests the heavy youth, brilliantly. " What do you say to one of us going in by himself, and pretending to be in an ill-humor—pet—eh ? "

This idea meets with the silent contempt it so justly merits.

A pause.

"Stay—I have it," says Scrope, eagerly.

"Eureka! One of us must be a *baby*—a dear little *pet*, you know; and some one else must carry us in, squalling and hallooing. I say, who will be the baby? Do not all speak at once!"

The warning is unnecessary.

"Well, I suppose, if nobody else will, I must," says Major Webster, rather ruefully.—"Scrope, you are the biggest; will *you* carry me in? *Are you sure you can?*" eying him rather doubtfully.

"Of course I can, my dear fellow, as soon as look at you. Up with you!" answers Scrope, stoutly, and so stoops promptly down to embrace his nursling's legs.

"Stop a bit!" cries the other, gravely, stroking his red beard. "I must have something on—must not I?—or they will not know I *am* a baby."

Scrope looks round on the properties scattered about—umbrellas, hats, door-mats, sheets, carving-knives.

"Here you are," he says, snatching up a white table-cloth. "This is the very thing for you.—Who has got a big pin?"

Having pinned the table-cloth round his waist, and tied an antimacassar over his head, Major Webster stands complete, ready to represent smiling infancy. There is some difficulty in getting him hoisted up; the table-cloth *will* get under Mr. Scrope's feet, and trip him up.

"For God's sake, don't drop me!" cries Webster, nervously. "Perhaps we had better give up the idea."

"Not a bit of it! Get up on the chair; I shall have better *purchase* of you."

"And what am I to do?" asks Lenore, beginning to laugh by anticipation. "Have I no *rôle*?"

"Oh, you must be nursery-maid, don't you know?"

says Scrope, panting, and clasping the major's legs as he stands on the chair, " and give him the bottle when he halloos. There, take that hearth-brush, and shoot it out at him ; that will do as well as any thing else."

" But a bottle does not *shoot out*," objects Lenore, whose acquaintance with the ways and appurtenances of infancy, though meagre, is apparently more exact than the young man's.

" What does that signify·? " says Scrope, breathlessly, having with one final effort heaved up his bearded baby. " One must leave *something* to the imagination."

" For God's sake, mind the step ! " cries Webster, gloomily, looking down with apprehensive eye from his unnatural elevation.

It *is* nervous work, but they get through it triumphantly. Mr. Scrope staggers along, with laboring breath, and arms firmly clasped round his baby's table-clothed legs, who, for his part, clutching Scrope convulsively round the neck, while his bronzed face and beard emerge absurdly from his antimacassar, gives utterance to a series of the dismallest deep *yells*, supposed to represent the faint cries of infancy. Lenore walks gravely alongside, occasionally shooting out her hearth-brush at him; whether or not the audience discover that it is the mystic symbol of an " Alexandra " bottle will never be known till the Last Day. Having completed the circuit of the room, and made a playful feint of depositing his " *pet* " in Jemima's lap, Mr. Scrope and his coadjutors retire.

" I thought it was *Dumb* Scrambo," says Paul, dryly, as Major Webster's last *bellow* dies on the ear.

" I suppose that only applies to articulate sounds," replies Jemima, who is on his other side. " Bah ! " (wiping her eyes) ; " it is an insult to one's understanding to laugh, but one cannot help it. After all, it is not half so good as charades."

"Paul should have been at the Ansons' the other night," says Sylvia, with a little coy hesitation and stumbling (both quite thrown away) over his name; then, turning to him:

"You should have seen Lenore, as *bar-maid*, running about and saying all sorts of impertinent things to the gentlemen, in a Breton cap. Do you know, she has got an *immensely* becoming Breton cap! I tell her that it is too matronly for her, and that she ought to give it to me. Do you give your consent?" (opening and shutting her fan bashfully).

"A *bar-maid!*" repeats Paul, with a slightly-clouded face. "Very entertaining, I dare say; and who *were* the gentlemen that she said impertinent things to?"

"You need not be jealous," interposes Jemima, with a rather dry laugh. "Only old Mr. Anson; he came in as *Boots* in a pea-jacket. Now, if there is an absurd sight in the world, it is an old fat man in a pea-coat."

"Ah! true, so it was!" says Sylvia, languidly. "*Inconstant*, you know, was the word; that was *inn*, and *constant—*"

"How long they are in coming this time!" cries Jemima, hastily interrupting. "What *can* they be doing?"

"And *constant?*" says Paul, leaning forward, while his eyes shine with a rather doubtful expression. "How was *that* acted?"

"I don't think I will tell you," says Sylvia, with charming archness. "You know, 'when the cat's away, the mice will play.' Well, Lenore was supposed to be engaged to Charlie Scrope. Poor Charlie! he torments me out of my life to act, too; but I said, 'No! no! no! not my line at all!'"

"Well—but about Lenore?" interrupts Paul, impatiently.

"Oh, yes, to be sure. Charlie was supposed to have

been away for five or six years, and to come back suddenly, and then they rushed into each other's arms; of course " (tapping him playfully with her fan), " it was only a *stage*-embrace—*cela va sans dire*—but it made us all laugh ! "

The cloud deepens on the young man's forehead.

" It must have been almost better than the bar-maid," he says, grimly, turning away.

Meanwhile, the ingenious *troupe*, still at fault for the right word, have hit upon another wrong one—" *Wet.*"

" *You* carry in a candle," says Major Webster to Lenore, thrusting the weapon indicated into her hand, " and pretend to catch fire; blow out the candle and drop it, and begin to scream like mad; and then—don't you know?—we will all rush in with buckets, and put you out."

" But must I scream much, or little ? "

" Oh, the louder the better ; and you must go on screaming till we come."

Lenore does exactly as she is bid. Shrieking at the pitch of her high, clear voice, imaginarily burning, and as imaginarily being extinguished—with one of Mrs. Webster's best silver candlesticks lying dinted and doubled up at her feet—her joyous eyes seek her lover's face for applause; but, as soon as they light on it, both her laughter and her screams together die. Unmindful of her assistants, she hurries back into the dining-room.

" You stopped *much* too soon," says Major Webster, reproachfully; " you ought to have gone on for a quarter of an hour longer."

" Is your dress damaged? Did any of the wax fall on it ? " asks Scrope, eagerly, falling on his knees before her, and catching hold of the silk. His back is turned to the others, who have already fallen into fresh wranglings and janglings; nobody sees him; he stoops his head hurriedly, and brushes one of her smart lace-flounces with the silky gold of his mustache.

"What are you doing?" she cries, angrily, twitching it away from his clasp.

"I am playing a Dumb Scrambo of my own," he says, lifting his eyes with a defiant flash to hers. "Why do you stop me? It amuses me, and it does you no harm."

"I hate Dumb Scrambo!" she cries, passionately. "It is a vile game. Why did you play at it?—who wanted you? There were plenty without you."

"I played," says the young man, raising himself from his kneeling posture, and growing rather white under these amenities, "because I have a benighted idea that, when you go to other people's houses, you should conform to *their* amusements, and not consult *only* your own, as some people do."

"Is that meant for a sneer at Paul?" asks Lenore, in a fury.

"Do you think," continues the young man, incisively, "that I *enjoyed* crawling along a beeswaxed floor in my dress-clothes?"

No answer.

"Do you think that I *enjoyed* hauling about that Jack Pudding" (with a glance at Major Webster's broad back) "for the amusement of half a dozen old women?"

"Of course you did, or you would not have done it," answers Lenore, brusquely.

"It, at least, had the good effect of rooting you out of your corner," says Scrope, with a bitter laugh. "Perhaps it *was* worth while breaking one's back, and spoiling the knees of one's trousers, to accomplish such a result."

"Why on earth could not you leave us there in peace?" cries the girl, angrily. "*You* might have sat in a corner till the crack of doom, and I would not have put out a finger to move you!"

"You are *in disgrace*," says the young man, speaking in a low voice, but with an eager flush; "I know it—so do you! we saw it in his face—*in disgrace*, because I poured an imaginary bucket of imaginary water over you! Such being the case, I wish you *joy* of your future life!"

·   ·   ·   ·   ·   ·   ·   ·

WHAT JEMIMA SAYS.

We are in the omnibus, going home. There is not an earthly vehicle that makes a more deaving din than an omnibus—a sort of steam threshing-machine in one's head; yet we are all talking—at least not all—four of us *à qui mieux mieux*.

"Very stingy with their champagne; did not half fill one's glass."

"Very bad oyster-sauce!—something oily about it!"

"The fricandeau was good; I am always fond of a fricandeau."

"I think that, considering they have a three-hundred-guinea *chef*, and three in the kitchen besides, they *might* give one better bread-sauce."

"I am sure Major Webster has got a temper! I saw him scowling at one of the footmen at dinner."

These are some of the severe and spirited strictures that we are passing on the entertainment we have just quitted.

"I almost wish that we had asked Mrs. Webster to wait for us in the cloak-room, at the ball on Friday night, so that we might all go into the room together," says Sylvia, with what I *feel*, though I cannot *see*, to be a simper. "Of course I am *really* quite an efficient *chaperone*, but people make such stupid mistakes! The man who took me into dinner asked Miss Webster whether I was *out!* Just fancy!"

"How differently people see things!" I say, with my usual malevolence. "The man who took *me* into dinner asked me which was the older, you or I?"

Meanwhile Lenore says little, and Paul nothing, though they are sitting side by side. As we clatter and rumble with redoubled noise through a village, a light from a window darts a ray into our darkness. I see that Lenore's face is turned toward him, and that the hand nearest him lies ungloved on her knee, as if wishing to be clasped by his. Under cover of the others' chatter, I listen treacherously to their whispered talk:

"Paul, are you *dead?*"

"No."

"Are you asleep? I cannot see your eyes."

"No."

"Are you angry?"

"Yes."

"What about?"

No answer.

"Would you be less angry if I told you (stoop down your head) that I have been in Gehenna all the evening, and that I think *him* a greater bore than ever?"

The next lamp-post that we pass reveals the white hand nestling in its owner's.

CHAPTER V.

WHAT THE AUTHOR SAYS.

"IF there is a thing in all this wide world that gives me the horrors," says Sylvia, with a little shudder, "it is mutton dressed lamb-fashion. I know my temptation lies in quite the other direction, to make a *grandmother* of myself!"

This is at luncheon, on the day succeeding the Dumb Scrambo; the friendly criticisms on the entertainment and the entertainers are being renewed and carried on with a spirit hardly less piquant than the sorrel-sauce that is flavoring the interlocutors' cutlets.

"Poor Harriet Webster! a white book-muslin *frock*—one can call it nothing else—and a pink sash, *low*, too, nowadays, when no one thinks of being *décolleté* except at a ball!"

"She only wanted a *rattle*, and to have her sleeves tied up with coral, to be the complete infant," says Lenore, laughing maliciously. "If she had thought of it, Mr. Scrope, you might have carried *her* in last night, instead of her brother; she would have been several stone lighter."

"And the way she kept hoisting up those wretched little shoulders, too, to her ears!" says Jemima, putting in her oar. "I really *trembled* for the string of her tucker. I wonder her brother does not remonstrate!"

"Pooh!" cries Lenore, carelessly. "I do not suppose that he knows whether she *has* any shoulders, or any tucker either—brothers never do!"

A little pause while the first sharpness of hunger is appeased; then Lenore recommences:

"What bushy black brows *your* lady had, Paul! Poor

fellow! I *did* pity you; and they met so amicably in a tuft on the top of her Roman nose!"

"*I* did not think much of Miss Jemima's friend," says Scrope, laughing; "he looked as if he had been run up by contract—hands like feet, and feet like fire-shovels."

"And his wife?" says Jemima; "did you see her? No?—a little bunchy thing, who never says any thing but 'Fancy!' and, if you are *very* intimate with her, 'Just fancy!'"

"Then, like her, I cannot imagine why," says Sylvia, languidly, "she has a way of *looking down her nose.*"

"Paul, why don't you speak?" cries Lenore, with a pout. "We have all said something clever; it is quite your turn."

"Is it?" says Paul, lazily. "Mine is a long time hatching; it will come presently; but, you see, you do not know any of my best friends; so it will lose all its point, I am afraid."

"I am sure we have not said any thing that was not perfectly good-natured," says Sylvia, with an air of injured innocence; "and, as to that, I have no doubt we are quite quits. I dare say they have made quite as many comments on us—not that they *can* say *we* are *décolleté*—as we have on them."

· A diversion is here effected by the depravity of Tommy, who, being dissatisfied with his dinner, insists on saying, "Thank God for my hasty pudding!" instead of the authorized form of thanksgiving. He is instantly degraded from his high chair, and borne off wriggling like an eel, and kicking the footman's shins.

"Let us go out," says Lenore, laying her hand on her lover's coatsleeves, as she passes out of the dining-room. "Let us go into the wood. I love a wood in winter. I *love* kicking the dead leaves. If you are good, you shall kick them too."

Five minutes later she has joined him as he stands in the wintry garden puffing at his pipe.

"Wait a minute!" she cries, her eyes flashing gleefully. "Look at the children going out walking. Did you ever see any thing so be-comfortered and be-gartered? I *must* run and knock their hats over their eyes!" She springs away from his side, and in two seconds is back again. "It is such fun!" she says, breathlessly; "it makes them hate one so!"

And now they are in the wood; above them the high brown boughs meet in wintry wedlock; each little pine-twig, no longer hid by leafage, asserts itself, standing delicately out against the softly-travelling, sad-colored clouds beyond. Underneath all the trees dead children lie heaped; there is no wind to stir them. There they lie! One can hardly tell one from another now—the horse-chestnut's broad fan, the beech's pointed oval, massed together in one bronze-colored death. They are over Lenore's ankles, as, with all the delight of a child, she ploughs through them, kicking them up, laughing, and insisting that her lover shall kick them too.

"What a good smell they have when one stirs them up!" she cries; "something half-pungent! Smell, Paul, smell!" Paul obeys, and stands docilely inhaling the autumnal odor. "And now," she says, clasping her two hands round his arm, leaning a very considerable weight upon him as they again pace slowly onward, "talk a great deal. I seem hardly to have heard your *real* voice yet; yesterday was all church and plum-pudding and scolding, and to-day we have done nothing but dissect the Websters. Talk! talk! talk!"

"How *can* I talk?" he says, laughing. "You will not let me get a word in edgeways."

"Tell me all about every thing," she says, comprehensively. "Begin at the beginning, like a story—at the very moment you stepped off the Dinan boat—letters go for nothing. Were you very sea-sick? I believe you were, though you would not own it."

"Frightfully, since you insist upon it," replied Le Mesurier, with a mendacious smile. "I lay on deck on the small of my back, with a livid face, praying for shipwreck—that is the right feeling, is not it?—while, to add to my sufferings, everybody kept stumbling over my legs."

"And when you got home," continues the girl, eagerly, taking this statement for what it is worth, "were they all very glad to see you? Did they all rush out to the door to meet you?"

"The butler came out, I believe; I do not think that even he *ran ;* certainly no one else did."

"And when they saw you" (speaking very rapidly), "how did they look? Did they look *odd?* What did they say to you?"

"Oh, I don't know; much the same as they always say —nothing different—why should they? they did not know any thing *then ;* they said, 'Oh, here you are!' or something equally brilliant; and my father said: 'For God's sake, do not touch me! I have got it in both hands.' He meant the gout."

"And then you kissed them all," says Lenore, a little envious at this part of the programme. "Do you kiss your father? Some grown-up men do."

"Do they?" replies Paul, grimly. "How very unpleasant for both parties! No; I do not, certainly."

"And—and was there no one there besides just your own people—just your father and sisters?" asks Lenore, with wily suavity.

"My cousin, of course" (with a tone of airy *nonchalance*).

" And " (laughing not quite so easily as before)—" and what was *she* doing ? "

" My dear soul " (with slight symptoms of impatience), " it is six months ago ; how the mischief can I remember ? " —then, seeing her countenance fall a little—" stitching, I fancy ; making a flannel petticoat for some old woman."

" Which she ostentatiously thrust into a cupboard the moment you appeared," says Lenore, sarcastically, turning down the little red corners of her mouth—

" ' Did good by stealth, and blushed to find it fame.' "

Paul lets this thrust pass in silence.

" And did you bring me on the *tapis* that night, or did you keep me till next morning ? " (looking anxiously up in his face).

" I kept you for several days," he answers, smiling— " very much against my will, I can tell you ; but I knew that, as long as IT remained in his hands, there was no use broaching the subject."

" But the girls had not the gout !—you told them, did not you ? " (with great animation).

Paul looks down, and his expression is embarrassed.

" Yes," he says, slowly, " I did."

" And showed them my photograph ? "

" Ye—es."

" I hope you told them that my hair was not so dark as it looks there " (very anxiously). " Did not they think it pretty ? Did not they say what a good figure I must have ? "

" I dare say they would not have thought it polite to make personal remarks about you to me," Paul answers, looking thoroughly confused ; " and they never *are* girls to say civil things, don't you know ? "

Lenore puts up one dog-skin-gloved hand and hides her

mouth; it is the mouth that, in its altered and quivering lines, betrays mortification most.

"Did not they—did not they say *any thing?*" she asks, in a blank voice.

"They looked at the name of the photographer on the back," he answers, with a smile of recollected annoyance, "and said, 'Oh, yes; he was a good man, they knew.' I remember *that*, because it made me so savage."

"And—and your *cousin*—what did *she* say?"

"She was not there."

"But—but when you told her you were going to be married—what did she say *then?*"

"Pshaw!" cries he, impatiently, reddening slightly. "What extraordinary questions you do ask! What can it matter to you or me either what she said? She said the —the—usual thing, I suppose" (turning his head half-way, and viciously knocking a big fungus-head off with his stick).

"I do not believe a word of it!" cries Lenore, in a fury. "Why do you hate talking about her? Why do you always slide away from the subject when I lead to it? You do not *look* as if you were telling truth! I believe she—she—she—wanted to marry you herself."

Sometimes the innocent wear the pale livery of guilt, by some ingenious freak of nature. At this audacious statement Paul certainly looks whiter than his wont.

"You are talking nonsense," he says, brusquely; "childish, unladylike nonsense," and, so speaking, he drops her arm, and stalks on by himself.

She rustles after him through the dead leaves, half penitent, half suspicious, till they reach a stile that gives egress from the wood into a meadow—a December meadow—a very different matter from one of June's buttercup gardens —a meadow flowerless, gray-colored, and drenched. There, having overtaken him, she lays a hand on each of his arms.

"Why *will* you insist on rousing my devil?" she says, impulsively. "Do you do it on purpose? I do not know whether other women have a devil, but I have, I know."

"It is so remarkably easily roused," he answers, drily.

"There is not a *gooder* woman in the world than I am sometimes," she continues, naively. "Why will not you let me always be?"

"*Let* you," he repeats, laughing, a little ironically, but looking down with a mollified expression at her repentant, fond face, freshened by the cool, moist wind. "I am sure I do not know what I do to hinder you; I wish to Heaven you would be!"

CHAPTER VI.

WHAT JEMIMA SAYS.

THAT evening, Fate, in the shape of a sleek little widow, wills that we shall have a small dinner-party. We should all have much preferred to have kept to our family circle, and, lounging in our chairs, have wooed little contraband sleeps, in recollection of our last night's fatigues, and preparations for those of the next. But Sylvia is obdurate. "Say what you please," she says, pronouncing each word very distinctly. "Call me a prude if you like—it will not be the first time—I cannot help it, but it does feel so *odd*, we three quite young women sitting down and hobnobbing with those two young men; nobody *belonging* to anybody else, don't you know."

"I beg to say I *do* belong to somebody," interrupts Lenore, holding up her head.

"I am sure nobody can feel more kind and sisterly than

I do to Paul," continues Sylvia, with an air of conscious modest merit; " but still there is no use denying that he is a comparative stranger, and I confess I *should* like him to see that we have *some* idea of civilization."

So, to prove our civilization, we enlarge our little circle by the addition of the three Websters, of a couple of stray marauding girls, and of three diffident foot-soldiers from the —— Barracks.

"We used to have really *nice* regiments always," Sylvia says, in apology for these poor young gentlemen, before their arrival, as she stands with one round white elbow leaning on the mantle-piece, looking up with her large appealing eyes to Paul—Sylvia's eyes have appealed and besought and implored all their life, but what for, nobody ever could make out—" really *nice* regiments—the Enniskillens, and the 9th Lancers, don't you know; but now we have only those nasty walking things."

Paul laughs: "I like nasty walking things; I was one myself."

There are no mistakes as to pairing to-day. I, who have no claim upon anybody—I, to whom it is absolutely indifferent *who* leads me, so that I ultimately reach the savory haven of dinner, and Mr. Scrope, who also has no right to anybody present, march in together. During soup he tries to make feverish and unnatural love to me, which I rightly attribute to the fact of Lenore's blue ribbons and sweet peas being fluttering and flowering opposite; but, as I indignantly decline to be the victim of any such imposture, he relapses into a sulky silence, and I into my usual trite vein of moralizing.

If people could but hear the comments made on them! For instance, if Miss Webster had but lurked behind the window-curtains at luncheon to-day, how clothed and lowered and quiet would her shoulders be! I look: they are still playfully shrugged and lifted in all their lean and virgin nakedness.

It is evening. Tea has reunited those whom claret parted. The footmen have wheeled in the card-table, and are now clearing another table for a round game—that noisy refuge of those who cannot talk—whereat loud and inarticulate sounds, like to the bray of the ass, the shrill clucking and calling of a distracted hen-roost, take the place of low-voiced and rational conversation. We are all making our selection between the two games: there are far more candidates for the boisterous mirth of the one, than for the silent dignity of the other. The infantry, and their attendant houris, the Websters, in short, all the *externes*, distinctly decline a rubber.

Major Webster has arrived at the age when a man insists on being classed among "the young people." Being ten years his sister's senior, he is almost as old for a man as she for a woman. He likes to get near the youngest girl in the company—he *loves* bread-and-butter, that surest sign of advancing age—to bank with her, look over her cards, and tell her all about himself. Paul chooses whist: I am amused to hear Lenore (the amount of whose knowledge of the game I am acquainted with) follows suit. Mr. Scrope does the same; so does Sylvia. As for me, I am nobody. I have been a spectator all my life. I am a spectator still. Lenore has walked over to a cabinet, close to where I am sitting, to look for some whist-markers. Scrope has followed her on the same pretence.

"Why do not you join the round game?" I hear her ask him hurriedly, in a low voice. "I wish you would—three-lived commerce and a pony—just the game for a nice little school-boy."

"Just" (flushing a little and looking rather mulish).

"*Do!* there's a good boy!" she says almost imploringly; "I'm really in earnest."

"I will play *bézique*, if you like," he says, eagerly; "let me get the little round table; you shall deal every time."

She does not speak in answer, but only turns down the corners of her mouth, with an expression of the completest scorn.

"What are you two whispering about over there?" cries Sylvia, playfully, from the table; "no whispering allowed!"

"Let us cut for partners," says Scrope, eagerly advancing.

"It is not much use," replies Lenore, bluntly; "for, whoever I cut with, I mean to play with Paul."

They begin. It is Sylvia's deal—Lenore to lead. It is some time before she realizes this fact.

"Oh! is it *me?* What a bore! What on earth shall I play? I have no more idea—Paul, I wish you would suggest something?"

Paul looks resolutely, gravely impenetrable.

"When in doubt, play trumps!" suggests Scrope, laughing.

"*Trumps?*" (with a expression of profound contempt). "Very likely!—as if I did not know that one ought always to keep them to the *very* end!"

Having half-played several cards, and withdrawn them —having gazed imploringly at Paul, who ill-naturedly will not lift his eyes—having tried to look over Scrope's hand, she at length embarks on the ace of diamonds. The others play little ones to it, and the trick is hers.

"Oh! it is mine again, is it?" (with a tone of annoyance). "If I had thought of that, I would not have played it. Now it is all to come over again. I suppose" (looking vaguely round for counsel) "that it is not a bad plan to play all one's big ones out first, is it?"

Paul conscientiously tries to veil the expression of ex-

treme dissent that this proposition calls into his countenance, and so successfully, that the ace of hearts instantly
and confidently follows his brother. He is succeeded by
the ace of spades.

"You have every ace in the pack," Sylvia says, pettishly.

"*That* I have not!" answers Lenore, glancing up with
a mischievous gayety at Scrope. "*You* know better than
that, do not you, Charlie?"

At the unnecessary and illegal candor displayed by the
first half of the sentence, Paul shudders slightly; but, at
the familiar abbreviation of his friend's name, he forgets all
about his cards. He would not look at his betrothed before, when she sought mute counsel from him. He looks
at her quickly enough now, with an expression of the most
unfeigned, displeased surprise. But, unluckily, she does
not see it. Her gaze has strayed to the other table, and
she is whispering to Scrope.

"Look at the major—we always call him ' *The* major,'
as if there was only one in the world. He is telling that
little miss beside him how a cricket-ball once hit him in
the left eye, and asking her to look in and see the mark."

"How on earth can you tell at this distance?" asks
Scrope, eagerly, answering in the same tone, and playing
at hap-hazard the first card that comes.

"I know his little ways," she says, laughing. "Once
I used to be invited to look into his eye. "Ah! '*Nous
avons changé tout cela.*' I am too old now."

"Would you mind going on when you are quite
ready?" Paul asks, with an extreme politeness of tone a
little contradicted by the unamiable expression of his countenance. Let those who blame him recollect that he loved
strict whist, and the rules of the game, with a love hardly
inferior to that of the renowned Mrs. Battle.

10

" *My* turn ! " cries Lenore, returning to the consideration of her cards. " You do not say so ! It is *always* my
turn. Now what next? Have spades ever been out before ? Surely not."

She herself, as I have before observed, led the ace three
minutes ago, and Sylvia threw away her queen on it. She
now boldly advances her king, which is naturally trumped.
At this catastrophe she expresses the extremest surprise,
which she calls upon Paul to share. In another quarter
of an hour, not only the game, but the rubber is ended.

" Absolutely *thrown away !* " cries Paul, tossing down
his last card, with a gesture of unrestrained irritation.
" Two by honors, and excellent playing-cards ! It is
enough to make a saint swear ! "

" I do not know what you mean ? " cried Lenore reddening. " I am sure I did nothing wrong, did I ? " (appealing to her adversaries). " I did not revoke, and I
returned his lead whenever I remembered what it was, and
I led out all my big things. One cannot expect too much
with those little nasty twos and threes ! "

" Let us change partners," cries Scrope, his broad blue
eyes flashing eagerly. " *I* am the worst player in Europe."

" By all means," says Lenore, with *empressement*, glaring angrily across at Paul, though there are tears in her
treacherous eyes. " I should like nothing better."

" *Not for worlds !* " says Sylvia, with a little emphasis
on the words, rising, and gathering together her gloves,
fan, and scent-bottle. " I would not expose my poor little
manœuvres to *Paul's* criticism for any earthly consideration ; I do not mind *you ;* you are a child ; you are *nobody !* "

The guests are gone—" Good-night time " has come—
we discreetly issue forth into the hall, and drink claret and

sherry-and-water, while Paul and Lenore are saying it in the drawing-room. They do not, however, speak very low, as I overhear them.

"One thing is certain, Paul," says Lenore, playfully, but with a sort of uneasy dignity in her tone, "and that is, that, when we are married, we will not play cards; I wish you would not be cross to me *before people.* I do not mind when we are by ourselves."

"I wish you would not call men by their Christian names under my very nose," Paul answers, in a tone that sounds half jealous, half ashamed.

"Do you?" (rather coquettishly).

"Lenore, how many men *do* you call by their Christian names?"

She laughs mischievously. "Ever so many; but I only do as I am done by; almost every man I know calls me Lenore. No! no!! no!!!" (her tone suddenly changing to one of repentant alarm); "do not look so furious—I am only joking; nobody does that I am aware of—hardly anybody!"

CHAPTER VII.

WHAT JEMIMA SAYS.

"A CHILD might play with me to-night, I feel so bland," says Lenore. "Tommy, Bobby, now is your time; never, probably, will you find Aunty Lenore in such a frame of mind again; drive her hair-pins into her skull, throttle her with your fat arms, ride rough-shod over her prostrate body; she will not utter a groan!"

It is the day following Sylvia's dinner-party. Lenore is sitting on the white hearth-rug of our sister's boudoir, an *immoral-looking* little up-stairs room. Looped rose curtains; lazily low chairs; mirrors gleaming through festooned white muslin; flowers that give out their scent delicately yet heavily to the warmed air; and outside the storm-rain scouring the pane, and the wind shaking the shutters with its strong, rude hands. "Had ever any one better cause to be happy than I?" says the girl, while her eyes dance in the firelight. "I am nineteen, I am handsome, I am going to a ball, and shall dance all night, and eat ices, and sit in corners with the dearest fellow in all the world, who is extremely pleased with me."

"Instinct tells me that he dances like a pair of tongs," reply I, amiably.

Lenore reddens.

"Poor Jemima!" she says, with a sort of resentful pity. "No wonder you say spiteful things! You are twenty-nine; you are *first* with nobody! how can you bear to go on living? what *can* you have to think about all day and all night?"

"Think about!" repeat I, cynically. "Oh! I do not know. Sometimes my latter end, and sometimes my *dinner.*"

"Poor old Jemima!"

"It is a mercy," continue I, reflectively, "that one's *palate* outlives one's *heart;* one can still relish red mullet when one has lost all appetite for moonshine."

"Bravo, Miss Herrick," cries a voice, as Scrope emerges from behind the *portière,* which hides a little inner room, and lounges with something of his old sleepy manner to the fire. We both start.

"Who gave you leave to come here?" asks Lenore, sharply. "Why did not you cough, or sneeze, or sigh, to let us know you were there, instead of meanly listening to all we had to say?"

"Neither of you said any thing either confidential, or that demanded contradiction," replies the young man, leaning his back against the chimney-piece, and looking down with *insouciant* defiance on the girl at his feet. "*You*, Miss Lenore, modestly observed that you were nineteen and very handsome, while Miss Jemima remarked that red mullet were better than moonshine, and that Le Mesurier danced like a pair of tongs; in both cases I have the good fortune to agree with her."

"You have, have you?"

"You are wasting all the life out of that bit of deutzia in your dress," says the young man, indicating with a slight motion of the hand the white flower that, resting on Lenore's breast, contrasts the dark folds of her serge gown; "suppose you give it to me?"

"Suppose I do not!"

"You will really, won't you?" (stooping forward a little, and stretching out his hand to receive the demanded gift).

"*Most certainly not!*"

"All right!" (resuming his former position, and speaking with languid indifference); "it is a half-withered little vegetable, and I am not sure that I would take it now if you offered it me; but all the same, I have a conviction that before the evening is over it will be mine."

"You have, have you?" cries Lenore, with flashing eyes; "sooner than that *you* should ever have it—look here!"

She runs to the window, unbolts the shutters, and opening the casement throws the flower out into the wild sleet. Thrice the winter's cold gust drives it back against her, but the third time it disappears. Then she shuts the window, and returns to the fire.

"What a fine thing it is to have a spirit!" says Scrope,

walking to the door. He does not look particularly vexed, but his cheek is flushed.

When he is gone, I retire behind the *portière* to write letters; Lenore maintains her former position, thinking, smiling to herself, and curling the pug's tight fawn tail round her fingers. In about ten minutes the door reopens, and Mr. Scrope again enters. His boots are miry, his shooting-coat is drenched, large rain-drops shine and glisten on his bare gold curls, but in his hand he holds the bit of deutzia, muddied, stained, dispetalled almost past recognition, but still the identical spray that floated out on the storm-blast through the open window.

"My presentiments seldom deceive me," says the young man, advancing to the fire, speaking with his old drawl, and wiping the luckless flower with his pocket-handkerchief; "feel how wet I am" (extending his coat-sleeve).

Silence.

"I am sorry I was so long," continues he, spreading his hands to the blaze; "but it was ill work grubbing among the dark, wet garden-borders; the rain put out my eyes, and hissed in my ears; but, don't you know, one hates to be beaten."

I peep at them through the *portière*. Lenore has sprung to her feet, and stands facing him. "Give it me back!" she cries, imperiously.

"Most certainly not, as you tersely observed just now."

"Give it me *this instant!*" with a stamp, advancing a step nearer, and trying to snatch it out of his hand.

"*Au contraire*" (holding it high above her head). "I mean to dry it in silver paper, and inscribe upon it, '*Souvenir* from Miss Lenore!'"

"I will give you *any* other instead of it," says Lenore, dropping her Xantippe tone, and growing conciliatory. "I will even fix it in your coat to-night. There!"

"Thanks. I have contracted a particular *penchant* for this one."

She does not repeat her entreaties, but I see her face working.

"Why are you so anxious to have it back?" asks Scrope, tormentingly, standing close to her on the hearth-rug; "don't snatch—it is unladylike—it is wet, it is limp, it is deader than a door-nail."

"Paul gave it me!" cries the girl, bursting into a storm of tears, "you know he did; and he will be so angry when he sees you with it."

He tosses it contemptuously to her: "Take it! I would not have it as a gift. You told me once that you never cried, and this is the *second* time in two days that I have seen you in tears."

They have forgotten all about me. He is leaning his elbow on the mantel-shelf, and staring morosely at her, as she wipes her eyes.

"The *second* time!" (looking up at him with the tears still sparkling on her lashes). "What do you mean?"

"Do you think I did not see your red eyes at luncheon, yesterday?" asks Scrope, scornfully. "You sat with your back to the light, and laughed more than usual, but you did not deceive *me*."

She turns half away, looking put out at the accusation, which she is unable to rebut.

"What had you been quarrelling about?" asks the young man, eagerly; "as usual, about *me?*"

"You are right," she answers, turning her great angry gray eyes upon him; "it *was* about you; it is *always* about you; if it were not for you, we should never have a word! Why do you insist on *thrusting* yourself between him and me? Why do you not go away? There are a dozen other places where, I dare say, you would be welcome. Why

cannot you leave this one, where you *must* see that you
are in the way?"

"May I ask how?" His voice is cold, but it is the
cold of strangled emotion.

"Did not I tell you a hundred times, at Dinan, what a
bore and a nuisance I thought you?" asks the girl, half in
bitter jest, half in earnest. "Why do you make me say
these rude things to you over again?"

He looks at her steadfastly. "You mean them *now;*
you did *not* mean them then."

"Did not I?" (indignantly); "ask Jemima."

"Lenore" (his lips growing white), "you said 'go,' but,
as I stand here, I swear your eyes said ' stay.' "

"They did not!" she cries, passionately; "they *never*
did; if they had—if they ever had been so unfaithful to
him, I would have *torn* them out?"

"Did you think me a *bore* and a *nuisance* when I lay
at your feet those summer mornings under the chestnuts
on Mont Parnasse, and read 'Manfred' to you?"

"*That* I did," she answers, with vicious emphasis.
"Why, I *slept* half the time, and dislocated my jaw with
yawning the other half! Not one man in a hundred can
read poetry, and *you*" (bursting out into angry laughter)
—"you rolled your *R's,* and ranted with the best of them."

Mr. Scrope turns sharply away, to hide his bitter mortification.

"Why do not you go?" continues Lenore, with her
startling candor; "it cannot be very amusing to you being
here now; the partridges are so wild that you cannot get
near them, and Sylvia never has any pheasants—go!
go!"

Again he turns and faces her. "Are you serious?"
he says, while all his boyish face twitches. "I know you
never stick at saying any thing that will hurt your fellow-

creatures' feelings, but do you really mean that you wish me to leave this house ? "

" I do, *distinctly.*"

" That the sight of me takes away your appetite, or *his*, which is it ? "

" Both."

" Miss Lenore " (dropping his sneering tone, and trying to take her hand), " I have been impertinent to you. I own it. I had no right to sneer at him behind his back —it was mean and womanish of me; but—but—you were a little friendly to me at Dinan, and it is hard to be shelved all in a minute."

" At Dinan you were never any thing more than a *pis aller.*"

" If I promise never to address you unless you first speak to me," says the young fellow, entreatingly ; " not to look at you more than I can help ; to be no more to you than the footman who hands you soup, will you let me stay then ? "

" Fiddlesticks ! " replies she, with plain common-sense ; " nobody can *efface* himself in the way you describe ; staying in the house with a person, one must be brought into constant contact with him. I say again—I say it *three times—go! go! GO!*"

" I will go, then," answers Scrope, steadying his voice with a great effort, and speaking with cold quiet; " but I will not go unpaid. Yes ; I will go, but on one only condition."

" What is it ? "

" That you dance with me to-night—not a beggarly *once*, as you might with Webster, or any other bowing acquaintance, but *three—four* times."

" I will do nothing of the kind ; I will have no bargaining with you," replies Lenore, with dignity.

"Then I will stay!" cries Scrope, with angry excitement. "Miss Lenore, it is not *your* house; you cannot have me turned out-of-doors, much as you would wish it. Eyesore as I am to you, I will stay!"

"Do!" she says, with a contemptuous sneer; "it will be a gentlemanlike act, of a piece with the rest of your conduct."

("That was a nasty one," think I, from behind the *portière.*)

There is a moment's silence.

"Say no more bitter things," says Scrope, in a changed, rough voice; "if you tried from now till the Judgment-day, you never could beat that last; and the worst of it is that it was true—it *was* ungentlemanlike; but, when one has gone mad, one is not particular about one's manners, as perhaps *you* will discover some fine day."

Lenore is silent.

"Make your mind easy, I will go—to-night, if you wish."

"There is no such wonderful hurry; to-morrow will do perfectly."

"To-morrow, then."

"Thanks."

"Lenore" (speaking with cutting emphasis), "you are the handsomest woman in the warld, and the one who has the knack of saying the nastiest things. If your face drives men mad, your tongue brings them back to sanity pretty quickly. Other women's sharp speeches pour off one like water; *yours* bite and sting."

"Perhaps" (indifferently).

A little stillness.

Again I peep. Scrope has sat down by the table; his elbows rest on the Utrecht-velvet cover, among all Sylvia's silly little knick-knacks; his hands shade his face.

"Don't look so tragic," says my sister, in a mollified voice, sidling up to him. "I own that I thought of myself *first;* I always do; it is my way; but, if you could have sense to perceive it, you would see that it is quite as much for your interest as mine that you should go. My dear boy" (laying her hand on his coat-sleeve), "I have a horrible suspicion that you are *crying!* Please disabuse me of it."

"Nothing is further from my thoughts," says Scrope, lifting his head and showing his beautiful face, undisfigured, indeed, by tears, but paled and altered by anger and pain. " Good God !" (looking at her fiercely) "a man *would* be a fool to cry about you. Would you ever cease laughing and jeering at him ? "

"Stop raving at me !" cries Lenore, whose patience is fast oozing out. "I have done nothing ; you have been a fool, and you must pay for it. Perhaps" (speaking very slowly, as if the words were not sweet to her lips), " I wish to be quite fair—perhaps—at Dinan—I *helped* you to be so —a little."

He does not speak.

" Charlie ! look here" (speaking with a soothing, sisterly tone), "*you* know, and *I* know, and Jemima knows, and I am afraid Paul knows, that sixty times a day you are on the verge of making a fool of yourself. Is not it better that you should go, before you tumble over the verge ? "

" All right," answers he, impatiently, shaking off her hand; "I am going. Having gained that point, I think the least you might do is to leave me alone."

"But—but you will come to the ball to-night ? "

" No" (very curtly).

" You *must ;* it will look so *odd !* "

"Odd it *may* look, then. At the present moment"

(laughing disagreeably), " my whole life looks oddly enough, I can tell you."

"But supposing I give you *one* dance, a quadrille?" (unable, womanlike, to let well alone, and kneeling down on the floor beside him).

"I would not walk through a quadrille with you" (speaking very loftily), "if you were to go down on your knees to me."

" As I am doing at the present moment," replies Lenore, laughing. "A waltz, then?"

"Are you serious? Do you mean it?" (catching hold of her two hands, while his eyes light up) " or are you only making a fool of me, as you have been doing without intermission for the last six months?"

" One never knows what may happen," replies the girl, oracularly, already rather repenting her concession; " perhaps—the fag-end—the very fag-end of a galop, if you will not expect to take me into tea afterward."

" Do not!" cry I, dropping my pen, and hurrying from my lurking-place. "Lenore, for the first time in your life, take advice! Let this poor boy go to-night!"

As I had surmised, they had forgotten my existence. Both look at me with the partial fondness with which it is usually an interloper's fate to be regarded.

"Meddlesome Matty!" cries my sister, with her usual amenity, "who asked *your* opinion?"

"Miss Jemima," says Scrope, reproachfully, "I thought *you* were my friend."

"So I am," I say, smiling and turning to him. "If she dances with you once, twice, a dozen times, to-night, how much the better will you be to-morrow? You will have set us all by the ears, while you—" I pause.

Neither speaks.

"It is useless disguising from ourselves," continue I,

with my usual excellent common-sense, " that Paul will be displeased."

"Let him be displeased, then, if he can be so irrational ? " cries Lenore, cheeks on fire, and eyes burning. " But no ! what am I talking about ? Paul has perfect confidence in me ; if I were to dance all night with Charlie Scrope, or Charlie anybody else, he would not mind—he would understand."

" Time will show," reply I, mystically, walking to the door.

" I will give you *four* dances, four *round* ones—there ! " says Lenore, with a brilliant smile, and a triumphant glance at me as I leave the room. " *Vogue la galère !* "

CHAPTER VIII.

WHAT THE AUTHOR SAYS.

It is time to go to the ball; all are ready; all are in the hall, save Lenore. The men have each two pairs of white-kid gloves in their pocket; one has plain gold studs, the other diamond and black enamel; but, oh, how poor, how small, are man's highest adornments, compared to woman's ! At his best, in his dress of greatest ceremony, he is but a scrimping, black-forked biped, compared to the indefinite volume, the many-colored majesty, of beflounced, belaced, beflowered woman.

" Did you tell her we were all waiting ? " asks Sylvia, in a tone of impatience.

" I did," replies Jemima, stepping leisurely down-stairs with a large mat, which her train has carried down from the upper regions, attached to her tail.

" And what did she say ? "

" She said, ' Hurry no man's cattle ! ' "

" Was she nearly ready ? "

" I don't know."

" What was she doing ? "

" She was advancing and retreating before her long glass, ascertaining whether her petticoats were all of a length."

" There is plenty of time," says Scrope ; " not ten yet. I remember once going to a ball in the country, and finding myself the first person there. It was an awful sensation ! "

" Are you sure that I should not look better with a *fichu ?* " says Sylvia, in an anxious aside, to her sister, getting out of ear-shot of the men, and craning her throat to get a view, over her shoulder-blades, at the back of her own neck. "Am I too *décolletée* behind ? You know that there is nothing in life I have such a horror of as being called a ' frisky matron ! ' "

" It does look rather *juvenile*, perhaps," replies Jemima, unkindly saying the exact reverse of what she knows is expected of her.

Sylvia's countenance falls a little.

" ' *Juvenile !* ' Oh, that was not what I meant in the least ! I asked Charlie Scrope what he thought" (smiling a little), " and he said, ' You look *awfully jolly !* ' He said it *quite loud.* I am sure I don't know what Paul could have thought. I suppose one ought not to have asked him his opinion, poor boy, because he *always* thinks one looks nice, whatever one has on."

" Does he? Jemima " (lowering her voice, and speaking with eager sincerity), " promise to tell me every thing that you hear anybody say of *me* to-night, and I will promise to tell you every thing I hear anybody say of *you.*

Jemima does not answer; her eyes are fixed on the stairs, on which a vision has appeared, above whose head two lady's-maids are triumphantly holding flat candlesticks, to aid the bright gas-light which is already illumining her —a vision, like a summer-night, dark, yet softly splendid— Lenore, all in black, with great silver lilies starring her hair, shining on her breast, garlanding her skirts. As she comes stepping daintily down, she does not look conscious —*very* handsome people seldom do; it is a prerogative re- served for faintly and doubtfully pretty ones. In her hand she carries a huge bouquet of white and purple flowers. All stare at her; but she seems to see only Paul. She goes straight up to him, her eyes shining like soft lamps, and her cheeks all rosy with happiness.

"Thank you *so* much!" she says, in a low voice. "I was surprised—and yet *not* surprised—when Nicholls came to my room and said, 'Here's a bouquet for you, ma'am.' I knew in a minute, of course. I did not even take the trouble to ask whom it was from; I *knew*, naturally."

As she talks, Paul's complexion varies, and his counte- nance changes; but she goes on, without giving him time to speak:

"How did you come to know all my favorite flowers? Was it intuition, or did I ever tell you? I forget. Vio- lets, Roman narcissi, white hyacinths—all the scents that I am most wild about. There" (holding up the bouquet to his face), "you may have *one* sniff, one *little* sniff, at it— only a little one, mind!"

"Lenore," says Paul, in a mortified voice, looking red and miserable, "it was not I. I know nothing about it. To tell you the truth, I never thought of such a thing!"

Had they been alone, he would have added fond apolo- gies; would have told her—what was the truth—that, had he thought they would have given her pleasure, he would have bought her a thousand bouquets, each much bigger than a haystack; would have sent to Kamtchatka for them, did bigger, fairer flowers grow there than here; but, as three people are by, his pride restrains him.

"*Not you?*" repeats Lenore, in a blank voice, as her arm and the now valueless posy drop to her side. "Who was it, then? Oh, of course" (following Scrope, who has turned to the fire to hide the scarlet tinge that has spread from the crown of his head to the nape of his neck) "it was *you!* I am right *this* time! Thanks so much for thinking of me."

She stretches out her hand to him, but her voice quivers.

These little disappointments are sometimes acute, as a needle, though but a small weapon, can give a sharp prick.

There is nothing further to delay the cloaking and shawling, which forthwith takes place. Paul and Lenore stand together alone for a minute.

"They have no longer the same smell," says the girl, eying her nosegay with a disenchanted look; "the narcissi's petals are already beginning to yellow and the maiden-hair to shrivel. Oh, you bad, *bad* Paul! just as I began to think that you must really be getting a little fond of me!"

"Don't talk such nonsense," replies Paul, brusquely; "cannot you see with half an eye, that I am in a greater rage with myself than you can possibly be with me? But Lenore" (hesitating a little), "now that you know that *I* —fool that I was—did not get it for you, are you still going to take it?"

"Of course I am," replies Lenore, decisively; "though it is the bouquet of disappointment, it gives a nice finish to one's toilet; if" (with a coquettish pout) "one is not provided with *legitimate* bouquets, one must console one's self with illegitimate ones."

It is an Infirmary Ball; one of those balls, therefore, at which, in *theory*, gentle and simple meet and frolic with happy equality and unity; at which, in *practice*, the gentle glide gracefully about at the top of the room, and the simple plunge and caper at the bottom. There is more air, more space, more every thing that is desirable, at the lower end near the doors, but to remain at that end is to confess an affinity with the butchers, the bakers, the haberdashers, of the good city of Norley. At the expense of any amount of elbowing, pushing, bruising, one must work one's way up to where one's peers sit enthroned on red-cloth benches. They are rather late. Slowly they work up. Paul escorts Lenore; Scrope, Sylvia; Jemima, herself. A galop is playing, and a hundred, two hundred people, are floundering, flying, and bounding round, as Nature and their dancing-master have taught them. Little women burying their noses in big men's coat-sleeves; big women trying not to rest their chins on the top of little men's heads; men who hold their partner's hand out, like a pump-handle, sawing the air with it up and down; men who hold their partner's hand on their own hip, describing an acute angle with the elbow; men who hug their partners like polar bears; men who hold their partners uncomfortably tumbling out of their arms, as if they were afraid of coming near them; men who run round their partners, men who kick, men who scratch, men who knock knees—every variety, in fact, of the human animal, rushing violently round, doing their best to make themselves giddy and tear their clothes.

"Are you going to dance this with me, or are you not?" asks Lenore, impatiently; "because, if not, I will ask some one else—I mean, I will make some one else ask me."

"Of course I am."

" What are you waiting for, then ? why don't you start ? I am mad to begin! Tum te tum! if they play this air when I am in my coffin, I shall jump up and galop in my shroud ! "

In a second more, the black and silver gown has joined the merry mad rout of reds, and blues, and greens, and whites. After half a dozen turns, Lenore pants a little, and says :

" Stop."

" That means that I dance badly," says Paul, releasing her from his arms.

" It means that I am never long-winded ; doctors often say that I ought not to dance."

" Not really ? " incredulously looking at her cheeks, carnationed by the movement of the dance—at her great clear eyes. " I say, Lenore, do I dance very atrociously ? It is a thing that I do not do once in a month of Sundays."

" Not *very*," replies Lenore, rather slowly; " you have not quite got into my step yet, but that will come." (Then, seeing him look a little mortified :) " You are not like Major Webster, who leaps his own height in the air every step he takes, and gets round the room in three *bounds*, like a kangaroo."

Paul laughs.

" That *is* modest praise."

Meanwhile Sylvia has been safely piloted to the top of the room, and enthroned between Mrs. Webster and another diamonded dowager. Jemima and Miss Webster remain standing. To take a seat is virtually to confess yourself shelved ; to remain standing, is an advertisement that you are still to be had.

" You won't take a turn, I suppose ? " Scrope says to Mrs. Prodgers, as he prepares to saunter away.

She has so often announced her intention of not dancing that he thinks the invitation—in itself dissuasively worded—may be safely hazarded. But human prescience is often at fault.

"Would you mind holding my bouquet for me, dear Mrs. Webster?" says Mrs. Prodgers, getting down with some alacrity from her bench. "Thanks so much! You see" (with a little affected shrug), "I am fated not to be left in peace. It seems a little hard upon the girls, doesn't it? but one cannot *pass on* one's partners, can one? they would not like it. I assure you I had no more idea of dancing—but one gets so tired of saying 'No,' 'No,' 'No'—such an old friend, too—you need not smile—he is *really !* "

"Quite right, my dear, quite!" replies Mrs. Webster, nodding good-humoredly. She is very comfortably perched herself, and she has long given up her daughter as a bad job. "I only wish that Miss Jemima could find a partner too—where is James?" (standing up on the raised footboard, whence she can get a commanding view over the company's head); "he was here a minute ago, and he had no partner then—his had thrown him over—I am sure he would be most happy!"

"Oh, no, no, no, thanks!" replies Jemima, in a frenzy at the thought of being crammed down James's unwilling throat. "I am quite happy, I assure you! I *like* looking on; it amuses me, and some one will be sure to turn up just now."

Miss Webster smiles; she always does; she has smiled through eight-and-thirty years of hope deferred. Callow boys and fat old married men are her sheet-anchor, and she is on the lookout for such now.

The dance ends; the sound of scampering and shuffling ceases suddenly; people's voices drop from *bawling* pitch to their natural key; everybody streams to the doors. The house seems to have been built for the express purpose of furthering love-making. From the ballroom long corridors diverge in every direction, dimly lit; and out of these corridors open many quiet rooms, also dimly lit.

"Let us go into the passages!" cries Lenore, "and I will show you all the holes and corners, where I perpetrated my worst atrocities in flirtation last year."

"On the same principle, I suppose," replies Paul, laughing, "which makes a man always take his second wife to visit the tomb of his first?"

They find a bench, retired, yet not lonely, where, in shade themselves, they can see men and girls, men and girls, men and girls, go trooping by: couples flirting, couples not flirting, couples trying to flirt, couples trying *not* to flirt. It is a bench that only holds two people; well armed, well cushioned, where, half hidden behind Lenore's spread fan, they lean together and whisper gayly.

"Paul! Paul! do you see that girl?—how dirty the body of her dress is?"

"Cannot say that I remarked it."

"It *is*, though; as dirty as the ground! She and her sisters always make a point of coming to these balls in filthy dresses, to mark the distinction between themselves and the clean, crisp, townspeople."

"It is patrician dirt, is it? I respect it."

"Do you see that big person in pink? Last year she went to the Assembly in a wreath of *mistletoe;* you may imagine the consequences."

Paul laughs.

"Her partner always gets very drunk! Last time I saw him was in the Ansons' supper-room; he was sitting on a lump of ice, crying bitterly."

"Lenore, why are you hiding your face?"

"Hush! hush! young Anson is coming this way; he

would be sure to ask me to dance, and dancing with him is like going into a *battle*, without the glory."

Young Anson passes safely by, looking neither to the right hand nor the left.

"I breathe again, Paul!" (edging a little nearer to him, and dropping her voice, more for the pleasure of whispering than from any dread of being overheard). "Paul, do you mean to let me dance when we are married?"

"H'm! I shall see."

"We shall not be able to go to many balls," says Lenore, sighing, "for we shall have no clothes."

"Speak for yourself."

"We must stay at home, and have tea and shrimps; of course, we shall not be able to afford dinner."

"Shall not we?" (looking rather aghast). "Does dinner cost more than tea and shrimps?"

"Of course it does: shrimps are only fourpence a pint!"

Paul shudders.

"Could not you make it *prawns?*"

"Certainly not; tea and shrimps it must be—perhaps water-cresses in the height of the season—and, after tea, you will read the paper in carpet slippers—not the *Times* —we shall not be able to afford the *Times*—but some penny paper—and I shall sit opposite you, with my hair *flat to my head, and low down over my ears*—is not that it?—hemming a duster!"

"I do not believe you *can* hem."

The music has struck up again: Lancers, this time. Fewer couples trail and saunter by: most have returned to the ballroom. The fiddles' sharp, loud squeak comes more softly to their ears; the merry cadence and marked time of the Lancers; then the little pause in the music, that tells one, without one's seeing, that the girls are all courtesying, and the men, with arms linked together, are galloping madly round, like savages before a wooden god.

Lenore's eyes dance softly, too, in this dusk place.

"Lenore, I have a favor to ask you."

"Not a very big one, I hope."

" *You* will think it immense."

"What is it?"

"That you will dance with no one but me, to-night."

He had expected her to accede with eager alacrity, but, on the contrary, she says nothing.

"I know that I dance badly, *vilely*," continues Paul, coloring a little. "I have long suspected it, and to-night" (laughing a little) "I learned it *for a certainty*, from your face, and from the eagerness with which you engaged me in conversation in the pauses of the dance, to hinder me from starting afresh. But why *should* we dance? *Could* we be better off than we are now?"

"Not easily," she says, and says it truly; but she still evades replying to his request.

"I want to have a feast of your society to-night," says Paul, earnestly. "Think what a fast I have had!—six months! We seem to know each other so little yet, and even *there*" (giving a vague nod to express Sylvia's abode), "jolly as it is, we never seem to get five minutes' talk without Jemima bouncing in at one door, or Sylvia ambling in at another, or those imps of Satan rushing in and playing the devil's tattoo on one's shins."

"Children of Belial!" says Lenore, tersely. "Good Heavens, Paul! how I hate the young of the human species! Don't you?"

Paul looks rather shocked.

"Don't say that—it is unwomanly!"

"Of course," retorts she, sarcastically, "to a man they

may be imps of Satan, but to the ideal woman they must always be cherubs—biting, kicking, scratching cherubs, but *cherubs* always. By-the-by, Paul" (with a sudden change of tone), "how *is* the ideal woman? Have you seen her lately?"

Paul turns his head away, and says:

"Fiddlesticks!"

"Paul, Paul! I have an idea! How red you are! Look me in the face—don't turn the back of your head to me. Is it *she* that wears her hair flat, and eschews *frisettes?*"

Paul turns round as bidden. His face is undeniably red; he is not laughing, and his eyes are rather defiant.

"What if it is?"

"Does she wear a poke bonnet?"

"Perhaps!"

"And a gray cloak down to her heels?"

"Well?"

"I know all about her," says Lenore, resentfully, her eyes flashing and cheeks ablaze. "A puritanical little prig!"

"I do not see what good it does you abusing a person you have never seen," says Paul, in a rather surly voice; "nor what it has to say to whether you are willing to sacrifice this one evening to me or not."

"Certainly not!" replies the girl, angrily. "Why should I? What have you done to deserve it? Yesterday you scolded me till I cried; everybody saw my red eyes. To-day you forgot the common civility of getting me a bouquet; and you are always trotting out another woman's virtues and beauties at my expense. *Certainly not!* I will dance like a Mænad with all my old friends."

Paul's forehead wrinkles into a frown, and his mouth turns down, as is his way when extremely vexed.

"All right! Do!" he says, in a constrained voice.

She had spoken with petulant half-meaning, had expected to be coaxed, entreated, scolded even, out of her perverse determination; but he employs neither coaxings, entreaties, nor scoldings—he acquiesces with dumb pride. They sit side by side in sullen silence, till disturbed by the sound of approaching voices, feet, and the long rustle and swish of a woman's infinite gown.

"You must take me back to the ball-room," Sylvia is saying, as she flutters her fan and smiles; "you must, indeed. If people come out and find us sauntering about here, they will be sure to say that I am flirting with you, and there is nothing in life that J should dislike so much as that—oh! here you are!"

Both are too sulky to answer.

"Not been dancing? Very wise of you! Look how much better you have come off than I!—in ribbons—absolutely in tatters! And Charlie has got a yard and a half of me in his pocket—have not you?"

She looks up at him playfully, with round, complacent eyes, and then stops suddenly.

To even Sylvia's comprehension, it is evident that he has not heard a word she has been saying. His eyes are fixed with steady intentness on Lenore. Paul is gazing vacantly down the long vista of the fast-refilling corridors.

"Are you engaged for the next dance, Miss Lenore?"

"What is it?" (nonchalantly) "a quadrille?"

"It is a waltz."

She peeps at Paul out of the corner of one eye; not a sign of relenting on the ill-tempered gravity of his face. Well! she can be as cross and sulky as he, at a pinch.

"No—I am not."

"Will you let me have it?"

"Certainly."

" Shall I be likely to find you here still after I have taken Mrs. Prodgers back to the ballroom ? "

"I will not trouble you," replies Sylvia, rather offended at the slight hint of anxiety to be rid of her unintentionally implied in these last words. "I am going" (with a coquettish smile) "to put myself under Paul's protection.— Do you hear, Paul ? I am going to put myself under your protection. You are not going to dance? No? Neither will I! We will sit here and criticise everybody—yes, we will talk you both well over" (shaking her bouquet at Scrope); "if your ears burn, you will know what to attribute it to."

Lenore has risen, and, while Sylvia is speaking, she bends and whispers maliciously to Paul, "Pleasant meditations on poke-bonnets and flat heads to you!"

He does not take the slightest notice.

She puts her hand on Scrope's arm, and walks off. Twice, thrice, she looks back, but not once has she the satisfaction of detecting her lover's eyes wistfully seeking hers. Silently they enter the ballroom and join the just-beginning whirl. Lenore is thoroughly out of tune—angry with herself, enraged with Paul, furious with Scrope. If any hole can be picked in his performance, he may be quite sure that she will not spare him. She is, however, deprived of that satisfaction. Scrope's performance is as much above praise as Paul's was below blame. He dances superbly. It is a small accomplishment, and does not add much to a man's social value, but in a ballroom it is the giver of great joy. Once in his arms, a delightful sense of security and strength comes over Scrope's partner; a blessed certainty of immunity from jostling; of being borne along steadily, rapidly, buoyantly, with the swift smoothness of a swallow's flight; all trouble taken off her hands, and only pleasure left. Lenore loves dancing *intensely ;*

11

with an intensity, indeed, seldom met with among sad and
sober Englishwomen.   On her the mere music, motion, and
measure of the dance, have an effect verging on intoxica-
tion.   Down the long room they fly together; the floor
seems nothing to them; they are floating on air, while the
music swells loud and sighs faint, bursts into mad merriment, and dies in voluptuous complaints.   Lenore has forgotten her anger—has forgotten even Paul; all feelings are
merged in one of acute, sensuous enjoyment—a feeling
languid, yet exciting; luxurious, yet exhilarating.   Many
couples, who set off at the same time as they did, are
standing still to rest, panting and breathless; but they still
fly on with untired, joyous grace.

   "Shall we stop?   Am I tiring you?" Scrope asks.

   "No, no!   Go on, go on!"

   "I wish to Heavens it could go on *forever!*" says the
young man, losing his head, and foolishly whispering into
the white ear that is so temptingly close to his face.

   The spell is broken.

   "Stop!" says Lenore, imperatively.

   He obeys, and stands gravely beside her, his broad
chest heaving a little with his late exertions; some strong
suppressed excitement giving an expression painful yet
eminently becoming to his straight-cut Greek face.

   "I thought you said you were not tired?"

   "No more I am."

   "Why did you say 'Stop,' then?"

   "Because you were beginning to be a fool."

   "I began that long ago; six months ago, in church; in
Guingamp Cathedral—if you wish to be exact."

   "You insist on being a fool, then?"

   "I said that I wished this waltz could last forever, and
I stick to it," says the young man, doggedly.   "I do wish
it."

"Tastes differ," says Lenore, scornfully. "I know nothing that I should dislike more than an eternity of capering with you."

He bites his lip hard, but attempts no retort.

"Shall we take another turn?" says Lenore, presently; mollified by his silence, after an interval spent by her in tapping with her feet and beating time to the music. "That is to say, if you will promise not to be a fool."

"I promise nothing."

"Well, then, we must risk it, I suppose," replies she, with a careless laugh. "Mind, it is no compliment to you. It is solely for my own satisfaction; for, though you may be a fool, you dance like a seraph, and I cannot bear to lose a bar of this."

Away, again, light as a feather; as if blown by the breath of the music. Once off—her anger unroused again by any rash remarks from her partner—the same sense of delicious enervation as before, steals over Lenore. It is like floating on a summer sea, as the music whispers, whispers, then laughs out and triumphs, in a loud, glad clash.

And Scrope—"Every dog has his day," they say, and this is his. It is a wretched little day; but still it is his! She may be Paul's for all after-life—nay, she will be, of course; who can hinder her? But for these divine, mad minutes she is his! It is not *Paul's* arm that is round her waist; it is not *Paul's* heart against which hers is panting; it is not *Paul's* shoulder on which the milk-white beauty of her arm is lying. All earthly pleasures must end, and a waltz is, in its very essence, one of the shortest; the music ceases. As they turn toward the door they come face to face with Paul. He makes as though he would pass them without speaking; but Lenore addresses him:

"What have you done with Sylvia?"

"She is dancing."

"And you? Why are not you?"

"Because I *hate* it!" (emphatically).

"You might have given Jemima a turn; she very seldom gets a partner, and she likes dancing."

"Even with *me?*" (with a sneer).

"I wish you a better temper," says Lenore, hastily, moving on.

They pass out into the passage.

"Why have you come here?" cries the girl, fretfully; "it is draughty. I shiver; let us go back to Sylvia—to Mr. Webster—*anywhere!*"

"You do not shiver when you are with other men," says Scrope, resentfully.

"*Other* men do not stare at one, as if they were going to *eat* one!" cries the girl, indignantly. "Good Heavens! Charlie, how much better I liked you when you were only a stupid, silent, sulky boy, before you adopted these unpleasant man's airs."

In defiance of appearances, Scrope stands stock-still; he is young enough to be galled by allusions to his age.

"Lenore," he says, almost imperatively, "stop gibing at me; after to-night, I give you a *carte blanche* to abuse me as much as you please behind my back—to mimic me for your friends' amusement—to show me up in as humiliating a light as it pleases you—you are quite capable of it —but, *for to-night, be civil.*"

"Mend your own manners, then," cries the girl, tartly. "Who gave you leave to call me 'Lenore?' For the last few days I have remarked that you have been slurring over the 'miss;' please to replace my style and title immediately."

"Is it worth while," asks the young fellow, more calmly, but with great bitterness; "is it worth while accustom-

ing one's self to call you 'Miss,' when you will so soon be
'Mrs. ?' For all my future life I swear to you, I will try
to think of you only as 'Mrs. Le Mesurier;' but, for to-
night, be *Lenore*, plain *Lenore !*"

For all answer, she bursts out laughing. "Excuse me,
it is rude, I know; but you reminded me so forcibly of the
tale of the man at a ball, who, when the music stopped
suddenly, was heard saying to his partner, at the top of
his voice: 'Do not call me Mr. Smith; call me *plain William !*' and, as he was remarkably ugly, he was called
'*plain William*' ever after."

CHAPTER IX.

WHAT THE AUTHOR SAYS.

IN the mean time, Mrs. Prodgers has been restored to
her eminent position on the bench : she has been danced
and talked and walked about, into a state of even more
than her usual complaisance.

Jemima still stands where she left her.

"Have you been dancing, dear? Yes? Oh, I am *so*
glad—I thought you would—I don't know what has come
to the people to-night; they would tear one in pieces, if
one would let them! *one* thing I *do* set my face against,
and that is, those passages. I said to young Anson, 'There
is no one fonder of laughing, and talking, and fun, than I
am, but if you talk from now till Doomsday, you will not
persuade me to sit out with you.' I dare·say there is no
harm in it *really*, but people do let their tongues run on
so, when a person is young and tolerable looking."

Jemima makes no answer.

Sylvia's conversation is like a Gregorian chant; there is a certain sameness about it.

Miss Webster has been waltzing with an Eton boy, in a round jacket: her shins are black with bruises, her elbow is scratched, but at least she has not been a wall-flower.

Another *galop* strikes up. Sylvia's talk drops into silence; she fiddles with her bouquet, and tries to look as if she would not dance if she were asked. Men hurry hither and thither, seeking for their promised partners; raising and dashing in the same instant false hopes in unengaged girls, by making apparently straight for them, staring hard at them, and then flying off at a tangent on discovering that they are not the right ones. Jemima scans the crowd to see whether she can discover any one likely to ask her (in many women the love of dancing survives the probability of being invited), but, finding no one, resigns herself with philosophy to her fate. Other people's enjoyment is not so good as one's own, but it is perhaps better than none. It is some people's lot to be spectators through life. She looks on. The pink calico, the laurels, the mirrors, the pretty rose-red ladies, the plunging grocers and floundering groceresses; a tremendous *thud!*—two people fallen like one log; now sprawling in a confused heap of broadcloth and illusion on the floor; the lady has ingeniously wound herself, like swaddling-clothes, round her squire's legs; she is unwound, feels for her head, settles her wreath, and off again! There are so many people, and they go so quickly, that it is difficult to follow any one: a blue couple, a pink couple, a white couple; they dazzle the eyeballs with the celerity with which they shoot across them! A black couple—taller than most of the others; the soft sparkle of silver flowers flashing like meteors down the room.

Why, it is Lenore! Lenore and Scrope again!

"I thought I had understood that your sister's *fiancé* was a *plain* man," says an old woman, who, unable to find room on a bench, is standing behind Jemima, and tapping her on her bare shoulder to attract her attention.

"Quite the contrary" (with a complimentary smile). "Have you ever seen him?" asks Jemima.

"Is not it he with whom she is dancing?"

"Oh, dear no!"

"Really! what a stupid mistake! I thought it must be, because I have always seen them together. A cousin, no doubt?"

Jemima does not relieve her curiosity. She affects not to hear.

Turning her head aside a little, she finds Paul at her elbow. Judging by his face, he has heard, apparently.

"Oh, there you are!" cries Sylvia, catching sight of him at the same moment, and resuming her animation. "You are in disgrace, do you know, *deep* disgrace? You have not asked me to dance *once* to-night" (looking at him with large, round eyes, and smiling archly).

Paul smiles, too, but not very cheerfully.

"My dancing is such that it is only on *very* old acquaintance that I dare inflict it."

"I saw you dancing with Lenore."

He shrugs his shoulders.

"I believe I *did* shamble round the room once or twice, but it was not a very successful experiment."

After the dance, which is surely ten minutes longer than any *galop* that ever was played before, after a prolonged stroll in the corridors, after tea, Lenore returns to her *chaperone;* returns, laughing and flushed, but with a look of uneasy excitement underlying the surface-merriment of her face.

Paul has been waiting, with no outward sign of impatience on his grave, sad face. He goes up to her.

"May I have five minutes' talk with you?" he asks, formally.

She takes his arm, and they walk off.

Neither speaks till they reach the bench on which, in the earlier and happier part of the evening, they had sat together, gayly chattering. Then Paul addresses her with cutting, cold politeness.

"May I ask, Lenore, what is inducing you to make yourself so remarkable with Scrope to-night? Is it solely for your own satisfaction, or for the double pleasure of amusing yourself and annoying me?"

The opening is not conciliatory. The color rushes red and headlong to Lenore's cheeks; she flings up her proud head.

"I killed two birds with one stone," she says, in angry jest: "he dances like an *archangel*, and it makes you jealous."

"I do not doubt your first assertion," says Paul, more coldly than ever, "and I fully agree with your last; perhaps I am more prone to jealousy than other men. I have not been so used to women and their ways. But I confess I do not enjoy seeing my future wife hauled about by a man, who is (as is evident to the most casual observer) making passionate and unrestrained love to her."

She is about to interrupt him, but he stops her.

"I confess I do *not* relish seeing him pointed out as occupying the position which, till to-night, I supposed was mine."

"What do you mean?"

"I mean" (in a tone where the persuasive is quite swamped in the imperative) "that I distinctly *object* to your dancing with Scrope."

"That is unfortunate!" retorts Lenore, to whose ears the imperative has been, from her youth up, an unknown mood, and whose gorge has always risen at the faintest attempt at coercion; "for I have every intention of dancing with him again—once—twice—if not more."

"After the opinion I have just expressed?" cries Paul, his anger effectually breaking through the armor of his coldness, voice raised, and gray eyes lightening.

"Most decidedly," she answers, with distinct emphasis. "I am not in the habit of breaking my word, and last night I promised him that, on condition that he leaves Sylvia's house to-morrow, I would waltz four times with him to-night—and waltz four times with him I will!"

"You *promised* him!" repeats Paul, hardly any longer master of his indignation. "Am I to understand that you have been *making terms—bargaining* with him? How ought his comings or goings to affect you?"

"In this way," she answers, her lips quivering with anger, but articulating with slow clearness. "I have, or fancy I have, a considerable regard for you and a slight regard for him, and I have no wish to see you kick each other down-stairs—a *dénoûment* which is only a question of time as long as you are in the same house."

"Lenore!" (snatching her hand, and holding it with almost painful tightness, while his eyes glow bright and deeply angry in this dim place,) "are you mad, or are you bent on driving *me* mad? After what has often passed between us about that fellow, can you *dare* to tell me to my face that you have a regard for him?"

Whom the gods wish to destroy they first deprive of understanding.

"*Dare!*" she says, while her eyes meet his unflinchingly, though, within, her spirit quails—her heart yearns to him in his honest anger. "What an ugly word! Yes,

I *do* dare! why should not I?   He is handsome, and I love
to look at beautiful things and people; he admires me
blindly, and admiration is food and drink to me; he can
see no fault in me, and I hate to be eternally carped at and
picked holes in!"

"I see," says Paul, dropping her hand, and speaking in
a tone of smothered resentment, which (if she could but
have understood it) was more alarming than his outspoken
anger, "I understand; you cannot see our unsuitability
more clearly than I do; from the first, I felt it profoundly,
and every day I live I feel it more.   But, Lenore, why,"
(grasping her arm with unconscious fierceness)—"why—
if, from the first, you only meant to torment me—why did
you *make* me love you?   There were hundreds of other
victims that would have done you more credit!   Why
could not you leave *me* alone?"

"*Leave you alone!*" (turning as white as a sheet);
"what do you mean?"

"I mean," he answers, firmly, "what you know as well
as I do, that you could have hindered me from loving you,
if you had wished; I was not given to falling in love; till
I met you I hated ladies' society; I avoided women; I did
not understand them, and they thought me a bore.   I left
them alone, and they left me alone; until you—solely for
the gratification of your own vanity, as I now see—*made*.
me love you, against my wish, against my better judgment,
as, for the same reason, no doubt, you have now made
Scrope."

She sits, with her head bent, silent; she cannot command her voice to answer.

"He is a more creditable conquest than I, I own," continues Paul, bitterly; "but for all that you will be the ruin
of him!   When he joined me at Dinan he was as nice a
boy and as good a fellow as ever lived; I looked upon him

as a brother, and *he*—he swore by me! You have made him hate me! You have made me detest the sight of him! I congratulate you on your handiwork!"

She lifts her eyes to him, all the softness gone out of them, scintillating with anger. "Have you done?" she asks, in a choked voice; "have you insulted me enough for one day?"

"I have not insulted you," he answers, resolutely, "unless God's truth be an insult; I never was a good hand at telling smooth lies; my love for you has never been blind enough to hinder my seeing that you are, in some respects, different from what I could wish you to be; if it is an insult to tell you so, I can only say it would have been a thousand times better if we had never met!" •

A pain like a knife goes through her HEART, but she makes no sign.

"I quite agree with you," she answers, commanding her voice into calmness by an immense effort; "will you be so kind as to take me back to Sylvia?"

He gives her his arm, and they begin to retrace their steps; but before they have gone six paces he turns aside into one of the rooms that open out of the passage. It is empty; he shuts the door. His soul is in a tumult; full, not indeed of the unnamed pain of Lenore's, but of confusion and doubt. If he marries this woman, he will be a miserable man; he has long suspected it, and choked back the suspicion; to-night he has realized it—but yet—but yet—she is as beautiful as a summer moonrise—he cannot give her up without an effort. They are as much alone as if they were on a desert island; he stands facing her.

"Lenore," he says, earnestly, "let us understand one another. If this is only a silly quarrel, for Heaven's sake let us make it up; if it is only a capricious way of trying how much I can stand, I tell you candidly that I am at the

end of my tether; I will not bear a feather's weight more!
Lenore, am I unreasonable? I like a quiet life, and I want
to trust my wife absolutely, and to believe in her as I believe in God. Tell me, did you mean the things you said
just now, or were you only angry? If you were, I am the
last person that has any right to blame you. Oh, my dear,
think before you answer me! Our whole two lives hang
upon it."

She looks at him. His face is stern, and resolute, and
deeply angered; but is it not also tender? She is all but
melted; in a second more she would have been sobbing on
his heart, but in the instant of hesitation his former words,
" You *made* me love you," recur to her, bringing profound
resentment with them.

"I *did* mean them," she answers, passionately. "I *do*
mean them; it is so pleasant to me to find any one to like
me *spontaneously* that I naturally prize their society."

His face pales and changes, it is no longer tender; it is
only stern.

"All right," he says, coldly; " you are at least explicit.
It has come to this, then, Lenore—you must choose between Scrope and me. I am far from saying that he is not
a fitter mate for you than I. He is young, he is good-looking, he is rich, he has every thing to catch a woman's eye
and gain a woman's heart; and I—" (looking down and
sighing), " well, I suppose I have not much. It has been
as great a wonder to me as to the rest of the world what
you could have seen in me—you know, I told you before
I'm not up to woman's ways—but one thing is certain"
(lifting his head again, and speaking with firm emphasis),
" *I will go shares with no man;* I will have *all* or *none!*
As long as you are my betrothed wife, I *forbid* you to
dance with Scrope."

"And I decline to be forbidden," she cries, maddened

by rage—by the internal knowledge of being in the wrong, and—oh, far worst, cruellest of all—by the conviction that he does not love her well enough to take her, faults and all—that he will have her on his own terms or not at all, that he is going—if she persists in her pride—to give her up, and that the giving her up will not cost him his life—will not break his heart, or even cause it any very mortal pain. "I deny your right to employ such a word to me; if I were a hundred times your wife, I should refuse to be ordered about like a dog! If you expect the tame docility of a slave, you had better go to your cousin for it, for you certainly will not get it from me."

He bows gravely.

"It is fortunate, at least, that we have discovered the discrepancy of our ideas of marriage before it is too late. Thank you, at least, for telling me now, instead of later."

"Yes," she answers, breathing hard and short; her face altered and contorted by the fatal excitement that is hurrying her to her destruction; "if I *made* you love me, as you generously say, I will, at least, not *make* you marry me."

He stands mute, all his face white and quivering, unable to master himself enough to reply to her gibes with calmness, and not willing to descend to the unmanliness of re-crimination. Then, at length, he speaks, with a slow and bitter smile:

"You have given me a lesson that I shall not forget in a hurry. I confess that I had not thought myself a vain man, but to-night has proved me to have been egregiously misled by my own conceit. Do you know—you will hardly believe me—laugh at me, I give you leave—but for the last six months I have been reproaching myself with the thought that, well and heartily as I loved you, you loved me even better—that you were giving more than you received? I am disabused, Lenore" (speaking very slowly, and planting each word like a sword-thrust in her heart); "you are incapable of loving any one but yourself—any thing but your own will. *I have done with you!*"

As he speaks, unmindful of the usages of society, forgetting that she has asked him to take her back to her *chaperone*, he turns to leave her. At the door he pauses to take one good-bye look at the fair, proud woman he has resigned. Her eyes are gazing vacantly at him, and her lips seem moving. In a moment more he is gone. She remains in the same position in which he left her: she does not move a finger. Her great, wide eyes keep staring at the door by which he went out, and her lips repeating his last words, "I have done with you—done with you—done with you!" They do not convey the slightest meaning to her mind. By dint of saying them over and over again, they grow to sound unfamiliar, grotesque. She half laughs. How long she remains in this semi-stunned state, she does not know. The fiddles squeak distantly, and the people pass and repass; but she heeds neither. She is recalled to herself, at last, by the entrance of a man, who first looks in uncertainly, and then comes in joyfully—Scrope.

"Why, here you are!" he cries, cheerfully. "I have been hunting high and low for you. I thought you were with Le Mesurier. This is our dance—Good God!" (with an abrupt change of tone) "what has happened?"

His voice brings her back to her right mind—brings the bitter, bitter truth rolling over her soul like a black flood. Paul gone—gone for good!—gone with a look of inexorable displeasure on his face, and she herself has thrown him away!

"What has happened?" she says, in a sharp, harsh voice. "Do you ask that? Why, just this" (laughing rather wildly)—"I have been amusing myself cutting my own throat. That is what has happened, and I have to thank *you* for it."

He looks at her in unbounded astonishment. Has she gone mad, as her words seem to imply?

" What do you mean ? "

" I mean," she answers, speaking more collectedly, " that Paul is gone—he does not like me any longer—he has *done with me !*" (falling unconsciously into his own form of expression).

" WHAT ! "

" Don't look *glad !* " she cries, excitedly. " How dare *you ?* If you look. glad, I shall *kill* you ! "

" I am not looking glad. What should I look glad for ? I don't know what you are talking about."

" You have got your wish," she says, rising and speaking with slow vindictiveness. " You have parted us ! It is what you have been aiming at all along. I hope you are pleased."

" Do you mean to say that you have been quarrelling about me again ? "

" Yes, I do ! " she answers, panting, and looking at him always with dilated eyes. " You knew we should. That was why you remained here when I *begged* you to go, when any *gentleman* would have *died* sooner than stay."

The young man bites his lip till it bleeds; he clinches his hands convulsively ; he writhes under her insults ; but he makes no retort.

" Was it because you danced with me ? " he asks, quietly, after an interval.

" You know it was," she answers, petulantly. " Why do you keep worrying me with these questions? He told me not to dance with you, and I said I would ; I thought it was fine to have a spirit—you have always told me, all of you, what a fine spirit I had. Well, God knows " (laughing harshly), " I have been spirited enough to-night ! "

A little silence.

" If he had but known," she says, looking scornfully at her companion, " how *small* the sacrifice was that he asked of me, he would not have insisted so much upon it."

Scrope's endurance fails a little.

" You are making mountains of mole-hills," he says, impatiently. " As far as I can understand, you have had a little misunderstanding—I do not see how any one could well live with you without having them—a misunderstanding which you will make up within the first five minutes of your next meeting—that is all."

" It is *not* all ! " she answers, persistently. " We have had a hundred such misunderstandings as you describe—they were always my fault—always—and made them up again; but this was different. When he turned at the door and looked at me, I felt that it was all over with me."

As she speaks, she sinks upon the sofa again; her arms fall heavily to her side; the listlessness of despair is expressed in her whole attitude.

" Fiddlesticks ! " replies Scrope, brusquely. " A man throw a girl over to whom he is passionately attached, because she says a few nasty things to him—more especially " (smiling, a little maliciously), " when she has rather got into a habit of saying nasty things to everybody ! A very likely tale. No, no; though you are engaged to Paul, and I am not, I think I know him a little better than you do, still."

She shakes her head; his words convey neither conviction nor comfort to her mind.

" Listen ! " says the young man, eagerly, sitting down on the sofa beside her. " Since I came into this room you have been unciviller to me than ever woman was to man before; once or twice I have felt as if I should like to kill you, or myself, or both; but you said one true thing—it *is* I that have brought this on you; and so, I suppose" (rather ruefully) "the least I can do is to try and put things straight again for you; I will go and look for him—he cannot have gone far—most likely" (sighing a little derisively) "I shall find him in the supper-room—and I will bring him back to you, see if I don't."

"Will you?" she says, with a bitter smile. "There will be two to that bargain!"

Before she can say more he is gone.

The minutes pass: five, ten; she sits with her eyes riveted on the door, saying over to herself, "There is no hope, there is no hope," but all the while, hope is there. After a space, which the clock announces to be a quarter of an hour, but which is marked on the dial-plate of her heart as ten years, Scrope reënters—alone.

"I could not find him anywhere," he says, advancing with his eyes on the ground; "he has gone. For Heaven's sake, keep up" (seeing her face change and quiver convulsively). "Don't look so miserable! It is only the delay of a few hours—it will be all right to-morrow morning."

"It will *never* be all right again," she cries, bursting into violent weeping, and throwing her head down on the hard horse-hair bolster of the sofa. "O Paul! Paul!"

The sight of her misery sets him beside himself. He flings himself on his knees beside her, catches hold of one of her hands, that is hanging down limp and nerveless, and, rashly trusting to her absorption, kisses it over and over again. After all, it is only white kid that gets the benefit of his caresses.

His action rouses her—she sits upright; the lightning flashes at him from her drowned eyes; the hot carnation scorches up the tears on her cheeks.

"How *dare* you?" she cries wildly, tearing her hand out of his grasp. "I shall always *hate* my hand for having been kissed by you—*you*, who have brought me to this! If I did not know that it was useless to ask any favor of you, I would beg you, at least, to relieve me of the sight of you."

He rises to his feet; a spasm contracts his angry, beautiful face.

"I'm going, never fear. I begin to agree with you, that I cannot be a gentleman, or I should have gone long ago." After a pause: "I have sent for my things from your sister's house. I shall go to London by the next train."

"Thank God, at least for that!" she says, fiercely. "The last and only boon I have to ask of you is, that I may never set eyes on you again."

He bows.

"I promise you that you shall not *unless you send for me!*"

She laughs insultingly.

"You will wait some time, if you wait for that."

"Lenore" (taking her hand, whether she will or no, while his eyes burn, savage and passionate, into hers) "you will make some one *murder* you, some day. Good-bye!"

CHAPTER X.

WHAT JEMIMA SAYS.

"QUITE incomprehensible," says Sylvia, slightly shaking her head, and turning the tap of the urn on to the recipient teapot.

We are at breakfast; breakfast after a ball is a languid feast: one looks green, one is yawning, one drinks two cups of tea instead of one. From another evil, to which some people are subject, I am free—I never suffer from the cramps that result from over-dancing. Sylvia and I are the only ones that have yet made our appearance: after all, there are only two more to appear—Paul and Lenore—for Mr. Scrope has gone overnight, or rather this morning, and it is *à propos* of his departure that Sylvia is, for the fiftieth time, expressing her astonishment, her displeasure, her remorse.

"So ill-bred," she continues, nibbling a piece of toast; "so unlike him. I have always said what a particularly gentlemanlike boy Charlie Scrope was! Do you know, Jemima, it has struck me once or twice that perhaps he was hurt at my refusing so point-blank to sit out in the corridors with him? Very unreasonable of him if he was so, for I meant nothing personal to him; I said the same to them all."

I shake my head with an air of superior information.

"It was not quite such a sudden thought as all that; earlier in the day he had settled to go."

"And never mentioned it to me?" cries my sister, raising her voice a little, and coloring. "Most extraordinary! Now I come to think of it, Jemima, he has been very odd and *distrait* for a week past; several times when I spoke to him, he answered quite *à tort et à travers*, and once or twice he did not answer at all."

I shrug my shoulders.

"They are all alike; determination of *Lenore* to the brain; when Lenore is in the room, they *never* answer me. I am quite used to it; are not you? For the last five years I have walked through life with a gooseberry-bush in my hand."

"She is very nice-looking, of course," says Sylvia, in a rather demurring voice, not seeming particularly to relish the being put, by implication, in the same boat with me.

"I am sure I am the last person to gainsay that; nobody *can* accuse me of not being willing to admit other people's good looks; but there is no denying that she is on too large a scale to suit some people's tastes: many *men* prefer something more *petite* and *mignonne*."

"Do they?" say I, skeptically. "I do not know. It seems to me that most men like a woman that there is a good deal of."

"I do not think I quite liked the way she did her hair last night," says Sylvia, taking some honey, and looking at it pensively as it slides in a long string from the spoon; "too much scratched off her face."

With what clever stroke of caustic wit, or incisive irony, I might have parried this thrust will never now be certainly known, for at this moment a footman enters with a note, which he hands to Sylvia. She opens it and reads; apparently it does not take long to peruse.

"Are *all* the people run mad?" she cries, in a tone of peevish astonishment, tossing it over to me. I pick it up.

"DEAR MRS. PRODGERS: I must apologize to you for leaving your house so suddenly, and at so untimely an hour; but, the fact is, I am unavoidably called away. Thank you over and over again for all the kindness and hospitality you have shown me.

"I remain, yours very truly,
"PAUL LE MESURIER."

"Is Mr. Le Mesurier gone?" cry I to the footman, who is in the act of leaving the room.

"Yes, 'm."

" What time did he go ? "

" About seven, 'm. I heard him telling the driver that he must catch the 7.25 up-train from Norley."

" I wonder did he and Charley travel together," say I, *sotto voce*, tickled, despite myself, by the notion of the rivals boxed up together, within the narrow precincts of a smoking-carriage, for all the long transit between Norley and London.

" Did he leave nothing besides this ? " cries Sylvia, in indignant excitement, holding up the little billet between her finger and thumb; " no message—nothing ? "

" I believe, 'm, there was a letter for Miss Lenore."

" Where is it ? what has become of it ? Bring it here."

" If you please, 'm, I think Nicholls took it up to Miss Lenore an hour ago."

He retires, inwardly amused, interested, compassionate, no doubt; outwardly as absolutely indifferent to the joys, the sorrows, the deaths, the marriages, the jiltings and being jilteds, of his family, as is incumbent on any servant who wishes to keep his situation.

The urn sputters and fizzes; the pug sits on his haunches, with his blear eyes rolling, and gives a short, suppressed bark, that means " Muffin." We stare at one another.

" I thought there was something wrong last night, when Lenore said he had gone home with a headache," say I, with that sort of back-handed prophecy—that " told-you-so " wisdom—for which women are so remarkable.

" So did I," says Sylvia, determined not to be behind-hand in sapience.

Again we stare at one another, with our toast dropped from our fingers, and our tea quickly cooling in the frosty morning air.

" I think I will go and see how she is getting on," I say, rising.

"So will I," says Sylvia, rising, too.

This is not quite what I wish, but it cannot be helped. As we pass the nursery, the children, hearing our footsteps, shoot out like bomb-shells, and join us.

By the time we reach Lenore's door we form a quite considerable *cortége*, both as to noise and numbers.

I knock—no answer. I knock again. "Lenore, may I come in ?" Still no answer. I try the handle—it is locked. I announce the fact.

"How very odd !" says Sylvia, rattling the handle in her turn. "Lenore! Lenore! we are all come to see you. Let us in !"

I do not myself think this form of request likely to invite compliance; but, whether it is or not, it meets with no better success than its predecessors.

"Do you think she can have got out of the window ?" suggests my sister, beginning to look rather tragic.

"Absurd ! Why should she ? "

Again we knock and rattle, each one in turn, and then altogether. No result.

"Suppose you look through the key-hole, Jemima ?" says Sylvia.

I comply. A key-hole is an unsatisfactory vehicle for exercising sight. At my first glance, I see nothing ; at my second, I dimly discern what looks like a rose-colored heap lying on the hearth-rug—Lenore has a rose-colored dressing gown.

"She is lying on the hearth-rug," I announce in a whisper. "Poor soul! I am afraid that she is taking it sadly to heart."

"Lying on the hearth-rug !" repeats Sylvia, turning rather pale, and clutching my arm.

"Good Heavens ! Jemima, I hope she has not—has not—put—put an end to herself !"

" Fiddlesticks ! " cry I, angrily. " Why should she ? How could she ? Swallowed the poker, I suppose, or cut her throat with a small-tooth comb."

Sylvia applies her eye, in turn, to the key-hole.

" Lenore ! " (raising her voice), " why are you lying on the hearth-rug ? What are you doing ? You are frightening us all out of our wits. Open the door this instant."

We hear a noise inside; in a moment more the door is flung roughly open, and Lenore confronts us in her dressing-grown—her undressed hair falling in a long, bright-brown shower about her face, which is ash-white. Her eyes are red, and her eyelids redder—the first are half and the latter *double* their normal size.

" What do you want ? " she says, hoarsely. " Why are you making this noise ? What has brought you all here ? "

A daunted silence falls upon us for a moment, then Sylvia speaks :

" Nothing particular, dear ; we only wanted to know what has made Paul take himself off so suddenly, and we thought you might be able to tell us."

" I neither know nor care," she answers, fiercely; but I see both lips and eyelids twitching.

" Aunty Lenore, how red your nose is ! " cries Bobby, with all that delicacy for other's feelings, that charming reticence, so characteristic of infancy ; staring at her the while, with eyes as black and round as the plums in a Christmas pudding. The last straw breaks the camel's back.

" Had not you better send for the servants and the stablemen, the dogs and the parrot ? " cries Lenore, turning savagely to Sylvia. " It is a pity that you should not have every living thing in the house to gape at me."

" Go down-stairs," say I, pleadingly, " and take the

children with you. I will be down directly; perhaps she will let me speak to her myself."

With many demurrings, both of word and look, Sylvia complies, and retires with her offspring.

I follow Lenore into her room, and close the door.

"Is. it true?" I say, compassionately, taking her hot, reluctant hand.

"Is what true?"

"That he is gone."

" I really cannot say; I have not been to look for him," she answers, in a devil-may-care voice, averting her eyes.

"Lenore!" I cry, reproachfully, "what is the good of keeping up this affectation with me? It is all very well before Sylvia; but have you forgotten that night at Morlaix, when you were so happy, and when you came and told me all about it?"

"I remember," she answers, with a hard laugh; "and how pleased you were at being waked out of your beauty-sleep, and how kind and complimentary you were about him."

"I was not kind," I answer, rather crest-fallen. "I was sleepy, and very ill-natured, and rather envious; but I am not ill-natured now. I would help you, if I knew how; and, though you are determined to hide it from me, I know what you are feeling."

"Then you know more than I do myself," replies my sister, quite collectedly. "I give you my word of honor, at the present moment I feel absolutely nothing."

I am not generally short of words, but I can find none now.

"When I first got *that*," she continues, nodding her head toward a note which lies open on the dressing-table; "you know I had been buoying myself up with hope all night, because he came back here, instead of going straight away—I thought it a good sign—but when I got that I think I must have gone mad for five minutes—do people ever go mad for such a short time ?—I found myself down on the hearth-rug, beating my head against the floor. That was wise, was not it? So likely to bring him back. Jemima!" (grasping my arm with her burning hand), "I am going to tell you a secret; if I could have found any thing to do it with, I should have tried to put an end to myself. I should have done it in a bungling, journeyman way, and very likely, when I got into the other world, I should have been sorry that I had not stayed here; still, I should have tried; but you see" (laughing) "it is difficult for the best-intentioned person to commit suicide with a cake of Windsor soap or a back-hair glass!"

"Lenore!" I cry, angrily, "you frighten me! Why do not you cry? Why do you laugh? I wish you would not look so odd!"

"Do I look odd?" she says, rising and going over to the long *cheval* glass. "Well, yes" (making a derisive bow to her own swollen, disfigured image), "a charming-looking person — the belle of the ball! I always told Paul" (a sharp contraction of the muscles of her face as she speaks his name) "that I looked nothing without my plaits."

I stand stupidly staring at her, with my hands clasped.

"If you want to ask any questions, *now* is your time," she continues, calmly; "it will be back on me just now—rushing, tearing back; but for the moment I feel as little as you do, or, if possible, less; I say over, 'Paul is gone!' and then 'Charlie is gone!' and the one fact seems as little afflicting as the other."

"Lenore, are you speaking truth?" I cry, incredulously. "You look as if you were! Tell me, if you are sure you

12

can bear to do it, how was it? You know I am quite in the dark. How did it come about?"

"Incompatibility of opinion about Mr. Scrope," she answers, with a forced laugh; then, sinking down on the floor, hiding her face in the folds of my gown like a child: "I do not think I *will* tell you, after all," she says, moaning; "when one's ship has gone down, what is the good of going into the details of the wreck?"

At the last word she breaks into tumultuous weeping.

"Perhaps it has not gone down," say I, eagerly. "Who knows? Let me see the note. May I?" stretching out my hand to take it.

"If you like." Then, laughing again painfully between her sobs: "It is not so affectionate that one need be ashamed of showing it."

I pick it up eagerly. It is not very tidily written, scratchily rather, and shakily; several of the little words are left out:

"December 28th, 5½ A. M.

"I would not have come back here last night, if I could have helped it; but it was unavoidable. I shall, at least, not intrude upon your sight again, as I shall be gone hours before you are up. I will send back your letters in a day or two; also, if you *insist* upon it, your photographs. Do not send back *any thing* of mine—it is the last favor I ask of you.   P. LE M."

I touched Lenore's heaving shoulder.

"Look up!" I say, cheerfully. "I am in better spirits. There is hope!"

She lifts her heavy head.

"Hope of what?"

Poor soul! The tears are running flat races down her

cheeks, coursing down her nose, and making hot wet spots
on the breast of her smart rose dressing-gown.

"He is angry," I say, smiling; "there is always hope
when a man is angry."

She does not answer in words, but she draws herself
up into a kneeling posture, and clutches my arm with painful tightness, while a little red creeps into her cheeks.
There is already plenty in her nose and eyes. With her
loose streaming hair, and upward wet eyes, she looks a
Magdalen all over. The old painters, if you remark, have
a knack of making their Magdalens' noses a little red.

"If you wish it, and are willing to take him on his own
terms, I believe you may get him back."

Still she says nothing; only the clasp on my arm tight-
ens, till I wriggle uncomfortably under it.

"You must, of course, write at once," I say, in a matter-of-fact voice, "and tell him that you are sorry, and that
you will not do *it*—whatever *it* was—again."

"*Say I am sorry!*" cries Lenore, starting to her feet.
"Eat dirt, and go, like a whipped child, with its finger in
its mouth, and say, 'I'll be good!' *Not if I know it!*"

She no longer looks like a Magdalen, or, if she does, it
is a very restive one.

"Very well," say I, coolly, "if you prefer your pride to
your lover, of course it is a matter of taste which is best
worth keeping. I have no more to say."

No answer.

"I see," continue I, with affected enthusiasm, "you are
conscious that you were in the right, and that he was so
completely in the wrong that the first advance *must* come
from him. I understand, of course! I respect you."

"Do not!" cries Lenore, gruffly. "I was not in the
right—am I ever? But the knowing that one is in the
wrong does not make it any the easier to say it."

" There are so many ways of implying a thing without exactly saying it ! "

Silence.

" My dear child," say I, stretching out my hand to take one of hers, which is twisting and turning its fellow about, "the question is, how can you live best : with your dignity and without Paul, or with Paul and without your dignity ? "

She falls on her knees beside me again ; she buries her face in my lap.

" Jemima, never tell anybody, and, if you are asked, say that it is not so ; and never remind me, when you get angry, that I have said it ; but—but " (very indistinctly) " I would eat all the dirt that ever was in all the world to get him back again—there ! " (Looking up and coloring violently.) " Was there ever a case on record of anybody having said any thing so mean ? "

I shrug my shoulders.

" What does it matter about being mean, so as one is happy ? " say I, with a philosophy of doubtful morality, if carried out to its final consequences. " Write ! *write!* WRITE ! and, if possible " (picking up the note again, and laughing), " write with a better pen than he did, Lenore " (examining it more narrowly). " I do believe he *cried* over it. Look ! what a suspicious blot over the ' P.' ! "

" Only a sputtering pen or bad blotting-paper," replies Lenore. But she is laughing, too, and there is an alertness in her gait as she walks across the room in strong contrast to the heavy droop of her attitude five minutes ago. " Jemima " (her poor red eyes sparkling again, and a tender tremor about the quivering corners of her mouth), " I will write. God knows what will come of it, or how I shall bear the waiting for the answer ; but—I will write."

" Do," say I ; and then I draw an arm-chair to the fire,

and Lenore sits down to the writing-table. The opening
sentences seem to be hatched with difficulty, but after them
her pen runs glibly enough; it is going to be a longer letter than his. "Lenore," say I, presently, turning my head
round, and speaking diffidently, "I think that, on the sup-
position that this may not bring him back—a most improb-
able one, but still possible—I—(do not be angry)—I would
not make it *too* affectionate." She flushes scarlet, reads it
hastily over, then tears it into a thousand bits, and, running
over to the fire, tosses the fragments in. "Nor too cold,"
I subjoin, rather startled at the effect of my caution. "Do
not you understand?" I continue, eagerly. "The kind
of letter you should write is one that, if he is so disposed,
will bring him back again; and that, if he is *not* so disposed, will not make you hot to think of having sent it."

To compose such a letter as I have thus described
seems a hard task. The hearth is strewn with little shreds
of paper, before one that hits the golden mean between the
fond and the frigid, is written fairly out without blots or
erasures.

"Will you read it?" asks my sister, holding it out rather
reluctantly to me, when it is at length finished. "I think
I had rather you did not, but you may, if you wish."

I shake my head, and swallow down my curiosity:

"Why should I? It is between you and him; what
has a third person to do with it?"

She turns away relieved, folds it up, directs it, and fast-
ens the envelope.

"Jemima," she says, clasping my arms with her two
hot slender hands, while her great solemn eyes fix themselves, feverish and miserably excited, on mine, "the re-
sponsibility of this lies with you. I do not know whether
it is affectionate or not; I cannot judge—I hardly know
what is in it; but if it fail, the shame of it will *kill* me."

CHAPTER XI.

WHAT JEMIMA SAYS.

AT the lowest calculation there must be forty-eight hours between the sending of any letter by post and the receiving of the answer. In most cases sixteen or eighteen of these hours are slidden over in sleep; but in a great anxiety, who *can* sleep? In heavy grief one *may* sleep— probably one will; when Hope has stolen out of sight, and Despair sits by us with veiled head, then one sleeps most deeply. Sometimes, in slumber, God gives us back our dead: him that but yesterday we coldly kissed in his strait shroud, we see coming toward us with life-colored lips, and open eyes: the dead never come back to us *dead:* always they are alive—talking, smiling, occupied in some commonplace employment, making some foolish, tender jest. But Sleep refuses to come to the troubled, who have yet an uneasy hope: she will not be made use of merely as a bridge over obnoxious hours: she will be loved and wooed for herself, or else she will stand relentlessly apart. I think that there are very few of the thousands of minutes that constitute those forty-eight hours that do not find Lenore consciously, broadly wakeful. She refuses all proposals that tend to divert her thoughts by exercise or employment: she will not walk—she will not drive; she will not even come down-stairs. All day long she sits in the window-seat in her room—sits there, with drooped figure and carelessly dressed hair; her eyes fixed alternately on the brown winter outside, or the avenue by which all carriages and all foot-passengers must approach the house, and on the watch which lies on the table before her; as if by looking, looking, she could make the slow hands pass more

swiftly over the dial-plate. O unwise Lenore! to wish to
hurry the feet of the swift minutes! They may seem un-
sweet, nay, most bitter, according to our present gauge of
sweet and sour; but oh! are they worse than the deep,
timeless grave, and the leaden-colored shores of Eternity,
toward which, in their flitting, they carry us? Once, coming in suddenly, I find her with all Paul's letters strewed
round her: she is reading them all through in order—from
the first sea-sick note he wrote her from Jersey on his
homeward journey, to the three scrawling, galloping lines
which, less than a week ago, announced the train and the
hour which were to bring him back to her. I think, poor
soul! she is trying to extract more love than is in them,
from the loving phrases that fill them. The short winter
day treads heavily past to his rest, and the night comes—
the winter night in its dull endlessness—then the dim, late
morning light. Lenore makes no complaint, and cuts me
short when I begin inquiries; but I *know* she has not slept.
The postman comes and goes without any special interest
attaching to him; it is impossible that he can bring any
thing yet.

Another day walks past with lagging feet. Lenore will
not move, will not eat: all her life seems to have passed
into the eyes which *grow* to the face of the watch that ticks
ever before her. She has turned Paul's picture, which
hangs opposite her bed, to the wall; when I ask her why
she has done it, she answers that, unless he is hers, she has
no business to look at him.

The second slow day dies: its life is so faint and dark
that there is but little difference between it and its death.
Sylvia and I dine *tête-à-tête*, and get over our dinner with a
surprising and feminine celerity. It is astonishing how the
presence of even one man prolongs the duration of dinner;
is it from the comparative immensity of man's appetite, or

from the stimulus and gentle fillip that his company gives to conversation? We yawn through the evening, and at ten retire to such warm depths of silky sleep as one experiences only in frosty weather.

It is rarely indeed that others' griefs keep one awake. Our letters arrive mostly at half-past seven: it is some time before that hour, and in my curtained and sheltered room absolute darkness still reigns, when I drowsily hear a footstep passing along the corridor outside my door. From some half-conscious, half-dreamful impulse, I jump up and run to the door, open it, and look out into the black chillness outside.

"Lenore, is that you?"

"Yes."

"Where are you going?" (my teeth chattering so as to make me almost entirely unintelligible).

"What is that to you?" Tired of her incivilities, sleepy and shivering, I prepare to shut the door in a huff. "I am going to see whether the postman is *dead*, that he is so long in coming," she says, in a quick, excited voice.

"It is not nearly time for him!—it is the middle of the night!"

"It *must* be time for him," she says, petulantly; "it must be *three years* since he was here last!"

"You will be frozen," I say, laying my hand, in the dark, on the thin shawl that covers her shoulders; "have my seal-skin!" She does not heed me.

"Jemima" (I cannot see her face, but I hear the quick sobbing breaths with which she speaks)—"if it does not come to-day, my reason will tell me that it is because he is not at home, and that it has had to be forwarded to him; but all the same—reason, or no reason—if it does not come, I shall *go mad!*"

Before I can reply, she is gone. I shiver back into bed;

I find it as deeply, downily warm as I left it; but the delicious languor, the semi-unconsciousness, fast melting into total unconsciousness, that such warmth and softness woo, declines to come again. I find myself, with my head raised every minute from the pillow, listening for that back-coming footfall. It seems a long time coming; perhaps it is only half an hour really: at last I hear it—I spring to the door.

"Well?"

A gray figure runs past me, with its head bent, but answers nothing. I snatch up a dressing-gown, and run, *ventre à terre*, after it, half afraid of finding the door locked, when I reach my sister's room. It is not—it is ajar; I enter. The sick dwarf light creeps in by the latticed window-panes; the dead fire's ashes lie whitely gray upon the hearth; the table is gray, the chairs are gray, and on one of them a gray figure lies still and stiff, with gray hands covering its face.

"What is it?—what is it?" I cry, horribly excited, running up to her. She drops her hands into her lap; in the dim light I see her great shining eyes, brimming over with anger and despair, flame into mine.

"It is all your fault!" she says, hoarsely; "*you* did it! I have lain down in the gutter, and he has walked over me, and it is *your* doing!"

"*What!*"

"If you had left me alone, if you had not meddled— you were always a meddler, always—I might have gone through my life, hating myself, knowing that I had been my own death, finding no taste in any thing; but at least I should not have had to get red whenever I thought of myself—at least I should not have made overtures that have been declined. I should not have asked a man to marry me, and been politely, but firmly, *rejected*—Good God!" (breaking off suddenly, and clinching her hands above her head)—"it cannot be *me* that this has happened to—it *must* be somebody else. *I* that always held my head so high!"

"What are you talking about?" I stammer; "he cannot—he has not—"

"Has not he?" she answers, bitterly, "There!—read! Can you see?" (walking over to the curtain and pulling it back) "——'*My dear Miss Herrick!*' When I got as far as that I knew it was all over with me! His 'dear Miss Herrick!' 'My dear Miss Herrick!'—'my dear Mr. Le Mesurier!' Oh, my God!"

She throws herself on the floor, and buries her face in the carpet, while her hands dig themselves into it, like those of a man in the death-agony. After all, why should the soul's death be accompanied with throes less bitter than the body's?

"How can I read it?" I cry, impatiently, "you are holding it!" and, indeed, as she lies prostrate on the floor, it is crumpled up in one of her clinched hands. She raises herself, and straightens out the creased paper.

"Look!" she says, striking it with her forefinger. "See how straight the lines run—how firmly the letters are formed—it might be a thesis instead of a death-warrant! Do you see any blots *here?*—do you think he cried over *this?*"

"Give it me!" I say, eagerly stretching out my hand; "let me see it!"

"*Never!*" she answers, tearing it sharply across, and then again across, and then again; "it is between him and me—the last thing that ever will be!"

I kneel down beside her in silence in the cold gray dawn, and put my arm round her.

"Be satisfied with knowing the upshot!" she says, with a dreary smile. "He says it very kindly, very prettily, in a very good, bold hand, and he takes six pages to say it in; but, all the same, the drift is, 'I have had enough of you!'"

"Is it possible?" I exclaim, with a gasp, and a bitter sense of regret at my share in the business.

"It was not his *real* reason for leaving me," says Lenore, sitting on the floor, and rambling on to herself, half under her breath. "It was only a blind—how dull of me to be taken in!—a pretext for getting back to *her*. Yes, I understand—I understand. I suppose I do get wearisome after a time, but" (with a long, low moan) "it was such a little, *little* time."

A pause.

"She made good use of those six months, did not she? —did not cry at him, and throw herself at his head, as I did; but stole up to him, modestly, with her eyes down, so that he did not find it out—she always *was* his *beau idéal* of feminine excellence—yes, yes" (running dreamily over in her mind his long-past phrases), "'Eyes like a shot partridge;' 'Not at all clever;' 'Does not say much;' 'Very loving.' Yes, his *beau idéal*—meek, dowdy, mealy-mouthed! He would have kept to her always, if I had let him alone. I am glad I did not. I had my day—I had my day!"

Her hands embrace her knees; she begins to rock gently backward and forward.

"Stole him away, bit by bit, bit by bit!" she continues, sighing softly. "Jemima!" (her tone altering, and her eyes glittering with a passion of despairing jealousy), "that cousin is a sweet woman—I know she is—charitable as Dorcas, patient as Griselda, she will help him in every thing good, and hinder him in every thing ill. If I thought she were a bad woman, and that he would repent it, I could bear it better. Oh, my God, he will never be punished!—men never are. Every day of his life he will be gladder and gladder that he is rid of me—he will tell her so—while I—while I—"

She raises her voice wildly at the last words.

"Stop!" I cry, angry and frightened. "Don't look so odd! For God's sake, see him as he is—look at him as other people do—a man your inferior in every respect, and who never really loved you."

No sooner are the words out of my mouth than I see that I have been guilty of one of my many breaches of tact.

"How *dare* you say that?" she cries, griping my arm. "If you wish to say such things, say them to some one else!—do not *venture* to say them to me! If you are going to tell such cruel lies, leave my room this instant! *Never really loved me!* Much you know about it—you, whom nobody ever loved. Do you think *I* could have been mistaken—I, who was with him all day—who watched his face ever minute? He *did* love me! he *did!* he DID! Not blindly, not foolishly: he saw—he could not help seeing—that every second thing I did, every second word I said, was wrong and unladylike; but he was making me better—every day he was making me better! If he had married me, I should have been a good woman, and he would have taken me to heaven with him!"

"I am not so sure that he is going there himself!" I say, spitefully.

"Say that you did not mean it—say that you do not think it *really!*" continues my sister, with an anguish of entreaty in her tone, and in the haggard loveliness of her face. "You mean" (with a wild smile) "he has taken away the present and the future! If you take away the past, too—if you take away that day at Huelgoat—that day—that day" (wandering off into memory again) "when I knelt on the cushion of little marsh-flowers by the brook, and the children went by to pick bilberries: if you take away *that* day, and the days at Morlaix, and the day when we stood by Châteaubriand's tomb, and saw the waves and the sea-mews below us, and planned how we should walk on through life, and to heaven together—if you take *them* away from me, what is there left me but to curse God and die ?"

I shudder, and cry, " Hush, hush !" but she pays no attention to me.

" She might as well have left him to me," she continues, presently, pushing Paul's betrothal-ring absently up and down her finger; " she could have done so well without him ! She is a good, religious woman, and has another happy world to look forward to, while I—I have only this. You see, Jemima, it is only we wicked people that *can* lose all at one blow."

" My child, my child !" I cry, snatching her two hands; " what are you talking about ? I do not want to preach to you, and you would not listen to me if I did, but you frighten me ; it is like *daring* God to do worse to you. How *can* you have lost all as long as you are still within the bounds of His great clemency—as long as you are still outside hell's gates ?"

" *Am I ?*" she says, with a flickering, haggard smile; " are you so sure of that ? As I came along the meadows this morning, I have an idea that I had a good notion how they feel down below. Bah !" (jumping up and walking to the window), " do not look so scared ; not sleeping and not eating make one light-headed. I am getting quite rantipole. Get me something to drink—cognac— sal-volatile — it does not matter what, so that it is strong !"

I hurry back to my own room, pour some sal-volatile and water into a glass, and return with it to her. I find her lying languidly back in an arm-chair, pale and worn out, but with open eyes and a set, stony face.   She drinks eagerly, and then gives a long, low sigh.

"Poor soul, poor soul!" I say, pitifully, stroking her loose, tossed hair.   "I dare say you think it is easy enough to bear other people's troubles, and, as you said just now, since I never was loved myself, I cannot enter into your feelings; but still, do you know, Lenore, I think no one can well be sorrier for you than I am?"

"Really!" (with an air of most weary indifference).

"Lenore, you are not a weak woman, I know that; don't let him have the satisfaction of thinking that you take it to heart!   Show him what stuff you are made of, by bearing it brávely!"

"Make an effort, in fact, like Mrs. Dombey," says my sister, smiling sarcastically; "or rather *unlike* Mrs. Dombey.   Never fear!   Have you lived with me nineteen years, and have you yet to learn that I am not the sort of woman to go about with my pocket-handkerchief to my eyes, whimpering because I have been *jilted*—yes, let us call things by their right names—*jilted!*"   As she speaks, a deep carnation flush of shame spreads over her white cheeks.   "Go now," she says, imperatively; "leave me!   There, you need not look toward the windows as if you thought I were going to throw myself out of one of them —see, they are all bolted—and I would not make such a clumsy ending for the world."

I move, unwilling and slow, toward the door.   She calls after me:

"Jemima, if ever you tell any one how you have seen me, and what things you have heard from me, during the last forty-eight hours, I will kill you.   Let them think I have had influenza—mumps—any disease you choose; but let no one ever guess that I have been pining three whole days for *love*.   Bah! it makes me laugh to think of it!"

"Are you *sure* I can do nothing for you?" I ask, staring uncomfortably at her forlorn, wild face.

"Certain!" she answers, emphatically. "I must fight it out by myself; it is a case where neither man, woman, nor child, can help me!"

"If neither man, woman, nor child, can help you," I say, hesitatingly, yet eagerly, "why not go to *God?*"

She shrugs her shoulders: "It is a sort of trouble that God would not care about!"

"What are you saying?" I cry. "Is God, like a man, *capricious* in His pity?"

"I think so," she answers, listlessly; "at least I know He does not pity me."

I am too shocked to make any rejoinder.

"I have set up an idol in the place of God," she says, gravely. "Can I expect God to be sorry because it is knocked down? There—go! You are a good woman in your way, and I rather like you; but you'll never make your fortune as a preacher!"

Sadly I obey her. During the long, weary day I go about heart-sore and anxious. I do not go near her room myself, nor do I allow any one else to do so; but my heart is gnawed by a painful curiosity to know what terrible death-fight of the soul is raging within those quiet walls.

As Sylvia and I sit moping and flat by the drawing-room fire before dinner, what is my surprise to see the door open and admit Lenore, who enters with a brisk step and a matter-of-fact air!

"Good-morning, Sylvia; rather late in the day to say 'good-morning'—is not it? I have registered a vow never to go to a ball again; it has taken me three whole days to recover from that last one!"

She says it rather as if it were a lesson learned by rote; but she looks alert and upright; her cheeks are colored with pink, and her eyes are neither lack-lustre nor wet.

"Aunty Lenore!" cries Bobby, who has been raging round the room with a luckless kitten (mewing with pain and exasperation, and with all its claws out) clutched round the neck with strangling tightness in his cruel little arms. He drops the kitten, which instantly makes off with its tail straight up. "Aunty Lenore!" rushing at her, and boisterously embracing her knees, to the injury of her crisp muslin dress: then, with a sudden and ingenious connection of ideas, "Where is Uncle Paul?"

With a sudden impulse she pushes the child violently away. I see her face writhe, and the pupils of her eyes darken and flash; but, in an instant, controlling herself, she speaks, calmly:

"He is gone! He is not 'Uncle Paul' any longer—and—and—don't bother about him!"

As we pass through the hall to dinner, I see a letter, in Lenore's handwriting, lying on the hall-table. I glance inquisitively at it: it is addressed to—

"CHARLES SCROPE, ESQ.,

"Limmer's Hotel."

CHAPTER XII.

WHAT JEMIMA SAYS.

IF I imagine that Lenore's composed cheerfulness and equable serenity are the result of a strain so strong as to be unable to be kept up beyond one evening, I am mistaken. I find her the same the next morning, and the morning after that, and the morning after *that*. She talks

more than usual; ordinarily, indeed, she is too lazy to take
the trouble of talking merely for the sake of contributing
her share to the general stock that forms family conversation; but now she talks resolutely to any one who will
talk to her. She lounges away less time than usual in her
own rooms; always she is to be seen in the general sitting-
rooms, by all comers and goers, working and reading tran-
quilly. She drives out with Sylvia to pay morning-calls;
she walks out with me into the village, carrying broth and
jelly. Sometimes I try to surprise her face *off guard*, to
see her features fall into the haggard lines of hopeless
angry grief in which I saw them so lately; but I fail; her
face seems to be never in dishabille. She actually *plays
with the children!*—gambols which, I confess, remind me
of the millennium, when, we are told, the weaned child
shall play on the cockatrice's den. On the third day, I am
sitting pondering these things in the drawing-room, which
Lenore has just left with a light and buoyant tread. Sylvia, with one of her spasmodic fits of maternity upon her,
is trying, with alternate peevish coaxings and caressing
abuse, to lead, or rather push, pull, and mildly flagellate,
her offspring along the rosy path of learning. In this case,
it is theological learning, as represented by the "Peep of
Day." Bobby is leaning against her knee, while in the
corner—why such peculiar ignominy should attach to the
corners of a room tradition saith not—stands Tommy, committing to memory these soothing lines:

> "Now if I fight,
>   And scratch, and bite,
>   In passions fall,
>   And bad names call,
>   Full well I know
>   Where I shall go."

Now and again, as the thought of the gloomy regions

whither his iniquities are hurrying him comes home to his mind, he blubbers suppressedly. What amplest enlargement on the horrors of hell could equal that portentous hint ?—

> " Full well I know
> Where I shall go ! "

Sylvia to Bobby: " Has God been kind to dogs ? "

Bobby to Sylvia, doubtfully : " Ye—es."

His round eyes are fixed on Toby the pug, basking in the fire-warmth, and chasing the lively flea through the preserves of his soft fawn hind-quarters, and his mind is wandering from the typical dog of the fable to the *actual* dog of real life.

" Is the dog's body like yours ? "

Bobby (thinking it safe to stick to the affirmative) : " Yes."

" *The dog's body like yours ?* What are you thinking of, child ? Are *you* covered all over with black hair, and have you got a big, bushy tail ? "

Bobby glances down uncertainly at his small person ; but, seeing no caudal appendage, shakes his head.

" Are the chicken's legs like yours ? "

Silence.

Mrs. Prodgers is reduced to answering herself from the enlightened page before her: " No ; the chicken has very thin, dark legs."

Bobby does not appear sufficiently impressed with gratitude for the essential difference between his own fat, chubby supporters, and those of the benighted chicken. He is still watching Toby, who has abandoned the flea-chase, and runs barking toward the door.

" Mother, dear, there is a ring at the door-bell."

Prospect of emancipation, and consequent elation of tone.

"Nonsense, darling; attend to your lesson. Has the pig a—"

Whether the next word was soul or tail, gizzard or imagination, transpires not.

"But there was, *really*, mother. I hear Morris going to open the hall-door."

Mrs. Prodgers listens. "So there is !"

She jumps up hastily, while the "Peep of Day," with all its mingled treasures of piety and natural history, rolls unregarded on the floor, as she stands before the pier-glass, tweaking the black-ribbon bow that ornaments her head, and smoothing away the hair behind her ears. By the time the butler's solid footstep is heard nearing the room, she is *à quatre épingles.* The door opens : "Mr. Scrope." My mouth opens, too; my jaw falls. The stocking I am knitting tumbles into my lap.

"*Charlie!* "cries Sylvia, with a little scream, half real, half affected, of surprise, running forward, with her hands clasped.

Mr. Scrope enters, looking rather sheepish and somewhat dishevelled. There are black marks under his eyes; his yellow curls are tossed and dim; he looks unslept and night-travelled.

"You did not expect to see me, did you?" he says, with a rather embarrassed laugh. "Thought you had got me clear off—that you were rid of me at last? But you see I have turned up again, like a bad sixpence."

"It *is* a surprise, of course," answers Sylvia, looking modestly down, and fondling Bobby; "but—but *quite* a pleasant one. We were getting to hate each other, as only two sisters *tête-à-tête* can ; were not we, Jemima? "

His face falls.

" *Two* sisters ? "

Nobody explains: I, from malice, Sylvia from preoccupation.

"The fact is," continues Scrope, seeing that some explanation is looked for from him, "that I—that I thought—in fact, I found that I could get away for a day or two, so I thought I would run down and look you all up."

"Why did not you telegraph? Why not write? I would have sent to meet you?" asks Sylvia, raising her bashful eyes. "What scatter-brained things men are!"

He does not heed her; his eyes are wandering round the room.

"Are you looking for Lenore?" I ask, in a matter-of-fact voice. "She is in the library, writing letters. I will tell her you are here."

"Do not," he cries, eagerly, almost pushing me back into my chair. "I will not give you the trouble; I will go and find her myself."

"How *very* extraordinary!" says Sylvia, as the door closes upon him, smiling consciously, and leaning her elbow on the mantel-piece. "What *can* have brought him back? I have not the least idea; have you, Jemima? Poor, dear old boy, how pale he looked! I was *so* glad you were in the room. By-the-by, did I get very red? I felt as if I were turning all the colors of the rainbow."

"I do not know; I dare say."

"*Be sure you do not leave me alone in the room with him,*" she continues, volubly. "I shall always keep the children with me; there are no better *chaperones* in the world than children."

CHAPTER XIII.

WHAT THE AUTHOR SAYS.

As the young man opens the library-door a rush of cold air meets him; it is a bitter frost, black and pinching, yet one of the wide sash windows is thrown high up, and she whom he seeks is leaning out into the hard dull air. Her elbows rest on the sill; her dark, winter dress hangs in heavy, close folds about her, and her bright blond head leans languidly against the window-frame. The blotting-book is unopened, nor is any pen dipped in the ink. Lenore's correspondence will keep, apparently. Hearing the noise he makes in entering, she raises herself quickly, as one ashamed of her listless attitude, and they stand face to face.

"You sent for me," says Scrope—abruptly, without any preliminary hand-shakings, or "How do you do?"—"and I am come."

She nods familiarly to him, and smiles a little. "I knew you would."

"I was not in London; your letter followed me to the south of Ireland—the instant I got it I set off—I have been travelling night and day ever since. More fool I, you will say probably."

Again she smiles, coldly and sweetly.

"Since *you* have said it, *I* need not."

"And now that I am here," he says, brusquely, "what do you want with me? Tell me quickly."

Instead of complying, she turns her head round again, and looks out at the frosty black trees, while her fingers play still tunes on the sill.

"Tell me," he says, coming nearer to her, and breathing

quick and hard. "What? You will not speak? I know you—you would keep me on the rack a year, if you could. Why did you write and say, 'Come back.' It was for no good, I'll be sworn, or it would not be you who did it, whatever it was. Speak out, and put me out of my misery."

Then she speaks, but her words, at first sight, seem to have but small connection with his questions.

"Have you been in the drawing-room?" she asks, while the cold wind blows in on her cheek, and puts no additional color into it. "Have you heard Bobby say his hymn?— such a pretty one! Yes"—(putting her finger on her forehead)—"this is it:

> 'Now if I fight,
> And scratch, and bite,
> In passions fall,
> And bad names call,
> Full well I know
> Where I shall go.'

Does not it describe *me* exactly? I laughed so immoderately, that Sylvia said I was irreverent, and I had to leave the room." She throws herself into an arm-chair, and begins to laugh violently.

"What are you talking about?" he says, looking at her in half-scared amazement; "are you mad?"

She stops laughing.

"Last time we met," she says, gravely, "at the ball, don't you know?—*how* I hate balls!—I have an idea that *I* fought, and scratched, and bit; at least I know I—

> 'In passions fell,
> And bad names called'—

I called you a great many ugly names, and you did not like it; you were very angry. Well, I have sent for you all this way, just to say that—that—I am sorry."

" *What!* " cries the young man, breaking into un-governable fury, " is this the fool's errand you have sent for me on ?—to laugh in my face, and quote an idiotic nursery-rhyme to me ? By God, Lenore, it is too bad ! For the last seven—eight months I have been your butt, a football for you to kick about; but I tell you I am sick of the part. I throw it up ! Find some one else to take it, if you can."

He turns toward the door ; his broad chest is heaving ; his strong hands are clinched ; his deep-blue eyes flash and darken with uncontrolled anger—a passion much more be-coming to men's hard faces than soft and sawny love.

" Stay ! " she cries, rising hastily, and putting her back against the door to prevent his egress; " sit down, and, whatever you say, speak lower, for I have no special desire to be overheard. I *had* another reason for sending for you; but—but—I am *ashamed* to tell it you."

" What is it ? "

Big, upstanding, and exasperated, he does not look a man to be trifled with; but, after all, a man *may not* knock a woman down, so she may shoot all her little arrows at him with a smile and a quiet mind, and fear nothing. Her eyes drop to the carpet at her feet, and a color burns like fire on her cheeks.

" I sent for you to—to—to—ask you to *marry* me."

At the last words she raises her eyes, and looks him in the face. A deep and utter silence. He has staggered back against the wall, and is staring at her with wide, dis-believing eyes of utter astonishment.

" I have no reason for supposing that you wish to marry me," she says, collectedly, though her face is scarlet. " You never told me so; it is only an instinct—an instinct that perhaps has led me astray." Still complete silence. " It is not leap-year, is it ? " she says, with a forced laugh.

"No! Well, then, I have no excuse—none, except that I wished it; and you know, from a child, I have always asked for what I wished; and always—no, not *always*—not *always*" (stifling a sigh), "but *generally* I have got it."

"And—and Le Mesurier?" says Scrope, at last, in a rough and altered voice, trying to stand steadily on his feet, while his knees shake under him, and the room whirls round him.

"What about him?" she cries, sharply. "Why do you drag *him* in? If it was *anybody's* part to mention him, it was mine. You will hear no more of him; he is gone—it is all off, you know that; it was all off before you left—only, I suppose, it gives you pleasure to hear it again."

"And *you?*" says the young man, staring into her calm face, while he stammers and stutters; "you—you do not care; you—you are not cut up about it?"

She turns her face suddenly aside, but only for an instant: in a moment she is looking at him again—looking at him, and smiling.

"*Cut up!*" she says, laughing. "What an expression! It is only men that are *cut up!* Do I look very downhearted? Do you see any willow in my hand? No, no! I am not the sort of person that am ever *cut up* much about any thing."

Still he looks at her with a bewildered face, paled and quivering, as one but freshly waked from a heavenly dream, that knows not whether he yet sleeps or wakes; afraid to grasp within his hand the immense and utter bliss that her words seem to set within his reach, lest it should melt away like fairy gold. His emotion does not communicate itself to her; rather, it makes her more composed.

"Well," she says, with a pretty, chilly, mocking smile, "you have not yet answered me. How cruel to keep me

in suspense ! Does it require so much time to decide ?
The matter lies in a nutshell. Do you wish to marry me,
or do you not ? "

"Do I wish to go to heaven ? Did Dives in hell wish
for that cup of cold water ? " cries the young man, passionately, waking with a leap out of his trance, and flinging
his happy arms around her.

She shudders, and pulls herself away.

"Bah ! " she says, coldly, retreating several paces from
him ; "do not let us have any flowers of rhetoric ; and it is
too early yet to be affectionate. If Dives had got his cup
of cold water he would have taken it quietly, like a gentleman, and not *snatched* it."

"You were *not* in earnest then ? " cries the young man,
fiercely, with a revulsion of feeling as bitter as his former
triumph had been heavenly sweet. "I was a fool to be
taken in ! It was only an unfeeling, unwomanly joke.
Will you be kind enough" (coming close to her, and
breathing heavily) "to tell me where the wit is—where
the point ?—for, upon my soul, I do not see it."

"There is no wit—there is no point," she answers, with
perfect gravity and unflinching seriousness. "What wit
or point need there be in naked truth ? As I stand here "
(clasping her hands, and looking full into the fierce beauty
of his face), "I am in earnest. I *wish* you to marry me.
I *ask* you ! It is unmaidenly—immodest of me—I know
that, and so do you, but—I *ask* you ! "

. "God above ! " he says, in a whisper of intense excitement, "is it possible, Lenore ? " (catching her roughly by
the hand). "Turn your face to the light ; let me see your
eyes—I do not believe your *words ;* it seems so unnatural
to hear any kind ones from your lips. God ! when I
think that it is less than a week ago that I saw you standing here together, and you giving him such soft, kind looks,

13

to get one of which I would have sacrificed twenty years of my life, and thought it a cheap bargain—*you*, who never threw me any thing but mocks, and jeers, and ugly names—I *cannot* believe it. Say what you will to me—swear it, asseverate it—I cannot, I cannot!"

She does not answer: for the moment, I think, she finds speech difficult; she stands rigidly still, her face turned toward the bitter winter landscape, with lips tightly compressed, as one resolved *not* to weep.

"When I think," continues the young man, vehemently, "of how you smiled—of how happy you looked if he only touched in passing the border of your gown, less than a week ago—less than a week ago—can I believe that such love has all gone? *Gone?* Where can it have gone to? Tell me that! Does love disappear like a morning mist?"

"Hush!" she says, hoarsely, putting her fingers in her ears. "How many times must I tell you not to drag *him* in? If I ever cared for him" (she stops for a second, unable to manage her voice), "if I ever cared for him, that was between him and me; *you* had no concern in it; but now it is all over, *dead;* and, when things are dead, what is there to do but to bury and forget them? Take me or leave me, as you choose, that is your business—I know which you would do if you were wise—but, for God's sake, leave that old story alone! It is *my* old story, not *yours*, and I—I have a short memory" (smiling faintly); "I am fast forgetting it."

"But *are* you," he cries, with a painful skepticism, hardly to be wondered at, "are you *sure* of that? Are you sure that, if you saw him coming in *now*, *this minute*, at that door, you would not run to him, as you ran out into the cold to meet him that first night he came, and leave me to cut the brilliant figure I have always done, ever since the unlucky day at Guingamp, where I first saw you?"

At his words she shivers again, and shrinks, as if touched by a hot iron.

"What are you talking about?" she cries, passionately. "Why do you persist in indulging in these idiotic suppositions? He will *not* come back, I tell you. Do dead people ever push up their coffin-lid, and come walking back again? If they do, I never saw them. Well, they are more likely to come back than he is—much more likely. He is *done with*" (spreading out her hands); "so, for God's sake, try and help me to forget that there ever was such a person, instead of always throwing him in my teeth."

At the last words she catches her breath sobbingly, but resolutely forces back the tears that come crowding thickly under her hot lids. He stares at her stupidly still.

"He only liked me when I was on my good behavior," she continues, with a hard, wan smile, "and you know how seldom *that* is. I had an idea that *you* would take me whether I behaved well or ill, or not at all; and so—and so—I sent for you."

She stretches out her hand to him, smiling friendlily; and he, catching it between both his own broad ones, covers it with silent kisses, then, after a while, speaks slowly and diffidently, blushing like a school-girl:

"And you—you can tolerate the idea of being my wife? You—like me a little?"

"Like you?" she says, carelessly, with a forced laugh. "Of course I do. What a question! Have not I asked you to marry me? What better proof could I give? Why should I not like you? You are young, good-looking, and a *parti.* Of course, I like you."

He does not look very much satisfied with this expression of faith.

"You do not believe me?" she says, interrogatively.

" Well, I have already given you one proof; I will give you another. I have asked you to marry me. I now ask you to marry me *soon*. I'm aware " (laughing) " that it is not usual for such a proposition to come from the lady; but, as I have begun by taking the initiative, I suppose I must go on."

The look of wild, incredulous astonishment intensifies on his face and in his bold, bright eyes. Are his ears faithful carriers of the words intrusted to them, or does his brain interpret them untruly ?

"Lenore," he says, impetuously, throwing himself on his knees beside her, as she sits leaning back in an arm-chair, " forgive me for being such a fool, such an unmannerly brute, as to disbelieve what you say to me; but are you *sure*—I will not be angry if it is so—upon my soul, I will try not to be—but are you *sure* that it is not a *joke?* —that you have not made me the subject of a bet, that this is not some trap that you are drawing me into ? Confess—*confess* that it looks like it. Five days ago, you told me that the only boon you had to ask of me was that you might never see my face again—and, by Heaven, if ever any woman looked as if she meant what she said, you did then—and now—*now*—did I hear aright ? I am afraid to think so—you ask me to marry you *soon?* "

She hangs her head a little, as if ashamed, but says nothing.

"Is it any wonder," he continues, excitedly, " that, when I have been crying for the moon for the last six months, and hating my life and myself, and even all my own people, because I could not get it, that, when it falls down on a sudden at my feet, I should wish to know what brought it there ? Is it any wonder that I should wish to see the *dessous des cartes?* "

"There is no *dessous*," she says, naïvely. " What can I say ? I am sick of asseverating ! As I believe in God, and am unutterably afraid of Him" (looking solemnly up, and shuddering), "I am speaking truth! What reason *can* I give? I have none. I am tired of being Lenore Herrick, that is all. It is a name that has brought me no luck; perhaps Lenore Scrope will bring me better."

"God grant that it may!" he says, earnestly, drawing her toward him, into his arms and to his broad breast. "Sweet, give me one kiss, and I shall believe you."

So she gives him one kiss. Only five days ago! Only five days ago!

CHAPTER XIV.

WHAT JEMIMA SAYS.

Mr. Scrope returns to the drawing-room, as he left it, alone. As he enters, we both look up and smile, as one does smile with vague complacency at the sight of any thing young and specially comely.

"Did you find her?" I ask, as I kneel before the fire, giving it a vigorous and searching poke, for his benefit.

"Yes."

He says merely this—almost the shortest of all monosyllables; but there is something in the tone in which he says it that makes me pause, poker in hand, from my noisy toil, to examine him more narrowly.

"You have been quarrelling as usual, I suppose?" I say, with a wily attempt to come at the matter of their conversation without seeming too indecently curious.

"Lenore always quarrels with everybody," says Sylvia, patting the pug's fat stomach, as he lies on his back, with his eyes rolling awfully and a bit of rosy tongue showing between his black lips, in a state of Sybaritic enjoyment on her lap. "I tell her it is *her* way of flirting. She always maintains that she cannot flirt—does not know how; but of course that is nonsense. I suppose we can all do a little in that way, if we try?"—holding her smooth head rather on one side, and looking arch.

"Has she been saying any thing unusually exasperating?" I ask, as, under my successful labors, the frosty fire spires and races upward. "Never mind if she has; she is not in very good tune just now, poor soul, and one can hardly wonder at it."

While he speaks, Mr. Scrope has been stalking up and down in a fidgety way, making the boards creak. At my words he stops, and says abruptly:

"Why?"

"Have not you heard? Oh, of course not! Stupid of me! She would not be likely to mention it herself—it is not a very pleasant subject to talk about—but her engagement is all off, and she is naturally rather low about it."

"She is not in the least low; I never saw her in better spirits in my life," says Scrope, with a brusqueness that amounts to incivility; and, having delivered himself of this speech, he marches off to the window and turns his back to us.

"It must be *your* coming, then, that has cheered her," says Sylvia, laughing lackadaisically, "and indeed to tell you the truth, at the risk of making you atrociously conceited, I must say *I don't wonder at it.* It is a shockingly fast sentiment, I suppose, but there is something in the *timbre* of a man's voice that quite invigorates me; I suppose it is always having been so much used to men's society. I get on with them so much better than with women; *I* understand *them,* and *they* understand *me.*"

"Have you had any talk with her?" I ask, rising precipitately, and following him to the embrasure of the window, perfectly heedless of the fact that my sister is comfortably mounted on her .pet hobby—*self*, and is cantering complacently away on him. "Did she say any thing to you?"

"Listen!", he says, putting a hand on each of my shoulders, quite unconscious of the familiarity of the action—and indeed they might be posts for all he knows about them—and looking me rudely and triumphantly in the face. "She has been saying *this* to me, 'I will marry you as soon as you like!'"

"WHAT!!!!!!" Six marks of admiration but poorly render the expression I throw into this innocent monosyllable. I feel my face becoming a series of round *Os*—astonishment stretching and opening every feature beyond its natural destiny.

"Why do you keep staring at me?" says the young man, petulantly, giving me a little shake; "why do you stand with your mouth wide open? Why should not I marry? What is there to prevent me? Does not everybody do it? What is there so very surprising in it?"

Still I maintain an absolute silence; his hands have dropped from my shoulders, but I still stand before him, like a block of stupid stone. Neither does Sylvia speak; she is affecting to blow her nose, and has covered the nose part of her face with her pocket-handkerchief; what yet remains is excessively red. For once her hobby-horse has given her a nasty fall.

"Why do you stare at me like a wild beast?" cries Scrope, angrily. "Is this the way you always take a piece of news? Pleasant for the person who tells you, if it is. If I had told you that she had just fallen down dead in the next room, you could not look at me with greater dismay."

I cannot contradict it. Sputtering and breathless, I still face him, trying hard to speak; but, in all the wide range of good, noble, and useful words that the English tongue affords, I can find not one that suits the present crisis.

"Why don't you say *something?* " says the young man, with cheeks on fire and lightning eye. "The most disagreeable sentence you could invent would be better than this. Oh, come! I cannot stand it any longer—to be stared at by two perfectly silent women with their mouths open; it would make "—laughing fiercely—"it would make the bravest man in Europe run like a hare!"

He turns quickly to the door as he speaks. Then I find my tongue; its hinges are not well oiled, and it does not run smoothly, but it goes somehow. I catch hold of his arm or his coat-tail—I am not quite sure which—in my excitement.

"Stop, stop!" I cry, incoherently; "don't be cross! I mean to say something—I am going to say something—but—but—you take my breath away! It is so *sudden*—so *unnaturally* sudden!"

"*Unnaturally?* " repeats he, tartly, the painful consciousness that I have hit upon the joints of his harness making him defend the weak part with all the greater acrimony. "Why *unnaturally*, pray? If it does not seem too sudden to her or to me, I do not see why it need appear so to any one else."

"But—but—are you *sure* you are not mistaken?" I say, disbelievingly, mindful of the tear-swollen, desperate face I had seen lying among its tossed hair on my sister's bedroom-floor. "Are you quite sure she said those words? She is an odd girl—Lenore—very odd, and sometimes she has a random way of talking; I do not think she quite knows always what she is saying."

"Thank you," replies he, bowing formally, though his face flames. "You are, if not polite, at least candid. I understand. A woman must be slightly deranged to consent to be my wife."

My wits are still too far out wool-gathering for me to
be able to summon them back to compose some civil explanation and apology.

"You disbelieve me still?" cries my future brother-in-
law, greatly exasperated by my silence. "All right! do
—it does me no harm; but, if it should happen to strike
you at any time that I may, *by accident,* be speaking truth,
you have only to send for Lenore, and ask her."

"Poor dear Lenore!" says Sylvia, speaking for the first
time, and smiling sweetly. "She has not been long in
consoling herself, has she? I am *quite* glad."

Mrs. Prodgers . has finished blowing her nose, and her
face has laid aside its transient redness; but she now holds
her head quite straight, nor does she looks at all arch.

"You know, Jemima, if you remember, you laughed at
me—but I always maintained that Paul Le Mesurier did
not care two straws about her. I am sure I am the last
person to pretend to unusual clearsightedness, but one has
one's instincts!"

"It *is* sudden, of course!" bursts out Scrope, boyishly,
not paying any attention to my sister, but looking straight
and defiantly at me. "What is the good of telling me
that? How can I help it? Tell me that January is colder
than July—I know it is; but it is not my falt. If I had
had my way, it would not have been sudden—it would have
happened full six months ago. No one ought to know that
better than you."

"Ought I?" say I, vaguely. "I dare say—but to tell
you the truth—so many incoherences about Lenore—her
eyes, her ankles, and her inhumanities—have been poured
into my ears that I get them muddled together. I cannot,
at a moment's notice, assign to each lover his own several
Jeremiad."

"You are spiteful," replies the young fellow, laughing

a little, but looking offended. "If I had known how little you were listening to me, I would not have talked to you about her."

"Poorest, dearest Lenore!" repeats Sylvia, smiling a little patronizingly. "Quite the dearest thing in the world, and, mercifully for her, incapable of fretting much about any thing or anybody. What a gift!—if she could but give one the receipt!" (sighing and pensively passing through her fingers the beads of a great jet rope that she wears round her neck.)

"Jemima," says Scrope, impulsively, putting his hand again fraternally on my shoulder, "I do not suppose that they will do me any good—not a barley-corn—but still I have a morbid desire for your good wishes; they will be tardy and lugubrious, I am aware, but, such as they are, give them me. If *I*" (reproachfully) "had heard that *you* were going to be married, I should not have been so slow or so dismal in offering mine."

"That is a very safe position," reply I, dryly. "If you had seen me flying toward the moon, you would have complimented me on the ease and grace with which I flapped my wings. I *do* wish you good luck—there!—but whether you will *get* it or not is another matter."

"But—but—you—think that it *will* be?" says Scrope, with his whole eager heart in his voice. "Now that you have shut your mouth, and that your eyes no longer look as if they were falling out of your head, and that you can talk rationally—you *believe* it?"

"Upon my honor, I cannot say," reply I, laughing uncomfortably. "Lenore, as Sylvia truly observed just now, is quite the dearest thing in the world; but sometimes she goes round and round, like the sails of a wind-mill. I have a good mind to go and ask her myself."

So I go.

CHAPTER XV.

WHAT JEMIMA SAYS.

UP and down, up and down, up and down, with her hands behind her back, I find her marching in the ordered solitude of her own room, as I had expected.

"Good Heavens!" say I, entering, with my shoulders raised nearly to my ears, and my hands spread out.

She stops in her persevering trudge, looks me coolly over, and says—

"Après?"

I throw my eyes up to the ceiling, and shake my head several times, but words utter I none.

"You have heard, I suppose," she says, quietly. "I see he is running all over the house *button-holing* everybody, as the Ancient Mariner did the Wedding Guest. I hope he has told Norris, and William, and Frederick—it would be a sad oversight if he has not."

"It *is* true, then?" I say, gasping. "When he told me, I would not believe it—I said so—I said I would ask you myself."

"You might have saved yourself the trouble of the journey up-stairs," replies she, calmly, "but, as you are not 'fat and scant of breath,' like Hamlet, Prince of Denmark, I suppose it does not matter much."

"*Good* Heavens!" say I, for the second time.

"Try a new ejaculation," suggests my sister, smiling; "I am tired of that one."

"And—and—and your *reason?*"

"*Reason?*" repeats she, laughing rather harshly. "What extraordinary questions you do ask! Is not it on the surface? I am *in love*, to be sure—deeply in love."

I am on the verge of being delivered of a third " Good Heavens ! " but, recollecting myself, suppress it.

" If you remember, you did not approve of my first choice," says Lenore, with a bitter smile; " are you any better pleased with my second ? "

" *Much* better," I answer, emphatically; " far better— only it is horribly and *indecently* sudden—that is all ! "

Silence.

" As for the other," I continue, " you are right. I never *could* understand what you saw in him : a long nose, a yard of scarlet beard, and a sulky temper, seemed to me the whole stock-in-trade."

For one second her eyes flash with a furious pain, then grow quiet.

" Exactly," she says, composedly. " Now, in the case of the *present* nose, there is nothing to be desired, is there ? —nice and short, and runs straight down the middle of his face, without deviating a hair's-breadth to right or left; such *nice* curls, too, all over his head, as if they were put in curl-papers every night—and such *dear* little teeth ! "

" For shame ! " cry I, indignantly; " you are describing a *doll.* Lenore, Lenore ! what are you made of ? Beauty and love are thrown away upon you, and you have a perverted taste for ugliness and indifference."

She shrugs her shoulders.

" One may abuse one's own property, I suppose ? If you remember, he is *my* doll now—curls, and dear little teeth, and all ! "

I turn away, pained and disgusted.

" Stay," she says, laying her hand on mine; " do not be cross. I am serious—look at me ! I am sure I do not feel as if there were a joke to be got out of the whole of me."

I look at her, as she tells me—look with uncomfortable
misgivings at the bright beauty that has prospered her so
little : her cheeks are crimson, and the hand which holds
mine burns, *burns.*

"Attend to me," she says, imploringly. "I am *very*
much in earnest. I have done better *this* time, have not
I? I have been more wise at last."

I shake my head.

"How can I say?"

"This one is much more suitable to me, is not he? I
—I" (laughing feverishly)—"I begin to think that I did
not care *really* for the other so much after all; it was only
fancy—it was only my perversity. I wanted to get him
because I thought nobody else could. I—I was not *really*
fond of him, was I?"

She looks with a sort of wild wistfulness into my face
for confirmation of her words, but I do not think she finds
any.

"He is much more suitable to me," she repeats,
vaguely, as if trying to convince herself by iteration;
"much more in every respect. So much better-looking."

"Immeasurably," say I, emphatically; not that I see
what *that* has got to say to it."

"And better off," she continues, still holding and unconsciously pressing my hand with her hot, dry fingers.
"We should have been miserably poor, Paul and I—*miserably ;* and I hate poverty; I hate trying to make both
ends meet. They will meet now and *lap over,* without
any difficulty, will not they?"

"I imagine so."

"And in age, too," she goes on, eagerly, "we are far
better fitted; is it not so? Paul was old—older than his
age even—old in himself."

"He might well have been your father," I say, laughing vindictively, " except that no one would have accused you of emanating from so hard-featured a stock."

" No," she says, not in the least attending to my sarcasm, " of course not; altogether, you see," smiling mechanically—" altogether, you see, Jemima, it is all for the best. I am *nearly quite* convinced of it now, and, of course, I shall grow more and more convinced every day, shall not I ?" looking at me with imploring inquiry.

I make no response, and we both lapse into silence—a silence spent by Lenore in wandering aimlessly about, pulling the blinds up and down, disarranging the few wintry flowers in the vase on the toilet-table, altering the furniture. At last she speaks with sudden abruptness:

" It is to be soon—very soon !"

" He is wise there, I think," I answer, following her doubtfully about with my eyes. " Poor boy, he has not studied you for the last six months to no purpose; he knows what a weathercock you are, and is bent on making sure of you while you are in the vein. Who can tell when the wind may change ?"

" You are mistaken," she says, quickly, " it was not *his* idea at all; it was *my* suggestion. I suppose" (laughing with the same forced and hollow sound that had before pained me) " I suppose it is the first instance on record of such a proposition emanating from the lady, but it was. Yes, you may look as if you were going to eat me—I cannot help that—it *was !*"

" Good Heavens ! " repeat I, devoutly, lapsing unintentionally, for the third time, into my favorite ejaculation.

" Yes, soon—very soon !" she says, half to herself, pulling her rings on and off, lacing her fingers together and then again unlacing them; " and we will have a very smart wedding—very ! I hate sneaking to church with only the clerk and the beadle, as if one were ashamed of one's self. We will have all the neighbors, and men down from Gunter's, and a ball."

I stare distrustfully at her: her eyes are sparkling like diamonds at night, the splendid carnation that fever gives paints her cheeks.

"And you will have it put in *all* the papers," she says, laughing restlessly; "*all* of them—you must not forget— a fine, long, flourishing paragraph—do you mind?—in *all* of them."

"What an extraordinary thing to give a thought to!" I say, suspiciously. "If you had two columns of the *Times* devoted to you, how much good would it do you?"

"*Good?* Oh, none at all; but it is amusing. Flowers of newspaper eloquence are always entertaining, don't you know? And one likes one's friends—one's friends at a distance—to know what is happening to one."

A light begins to break upon me, but it is such an unpleasant one that for the moment I ask no more questions. A pause. There are so many things—true, yet eminently disagreeable—to be said, that I hesitate which to begin upon. Lenore presently saves me the trouble.

"If—if—if he were to see me now," she says, sitting down at my feet, and smiling excitedly up at me, "he could not think I was pining much for him, could he?"

The unpleasant light grows clearer.

"When he sees the account of my wedding in the papers—so soon—so immediately—such a brilliant marriage, too; I am so glad it is a good one—he will realize" (laughing ironically) "how irreparable an injury his desertion has inflicted on me, will not he?"

"*Is it possible?*" says I, with shocked emphasis. "I suspected it when you began to talk to me; I am *sure* of it now. Lenore! Lenore! you are going to be madder than all Bedlam and Hanwell together!"

"I am—am I?" speaking with listless inattention to my words, and still pursuing her own thoughts.

"Marrying one man to pique another always seemed to me the most thorough 'pulling your nose to vex your face,'" I continue, in great heat.

No remark, no comment on my homely illustration.

"Suppose he does hear of your marriage; suppose he does read every paragraph in all the papers about it; suppose he reads that you had twelve bridesmaids, and that you went off in a coach-and-six, how much the worse will he be or how much the better you?"

Still no answer; but she listens.

"He will feel a little stab of pain, perhaps—of mortified vanity, more likely; but it will be a very little one, not big enough to spoil his dinner (he likes his dinner); while you, my poor soul, where will you be?"

She has been lying with her head in my lap; at these last words she snatches it hurriedly up.

"What do you mean?" she cries, in a fury. "How dare you pity me? I am not a 'poor soul.' I am a very fortunate person—very much to be envied. Hundreds of people would change places with me; so would you, if you could."

"Hm! I don't know."

A pause.

"Lenore," say I, earnestly, putting my hand under her chin, and lifting her unwilling face toward mine, "listen to me, for I am talking sense. I never had a husband, which is more my misfortune than my fault, but all the same, I know what I am about. If you marry Charlie now, you will like him *at last ;* I am sure of that. I do not believe in the most perversely faithful woman *always* hating, *always* having a distaste for a handsome, manly, loving husband. Yes, you will end by liking him even better than he does you. It is always the way. But you will have to go through purgatory first; and, what is more unfair, you will have to drag him through too, poor boy!"

"Bah!" she says, with a scornful laugh; "it is nothing when you are used to it. If I have not been there, I am sure I do not know where I have been, ever since that accursed ball. Shall I ever again hear those detestable fiddles squeaking, and those vile wind instruments blowing and blaring, without going mad? I doubt it—I doubt it!"—putting her hands wildly to her ears, as if to shut out sounds of utter pain and horror.

"You rather dislike him than otherwise now," pursue I, pushing my advantage; "you are always better pleased to see him leave a room than enter it. Well, before your wedding-tour is over, you will *abhor* him. It requires an immense stock of love at starting to support the dead sweet monotony of a honeymoon."

She shudders.

"My dear child," I cry, with affectionate emphasis, "think better of it; if you *must* marry him—poor dear Charlie, I *am* sorry for him—at least put it off for six months; let us have a little time to breathe. If you will reflect a moment, I think you will see that to be handed on from one man to another within a week is hardly lady-like, hardly *modest!*"

At the last word the deep red on her cheeks grows yet deeper; but by the hard, defiant smile that curls her lips I know that I might as well have spoken to the winter wind that is howling and gnashing its angry teeth outside.

"Jemima," she says, calmly, "as I once before observed to you, you will never make your fortune in the pulpit; your sentiments are first rate, but they make one drowsy. See, I am yawning myself. As to *modest*, that is neither here nor there; you dragged in the word by the head and shoulders to prop your argument. As to *lady-like*, it is a matter of the most perfect indifference to me whether I am or not."

To this I say nothing. I only walk away to the window.

"Do not dissuade me!" she cries, falling from defiance to a tone of almost nervous entreaty, as she stands before me, twisting her hands. "Let me marry him in peace. Your little cut-and-dried saws are very neatly cut, very accurately dried, but they do not *fit*; you mean well, but one knows one's self best."

"Hm!"

"Do you think," she continues, with irritable impatience, "that I can go on *now* in the old groove—the old groove that I kept so contentedly to before—before the earth opened and swallowed all I had?"

No answer.

"Can I go on," she pursues, with deepening agitation, "watching you drop the stitches in your knitting, listening to Sylvia's weak cackle, hearing those awful children plunging and bellowing about? Do you know, Jemima, for the last few days, every time they have come blundering and shrieking into the room, I have felt inclined to scream out loud? I have not done it, because you would have put me into a mad-house if I had; but, all the same, I have felt the inclination."

I shake my head despondently.

"If he marries me," she says, her eyes wandering restlessly about, and speaking quickly and excitedly, "he will take me away to beautiful places, away from all the dreadful old things and people. It will be delightful—delightful! I shall begin all over again—my life over again! He will take me where there are no children—no Sylvias—no Jemimas—no self! Yes" (laughing uneasily), "I mean to leave *myself* behind. I mean to be a new, fresh person —a happy, prosperous person. I *wish* to be happy—I am *determined* to be happy. Jemima" (entreatingly), "for God's sake, do not hinder me!"

CHAPTER XVI.

WHAT THE AUTHOR SAYS.

PEOPLE cannot keep their mouths open forever—not even Jemima Herrick—they *must* shut them at last. Mostly they shut them very soon. No passion is so short-lived as astonishment. "A nine-days' wonder" is a hyperbolical expression. Who ever wondered at the awfullest murder, the most startling *esclandre*, the most unlooked-for turn of Fortune's quick wheel, during nine whole days? If walking on your head were to come into fashion, within three days it would excite no surprise to see people pounding along the pavement on their hats and bonnets, with their boots in the air. The neighborhood has been informed of Lenore's transfer from one lover to the other, and its "ohs" and "ahs," and head-shakings thereon, are over and done with. After all, they have been fewer than have been expected; people had so long made up their minds that Scrope was the right man that few of them had arrived at the knowledge that he was the wrong one before they were officially informed that he was the right one again. He has always been seen about with her; he is evidently her fittest mate in youth and comeliness; in this case all the sympathy goes with the successful lover. Does not he ride as straight as a die? Is not he as handsome as paint? Do not we know all his antecedents? Does not his property lic, does not his ugly old red abbey stand, in this our county ? Paul, unknown, plain, and saturnine, commands neither good wishes nor regrets. It has been announced that the engagement was dissolved by mutual consent—a course always adopted by the friends of the lady when the gentleman cries off. Lenore, however, is no party to this deception. Everybody's presents have been returned to him, and again sent back. On the principle of "To him that hath shall be given," the rich Mrs. Scrope's wedding-gifts are threefold greater and more numerous than those of the poor Mrs. Le Mesurier. On hearing of the change in her fortunes—if not for the better, at least for the more consequential—the Websters supplement their portly tea-pot with a cream-jug and sugar-basin to match. And Lenore, when she sees the teapot come back—the teapot out of which she was to have poured Paul's tea, in the little narrow house they had planned—she laughs violently.

"Do not let them send me any new congratulations— any of them," she says, dryly; "tell them the old ones will do; they need only alter the *initials*, as I am doing with my pocket-handkerchiefs."

Scrope has no father, and Lenore has no money, which two facts greatly facilitate the law arrangements. Whether *indecently* soon or not, the wedding-day is drawing on. Lenore has thrown herself into the business of *trousseau*-buying with an ardor more than feminine—with an artistic frenzy of a Frenchwoman, of a *petite maîtresse enragée*.

"Finery always *was* my snare," she says, laughing. "I loved even my cotton gowns and gingham umbrellas tenderly; but *now*—if being married entails such a saturnalia of fine clothes, I should like to have a wedding every year."

Lenore is very lively; she runs about the house all day singing; she walks, she rides, she plays billiards; she studies "Murray" and "Bradshaw" with avidity, making out routs to the ends of the earth; but she *never* sits still. Her cheeks are rosy red, and her eyes sparkle and glitter like beautifullest great sapphires.

"You are quite the most *eager* bride I ever saw," Sylvia says one day, with a doubtful compliment. "Poor Charlie toils after you in vain. *I* always imagined that impatience was the monopoly of the gentleman; I am sure" (sighing and looking down) "it was so in my case. I thought the days *raced* by—positively *raced;* if you remember, Jemima, I said so to you at the time."

"Did you? I dare say."

"Now, Lenore, on the contrary, seems anxious to *hurry* them. Fancy!" casting up her eyes and hands to heaven.

"I *am* anxious," says the girl, smiling rather wistfully. "I mean to be so happy—I want to begin. I am sorry it is not *en règle;* but I cannot help that. How many more days are there? One, two, three, four, five—bah!" (taking up two parcels that lie on the hall-table), "a couple more ivory prayer-books! Jemima, if there come any more prayer-books, you must send them back, and say that there is a glut of books of devotion."

The wedding-feast is to be gay and large; the house to be crowded and crammed from attic to cellar, chiefly with Scrope's people; mother, unmarried sister, married sister and husband, uncles, unmarried men, cousins.

"A perfect horde of barbarians!" says Sylvia, complacently swimming into the drawing-room, on the afternoon of the day on which they are expected, her little figure very upright, head slightly thrown back, and bust protruded, as is her way when the war-paint is on. "I have quite a good mind to run away and hide myself in a corner, and leave Tommy, as my deputy, to receive them.—Will

you, Tommy? How amusing it would be, and how astonished they would look!"

"One could hardly wonder at them," answers Jemima,
dryly. Jemima's head and bust are much as usual.

"As long as I have Charlie beside me I don't mind,"
continues Mrs. Prodgers, looking at herself over her left
shoulder in the glass, in one of Sylvia's strained and dis-
torted attitudes; "he is my sheet-anchor. Poor, dear, old
Charlie!" (laughing a little) "to think of his going to be
one's *brother!* It is *too* ridiculous!"

It is the evening before the wedding; the lit rooms are
gayly alive with many guests; not only those staying in
the house, but also dinner-guests. Many more are expected; some of them already uncloaking outside, for Sylvia
has decreed a dance.

"We must have a *band*," she has said, meditatively,
when making the arrangements. "There is no use doing
a thing unless you do it well. Yes, a band; they can go
so nicely in the recess under the stairs."

"It *is* dreary work pounding over a carpet, to the tune
of a piano, supported only by lemonade and negus," Jemima says.

"When people come on a *first* visit," says Sylvia, sa-
piently, "they always come to criticise. Did you notice
how they all looked me over, from top to toe, when they
came in to-day—*pricing* me, as it were? Well, I wish to
be *beyond* criticism."

"Don't have a band!" cries Lenore, hastily; "if you
do, I shall go to bed—that is all. I warn you. Those
dreadful fiddles, squeaking and shrieking, go right through
my head. Have a piano, and I will promise to play for
you from now till the Judgment-Day."

So a piano it is. The dancing has not yet begun, but
we all stand about in an unsettled way, that shows that

something is imminent. Detachments of people are being taken to be shown the wedding presents. The hot-red roses have to-night left Lenore's cheeks; she is very white —*deadly* white, one would say; only that it is a dishonor to the warm, milk whiteness of *living* loveliness, to liken it to the hue that is our foe's ensign. She is pale, but her eyes outblaze the star that quivers and lightens in Mrs. Scrope's gray head.

"I am so glad you are not a *Mourning Bride*," says Scrope's eldest sister, Mrs. Lascelles, a frisky young matron, pretty as hair like floss silk, Paris clothes falling off her soft, fat shoulders, and English jewels, can make her, looking with a sort of inquisitive admiration at the restless pale beauty of her future sister-in-law's face. "Not that *I* can say any thing" (laughing lightly); "I cried for three whole days before *my* wedding. Mamma said that my eyes looked as if they had been sewn in with red worsted.—Did not you, mamma?"

Mrs. Scrope smiles the placid smile of prosperous, stall-fed maturity.

"I did more than that," continues the other, still laughing; "I cried for a fortnight afterward! We went to *Brittany*" (making a disgusted face), "and Regy was ill all the way from Southampton to St.-Malo. I tried to look as if he did not belong to me. I am sure even the waiters at the hotels were sorry for me—I looked so *dejected!*"

At the mention of Brittany Lenore winces, and then begins to talk quickly and laughingly:

"*Must* one cry? I hope not. If it is indispensable, I will *try;* but I am afraid I shall not succeed. I am not a good hand at crying. I *never* cry."

They are to dance in the hall; the oak floor has been polished and doctored to the last pitch of slipperiness; the stags' heads have mistletoe wreaths. Plenty of light, plenty of warmth, plenty of space, plenty of men—what more can any rabidest dance-lover desire? To the general surprise, Lenore sits down to the piano; everybody remonstrates.

"Usurping *my* place!" says Jemima, cheerfully, putting her hands on her sister's shoulders. "Off with you!"

"On the contrary," returns Lenore, with a perverse smile, "I mean to adorn this stool till two o'clock to-morrow morning. Go away—dance—caper about, it amuses you. As for me, I hate it. *Va-t'en!*"

"Come on!" cries Scrope, half in and half out of his gray gloves, and looking radiantly happy and handsome. "What do you mean by settling yourself there? Jemima is going to play; she always does; she likes it.—Don't you, Jemima?"

Jemima smiles grimly. All very well to be conscious that your life-mission is to pipe for other people to dance, but a little hard to be expected to express *enjoyment* of the *rôle!*

"I am not going to '*Come on!*'" answers Lenore, pettishly. "I mean to stay here. Go away!"

"'*Go away!*'" cries the young fellow, leaning his arms on the piano, and looking desperately sentimental. "A very likely story!"

"For Heaven's sake, put your head straight!" she says, crossly. "When you cock it on one side like that, you look like a bullfinch about to pipe. I hate dancing—there!"

"Since when?" he asks, incredulously. "Not long ago you told me that you loved it better than any thing else in life."

"Not so *very* long ago, when I was cutting my teeth, I loved sucking an India-rubber ring better than any thing else in life. Do you insist on my sucking it still?" she says, dryly, turning over a heap of music. "Don't be a nuisance. Go away!"

He goes. In five minutes, all, not incapacitated by age and fat, and some even that lie under these disabilities, are scampering round. As there are plenty of men, several of the *chaperones* condescend to tread a measure. Lenore plays on dreamily; it is an air that the band played at Dinan one night last summer; as the brisk, gay melody fills her ears, the room, the people, the wax-lights vanish; she is in the Place du Guesclin again. How dark it is! The lights from the hotel show small and red; the *sabots* clump past. How close to our faces the green-lime flowers swing!

. . . .

She is roused by an eager voice at her ear.

"One turn—only one! I have danced with every thing that has any pretensions to age, weight, or ugliness. Pay me for it—only *one* turn!"

Scrope stands by her, panting a little. His broad chest heaves, and his wide blue eyes glitter with a passionate excitement. She shrugs her shoulders, but, as though it were too much trouble to argue the point, complies. Jemima takes her place, and they set off. After flying silently round for a few minutes, they stop. Scrope, even in stopping, unwilling to release her from his arms, gazes into her face with a passionate rapture, to see whether the delight he feels is at all shared.

"I *hate* it!" she says, irritably. "It tears my dress; it loosens my hair; it takes away my breath. Let us go to some cool place."

They saunter away to the conservatory. The Chinese lanterns swing aloft, their flames spiring up in dangerous proximity to the pink-and-green walls of their frail prisons. The daphnes and narcissi and lilies of the valley are uniting their various odors in one divinest harmony of scent, like a concert of noblest voices. Lenore throws her-

14

self wearily into a garden-chair, and begins to fan herself.

"Let me fan you," says her lover, tenderly, taking the
fan out of her hand and leaning over her; "it will save
you trouble. My darling, you look pale to-night."

"*My darling, you look red to-night!*" retorts she, with
a mockery more bitter than playful, glancing up at the
flushed beauty of his face. "For Heaven's sake, don't let
us register the variations in each other's complexion!"

An arrow shoots through the young man's bounding
heart. Is she going to change her mind? Now that the
prize is almost within his hand, must he lose it at this last
moment?

"Have I done any thing to vex you?" he asks, anxiously, kneeling down on the stone pavement at her feet.
"You know how idiotically fond I am of you; for Heaven's
sake, do not take advantage of it to play tricks with me!
What is the matter with you to-night? You are out of
spirits."

"What do you mean?" she cries, angrily. "I never
was in better spirits in my life. Everybody remarks it;
everybody says how lively I am. I talk all day, and I
laugh more than I ever did in my life before. Would you
have one always grinning like a Cheshire cat?"

"You talk and laugh, it is true," he answers, with a
grave air of anxiety; "but you are much thinner than you
were. Look at this arm" (touching the round white limb,
as it lies listlessly across her lap); "it is not half the size
it was three weeks ago."

"So much the better," she answers, with a laugh; "my
arms were much too big before. Sylvia was always
abusing them; it is much more refined to have smaller
arms."

"You will be all right when we get to Italy," he says,

fondly; "you will like that, will not you? Oh! sweet!" (leaning over her, with a passion of irrepressible exultation); "can I believe that I am waking when I think that long before this time to-morrow you will be my *wife?*— that at last—at last—we shall belong to one another, for *always?*"

She shivers a little.

"To-day is to-day, and to-morrow is to-morrow," she says, sententiously; "to-day, let us talk of to-day; we may both be dead by to-morrow."

"*Both!*" (smiling a little); "that is hardly likely."

"One of us, then; only the other day I read in the *Times* of a bride who was found dead in her bed on her wedding-morning. O my God!" (flinging out her arms, and then throwing her head down on her knees,) "if I had but the very slightest chance of going to heaven, how I wish I could be found dead in my bed!"

"What are you talking about?" cries Scrope, shocked and astonished at this unlooked-for outburst. "Lenore! look me in the face and say you did not mean it. I know you have a random way of talking, sometimes—Jemima says so; but, do you know, when you say such things you break my heart?"

"Do I?" she says, lifting her wild white face, unsoftened by any tears. "I am glad. Why should not I break it? I have broken my own—you know that well enough —why should not *you* suffer too? As for me, I suffer—I suffer always—all day and all night. I am glad to hear of any one else being miserable too. What have I done, that I should have a monopoly of it?" He stares at her, in a stony silence. "There," she says, after a pause, with a sickly smile, pushing her hair off her forehead, "I am all right now! I was only—only—*joking!* Pay no attention to any thing I said; I was only ranting. I think I have been overdoing myself a little the last few days. Suppose you go? I shall get well quicker if I am by myself."

So he goes, slowly and heavily. She has taken all the lightness out of his feet and out of his heart; it feels like a pound of lead. He makes his way up to the piano.

"Jemima," he says, in a low voice, "my sister will play for you; I want you to go to Lenore; she is not very well, I think—rather hysterical; she is in the conservatory, she would not let me stay with her."

So Jemima goes.

CHAPTER XVII.

WHAT JEMIMA SAYS.

"WHAT next?" think I, hurrying off, as bidden. "What new freak? Well, if I had been born with a silver spoon in my mouth I would not have spent my life in bewailing and lamenting that it was not a pewter one." In the conservatory no Lenore! Only two time-worn flirts of either sex, shooting their blunt little old arrows at each other's tough hearts, under a red camellia. I do not know why I do it, but I pass along, through the flowers, to a door at the other end that gives upon the outer air, and, opening it, look forth. It is snowing rather fast; great, shapeless flakes floating down with disorderly slowness, but it is not very dark. My knowledge of my sister has not been at fault, for, through the snow, I see her, at a little distance from me, walking quickly up and down a terrace-walk, with her head bent and her hands clasped before her. "How good for a person with a weak chest!" I cry, indignantly, skipping gingerly out on the toes of my white satin boots, and flinging the tail of my gown adroitly over my head. "Any one more unfit for death or more resolute to die than you, I have seldom had the pleasure of meeting."

I put my arm within hers and drag her along, back into the lighted warmth of the conservatory. A great tier of orange-trees and chrysanthemums hides us from the veteran lovers. I look at her: the snow-flakes rest thickly on her hair, on her flimsy dress; run in melted drops off her chilled white shoulders.

"It does not wet one much," she says, with a rather deprecating smile. "See, one can blow them away. How white they are! They will make the snowdrops that the school-children are to strew before me to-morrow look quite dirty, will not they?"

"Lunatic!" cry I, highly exasperated, shaking her; "fool! If I may be permitted to ask, what is the reason of this?"

"I was hot," she says, a little wildly, "stifled! Those flowers stifle me. Odious jonquils! Did ever any flowers smell so heavily? They are like the ones in that dreadful bouquet Charlie brought me for the ball."

I am shaking and flicking, with my best lace pocket-handkerchief, the snow from off her dress, so make no answer.

"You know, from a child, I was fond of running out, bareheaded, into a shower; I liked to feel the great cool drops patter, patter on my hair. I wish to God I could feel them now! Put your hand on my head" (lifting my cold, red hand, and placing it on the top of her own sleek head).

"My good child," say I, startled, "you are in a fever!"

"Jemima," she says, taking down my hand again, and holding it hard pressed between her two hot white ones, while her glittering eyes burn on my face, "I am quite happy, as you know, perfectly. No one has more cause to be so.   I am quite young; I am better looking than most people; to-morrow I shall be rich, very rich; which, after all, includes all the others; but, do you know, sometimes, within the last few days, I have thought—it is a ridiculous idea, of course, but sometimes I have thought I was *going mad!*   How do people *begin* to go mad?   Tell me."

Her voice has sunk to an awed whisper.

"Fiddlestick!" cry I, contemptuously.   "Do not be alarmed, only clever people go mad; no fear for you."

"If any one comes suddenly into a room, if any one bangs a door or speaks in a key at all louder than usual, I feel as if I *must* shriek out loud.   I told you so the other day, if you remember, talking of the children.   Sometimes I am afraid of lifting my eyes to your or any one else's face, for fear you should think they *looked* mad."

"Nonsense!" interrupt I again, now thoroughly angry. "It is all nerves.   Nerves are troublesome things, if you are not moderately careful of them, and you never give yours a chance; you never sit still, you never rest, and it is my belief that you never sleep."

"Not if I can help it," she says, feverishly; "not if I can help it. Sometimes, when I feel myself falling asleep, I get out of bed and walk about in the cold to wake myself thoroughly. I *hate* sleep; it is my enemy! As sure as ever I fall asleep, I am back in Brittany with him; we are as—as we used to be."

"If I were you," say I, with that sober eye to the main chance with which one regards life after five-and-twenty, "I should be glad to wake from such a dream to find how much more prosperous the reality is."

"So I am, so I am!" she answers, hastily, contradicting herself.   "Of course, it *is* prosperous, is it not? Everybody says so.   You—you are not *joking*, are you, Jemima, when you say I am so prosperous?" (her eyes resting distrustfully on my face).   "I am *really*, am I not?

But sometimes I think, when I look at you, that you are *pitying* me. Heaven knows why, for nobody needs it less. If you are, do not—that is all ! I hate being pitied; pity yourself instead."

" Dreams or no dreams," say I, trying to lead her from a theme which is making her painfully excited, " you *must* sleep to-night, if we give you laudanum enough to make seven new sleepers. If you do not, mark my words, to-morrow you will look as yellow as the little orange in your wreath." No answer, only a vacant plucking at her dress. "Dead-white in the morning," say I, with a judicious ad-hesion to the subject of millinery, " is almost always fatally trying to the best complexions, particularly when in juxta-position with snow." No answer. " Only this morning you told me that you were determined to look your very handsomest."

" So I am," she says, rousing herself, and speaking with quick interest; " so I am? You say right—I *must* look my best—I shall ; one always does when one wishes ; my veil will be down, too—they will not see me very clearly, you know ; but, however I look, you must be sure to have it put in the papers that I looked beautiful, and—and—radiantly happy. They say that sort of thing now and then, do not they ? "

" As to the being happy, never that I saw," reply I, snappishly. " A bride's happiness is taken for granted."

" I do not know whether I ever mentioned it to you be-fore," she says, with a hesitating, strained smile, " but I should like the announcement put into a good many papers besides the *Times*—the *Morning Post, Standard ;* but it must be in the *Times*, too, of course. People always read the births, deaths, and marriages in the *Times*, don't they ? "

She asks this last question with a keen anxiety, that would have puzzled any looker-on to account for.

"*Women* do," reply I, brusquely. "I do not think that *men* ever look at them."

"What nonsense you talk!" she cries, rudely. "Of course, they do. They always glance over them, at the least, to see whether there is any name they know. I have seen them, a hundred times. I have seen Charlie—"

"What about Charlie?" cries the young man, appearing round the screen of flowers simultaneously with his name. "He has not done any thing fresh, has he?" (trying to laugh, but yet speaking with a most anxious smile). "Jemima, how is she?—how are you now, my darling?" (taking her in his arms with as little heed to my presence as if I also were a prim dumb camellia).

"*How am I?*" retorts she, pushing him away with a gesture of distaste, and then, as if bethinking herself, accepting his embrace. "Why, how *should* I be? Much as I have been any time these nineteen years, with the exception of the solitary week when I had the croup. Reassure yourself—I have not the croup now, and I never have any other diseases."

He looks at her silently, with a pale, passionate wistfulness.

"You mean to be kind," she says, in a constrained voice, with a sort of remorse, "and you really are a very good fellow. I do think so always, though I show it rather oddly now and then, perhaps; but you must know that I have an inveterate aversion to being asked how I am. It is not confined to me. Many people have the same feeling. I really" (with a forced smile) "must draw up a list of prohibitions for you—'You must not do this,' and 'You must not do that'—before we set off on our travels, or we shall inevitably come to blows before a week is over."

"*Do I!*" cries the young man, eagerly, as one catching at a straw. "I do seem to be always blundering, don't I?

and saying the wrong thing? One would think I did it on purpose; but, as I live, I do not. I shall get better, however," he continues, hastily, as if afraid of her taking advantage of his confession; "every day I shall get better. Being with you always, I shall grow to understand your character better.—Dunce as I am, I cannot help doing that, can I, Jemima?"

"I really do not know," reply I, turning away with a dry smile; "there are some very sharp corners and unexpected turns in it, I can assure you."

"Jemima is right," says Lenore, gravely, gently unwinding his arms from about her. "You have got a very indifferent bargain, pleased as you are with it. To let you into a secret, you have overreached yourself. You will get a bad character of me from all the people I have spent my life with; I have the distinction of having everybody's ill word."

"I dare say" (defiantly, while his eyes recklessly, boundlessly fond, grow to her calm, chill face).

"It is not too late yet," she says, in a low voice that has yet nothing of the whisper in it; "it is one o'clock; I hear it striking. You have yet ten hours' grace."

"Ten hours!" cries the young fellow, mildly, throwing his arms again about her, and straining her, whether she will or no, to his riotous heart. "Lenore! Lenore! the nearer the time grows the farther you seem to get away from me. Are you going to slip away from me altogether at the last moment, as you did out of my arms just now? But no!—why do I put such ideas into your head? It is too late. You could not throw me over now, if you wished. Reckless as you are of all conventionality, even you dare not do that."

"What are you talking about?" she asks, petulantly, with a nervous laugh. "Why should I wish to throw you over? If I did, what could I do with all my fine clothes, and my otter-skin jacket? Do you think I could have strength of mind to send the Websters' teapot travelling back a *second* time?"

He continues looking at her, and holding her, but says nothing.

"I *like* you," she says, looking round at me with a sort of nervous defiance. "I do not care who says I do not. I am proud of you—I—I—I *love* you. Do not I, Jemima? Have not I often told you that I do?"

"You have told me a great many things in your time," I say, oracularly, "some that were true and some that were not. I will tell you one thing in return, and that is, that if you do not go to bed now, this minute, to-morrow you will be yellower than any orange."

CHAPTER XVIII.

WHAT JEMIMA SAYS.

IT is a circumstance never to be enough deplored by the female world that marriages and drawing-rooms are broad daylight ceremonies. Mature necks and faces, that the great, bold sun makes look as yellow as old law-deeds, or as the love-letters of twenty years ago, would gleam creamily, waxily white, if illumined only by benevolent candles, that seem to see and make seen only beauties, and slur over defects. Even the lilies and roses of youth—unlike the smooth perfection of their garden types—are conscious of little pits, and specks, and flaws, when Day holds his great searching lamp right into their faces. Day repudiates tulle and tarletane; they are none of his; and, as he cannot rid himself of them, he retaliates by behaving as glaringly and unhandsomely as he can to them. Nature is holding a wedding outside too, apparently; at least, it is all white, *white!* Heaven has sent down a storm of diamonds in the night, as a marriage-present to Lenore; wherever you look there is the glitter of myriad brilliants. Last night, at each iron gate there was a high, wide arch of evergreens, but during the dark hours the fairies carried the dingy things away, and replaced them by others of glistening white jewels. They are so bright, so bright, one cannot look at them; one turns away with winking eyes. I fancy that with some such lustre shine the archways through which the Faithful People go and come in the deathless white City of God.

There is a mystical stir and bustle in the house; everybody but the bride has been down to an early breakfast and has gone up again to put their best clothes on. The maid-servants are hurrying about the house in uniform gray gowns and white caps, all except the ladies' maids, who have the right of exercising individual will in the choice of their magnificence. The footmen have new liveries. The wedding-breakfast is laid out in the dining-room; I have been reconnoitring it. One has to look out of window to assure one's self that the season is winter. On the long glittering table summer and autumn hold their scented sway. Regiments of tall flowers—both white and vivid-colored; shady fern-forests; bunches of grapes, big as those fabulous ones swinging in gilt over an ale-house door, or as that mighty cluster represented in the illustrations to "Line upon Line," as borne between two stout Hebrews, slung upon a pole; odorous rough-skinned pines. I indulge in a pleased sigh, and glance at the *carte*, I draw a slight mental sketch of what my own share in the banquet will be. Truely, one waxes gluttonous in one's old age.

Since then I have been pervading such of the ladies' rooms as intimacy gives me the *entrée* to. I have seen twelve passably fair maids, in twelve gauzy bonnets, each with a murdered robin sitting on the top, as a delicate tribute to the season. Pretty, and clean, and white, the dozen look; but, alas! they will present but a drabby-gray appearance by-and-by out-of-doors, when contrasted with the wonderful blinding snow-sheet. I am not a bridesmaid; I have not been invited, nor, if I had, would I have consented to intrude the washed-out pallor of my face among this plump pink rose-garden.

Now I have returned to the bride-chamber, where Sylvia, fully dressed, and apparently laboring under some hallucination as to being herself the bride, has usurped the cheval-glass; at least, on my entry, I find a pretty little figure in violet velvet and swansdown, with bust protruded and semi-dislocated neck, gyrating slowly before it.

"How extraordinary one does feel in *colors!*" she is ejaculating, with a sort of uneasy complacency; "but for Lenore's sake, nothing should have induced me. I feel quite like a fish out of water; I really can hardly believe it is my own face—it seems like some one else's. What a fright one does look, Jemima!"

No contradiction from me.

"Does not one?"

"No, I don't think so," reply I, consolingly; "nothing out of the way. I don't see much difference."

"Violet always *used* to be considered my color," returns Sylvia, apparently finding my form of comfort not very palatable; "always, *par excellence*. How well I remember, the very last ball I ever went to with poor John —I was in violet *lisse*, with cowslips—overhearing some man ask, 'Who that lovely little woman in mauve was?' What a rage I was in!"

"And who *was* she ? " ask I, with interest.

" *Who was she ?* " (reddening.) "What stupid questions you do ask, Jemima! *Who was she?* Why *I*, of course."

"Mauve suits everybody, even *me*," say I, peeping over Sylvia's shoulder at my own unusual lilac splendor; "it was well-named the ' refuge of the destitute.' "

Having discharged this Parthian shaft, I turn away. The room is blocked with great imperials, packed and half-packed. A whole haberdasher's shop of finery is surging out of them, and a big white L. S. on each of their shiny black lids. L. S. herself sits before the dressing-table, but —difficult as it is to help it—she is not looking at herself in the glass. Her eyes are on the ground, and her brows gathered. She is fully dressed, with the exception of the wreath and veil—all dead white—dead white, like the doll on the top of a twelfth-night cake; only that the doll invariably compensates for the colorlessness of her attire by cheeks that outshine the peony, and *Lenore's* cheeks are dead white too. To my mortification, I perceive that, in spite of Worth's gown, and old Mrs. Scrope's Flemish point, my sister is looking as little handsome as a thoroughly good-looking woman ever *can* look. Hardly a touch of pretty red even on her lips, and a pinched blue look of cold and utter apathy about her face and whole attitude.

"If I am to arrange your wreath," say I, speaking sharply, "we had better begin; there is no use hurrying, and it takes some time to dispose it properly."

She does not move or change her position.

"Will you be good enough," continue I, ironically, "to look round and convince yourself that this is not a funeral?"

Still no answer.

"Lenore" (raising my voice), "are you dead? are you

dumb? are you cataleptic? For Heaven's sake, why do you not say something?"

"What *should* I say?" she answers at length, raising her heavy eyes, and speaking with harsh irritability, "why *should* I speak? I have only *one* hour more of my own now" (glancing with a sort of tremulous shudder toward the clock); "surely I may spend it as I like."

"That is better," rejoin I, not heeding the matter of her speech, but regarding her, with my head on one side, with an artist's eye. "When you speak you look ten per cent. better. I must tell you in confidence that as you sat just now, with your shoulders up to your ears and your nose resting on your knees, you had a near escape of being that anomaly in Nature, a plain bride."

No reply.

"For mercy's sake, say something," I cry, crossly; "do not lapse again into that utter silence! Dear me!" (taking the wreath gingerly out of its box) "how beautifully they do make these things nowadays! But for the scent, I really think they out-do Nature."

The wheels of the first carriage become audible; very faintly, by reason of the snow, but still audible, and Sylvia, after one final glance, shuffle, and whisk, swims out of the room. I become absorbed in an artistic agony, as I throw the lace, in a shower of costly flimsiness, over my sister's impassive head, and delicately insinuate the chilly nuptial flowers into their resting-place on the top of it.

Carriage after carriage rolls up: doors are opened; steps let down. My curiosity gets the better of me. I leave my nearly-finished task, and, running to the window, press my face against the frosted pane.

"The Websters," say I, narratively. "Ha! ha! ha! Old Mrs. Webster in a twin-gown to Sylvia; even to the swansdown on the body and tunic! Poor, dear Sylvia! she will never get over it; it will be the death of her."

As I stand there, laughing maliciously, I feel a hand on my shoulder. "What! are *you* come to look at them, too? Take care, they will see you. It shows a little want of imagination in Mrs. James making two dresses pin for pin alike, does not it?"

I turn toward her; but, as soon as I catch a glimpse of her face, my mirth dies, and I utter a horrified ejaculation. It is lividly white, and she is gasping.

"Open it wide!" she says, almost inaudibly. "I—I—I am stifling!"

"Good Heavens!" cry I, apprehensively and dissuasively, with my usual practical grasp of a subject. "You are not going to faint? Do not!—not till I get you a chair. You are so heavy—I never could hold you up."

As I speak I am struggling with the hasp of the window, which is old, rusty, and evidently constructed with a view to never opening except after ten minutes' of angry wrestling.

"Quick! quick!" she says, faintly panting, "wider! *wider!*"

But it is too late. As the frozen casement grates slowly on its hinges, her head, with all its smart paraphernalia of lace and flowers, falls back lifeless, and the whole weight of her body, in all the leaden inertness of Death's counterfeit, rests in my strained arms. No one knows, until they have tried it, how heavy dead and swooned persons are. I stagger under my sister's weight, and with much difficulty, and many bumps both to her and myself, get her down on the floor, where the little icy airs come and ruffle her useless laces and her soft tossed locks. Then I fly to the bell, open the door, and call mightily down the passage. "Louise!" I cry, "Louise!" as Sylvia's French maid comes floating airily along—not in the least hurrying herself, but rather throwing gallantries over her shoulder, as it were, to a strange valet in the middle distance. "Louise! Louise! Make haste! Mademoiselle Lenore is so ill! I do not know what has happened to her!—all of a sudden, too!—she has fainted, I think; I suppose it *is* a faint, is not it" (looking nervously in her face), "not any thing *worse?*"

Louise gives a little yell, and says "My God!" in her mother-tongue, in which flippant language that adjuration does not sound half so solemn. Then we kneel down, one on each side of her, sprinkle water in her face, considerably to the injury of her tucker—pour brandy down her unconscious throat—hold strong smelling-salts to her nostrils—roughly chafe her dead hands—use all the unpleasant asperities, in fact, that are supposed necessary to induce people to come back to that life which, as a rule, they are so loath to quit. But it is all to no purpose: she shows no sign of returning consciousness.

"I do not half like it," I say, looking apprehensively across at my coadjutor, and speaking in an unintentional whisper. "I have not a notion what to do next! Run, Louise, and tell John to go as quickly as he can for Dr. Riley—and—and—I do not like being left here by myself with her—send Mrs. Prodgers."

"What do you want with me?" cries Sylvia, pettishly, coming fussing in a minute or two later; evidently in complete ignorance of the errand on which I have sent for her. "I wish you would not send such mysterious messages. I am so nervous already that I do not know what to do with myself! I declare, just now, when Lord Sligo was talking to me, I had no more idea what he was saying—— Good God!" (catching sight of Lenore's stiff prostrate white figure), "what has happened? What has she done to herself now?"

"She has fainted," repeat I, briefly, "all of a sudden, before I could look round; and we cannot bring her to."

"Good gracious, how dreadful!" cries Sylvia, kneeling daintily down on the floor, too; not, however, before she had plucked up her violet-velvet skirts. "What does one do when people faint?—put cold keys down their backs—cut their stay-laces—hold looking-glasses before their mouths—oh, no, of course, that is to see whether they are —Heavens, Jemima!" (her face blanching) "you do not think she is—"

Mrs. Prodgers has an inveterate aversion for pronouncing the little four-lettered word, that, in its plain shortness, expresses the destiny of the nations.

"Nonsense!" cry I, angrily, again seizing the salts, and futilely holding them to her nose.

"Feel whether her heart beats," says Sylvia, looking very white, breathing rather short, and speaking in an awed whisper. "I am afraid to do it myself—I dare not!—you are feeling the wrong side, are not you?—they say it is nearly in the middle."

Complying with these anatomical instructions, I feel. Yes, it beats. Life's little hammer is still knocking feebly against its neighbor ribs.

"She will be all right, just now, of course; it is only that we are not used to this sort of thing. I never was the least frightened myself," say I, doughtily, but not altogether truly.

"I wish her eyes were *quite* shut," says Sylvia, peering into Lenore's swooned face with the horrified curiosity of a child; "they look so dreadful, showing a bit of the pupil."

"The wedding will have to be put off, of course," say I, rising, and walking toward the clock; "half-past eleven now; it is very certain that she will not be well enough to be married before twelve."

"But the *people!*" cries my sister, squatting in a dismayed purple heap on the floor, for the moment utterly oblivious of nervousness, swansdown, or even of the aptness of velvet to crease unless sat upon straight. "They are all come; everybody is dressed; most of them are already at the church; the bishop has been there half an hour."

I shake my head. "It cannot be helped."

"And the breakfast!" cries Mrs. Prodgers, as a fresh and worse aspect of the calamity presents itself to her mind. "Of course, the cold things do not matter; they will be as good to-morrow or the day after as to-day; but the soups, the *entrées!*"

I stifle a sigh. "There is no good in talking of it," I say, with forced philosophy. "You had better go at once and send them all away; there is no use in keeping them waiting in the cold. Charlie, too" (with an accent of compassion); "poor boy! what a bitter disappointment it will be to him!"

"As to that," says Sophia, with a slight relapse into the preening and Pouter-pigeon mood, "I do not suppose that a day's delay will kill him; men are often not sorry for a little reprieve in these cases. I am sure no one can feel more thoroughly upset than I do; if I were to follow my own inclinations, I should sit down and have a good cry."

"Do not follow them, then," I say, brusquely; "or, at least, send the guests away *first*, and cry as much as you please afterward."

By the aid of Louise, and with many appeals on her part to the French God, skies, and Virgin, I, heavily and with difficulty, lift Lenore on to the bed. Hours have passed, the doctor has come, Sylvia has resumed her black gown and giant rosary, the last carriage has rolled away with snowy wheels, before Lenore lifts the quivering white of her lids, and looks round upon us languidly, one after another. There are only three of us—the elderly doctor, to whom, from our earliest infancy, we have been in the habit of exhibiting our tongues and pulses; I, who am nobody; and, thirdly, a poor young man in a smart blue coat, with a kind, miserable, beautiful face, who has spent the last three hours and a half in clasping and kissing a limp, white hand, which, had its owner been possessed of consciousness, would hardly have lain with such passive weakness in his fond grasp. As her eyes open, he springs up joyfully to his feet, and bends over her. I do the same. With a faint gesture of distaste she turns away from him to me, and speaks in a weak whisper:

"I—I—I am at home, am I not?"

"*At home?* Yes, to be sure."

"I—I—I am not *married?*"

"No; not yet."

"I am so glad!"

Soon afterward she relapses into unconsciousness. All that day, and most of the following night, she lies like a plucked snow-drop in January's sleety lap, reviving from one swoon only to fall into another. Toward midnight she grows better, and sinks into a natural and healthy sleep.

"I wish you would change your clothes," I say to Charlie, in a whisper, as we stand staring at her with shaded light; "they look such a mockery" (touching the fine blue broadcloth). "Your poor bouquet, too."

"Not a very good omen, is it?" he says, with a melancholy smile, lifting with his finger the drooped and yellowed head of his gardenia. "Bah! who cares for omens? Only old women?"

"Only old women," repeat I, mechanically.

"She was not well *last night*," he continues, eagerly,

"was she? I told you she was not; it accounts for her talking so oddly, does not it? It shows" (peering anxiously into my face) "that she did not *mean* any of the things she said, does not it?"

I say "Of course," in a constrained voice, and try to turn away.

"Stay," he says, laying his broad hand on my shoulder, "do not go; I want to talk to you. I say, she was not quite herself when she woke up first, was she?—did not know what she was saying—*meant* nothing?"

I know that I am lying, but I answer: "Oh, dear, no! of course not!"

"Was it my fancy?" continues he, with a painful red spreading even to his forehead; "one gets odd notions—and these damned candles" (striking one viciously with his fore-finger) "cast such deceptive shadows — but it seemed to me, Jemima, that she turned away from me—as if—she had rather not look at me. Did not she like my being here, do you think? She is so—so—*maidenly;* she thought I ought to have stayed outside?"

"Nonsense," say I, shortly. "It is evident that you have never fainted; you do not understand how slow people's wits are in coming back. I do not suppose that she knew you from me, or me from the doctor."

He does not answer. I can hardly expect my logic to be very convincing, seeing that it has not convinced myself.

"Riley is not in the least surprised at this," I say, nodding slightly toward our patient. "When I told him about her not eating and not sleeping—it is my belief that she has not closed an eye for the last fortnight—he said that the only wonder was, that it had not happened before."

"Jemima," says the young fellow, turning me unceremoniously round so as to face him, while his eyes, in their searching truth, go through mine like swords; "tell me— I wish to know—what is it that has taken away her sleep and her appetite ? Is it *I ?* "

It is not, as I am well aware, but I maintain a stupid silence.

" Do not answer me," he says, with a sudden change of mood, pushing me away from him. " I do not want an answer; it was an idiotic question; this fuss and bustle have been too much for her, have not they ? and the hard weather has tried her. She will be all right again when once we get quietly off, will not she ? Jemima—I say, Jemima—do you think there is a chance of our being able to have it to-morrow ? "

I shake my head. " I doubt it."

" The day after, then ? " (very wistfully).

I have not the assurance to say " Yes," and I have not the heart to say " No; " so I say, " We will see."

CHAPTER XIX.

WHAT THE AUTHOR SAYS.

ALL the next day Lenore lies in bed, weak and white— it does not take much to pull her down—and, for the most part, silent. She asks for no one; expresses neither re-grets nor self-congratulations on the subject of her defer-red wedding—lies with her face, gentle and innocent as any saintly martyr's—what falsehoods faces do tell !—on the pillow, crowned by a bright, brown glory of hair—an aureole given her by Nature, not martyrdom. She is not ill, neither well; very still, and only turning restive under doses of brandied beef-tea, repeated *ad nauseam*. There are few of the minor diseases that are worse than beef-tea and brandy. The following day passes in much the same way; but, on the third morning, Jemima enters cheerfully:

"Riley says you may get up."

The communication does not seem to afford much satisfaction to the person to whom it is addressed. She turns her face away with a pettish jerk, and hides it in the pillow.

"He says you may dress and come down as soon as you like."

"*As soon as I like?*" repeats Lenore, ironically; "that would be a long time off. Why may not I stay here?"—(stretching out her arms lazily). "I am happy. I like to lie here all day long; the noises of the house seem so far off, and your footsteps outside sound so gently. I like to listen to the clocks, one after another, and count them as they strike. I feel nothing—I think of nothing. I have not been so happy for years."

"He says that staying in bed is very weakening."

"Then I like being weakened."

"Nonsense! Please talk like a rational being."

Never was toilet more slowly made than Lenore's—partly from weakness—for her illness, though brief, has told upon her; partly from a deep and innate unwillingness to return to the well and work-a-day world. At length there is no evading the fact that she is fully dressed; not only fully dressed, but established in an arm-chair before Sylvia's boudoir-fire: a banner-screen between her face and the flame; novels, work-boxes, point-lace, a pug—every thing that is necessary to make a rational woman's happiness—within easy reach of her hands. There is one other addition, without which, many rational women think happiness incomplete—a lover; and even he is not far off.

As a man's heavy step sounds muffled along the carpeted passage, as a man's fingers close on the door-handle, Lenore turns her head resolutely to the other side—like a child averting its face from the inevitable rhubarb and magnesia —and rests her cheek on the back of her chair.

He enters softly, and, afraid even of breathing over noisily, imagining she is asleep, stoops his waved gold head over her. He is soon undeceived.

"I wish," she says, in a most wide-awake voice, opening her beautiful, petulant eyes full upon him, "that you would not come creeping in, in that creaky, tiptoe way; nothing in the world fidgets me so much."

He starts upright again in a hurry.

"It was a stupid trick," he says, humbly, and then stops suddenly, afraid of rousing livelier wrath by further speech. As for her, she rolls her pretty, pettish head from side to side, and affects not to see him. He grows tired, at last, of standing with his back to the mantel-shelf, silent, and says, with eager tenderness, but in a rather frightened voice:

"You are better?"

"Yes, I am better," she answers, quickly; "at least, so they say; but I am still far from well—very far; it will be long enough before I am strong again, and—and—and up to any thing."

- "Riley says that there is nothing like—like *change of air*" (reddening guiltily).

"Riley is an old woman!" (reddening too).

"Lenore!" throwing himself down on his knees, on the rug beside her, and, in so doing, giving an unconscious buffet to the pug's black face, who forthwith departs howling, unheeded, and with his tail uncurled. "Lenore! why need we have half the county to see us married? Why need we put on smart clothes? Why cannot you come

quietly to church with me to-morrow, in your common bonnet and shawl" (Scrope is unaware that shawls are, for the
moment, extinct), "with only the clerk to say 'Amen?'"

"Where is the hurry?" she asks, tapping her foot
impatiently on the fender. "You talk as if we were two
old people, each with a leg in the grave. Supposing that
we put it off for a year, we should still probably have fifty
to gape opposite each other in."

"Even if we were sure of the fifty," he says, gently,
"I should still grudge the one; can one be *too long* happy? I never heard any one complain of being so."

"Do you like sickly women?" she says, abruptly, apparently half softened by his tone, and looking amicably at
him. "I think I am radically sickly—see how half a day
has pulled me down—my elbows stick out like promon-
tories" (pulling up her sleeve to show him)—"if you
married me you would have to be always *cosseting* me—
trundling me about in a bath-chair, and measuring out
physic in a spoon for me."

He is about to burst into a storm of protestations, but
she interrupts him.

"Do you know what Jemima said, that day, when I told
her I was going to marry you?"

"No."

"Well, she said it was *indecently* soon."

"I do not see what business it was of Jemima's," says
the young man, looking rather surly.

"Neither do I; but all the same it is true—*indecently*
soon—that is the very word that expresses it." As she
speaks, her face becomes spread with a hot blush, and his
own is not slow to repeat it in the deeper colors of manhood.

"What does this mean?" he asks, rising to his feet,
while a look of utter fear makes the red in his cheeks give

way. "What is this the preface to? Is it *indecently* sooner than it was yesterday, or the day before, or the day before that?"

"Do not be angry," she says, deprecatingly, stretching out her hand on which his own diamonds are flashing. "You know you are always reasonable—you always mind what I say, even when it is not reasonable; that is why I like you."

There is something of the turkey-cock about every woman; gobbling and swelling if a man is frightened and runs; small and silent if he stands still and cries "Shoo!" It is his turn now; there is no use in gobbling at him; he affects not to see her hand, and only says briefly, "Go on."

"You know," she says, sitting upright in her chair and straining her neck backward, so that her eyes may attain his face and watch it, "that I proposed to you—it is not a sort of thing that a man would be likely to forget. I try to think of it as little as possible, but it is true; and you accepted me; I suppose" (laughing awkwardly) "that you could not well have been so uncivil as to do otherwise."

"Go on."

"Well" (fidgeting uneasily), "I mean to marry you still —*fully*—but—but—it must be—not just yet—not now; a year—six months hence, perhaps—instead."

Unwilling to witness the effect of her words, she has dropped her eyes at the last clause; but, as the moments pass, and no sound comes, save that of a cinder falling from the grate, she looks up again.

"Have you no tongue?" she says, irritably; "are you *never* going to speak?"

"*A year hence!*" he says, in a low voice, turning a face, white as the face of the uncolored dead, toward her. "That means *never*. Thank you for leading me so gently

15

up to it.   Do you think I do not see what you are aiming
at ?   Do you think I have not watched it coming during
the last fortnight ?   I have prayed not to see " (striking
his hands together).   "I have entreated God to let me be
blind always.   Good God !" (flinging his arms down on
the chimney-piece, and hiding his face on them) " how do
men bear these things ?   Who can teach me ?"

"Bear what ? " she cries, rising hastily to her feet and
putting her hand on his coat-sleeve.   "What are you talking about ?   What is there to bear ?"

"So you have been tricking me all this time, have
you ? " he says, raising his ruffled head and looking deliberately at her, with a resentful calm in face and voice.
"At least, it can hardly be called trickery: it was so
lamely done, a child might have seen through the deception.

Silence.

"Of course you know best " (in the same polite, cold
tone) ; " but would it not have been simpler, and come to
much the same thing in the end, to have left me alone in
the first instance ?"

Left him alone! The very question, in almost the
same words, that Paul had once asked.

"I had gone clean away," he continues, in the same re-
pressed and sedulously quiet voice.   "Your polite speeches
had effectually rid you of me.   A man would not willingly
listen *twice* to some of the compliments you paid me at
that ball.   I had no intention of coming back; why did
you send for me ?"

Still no answer, no attempted defence.

"I can at least " (with a bitter smile, that sits ill on
his fair, smooth face) " pay you the compliment of saying
that you are not a *good* liar.   You are not apt at the trade ;
you bungle.   Every day, and fifty times a day, your *mouth*

has said to me, 'I like you—you are a good fellow—we shall be happy together;' and every day, and fifty times a day, your eyes and every movement of your body have said, 'I *loathe* you. I can hardly bring myself to speak civilly to you.'"

Still silence.

"Did it ever occur to you" (taking her by both slender wrists) "to make a rough calculation of how many falsehoods you have told me during this last month?"

"Stop!" she cries, wrenching away her hands from his grasp, which has more of the jailer than the lover in it. "Stop! you are very bitter to me—very. I can hardly believe that it is you; but you speak truth. I *have* told you many, many lies, but at least I have told them to myself too. I have said them over and over again, in the hope that they would come true at last."

He smiles a dry smile of utter incredulity.

"That was very probable."

"You do not believe me?" she says, passionately. "Well, *I take God to witness*—you will hardly disbelieve me now—that ever since that day in the library, when I thrust myself so immodestly on you" (she is crimsoner than any closed daisy's petals at the words), "I have longed and striven with all my heart and soul and strength to—to—care for you—as—as—you wish to be cared for."

"Well?"

"I have said over and over to myself all your good qualities, like a lesson. I have tried" (her face contracts with an agony of shame) "to wrench away all the love I ever had to give from—the—the person who once had it, and to give it to you instead."

"Well?"

"Sometimes, when I was away from you, I thought I had succeeded; but when you came near me, when you

touched me, good and kind and handsome as you are—"
She stops abruptly.

"Go on," he says, in a hoarse whisper. "Do not let
any consideration for my feeling stop you; it would not
be *you* if you did—*good and kind and handsome as I
am*—" (ironically repeating her words).

"It was too soon—too soon!" she cries, clasping her
hands in deep excitement, while the large scalding tears
drop hotly over her cheeks. "Jemima was right—it was
indecently soon. In the grief and shame of being so treated, I wonder, Charlie" (smiling painfully) "that you are
so anxious to marry a *jilted* woman. I thought I could forget all in a minute, but I cannot; nobody could. If I were
to go away to-day, and throw you over forever, could *you*
forget *me* all in a minute?"

"I would try my best," he says, with a fierce white
smile. "Perhaps it would be more correct to say, 'I *will*
try my best.'"

"Do you think I do not *wish* to forget?" she says,
taking his hand of her own accord, while her wet eyes
gaze wistfully upward, into the deep, angry blue of his.
"Do you think I remember *on purpose?* Does one *enjoy*
not sleeping and not eating, and being in miserable, uneasy pain all day and all night?"

He keeps silence.

"I am no great prize at the best of times," she says,
half sobbing. "My sisters—all my people—will tell you
that; but what sort of woman should I have been if I
could have jumped straight out of one man's arms into another's, quite easily and comfortably, without feeling any
shame? It was bad enough to be able to do it at all. O
Charlie! Charlie! knowing what you did about me, how
could you think me worth taking? How could you take
me?"

" *How could I take you ?* " he says, with a harsh, low
laugh, as unlike the jocund sound of his usual boyish mirth
as possible. " Do not you know that, when a man is *starving*, he is not particular as to having a *whole* loaf ? He
says 'thank you' even for *crumbs*. I tell you, Lenore,
that morning in Ireland, when I got your note, I had as
little hope of ever holding you in my arms as my wife, as I
had of holding one of God's angels. When I found that
there was a chance of my so holding you, judge whether I
was likely to throw it away."

He has put oné of his hands on each of her shoulders,
and stands gazing steadfastly at her, with a bitter yearning in his eyes.

" I knew that your *soul* was out of my reach," he continues, sadly ; " that I should get only your body, and
even *that* shrank away from me. Shall I ever forget those
first two kisses that you gave me—that I *made* you give
me ? They were colder than ice."

A little pause. The fire-flame quivers and talks to
itself ; the pug plucks up heart again, and, returning, lies
down, with his nose resting on his bowed forelegs.

" I suppose it is all for the best," says Scrope, presently, with a forced smile ; " at least, it is as well to say so,
is not it ? I was so idiotically fond of you that, if you had
been decently civil to me, I suppose I should have been
happier than any man can be and live."

No answer.

" Do you know," he resumes, in a tone of deep and
sombre excitement, " what has kept me up all this month,
what has hindered me from cutting my own throat or yours
—it was a toss-up which—what has made me smile and
seem pleased at words that *bit* and looks that *stung ?*
Well, I will tell you—listen, and laugh if it amuses you ;
it is true, all the same. I *knew* " (lifting his hands from

her shoulders, and framing her drooped face with them)—
"I *knew* that, if once I could get you all to myself, I could
make you love me; you would do your best to thwart and
hinder me, but I could *make* you. Lenore, I know it
still."

"Do you?" she says, sadly. "I wish you could; but I
doubt it."

"Tell me," cries the young fellow, emboldened by her
gentleness to take her once more in his arms, as if she were
his own—"it will do me no good to hear—be tantalizing,
rather—but still I think it would ease my pain a little—
tell me, if you had met me *first*—met me before you came
across *him*—do you think you could have liked me a little
then? Say 'yes,' if you can, Lenore" (with a suffering
accent of entreaty).

"How do I know?" she says, sharply, for once not
shrinking from his contact—not struggling in his embrace,
but rather coldly taking it for granted. "What is the good
of looking back? It seems to me now that, if I had not
met *him*, I should have gone on always, as I had gone on
before, laughing and amusing myself, and being happy in
my way, and not loving anybody *much*. I never was one
to fall in love *easily*—never!" (drawing herself up with a
little movement of pride).

"You fell in love with *him* easily enough," says Scrope,
roughly.

"Yes," she answers, almost humbly, though her face
flames, "you are right, so I did; it was a boast I had no
right to make."

"What on earth made you do it?"

"How can I tell? Perversity, I think; I always was
perverse from a child; they said I should pay for it, sooner
or later. I think I have now, have not I?" (smiling drear-
ily). A moment's pause. "Other people cared for me of

their own accord," she continues, sighing; "as for him, al-most every word I said *grated* upon him; I had to fight and battle even for his toleration."

" And *that pleased* you ? "

" Does one ever care for the things that one can stretch out one's hand and take ? " she asks, bitterly. " I do not, neither do you—that is evident, or you would not be here." After a little pause : "He thought very meanly of me from the first—very. He almost told me so in so many words, and I—I—well—I only meant to make him alter his mind; that was how it began. Bah ! " (breaking off suddenly, with a tempest of angry pain in her voice), "what does it matter how it began ? Is not it enough that it *did* begin, that it went on, and that now it is *ended ?* "

At the last word her raised voice sinks down, and dies in a sob. His hold upon her grows lax, he gives a long sigh of astonished, indignant grief.

" If that was the way to your heart," he says, with a sort of scorn, "no wonder I missed it." Silence. " Merci-ful Heavens ! " cries the young man, smiting his hands to-gether in a sort of wondering frenzy, " did one ever hear the like ? Must one hold you cheap, and have the ill man-ners to tell you so; must one cut you to the heart with frosty looks and words that *stab* like your own; must one love you tardily and leave you readily, before you will give one your affection? If so, Lenore, I tell you candidly that —stark, staring mad about you as I have been for the last six months—I tell you candidly that I had rather be with-out it."

" You are right," she says, coldly; " it is not worth having. After all, you agree with him; *he* thought it was not worth having, and so threw it away."

The moments flash past; the little moments, that tarry not to listen to brisk wedding chimes, or the slow passing-

bell. The two young people still stand opposite one another, each buried in thoughts, whereof it would be hard
to say whose share was the bitterer. Scrope is the first to
break the silence that has fallen on them.

"Tell me, Lenore," he says, breaking out into impetuous speech, "you have said so many disagreeable things to
me in your time, that *one* more will not matter; yes, tell
me—I will promise not to burst out into violence; I will
even try to look *pleased*" (smiling sardonically); is there
—is there—any talk of *his* coming back? Have you any
hope of it, that you are getting rid of me so quickly,
all of a sudden?"

"What do you mean?" she says, harshly, with a shrinking shiver, as if one had torn open a great gaping wound in
her tender body. "Do you think that if I had had any hope
I should have sent for *you*? He is not one to speak lightly,
to say one thing to-day and another to-morrow; I should
wear out my ears with listening before I heard the wheels of
his carriage coming back. No, no!" (with a low, sobbing
sigh), "I have no hope. It is humiliating to speak of hope
in such a case, is not it? I suppose I should not, if I had
any spirit."

"If you have really done with him *forever*, then," says
the young man, in a voice which is still half doubting, "Lenore—I do not want to be glad at what makes you sorry;
but how can I help it?—then, for God's sake, come to me;
what is there to stand between us? I *know* I can make
you forget him; even to-day—perhaps you will laugh at
me for saying so—you seem to hate me a shade less than
you did. O beloved, out of the great harvest of love that
you lavished on him—him who did not take it, who hardly
stooped to pick it up, who tossed it carelessly back to you
—have not you saved *one grain* for me, who have been
hungry and famished so long?"

There are tears in his shaken voice, though none in his eyes ; and indeed a man who *weeps* in wooing mostly damns himself. In a hairy, blubbered face there must always be less of the moving than the ridiculous.

"Say ' yes,' " he cries, with a passionate agony of pleading, twining both his arms once more about her. " I will hold you here until you say it. I will let no sound but ' yes ' pass those lips that have never yet given me a kind word or a kiss worth the taking."

" What am I to say ' yes ' to ? " she asks, holding aloof from him, as much as may be, with the old gesture of shrinking distaste. " Am I to say that I will marry you ? Well, I said that a month ago ; that is settled. Why must we go over all the old story again ? "

" But *do* we mean the same thing ? " asks Scrope, with distrustful vehemence. " That is the question. Will you marry me *now—at once*, without any senseless, causeless delay ? "

She has drawn herself away from him, and now turns, and, walking to the window, looks blankly out on the drear, white snow world—on the long, sharp icicles hanging from the leaves.

"Speak," he says, his voice sharpened and roughened, following her to the other side of the room. " I am waiting—I will wait on you as long as you please ; but if I keep you here to the Judgment-Day I will not go unanswered ! Will you marry me *to-morrow ?*—great Heavens ! if it had not been for this unhappy *contre-temps*, by to-morrow you would have been four days my wife !—or will you not ? "

She is trembling all over, and her cold, white face is twitched with pain, and wet with unwiped tears.

" Not *to-morrow !* " she says, with an involuntary shudder ; " not so soon—not quite so soon. Let me have time to draw my breath! I am not well; as I live, I am not well. See how thin I have grown" (holding out one hand, on which the wandering veins and the small bones indicate their places more clearly than they did last year). "I, who" (smiling) "used to be so afraid of growing too fat! I do not think I need be afraid of that now, need I? Let me get quite well—quite strong first. I shall be better worth your taking, then."

"Lenore!" cries the young man, seizing her by the arm, in an access of sudden and uncontrollable passion, "did you ever in all your life think of any one but yourself? What business have you to spoil my life for me? What business have you to make me a laughing-stock for everybody?—tell me that!"

"I have no business—none," she answers, drooping her long neck and sobbing.

"Will you marry me *to-morrow*, Lenore?" (speaking with the stern quiet of self-constraint).

"Not to-morrow—not to-morrow," she answers, mildly, turning her head restlessly from side to side. "I meant really to have married you on Tuesday—you cannot doubt that? Had I not my wedding-dress on? But see how ill the thought has made me. Give me six months. In six months I shall get used to the idea; perhaps I shall get the better of my temper. Six months is a long time; things that happened six months ago seem a long way off" (her eyes straying dreamily out to the still, white trees, and the square church-tower).

"I see how it is," he says, fiercely; "I have been very patient with you, and you think I shall be patient always. You are mistaken; I am sick of patience; I have done with it. I will marry you *now* or *never*."

At his words, her swimming eyes flash, and the wet carnation flowers hotly on her cheeks.

"Do you wish," she cries, violently, "for a wife who hates your touch?—who dreads being left alone with you? —who never hears your footstep without longing to fly out of sight—out of ear-shot of you? If you do, you have odd taste!"

He clinches his hands, and his teeth close hard on his under lip, but he does not trust himself to speak.

"Is not it my own interest to be fond of you—to marry you?" she continues, in strong excitement. "Are not you rich and prosperous? and have not I all my life been in love with ease, and wealth, and pleasure? Is it from choice that I wake all night? I am sick of being unhappy, and fretting, and hating everybody. God knows I would be happy if I could! Be patient a little longer—only a little."

But he only answers, "*Now* or *never.*"

"Well, then, it must be *never!*" she answers, vehemently—"there—you have said it yourself; it is *your* doing, not mine. It is *you* who have thrown *me* over—not *I* you."

"Very well," he answers, in a husky whisper, hastily averting his face, to hinder her from seeing the havoc that despair is working on its beauty; "you are right—it shall be *never!*"

Utter silence for a space—silence as deep as if they had been dead.

"Lenore," he says, at length, turning toward her for the last time his clay-white glance and the indignant agony of his eyes, "you make one say ugly things to you. Were you ever any thing but a curse to any one that you had to do with? You have cursed full six months of my life, but you shall curse no more of it: I *will* do without you. There is no lesson so hard that one cannot learn it in time, and I will."

She is silent.

"Even for a good woman, who had loved one, and whom one had lost by death, one would not mourn forever," he continues, in the same rough, unsteady whisper; "how much less for you, who have never given me any thing but unladylike insults—unwomanly gibes! Goodbye, Lenore! Yes, good-bye! But, before I go, give me one kiss—one *real* kiss. Since they were to have been *all* mine, spare me one!"

So speaking he stoops, and, for an instant, lays his lips upon her unwilling mouth. Then he goes. Thus she is rid of *all* her lovers.

NIGHT.

"Good-night, good sleep, good rest from sorrow,
To these that shall not have good morrow;
Ye gods, be gentle to all these,
Nay, if death be not, how shall they be?
Nay, is there help in heaven? it may be
All things and lords of things shall cease."

CHAPTER I.

WHAT THE AUTHOR SAYS.

AFTER Life's little hot day, comes Death's long, cool night; whether of the two is the pleasanter? Well, we shall know anon. Oh! patient friends, you have come with me so far, come with me yet a little farther. I will not keep you long. Already the shadows sketch themselves; the faint-colored even cometh. Summer is here again—early summer, early June, as when first, O reader, you and I met and panted together through the " endless days," when even night brought not darkness. Down in England, the meadows have a lilac tinge over them, from the ripe, heavy-headed grasses, and the horse-chestnut flowers' spikes have changed into little prickly green balls. But we are not in England, O reader, you and I; we are in Switzerland, in the high cold valley of the Engadine.

WHAT JEMIMA SAYS.

We are at the end of our day's journey, have stiffly descended from the huge dusty carriage in which we have crampedly sat all the long and shining day. To-morrow we shall reach our final destination, Pontresina. Meanwhile here we are, up among the mountains, the torrents, the pines, at this loveliest village of Bergun. An hour has passed since our arrival, and we have dined, if you can apply that sacred word to the empty form of tapping with our knives a black-boned chicken's skeleton, and sipping a nauseous wine of the country, black as Tartarus, and with a flavor that is agreeably compounded of pills, slate-pencil, and ink. There is no denying—degrading as it is to the supremacy of mind over body—that a bad dinner has a depressing effect. Not one of us three but feels cross and empty. Sylvia tries to sit upon a hard-bottomed, straight-backed chair, as if it were one of her own padded easy ones, and fails. Lenore stalks to the window and looks over the balcony. I think that people grow after they are thought grown up, oftener than is usually supposed. Lenore has certainly grown within the last six months, or perhaps it is only her loss of flesh that gives her such a tall look. She used to have a good deal of the shapely solidity that constitutes a person's claim to be a fine woman—rather a butcher's term of commendation, at best —shapely she must always be, but *fine* she is no longer ; only very slender and willowy. I pick up the visitor's book, read the dreary waggeries, the lame rhymes, the consequential commendations of bed and board. I come to the last entry :

" Mr. Tompkins, London.
" Mrs. Tompkins,   "
" Miss Tompkins,   "
" Miss L. Tompkins, "
" Mr. J. T. Tompkins,"
" Miss Harris,   "

" Exceedingly pleased with the accommodation at this

hotel—the attendance excellent, rooms most clean, and food better than at any other hotel in the Engadine."

I read this aloud.

"There is a prospect for us!"

"You are not serious?" cries Sylvia, starting upright in her chair, and opening eyes as round as marbles in unaffected dismay. "That is not *really* there! You are only joking!"

"Read for yourself," I answer, handing the book to her, while I joined our junior in the window. Well, one must send all appetite to one's eyes; there is at least plenty of food for them. The pearly evening sky, cut by the cold lilac peaks; the mountains, that wear always round their waist and feet a girdle of great pines; a sombre army—rising, pointed top above pointed top, in their endless, fadeless green; the rough torrent-course, that furrows the hill's face, like the traces of a tearful agony; an evening glimmer of meadow-flowers; a flash of bright water. And right under us the little village street, the deep-roofed low houses, the tiny casements, out of which the lavish pinks and flowered picotees are hanging; the queer sententious inscription on the *chalet* nearest us:

"Das Haus stet in Gottes Hand,
Jan Peder Grigori
Bin Ich genand."

And is not that Jan Peder himself, sitting outside, on a log of wood? He is old and withered, and very much the worse for wear.

Insensibly I begin to forget the void feeling that ruffled my temper five minutes ago, as I listen to the soothing drip, drip, of the two-spouted pump, that is always pouring into a wooden trough. The pump seems to be the rendezvous of the village; the leisurely chatter, in this odd mongrel Romansch tongue, rises soft and subdued to our ears. A tinkling of slow bells, as a herd of lovely, smoke-colored cows come slowly treading down the street, and stoop their sleek necks to drink. If one could see the inside of these folks' lives no doubt one would find that they were as basely grovelling as those of our own lower orders —lives probably lightened only by garlic and beer; but looking now at the outside of them, on this quiet purple evening, it seems as if one had come upon a little sudden patch of old-world innocent Arcadia.

"I wish that Jan Peder Grigori would go in-doors," says Lenore, gravely; "it must be very bad for him, being out so late."

"There must be some one here besides us," I say, leaning over the balcony, and pointing to a second and smaller dusty carriage, drawn up behind our great lumbering ark.

"A man, too," says Lenore, with lazy interest, "if a portmanteau be a sufficient proof of masculinity."

"It is such a bran-new one, too;" continue I, laughing, "that he must be either a just-married man, or a man just about to be married."

"Who was it said that a new flannel petticoat was an infallible sign of a bride?" asks Lenore, languidly. "Does the same hold good of men and portmanteaus? I wish we could see his initials, but the hat-box hides them."

"Now that I think of it," I say, meditatively, "I have a vision of having seen vestiges of food on that table in the corner; let us make Kolb find out who he is, for, by his luggage, I feel sure that he is an Englishman."

I am right. An Englishman he is, name unknown; he has come down from St. Moritz, and is on his homeward road; he is to set off at cock-crow to-morrow, and he went out walking only five minutes before our arrival. This is all the information we obtain, all the food we get to keep alive our faint and flagging interest.

"Do you mean to stay fustily in-doors all evening?" asks Lenore, presently, with a yawn, "because I do not. I am sick of Jan Peder, and the pump, and the goats; I shall go and *explore*, like Mrs. Elton in ' Emma.'"

"Do not!" cry I, hastily, and dissuasively. "You know that going out when the dew is falling always brings on your cough."

"Pooh!" replies she, lightly. "What matter if it does? I am going to set up such a stock of strength at Pontresina that it would be a thousand pities not to be a little worse before I get there."

"At least put on your—" I begin, but she interrupts me.

"Did you ever know me to take advice in all your life?" she asks, with a petulant gesture. "I should not wonder if I met our unknown friend of the new portmanteau; I am not sure that I am not going to look for him. *Au revoir !* "

I gaze after her and sigh, with a line of " Elaine " running in my head:

"Being so very wilful, you must go."

CHAPTER II.

" There cannot be a pinch in death more sharp than this is."

WHAT THE AUTHOR SAYS.

AFTER all, she puts a shawl over her head; it is not a very thick one, but neither is the mountain air very keen on this softly-creeping summer night. It is red, and the

old men and the women sitting in the door-ways of the
dark little houses stare at it admiringly.   She passes
among them quickly—past the rickety little wooden bal-
conies, the piles of firewood, the numberless odd little
casements, like windows in a doll's house—it is not *them*
that she wants—till, at a sudden turn, the village is behind
her, out of sight—the laughing, leisurely, chattering village—and the river that she sought is before her. A great,
bold hill-shoulder rises in front of her against the dark
night sky, and beside her the river boils and maddens along
in riotous white play; it is so swift that the eye cannot
follow it; it tosses high its cold spray, and cries exulting-
ly, "O snow! I am as white as you."   Nobody sees her—
she is all alone; even the broad-faced moon has not yet
looked in silver and pearl over the hill.   When one is
alone one does many foolish things.   Lenore throws herself on her knees on a flat stone close to the brink—dashed,
indeed, by the stream's stormy white dust—and speaks out
loud to it:

"O good, kind little river! will you drown memory for
me ?—will you drown Paul ?"

Lenore is not always thinking of Paul; sometimes for
almost a day she forgets him; but, long as it is since he
cast her off, and short as was the time during which she
possessed him, the impulse still holds her, on seeing any
beautiful thing, to say, "I will show it to Paul;" on hearing any witty thing, "I will tell it to Paul."   Paul was a
cross fellow, cruel and cold, as she sometimes tells herself;
but he would have loved this mad river, biting and raven-
ing with fierce foam-teeth against the dark bowlders that
lie in its bed, and crying violently to them, "Let me
pass!"   If he were here now, among the yellow tree-foil,
his arm round her waist and her head on his shoulder!—
they two standing, in dumb ecstasy, with only the larches

waving their green plumes above their heads, and the water's endless, restless roar, that ceases not day nor night, January nor June, making a loud hubbub at their feet— alone with the river, the mountains, and God! She can almost feel his arm; she turns her eyes to look up into his, but then the dream flies; there are no kind eyes to look into—there is no Paul—none!

She starts up hastily, and hurries on. The gorge narrows; there is only room for her and for the river—the panting fury of the stream. "O river! you take my breath away. Tarry a little; I cannot keep up with you!" But the river makes answer: "I cannot tarry; I have an errand unto the great gray sea." On and on, on and on she saunters, not heeding how far nor whither, until at length she comes to a slight hand-bridge of planks that gives and vibrates beneath her. There she stands and leans over the slender railing, gazing, with eyes that try in vain to keep up with it, at the swirling torrent. The evening is both darkening and lightening: darkening, for the sun is gone farther and farther away; lightening, for the moon is coming—yea, come. Already she had washed the hills' faces with her cool silver flood: now her pearl-white feet have reached—have lightly trodden on the water—the wonderful water! Can it be all the same—the same when it lies in opal sleep, and when it plunges against and angrily smites its drenched rocks? If one had but some one— some dear person—to show it all to!

After crossing the bridge the path she has hitherto followed takes a sharp turning round the spur of a hill, and is immediately lost to sight. As she stands, still leaning over the rickety hand-rail, and watching the moon-colored bubbles, she hears a footstep coming along this unseen path. It is growing late; the moon is rising high; this place is inconceivably lonely. Her first impulse is to turn

and run homeward, but her second contradicts it.   Why
should she stir ?   Bah !   it is probably some innocent rough
peasant, clumping home to bed in his deep-eaved *chalet.*
He will stare at her cloak, and probably give her a Romansch " good-night," to which she will be puzzled to re-
spond ; so she stays.   Nearer and nearer comes the footstep,
and her heart beats a trifle quicker than its wont.   Her
eyes are fixed on the corner which will give to view the
owner of this slow and intermittent tread.   Here he comes,
out of the rock-shadow into the light !   He is not a peasant !   He is—surely, he is an Englishman !   He is—*Paul !*
O God in heaven !   it cannot be !   Men dress so much alike
—there is such a deceptive resemblance between all the
men of a class at a little distance.   He comes a step or two
nearer, then stops and looks upward.   The moon shines
down full and white on his upturned face—the honest,
shrewd face, that is neither gentle nor beautiful.   She sees
his cool calm eyes glitter in the moonbeams.   He is carelessly dressed, without any necktie.   His strong throat
rises bare and muscular, and his hands are buried deep in
the pockets of the old Dinan shooting-jacket.   Do you
think that she faints or topples over into the water, or
screams or laughs hysterically, or calls out loud ?   Not
she !   She only stands still, with one slight hand hard
grasping the hand-rail, and with a heart whose loud pulsa-
tions drown the voice of the triumphant foamy stream,
waiting for her heaven to come to her.   Has Death let her
slip by him, having seen her bitter pain ?   Is she already
in the blessed land ?   Paul is so busy moon-gazing that he
is close to her—his foot is upon the plank—before he perceives her.   Then he jumps almost out of his clothes—out
of his Dinan shooting-jacket—out of his skin.

    " LENORE ! "
She could not have cried " *Paul !* " in answer if you

had offered her all the kingdoms of the world as a bribe. He stoops his tall head till his eager face is close to hers; he stares hard into her eyes; he even stretches out his hand and touches her red cloak to assure himself that she is real. Yes, it is no ghost-woman; it is a real Lenore, with a face much paler, indeed, than the Lenore he remembers—a face grave with the gravity of intense emotion, touched with the trouble of overpowering wonder—that is looking back at him with wide and lovely eyes.

"Great Heaven! who would have thought of seeing *you* here?"

In the accents of intense surprise it is difficult to ascertain the presence or absence of joy or sorrow. One would be puzzled to say whether Paul was very glad or very grieved at this meeting at the world's end with his old love.

"Lenore!—*is it Lenore?*" (again narrowly scanning her white and quivering face). "How, in the name of wonder, did you come here?"

It is stupid to be so tongueless, is not it? standing dumb, with hanging head, like a child playing at being shy. But she seems to have lost the art of framing words.

"Will you not speak to me?" he continues, with an eager hesitation, mistaking the cause of her speechlessness; "will you not shake hands with me?"

She puts out her hand in a moment: does he feel how it is shaking as it lies in his cool clasp?

"You—you—are not *alone* here?" involuntarily glancing at her left hand). "You are with—with—"

"No, I am not alone," she answers, speaking every word very slowly and carefully, as if not quite sure whether the right words would come; "Jemima and Sylvia—"

"*Jemima!*" he says, pronouncing the word, with a

lingering emphasis, as if it carried him back into memory, and smiling rather pensively.

Both are silent for a few moments—only two voices are heard: the river's loud hoarse one, as it keeps calling always to the rocks and the dumb green pines, and the grasshopper's sharp and shrill—and infinitely content. If it could but last forever! They two standing on that narrow bridge, on a sheet of silver, the river—all silver, too—tearing and roaring below them; the larches softly tossing their small green feathers; the unsleeping grasshopper singing his pleasant song; and they two looking kindly into each other's eyes. But when could one ever say to any happy moment, as Joshua said to the docile sun, "Stand thou still?" He will not stand still; he could not if he would; he is jostled away by his pushing younger brothers.

"How often I have wondered whether I should ever meet you again!" says Paul, presently, with a long sigh; "after all, the world is small—and if I did, where and how? Certainly, this is the last place that ever would have entered my head; and yet, only five minutes ago I was thinking of you."

"Were you?" she says, softly, while her eyes shine gently back at him, like beautifulest dew-wet flowers through happy tears!

"You have forgiven me?" he says, anxiously catching hold of her other hand, and holding both in the same loose friendly clasp in which he had before held the one. "We are friends, are not we? At peace?"

She has no hands to hide her face; she cannot hinder him from seeing how her drooped eyes brim over—how the heavy great tears are rolling down over her smart scarlet cloak. In the tender gentleness of her small wet face there is not much war.

"Do not cry," he says, looking surprised and miserable, as a man always does, when a woman unexpectedly weeps. "What is there to cry about? I am not" (smiling rather awkwardly) "going to scold you this time. You know I always was a good hand at lecturing, was not I? Often and often since I have wished that I had not been quite such a good one. . . . I can hardly believe that it *is* you," he says, after a pause, again interrupting the river's and the grasshoppers' duet. "What have you been doing to yourself? Somehow you are different. You are too old to grow, I suppose; people do not grow at nineteen; but —but—surely you are thinner than you used to be! Have you been ill? Are you ill now?"

"Not very," she answers, lightly; "anybody else would have made a trifle of it, but you know I always make the most of things, and I have not much of a constitution—so they tell me."

He does not ask any other question for the moment.

"For my part, I am glad," she continues, with a restless laugh. "I never could see what use a good constitution was to any one, except to make them suffer more, and die harder when their time came."

"I suppose you have been threatening to break a blood-vessel again," he says, with a smiling allusion to what she had told him on one of the earliest days of their acquaintance. "Good God! can that be only a year ago?"

"Only a year!" she echoes, dreamily. "But a year is a long time."

"You are pale, too," he says, proceeding with his scrutiny; "are you always pale now? The only time that I remember you as pale as you are now was that night when I upset you into the Rance! How wet you were! How the water dripped from your long hair! I did not believe till then that women really *had* such long hair. I can see you now!" His gray eyes look kind and almost wistful as he thus travels back into the pretty dead past.

"Can you?" she says, almost inaudibly.

"It was all a mistake, I suppose," he continues, sighing, "a blunder—a bungle—but it was pleasant while it lasted, was not it?"

She cannot speak for tears.

"Lenore," he says, after another silence, in a tone of stronger excitement than any that he has yet used, "I am going to tell you something. Often and often I have wondered whether I should ever have the chance of telling you. Sometimes I have wished that I should, and sometimes I have hoped that I should not. It does not much matter what you think of me now, one way or another, but I do not think that it will improve your opinion of either my wisdom or my humility. Do you remember that last letter you sent me?"

She is not pale now; he cannot accuse her of it. No rose in any midsummer garden was ever so red; and her streaming eyes flash in the mild moonlight with the old angry spirit. Is he going to twit her with that poor little overture that miscarried so piteously?

"I did not believe in it," he goes on, still in hot excitement. "I was sore and mad from your galling bitter words. Lenore" (almost entreatingly), "why do you let your tongue cut like a knife? I thought it was only a flirting manœuvre to get me back and make a fool of me a second time. I hate being made a fool of! Nobody had ever taken the trouble to do it before. I hate being trodden upon. I like to walk upright and go my own way."

"Well?"

"You remember the answer I sent—I hope you burnt it—I am not proud of it," reddening through all his sun-

tan. "Well, when it was gone, I read your letter over
again, and, by dint of poring over it line by line, I grew to
think that there was a true ring in it. Lenore, it was very
clever of you! I do not know how you managed to get
that true ring. I began to think of—of—the dear old
time" (his voice, though he is a man, shakes a little). "I
began—you will laugh at me for thinking of such a trifle
at such a moment—to remember the old blue gown and
Huelgoat."

She turns away and leans over the bridge; and, unseen
by him, unseen by any one, her tears hotly drop into the
cold river, and are swallowed by it.

"I recollected things you used to say," he continues,
with a pensive smile, given rather to the past then the
present. "You had such a pretty, fond way of saying
things—well" (dashing his hand across his forehead, and
abruptly changing his tone), "the upshot of it was, that I
resolved to ask you to—to—to—kiss and make friends, in
short—I suppose one may as well word it in that childish
way as any other. I had even" (beginning to laugh
harshly, for one's laughs at one's own expense are rarely
melodious) "got a new pen, squared my elbows, and sat
down to write to you." She is trembling all over, and
panting, as one breathless from a long race.

"Why did not you?—why did not you?" she cries,
with almost a wail.

"*Why did not I?*" he repeats, looking at her with
unfeigned astonishment. "I wonder at your asking that.
Why? Because at that very moment, not a week after
you had composed that triumph of pathos" (with a bitter
sneer), "I heard of your engagement to Scrope. I saw
how much the *true ring* was worth then; I believe I
laughed. There is always something to be thankful for,
and I was heartily thankful that I had not written. There

16

is no use in eating more dirt than one can help in this world, is there ?"

"But I am not engaged now !" she cries, passionately. "I can hardly believe that I ever was really ; people exaggerate things so in the telling. I think it was always more play than earnest."

"*More play than earnest?*" he repeats, in utter and blank astonishment. "Why, I understood that the wedding-day had come—that you were all dressed—and that it was only put off on account of your having been taken suddenly ill !"

"Yes," she answers, incoherently ; "thank God, I was ill, very ill; that was what saved me! Thank God!— Thank God !"

"*Saved* you ?" he repeats, looking at her with unlimited wonder ; "how do you mean ? Surely it was your own doing ? It was only put off, was not it ?—it is still to be ?"

"Never !—never !" she cries, wildly. "Who can have told you such things? It was all a farce from beginning to end; it never was any thing serious. I—I—think I must have been a little off my head."

"And you are not engaged to Scrope ?" (with an accent of extreme surprise).

"Not I," she answers, vehemently ; "do not suggest any thing so dreadful."

"Nor to any one else ?"

"*Any one else!*" she echoes, scornfully. "To whom else should I be ? Must I always be engaged to some one?"

Now that it is all clear between them, now that all clouds of misconception have been swept away, now that they are all alone here in the moonlight, surely he will take her in his arms. Her head will rest on the shoulder of the old jacket, where it has so often confidently lain before. But he only turns away with something like a curse, and says, half under his breath, " God! what lies people tell! " A silence. When next Paul speaks, it is in a constrained and sedulously-governed voice.

" I did not bless either you or him that day, I can tell you—not that *that* did you much harm ; but this was quite at the first, quite. When a thing has sense and justice in it, one soon gives up pricking against it. I have long given up pricking against this ; I have grown so wise " (laughing nervously) " that I acquiesce in it contentedly."

" Do you ? " she says, and her throat seems to have grown suddenly dry, and to send forth only harsh and ugly sounds.

" Perhaps—perhaps you will come round to him yet," says Paul, speaking with a very white face, and a tremor in his deep voice ; " in time, you know ; time does surprising things—things that one would not believe ! You— you might do worse."

A fiery, searing pain goes through her heart.

" You are very good," she says, while the flame of her hot eyes dries her tears ; " but I really do not see what business it is of yours."

" None," he answers, almost humbly ; " none! I beg your pardon for having said it ; but you know you con- sented just now that we should be friends, and friends may take an interest in each other's future, may not they ? "

She does not answer ; she is listening to the grasshop- per—his sharp treble song seems to have grown very dis- mal all of a sudden.

" Lenore," cries the other, impulsively, again catching her small hands, " before we say any thing more, let me tell you—I *must* tell you—about—about my future."

" Well ? "

Her eyes, dry now, achingly dry, are staring back at him, with an unnamed fear.

" My people have been up at St. Moritz," he says, going on rapidly with his story, " so have I, for the last two months ; I am hurrying home now as fast as I can, to get things straight. I am going—perhaps you have heard it already—I am going to be married."

When one receives a mortal blow, sometimes one does not feel much pain at the first—so they tell me ; one is only stunned. I do not think that Lenore feels much pain, only her wits go a wool-gathering. Not for long, however. Even though one is light-headed from extremest agony, one has still the womanly instinct to draw a decent cloak over one's ugly yawning wounds. Not much more than the usual interval between question and answer has elapsed, before some one—some kind spirit, I think, who has crept inside her cold and quivering body—speaks in almost Lenore's voice—speaks with a stiff little smile :

" To your cousin ? "

" Yes, to my cousin."

A little trifling pause, that would not be noticed, so short is it, in any ordinary conversation ; a pause, during which Lenore is fighting more fiercely than ever the typical lioness fought for her whelps—fighting for a voice, for a laugh, for civil careless words ; and he or she who in one of these mortal battles fights strongly, with heart and soul, with decency and self-respect on his or her side, mostly overcomes. Only it takes a great deal of lint to heal the wounds afterward. Lenore overcomes. But the victory is hardly complete ; she cannot let him see her face. She leans over the bridge-side, as she leaned five minutes ago to hide her happy tears ; but there are no tears to hide now.

" The ideal girl ! " she says, with a sort of laugh. " The

woman with eyes like a shot partridge's—rather dull, but very loving ! You see I remember all about her."

Paul does not speak; he also leans over the bridge, and there is not much of the triumphant bridegroom in the eyes that are idly fixed on a pointed rock, gray, and shining with wet moonbeams, which every minute the stream deluges.

"If you remember, I always prophesied it," says the girl, feeling her words come more readily; "only, like Cassandra, nobody believed my prophecies."

" Why did you prophesy it ? " he asks, almost angrily. " There was no sense in such a prophecy—no ground for it. There was not such a thought in any one's head—no, nor ever would have—"

He stops suddenly. She does not speak, only she shakes her head gently. Her wits have come quite back; she has buried the pain in a shallow hole, out of sight, for the moment. When this is over—when he is gone—it will shake off the light covering of its temporary grave, and rise up like a giant. Then again she will have to fight; but now for the moment she has won a most numb quiet.

" Why do you shake your head ? " he asks, abruptly. " Does it mean that you do not believe me ? At least in the old time you used to give me credit for speaking truth —sometimes too much truth to please you; why should I deceive you now ?—*now* that no word that either you or I could speak could bring us one jot nearer each other ? "

Still, she only leans her arms on the rail of the bridge —leans heavily on it—and her drooped head sinks low down.

" When was it that you prophesied it ? " he asks, almost in a whisper, coming nearer her. " Was it at Huelgoat, or at Châteaubriand's tomb, as we stood and watched the waves and the sea-gulls? If you did, I compliment you; you were indeed far-seeing." (No answer.) "I never was one to care violently for anybody—never. The game never seemed to me worth the candle. It does not sound well, but I had always liked myself best; but—somehow I like to say it now, though there is not much sense in it (shake your head as much as you please)—but, before God, I did care for you beyond measure in my way —it was not a very pleasant way—only I tried my best to hide it. I knew your amiable peculiarity of never valuing what you could get; but I *did* love you—I did—I *did!*" (rising into an emphasis and excitement most unlike him as he ends).

"Did you," she says, faintly, a little spark of animation coming into her face and into her dull eyes. "I thought you liked me; afterward they all said you did not."

"Well, I love no one beyond measure now, I suppose," he says hastily, pushing the hair off his forehead with a cross and jerky movement. "My affections are quite within bounds—well in hand" (smiling ironically). "The other was the pleasantest while it lasted, but no doubt this is the healthier state." (Still, silence.) "It is much better as it is," he says presently, speaking vehemently, and as if more with a view to convincing himself than her. "If we had married then, how we should have hated each other by now! Did we ever look at any thing from the same point of view?—and you are not a woman to be shaped to a husband's liking. Good God! how I laughed at that idiot West's notion of *moulding* you! You would not have given in, neither should I. Yes, we should have been miserable."

"Miserable — yes, miserable — *most* miserable," she echoes very slowly and mechanically; but whether she applies the word to the hypothetical case he puts, or to her own actual one, is not clear even to herself.

"You agree with me?" he says, sharply, as if not much gratified by the discovery of her acquiescence. "Of course! I knew you did. Yes, it is better for both of us; specially better for *you*."

"Much better," she says, speaking with an immense effort, and even accomplishing a laugh. "As you say, when did we ever look at any thing from the same point of view, even during the short time we were together?—how short! how short!" (uttering the words in a dragging, dreary way). "Hardly a day passed that we did not quarrel. Yes, it was pleasant at the time—*quite* pleasant. I suppose that your—your—cousin" (with a tight, strained smile) "will not mind my allowing *that*, will she? But, no doubt we shall both do better—I, as you say, especially."

A little pause.

"Do you remember," he says, suddenly, "that day at St.-Malo; how I—"

She interrupts. "I remember nothing," she says, firmly, though her pale lips tremble. "I have the worst memory in the world." He looks mortified, and relapses into silence. "Tell me," she says, presently, with a nervous excitement in her manner, "tell me all about *yourself*; that is much more interesting. When is it to be—what day exactly? I should like to think of you, you know—to drink your health, and" (laughing hysterically) "I suppose I ought to send you a present, ought not I?"

"For God's sake, do not!" he cries, hastily, "unless you can send me your bad memory; I *should* thank you for that."

"You *never* quarrel with her, I suppose?" continues the girl, drawing strength even from the very intensity of her own misery to speak collectedly, and even smilingly.

"It is all smooth sailing, like a boat on a duck-pond! No doubt you can *mould* her, like a piece of clay, into whatever shape you like."

Paul reddens. "She is a good girl," he says moodily; "and when I am away from you I know that I shall be happy with her—at least" (sighing heavily) "I ought to be; at all events, I shall have peace—that is something. All my life before I met you I thought it was every thing." (After a pause) "Thank God, she does not know how to sneer!"

"And when is it to be?" she asks, still smiling; "you know you have not told me; tell me. I wish to know the day—the very day."

"Immediately," he says, feverishly; "the sooner the better. What is there to wait for?"

"Well, I will think of you," she says, commanding her voice with great difficulty, and stretching out her trembling hand kindly to him; "yes, I will—that is" (breaking into an unsteady laugh), "if—if—I do not forget."

"Do nothing of the kind," he cries, roughly pressing the slender cold fingers; "neither *then* nor *ever!* Let us make a compact, never to think of each other again. What pleasant thoughts can we have of one another? Least of all, think of me on that day," he continues, after an interval, speaking with the signs of strong excitement. "I ask it of you as a favor; if your face comes between me and the parson" (laughing harshly) "I shall not be very ready with my responses! Let me have one good look at you!" (after another pause, while his breath comes quick and short) "just one. It would be a pity quite to forget the face of the handsomest woman one ever knew, would not it? There! —there!" There is the pallor of a mad longing on his cold shrewd face, as he stands staring and stammering in the moonlight. "Good-bye, lovely eyes!" he says, in a hoarse whisper; "good-bye, lovely lips! you gave me no peace while I had you; but, yet I wish—O God! how I wish—"

He stops abruptly. His mad fond words have brought back the solace of all the sorrowful to her smarting eyes; they are shining with the soft dimness of tender tears, as they grow to his harsh and altered face.

"Wish nothing," she says, gently. "I have wished many things in my time—that you were dead; that I myself were; that one could have things twice over, or not at all—but you see they have none of them come true."

"Let me, at least, wish one thing," he cries, violently. "Whether you let me, or no, I *will* wish it! I will pray, and urgently entreat God for it—that this—this *hell*, that is just half a step off heaven, may not come over again! Lenore, pretty Lenore, what ill-luck makes us both live in England? What security have we that we shall not come across each other again, and yet again, and yet again?"

"There is not much danger," she says, calmly, "at least, not yet awhile; we are not going home; we are going up to Pontresina for many months—for all the summer."

"To Pontresina?" he exclaims, brusquely. "What are you going there for? Health or pleasure? Not *health* surely?" peering at her again with an anxious suspicion.

"Partly," she answers; and then trying to speak lightly and merrily, "I suppose being over-lively and over-amused wears one out as much as over-work or over-grief; I was so gay last winter—so gay—that I danced all the flesh off my bones."

He makes no comment on this announcement.

"I am going to lay up such a store of strength against next winter," she continues, laughing almost loudly, "for I mean to be gayer than ever then—gayer than ever."

The contrast between the words she is uttering and the black devastation that is laying waste her soul strikes her with such bitter force that she turns away sharply.

"Do you?" he says, fiercely. "I dare say! What is it to me? Why do you tell me?"

Higher and higher the fair broad moon has been sailing; she has reached her zenith; now, nothing escapes her; every larch-feather, every yeasty crown of froth, every daisy and fine grass-blade, she has daintily washed.

"I am going," Paul says, with rough suddenness. "What am I waiting for? Can you tell me that? If I stayed here all to-night and to-morrow, and the night after, what would be changed? This vile stream would still be thundering on, and we should still be standing here, eating our hearts out with longing for things that, if we had them, would not give us content."

"Yes," she says, and her own pretty, womanly voice is almost as harsh as his, "go! Who is keeping you?"

His face is white—so white—with the pallor of unwilling passion, that he is trembling all over.

"And must I leave you here, all alone in this desolate place?" he asks, in a husky whisper; "all alone, as I found you?"

And she echoes, "All alone!"

"You are not frightened?"

Again she laughs, though the muscles about her face seem tight and stiff.

"What should I be frightened at?"

Their hands are interlocked, and their eyes are fixed on each other's faces.

"This is the third time we have said 'Good-bye,'" he says, indistinctly. "The last was bad enough, but, for my part, I liked it better than this; and the first—Lenore, do you remember the first on the steamboat at St.-Malo?"

"I remember *nothing*," she says, breaking out into impetuous passion, while the blood runs headlong to her cheeks. "How many times must I tell you that it is an *accursed* word? I have torn it out of my vocabulary! I always look on — *on* — now" (speaking feverishly). "Surely there must be something pleasant ahead somewhere—somewhere!"

"Perhaps," he says, gloomily; "but one thing I am sure of—O Lenore! you are sure of it, too—and that is, that there is nothing so pleasant ahead as what we have left behind!"

These are his last words.

CHAPTER III.

WHAT JEMIMA SAYS.

AND now we have done with Bergun; in all probability we shall see its little eaves and deep doll's-house windows never again. How happily might one (one is not equivalent to *I* here) spend a honey-moon among its rocks, and pine slopes, and flowered fields, always supposing that one had brought one's own food with one. I confess to an opinion that the chicken's black skeleton, and the untold nauseousness of the Sasseila, would cool the ardor of the warmest pair that ever yawned and fondled through the conventional month. We are still, however, in the foodless land of the Engadine; we have reached Pontresina. It is a long name, is not it? But the name is longer than the place; it is only a cluster of houses, white as the defacer of all beauty, whitewash, can make them. If I had had

the world's reins in my hand I would have put him that invented whitewash to even a feller death than that which I
would have inflicted on the twin-demons who brought up
gunpowder and electricity from hell's lowest pit. At the
foot of a long, stern hill the village humbly crouches, while
round it stand a silent, solemn conclave of great mountains
—white-snow spires reaching heavenward—God's church-
steeples; while far off a gray-green glacier dimly shines.
O mighty mountains! you coldly awe me with your

" aloof and loveless permanence."

The trees cluster in the valley, but the great hills stand
bareheaded before God. Here we are at the little Hôtel
de la Croix Blanche, having taken root among the whitewash. We have been here a week, and we have yawned
a good deal. The season has hardly begun—at least for
the English—and it has rained an infinity. We have even
had the doubtful pleasure of seeing flakes of unseasonable
snow. There are no books to be got, and we have ex
hausted our few Tauchnitz novels. To-day we have grown
tired of our own sitting-room, and have strayed objectless-
ly up to the general *salon* at the top of the house. It is a
bare, light room, whitewashed, of course. A carpet would
be pleasant to-day, but no rag of carpet is there; only
aggressively-clean squares of deal, intersected with red-
pine. There has been a wedding-party in the house all
day; their all-pervading din and to us incomprehensible
Romansch mirth have had a large share in driving us upward. It is afternoon now, and, thank God, they are gone!
We have been standing out in the balcony, watching their
departure, as they pack themselves into their shabby-hood-
ed carriages, garlanded with dusty green wreaths. Yes,
they are gone; the arm of each gawky youth, with osten-
tatious candor, clasping the solid waist of his maiden.

Now that they are gone, Sylvia retires inside, grumbling and shivering.

"Had not you better go in, too?" I say to Lenore; "it is very damp. You will never get well if you do not take more care of yourself."

"Why *should* I get well?" she says, querulously. "I do not want to get well; what object in life should I have if I were well? Being ill is something to do. I can be interested in my symptoms and my tonics; I would not be well for worlds."

I look at her compassionately—at her sharpened profile; it is getting a look of pinched and suffering discontent. Where is its lovely debonair roundness? Alas! even since we left Bergun it has been slipping—oh, how quickly!—away!

"You may get me a shawl if you like," she says, presently, "and a chair."

I reënter the *salon* to fetch them. Sylvia is sitting with the landlord's book of dried plants before her, lamentably turning over the leaves. At the best of times nothing can be more melancholy than a dried flower—a colorless skeleton, without any likeness to itself. One ought to be in the best of spirits to look at such a collection as is now engaging Mrs. Prodgers's slack attention. I return with the shawl—a heavy and warm one—and wrap it about my youngest sister, and then remain by her side, vacantly gazing at the view. The rain has ceased, but the clouds still hide the top of the glacier-mountain; one tiny cloudlet has lost its way, and is wandering about near the hill-foot, slowly evaporating, and losing its thin life. The balcony where we are is much higher than the opposite houses; it can look magnificently down on their roofs. They are a queer little row; not in a line at all, but each seeming to be shoving and elbowing its neighbor, in order to get forwardest; in the narrow street below a man is leaning against a door-post, smoking a long pipe; another is sweeping the round stones of the pavement with a besom. Nor can one possibly get up any interest in either of them.

"I do not think Kolb behaved quite honestly about this place," says Sylvia's voice dolorously, from the interior; "somehow one never can get foreigners to speak *quite* the truth—he certainly told me distinctly, when I asked him, that one might always wear *demi-saison* dresses here."

We are both too much depressed to join even in abuse of Kolb's mendacity. Several more leaves turned over; a heavy sigh.

"I wish the Websters were here; they talked of going abroad this summer. I will write and advise them to come here."

"Rather a case of the fox that had lost his tail," I say, laughing dismally.

"Tell them not to bring any *demi-saison* dresses," subjoins Lenore, sarcastically.

Several moments of forlorn silence. Sylvia has finished her book, and with a vague and mistaken idea that we have got some little piece of amusement that we are privately *worrying* without giving her information of it, she issues forth a second time and joins us. We are all in a row, like three storks standing on one leg on a house-top. The cloudlet has quite melted; there is not a trace of it. I wish I could melt too. The man has stopped sweeping. Suddenly—no, not suddenly—gradually a sound of distant wheels and bells salutes our ears. A vehicle of some kind is approaching at a brisk trot from the direction of Samaden.

"Coming *here*, do you think?" I say, with a spark of animation shooting, as I feel, from my lack-lustre eye.

" No such luck," answers Lenore, gloomily.

" No doubt it is going on to ' The Krone,' " says Sylvia, peevishly. " Everybody goes to ' The Krone.' I wish we had gone there. It was all Kolb's doing."

The bells ring louder, the horses' hoofs stamp the stones more distinctly; it is in sight. Yes, a carriage, twin-brother to our own late one, only that it is shut on account of the weather; four horses, piles of luggage, dusty tarpaulin. A moment of breathless suspense; we all lean over the balcony as far as our necks and heads will take us. Yes!—no!—yes! Far down in the street, right under our eager eyes, it is pulling up.

" My heart was in my mouth!" says Lenore, smiling a broad smile of relief. " I thought it *was* going on to ' The Krone.' "

" We are too high up here," I say, excitedly; " we should see better from our own windows."

Hereupon we all rush violently, helter-skelter, down-stairs to our sitting-room, which is on a lower floor. Only one window gives upon the street; it is small, but we all huddle into it. M. Enderlin, the landlord, letting down the steps; Madame Enderlin courtseying; Marie and Menga hovering near, ready to carry out parcels.

" *Maid*, of course," I say, as the first occupant slowly emerges. " She looks rather wet; evidently she was in the *coupé* with the courier, and they only took her inside because it rained."

A man's legs and a wide-awake, then a great deal of golden hair and a plump, smart woman's figure. Being above them, we see none of their faces.

" Nothing looks so nice for travelling as those French lawns, trimmed with unbleached Cluny," says Sylvia, with pensive envy; " they never show the dust."

" Bride and bridegroom," say I. " What a bore! They

will not do us much good; they will be swallowed up in one another."

"They look like *people*, however," says Sylvia, by which expression she means to intimate a favorable opinion of the new-comers' gentility. "If they are nice," she continues, "I mean, really people that one would like to know—and Kolb could easily find out that—we might make a party to go up Piz Languard with them."

"There is some one else with them," cry I, eagerly. "Surely they cannot have taken their parents to *chaperone* them!"

"Like the people at Dinan," says Lenore, dryly, "who went a wedding-tour *à l'anglaise*, and took the bride's mother *and the bridegroom's* with them."

A fat but nicely-booted female foot slowly treads the step, and then the ground; it and its fellow support a form of shapely, mature portliness. Having descended, this last figure lifts its face to look at the little cross swinging out as the inn-sign in the street.

"Good Heavens!" cries Lenore, emphatically.

"Why that pious ejaculation?" say I, gayly, my spirits having gone up fifty per cent. at the prospect of human companionship.

"Did not you see?" breaks out Lenore, excitedly. "Do not you know who they are?"

"Not I. How should I?"

"Why, old Mrs. Scrope, to be sure—Charlie's mother."

"What! all three of them?" I say, derisively. "My dear child, you are dreaming.'"

"Impossible!" says Sylvia, straining her little neck out of the window to catch a last glimpse; but they are gone. "You have such a mania for seeing likenesses that no one else can! How could you tell? one only saw their backs."

"And should not I know my own mother-in-law's back among a hundred?" says Lenore, with sardonic mirth.

"Oh, if it was only her back," I say, with a sigh of relief, "I do not mind; all old women's backs are much alike."

"Are they?" says Lenore, with a grim smile. "I do not agree with you; there are backs and backs; but I do not confine myself to backs—I saw her *face*, and my ex-mother-in-law's it was, I am sorry to say."

"And the other two were the married daughter and her husband, I suppose?" I say, a painful conviction that Lenore is speaking truth forcing itself on my mind. "Now that I think of it, there was something familiar to me in the broad gold arrow she wore in her hair."

Silence for a few moments, while we stare at one another blankly.

"I wish they *had* gone on to 'The Krone' now," says Lenore, dryly.

"If we wait to go up Piz Languard till we go up with them," I say, with a vexed laugh, "we shall remain some time at the foot, I think."

"*How* glad they will be to see us!" cries Lenore, breaking out into violent merriment, that does not, however, express any equally violent enjoyment, "considering that last time they saw us they left us with the Elizabethan sentiment that 'God might forgive us, but they never would,' or words to that effect."

"I declare I do not know what you are laughing at," says Sylvia, pettishly, with her eyes full of tears; "it is a great thing to be easily amused; as for me, I see nothing amusing in it! This sort of thing never happens to any one but me; really *good* people, that one would have liked to know *en intimes*—"

"Listen," I say, leaving the window and approaching

the door, " they are coming up! I hear Madame Enderlin's voice."

" We shall be always meeting them on the stairs," says Sylvia, lachrymosely, " and I declare I shall no more know how to behave—very likely they will take their cue from me—whether to stop and shake hands, or bow and pass on—"

" Stop and shake hands with the man—bow and pass on to the women," says Lenore, promptly; " men are always kind."

" As for *you*," retorts Sylvia, turning upon her with a tearful spitefulness, " in your case there can be no difficulty; they will cut *you*, of course, out and out—*dead*—and really, considering all things, one cannot blame them."

" Of course they will," replies Lenore, calmly, though her color deepens; " I should think very meanly of them if they did not."

" And *you* " (speaking very rapidly, while the large tears still roll helplessly down her cheeks), " what will you do? how will you take it?"

" *Do?* " says Lenore, with a little dry laugh; " what *is* there to do? I shall *be* cut, I suppose, and try to look as if I liked it."

CHAPTER IV.

WHAT JEMIMA SAYS.

" MADAME *est servie!* " says Menga, half an hour later, opening my door, and putting her head in.

" Do not go without me!" cries Sylvia, eagerly; " wait for me. Did you ever see anybody so silly as I? I am trembling all over—like a leaf—feel!"

" Lenore is not quite ready," I say.

" We will go without her," rejoins Sylvia, quickly; why should not we? They will be more likely to speak to us if she is not by."

I shrug my shoulders. " I suppose one must begin to be civilized again," continues my sister, holding out one plump and shapely arm for me to clasp a bracelet on. " It is astonishing how soon one gets out of the way of it! Certainly it is cold; but bundled up in a shawl one looks as if one had no more shape than the Tun of Heidelberg."

We descend. The few visitors are collecting in the hard-scrubbed *salle à manger* round the snow-white table.

" How my heart is beating!" says Sylvia, as we stand at the door about to enter; " look and see whether they are down yet."

I peep. " Yes, there they are; and, as ill-luck will have it, their places are next ours; you need not have taken off your shawl; they have both shawls, and the husband— what is his name?—I never can recollect—Lascelles, is not it?—is in his great-coat. There is no help for it; if we wish for food, we must go into the lion's jaws to get it."

As we approach, it becomes evident to us that the fact of our presence has been previously revealed to the new-comers. As we reach the table they just look up, and bow—gravely and slightly, it is true; but still they bow. Old Mrs. Scrope holds her little hooked nose—gently, not Jewishly hooked—rather more aloft than usual, gathers her shawl with a chilly gesture about her, and says across the table to her daughter:

" I wonder why they do not light the stove?"

Mr. Lascelles rises and shakes hands heartily, and says:

" How are you? Deuced cold, is not it? How long have you been here?"

Everybody but Lenore is down; the little *bourgeois*

German family—father, mother, two daughters, the mild
and havering English old maid in noisome cameo brooch
and hair bracelet, who spends her life in marauding about
the Continent in virgin loveliness; the Cantab, who has
been climbing every high mountain in the neighborhood,
till all the skin is peeling off his blistered, scarlet face—
here they are, all of them, eating soup, if you like to call it
soup, after his several manner.   It is weak and nasty stuff
enough, one would think, but apparently too strong for the
German stomachs; at least, having nearly finished their
share, they call for hot water, pour some into their plates,
and begin to ladle it up into their mouths.

"I had better go and call Lenore," I say aloud to Sylvia, purposely speaking the obnoxious name to see what
effect it will produce.   "I cannot think what has become
of her."

As I speak she enters.   As she comes hurriedly across
the room with a sort of nervous defiance in her face, I look
at her curiously, trying to see her as a stranger would.
Surely there can be nothing very provocative of wrath—of
conciliation, rather—in her altered look.   Even to *me*, who
have watched her daily, hourly, she seems ill, shrunken,
drooped.   How much more to them who have not seen her
since—six months ago—she shone upon them in the healthy
bloom of her delicate ripe beauty!   Poor soul!   Now that
her strength is gone and her fairness waned, can· they be
angry with her still?   As they rather *feel* than see her approach, I am sensible of a sort of ladylike stiffening and
drawing up on the part of the two women.

Mr. Lascelles is fully occupied in making faces at his
soup.   The dead cut Sylvia predicted is imminent.   As she
slips into her seat, the only one left—one next Mrs. Lascelles—with eyes determinedly downcast, and an uneasy
red look, half challenging, half deprecatory, on her face,

curiosity gets the better of their dignity, and they both glance at her. I see them both start perceptibly. Yes, they have noticed it too. Alas! the change is too patent to escape the carelessest, hostilest eye. With a sudden impulse they both bow, as they had bowed to us, slightly, unsmilingly, without the smallest attempt at cordiality, but still quite politely.

"Deuced cold, is not it?" says Mr. Lascelles, turning with an air of the greatest friendliness to Sylvia; man-like, happily and sublimely ignoring the squabbles of his womankind; and, rubbing his hands, "when last I saw you, it was deuced cold too; we were as nearly as possible snowed up on our way back to London — do you remember, Blanche?"

At this happy allusion to our last merry meeting we all wax deeply, darkly, beautifully red.

"Is it always cold here?" asks Mrs. Lascelles, rushing hurriedly, and quite contrary to her original intention, as I feel, into conversation with me.

"It has been cold since we came, but we are hardly fair judges yet; we have only been here a week; I am told that it is a remarkably healthy climate," I answer, stiffly and tritely; my besetting sin always being a tendency to sink into an echo of Murray.

"It has been *arctic!*" says Sylvia, to her neighbor, with a plaintive upcasting of her eyes to his face, "positively *arctic!* How I envy your great-coat!—nothing so pretty as beaver" (stroking it delicately); "naturally, we left all our furs behind us."

"One peculiarity of the climate," say I, addressing everybody, in a monotonous recitative, "is, that meat killed in the autumn dries of itself in the course of the winter; it is considered an excellent thing for making blood, and looks like sausage."

"Is not it too cold for *you?*" Mrs. Lascelles asks, pointedly addressing her question to Lenore, and speaking with a compassionate inflection in her voice.

Lenore blushes furiously.

"For *me!*" she says, stammering, and looking surprised, "for—for all of us; we *all* shiver."

No one makes any rejoinder.

"It is a wonderful climate for consumption, I believe," continues Lenore, speaking hurriedly and hesitatingly, as if not at all sure of the reception a speech from her may meet with. "A clergyman in the last stage came to St. Moritz last year, and is now quite recovered; not" (looking round with a nervous laugh) "that *that* need be any great recommendation to any of us, I hope."

Again they look at her, with an unwilling startled pity in their healthy, prosperous faces. The German father is dexterously whisking his beef-gravy into his mouth on the blade of his knife, at the imminent risk of slitting his countenance from ear to ear; the Cantab is reluctantly turning his peeled nose and flayed cheeks to the old maid, who, gently blinking behind her spectacles, is addressing him.

. . . .

"A happy deliverance!" cries Sylvia, stretching herself on the sofa in our sitting-room, when at length we attained that haven, dinner being ended. "Nothing *prostrates* one so much as these little social ordeals! Did you see how I cultivated the husband? I do not think they quite liked it."

I am looking out of window, and contemplating Mr. Lascelles's back, as he stands on the door-step talking to Kolb, and banging his arms together like a cabman, to keep them warm. I can feel, by the expression of his shoulders, that he is for the third time remarking that "it is deuced cold."

"If he had his own way, he would be always with us, in and out, in and out," continues Sylvia; "one can foresee that. But no doubt he will not be *let*."

"What a thing it is to be thin!" cries Lenore, with a rather bitter little laugh. "If I had been fat and well-looking, they would have cut me dead. If I gain in favor in the same ratio in which I lose in flesh, they will soon be thoroughly fond of me." I turn from the window with a sigh at this speech. "There *is* something very affecting in having a thing like a. bird's-claw held out to you, is not there?" continues she, looking with a sort of pensive derision at her own hand, first opening it, and then clinching it, to see how strongly the knuckles and bones start out.

"Do not!" I say, crossly. "I wish you would not!"

"In books," continues she, "whenever people on their death-beds lift up their thin hands, or hold out their thin hands, one always begins to cry, don't you know?" I laugh, but not very jocundly. "If they could hear the way in which I cough at night, I am not sure that they would not kiss me," says the young girl, with a sarcastic smile.

"How extraordinarily like Charlie his sister is!" says Sylvia, sitting up on the sofa. "What are you looking at, Jemima? Any new arrivals? Thoroughly *bon genre* they all look. Say what you will, blood must show."

"As the old maid said when her nose got red," retorts Lenore.

"A plain likeness, of course," pursues Sylvia, not deigning to heed this profane illustration. "Blanche Lascelles is too much of a *peace-and-plenty-looking* woman to please me—too *redundant*, don't you know? I confess to liking to see people keep within bounds; but she is growing so enormously large, she will soon be all over everywhere."

" Perhaps it is *bon genre* to spread," says Lenore, mockingly; "who knows?"

" She put me so much in mind of him that it was on the tip of my tongue to ask after him," continues Mrs. Prodgers.

" I am very glad it remained on the tip."

" I wish with all my heart he was here," says Sylvia, continuing her monologue and yawning. " I wonder is there any chance of it?   One abuses them when one has them, but certainly life—travelling-life especially—is very *triste* without a man."

" Do you wish it too, Lenore?" I ask, walking over to where my youngest sister is listlessly lying back in the one arm-chair that the room affords.

"How do I know?" she answers, in a tone of weary irritability. " I wish a hundred things one half of the day which I unwish the other half. No, certainly I do not—not until I get my looks up again.   Jemima " (gazing wistfully up at me), "how long do you think it will be before I do?"

" My dear, am I a prophet?" I say, very sadly, stroking her hair.

" Evidently they thought me very much gone off, did not they?" she asks, with her eyes still fixed on my face, and a faint, a very faint hope of contradiction in her own.

" How do I know?" I reply, evasively. " If they *had* thought so, they would hardly have chosen *me* to confide it to."

" But they did," returns she, gently, shaking her head. " As Sylvia says, one has one's instincts." (A moment's silence.) " Who was it?" she continues, with a melancholy smile; " Madame du Barri, was not it, who said that she would rather be dead than ugly?   Pah!" (with a shudder), " it would be very disagreeable to be either."

CHAPTER V.

" The gods may release
That they made fast ;
Thy soul shall have ease
In thy limbs at the last ;
But what shall they give thee for life, sweet life, that is overpast ? "

WHAT JEMIMA SAYS.

AT last it is summer to-day ; the sun says, " Now it is *my* turn ! " With his strong right hand, he has swept the clouds away from the snow-peaks — away — away — anywhere ; he will have none of them. Those snow-peaks ! They dazzle one so that one cannot look at them, save through blue spectacles. It makes one's eyes drop water but to glance hastily at their shining magnificence. Oh, happy consummation ! it is too hot even for *demi-saison* dresses.

" I think Kolb is very tyrannical ! " says Sylvia, discontentedly. " What do I care about the water-fall, or the Mortiratsch glacier ? After all, when you have seen one glacier, you have seen them all ; and though nobody *can* be fonder of scenery than I am, yet of course there are other things in the world ; I had much rather have stayed at home to-day and found out what the Scropes' plans were."

We were all joggling along in a little chaise, drawn by a fat pony, which, however, is so far from us as to be almost out of sight, from the length of the traces—jiggling, joggling along through Pontresina, between the green sheltered white houses ; here and there a flourish of flowers —geraniums, cinerarias—out of their windows ; through the upper village, and along the hot high-road. On each

17

side of us is the lovely riot of the meadow-flowers; they seem to have rushed out, all at once, and all together, to answer to their names at the roll-call of the spring sun.

"At all events," say I, laughing, "Mr. Lascelles cannot say that it is 'deuced cold' to-day. Pah! how apoplectic it makes one's head! Oh, for a good honest British cabbage-leaf to put in one's hat!"

"There is one comfort," says Sylvia, pursuing her own thoughts, "and that is, that there is no one they *can* become *liés* with, in our absence, as I should think that they were sociable, sensible sort of people, who cordially hated their own society."

"Worse even than ours?" asks Lenore, with a cynical smile, from beneath the dusty little hood under which she is leaning back.

We leave the high-road; we turn into a by-way that leads to the glacier—leads through a company of larches. They have grown up, here and there, among the great strewn stones, of every shape and size — lichen-grown, green, forbidding. By-and-by we have to say good-bye to our carriage; it can go no farther; the road breaks off.

"This is quite the most *triste* festivity I ever assisted at," Sylvia says plaintively, as we dawdle and loiter hotly along.

"Bah! how the midges bite! As a rule, no one is more independent of men's society than I am, but in a case of this kind a man is indispensable to give a sort of impetus, a fillip, to the whole thing."

"Let us have luncheon," say I, with my usual material view of things; "eating always raises one's spirits, and we can eat as well as if a regiment were looking on."

So we lunch on the short sward. The smooth, smoke-colored cattle are ringing their bells vigorously, as they browse near us, though what they eat the Lord only knows, unless they have a taste for yellow potentillas, sweet-scented daphne, and dry white bents. Kolb has stretched a mackintosh for us to sit on, and brought spiced-beef that looks weirdly nasty, in sun-warmed slices, out of a marmot-skin bag; rolls, hard-boiled eggs. A bottle of Château Margot stands under a great rock, knee-deep in yellow violets. The glacier river, the Bernina, runs madly past us, hoarsely raving to its wide stone bed, in a torrent of dirty yellow-green-white. There we lie, couched comfortably as ruminating cattle, while at our elbows and feet the gentians open their blue eyes—bluer than any woman's, deeper than any sapphire.

"How pretty they would be if artificial!" Sylvia says, pensively plucking one. "A spray for the side of the head, you know, and another for the corsage; I am afraid we are too far off for it to carry well, or I would send one to Foster's in a tin box; he will always copy any flower you send him, exactly."

"Perish the thought!" says Lenore, with a sort of lazy indignation, laying her head down among a crowded little family of the yellow violets, under a great split rock.

"Dark blue is not a good night-color, however," says Sylvia, still pursuing her own train of meditation.

"How drowsy the river's roar makes one!" I say, yawning, and burying my hot face in my outstretched arms; "if you two will not speak, I shall be asleep in three minutes."

"How *hideous* it is!" says Sylvia, dropping her gentian, and gazing with a sort of disgust at the tearing flood. "Glacier-rivers always are. Did you ever see any thing so dirty in your life? It looks as if hundreds and thousands of washer-women had been washing in it with myriads of cakes of soap!"

After all, we never reach the glacier. If luncheon has

cheered, it has also enervated us. We content ourselves
with languidly strolling to the water-fall. Now we have
reached it; now exertion is at an end; now we lie, lazy as
lotus-eaters, on the dry, warm herbage—scant, yet so
sweet!—and gaze and listen, gaze and listen, for God
knows how long, to the loud, white beauty of the fall.
Down it comes from the top of the low hill in one long,
snowy plunge; then a smooth sliding over the polished
backs of the great stones; a curling of creamy wavelets;
then another foamy leap in lightning and froth; then a
green pool, where the sun is holding dazzling mirrors, too
bright to look at, to the pines' dark faces. The long roar
rings loud yet gentle in our ears, bringing to us a drowsy
joy. Even Sylvia's grumblings are stilled—at least we no
longer hear them, Lenore and I. We have climbed slowly
and intermittently up the rocks to a little plateau, whence
we can see the water's chiefest plunge. Who can stop it?
The air is full of its cold white powder; a great stone
opposite is forever wet with the cool damp dust drifted
against its shining sides. Little lilac primulas confidently
grow and bloom in its clefts. O torrents and hills and
flowers, you make me drunk with beauty! What can be
nobler than to watch the play. of God's imagination in
these silent places?

With elbows deep sunk in gentians, and head on hand,
we lie and lie and lie, till the sun is marching, in all his
afternoon heat and mellow glory, through the pale turquoise
sky. The pines above our heads smell divinely. There is
no flower, however sweet, that has a better fragrance than
that which the grave, flowerless firs give out at the bidding
of their master, the high June sun. For half-hours hours—
we know not which—neither of us has spoken. My eyes
have long been fixed on the little rainbow that the water-
fall has caught and held fast, with its faint green and

yellow and red, in her shining toils. Presently, and little
by little, I cease to see the tender colors of the prism—I
cease to hear the water's plunge and the pines' low sigh;
I am asleep. Whether my doze is long or short, I do not
know. I imagine, however, that it is not very long; but
it is broken at last by a sharp exclamation from Lenore.

"What are you making such a noise about?" I cry,
starting up and rubbing my eyes. "One may as well be
killed as frightened to death——*Charlie ! ! !*"

Am I dreaming still? No; the water-fall's voice has
come back to my ears, and the pines' woody fragrance to
my nostrils. Providence has granted Sylvia's prayer—for
a prayer it was; at least, it fulfilled the hymn's definition
of prayer:

'Prayer is the heart's sincere desire,
Uttered or unexpressed."

There he stands, three paces from me, among the juni-
per-bushes, solid and real, in the loose and untinted clothes
that summer Britons love—stands there in all the stalwart,
deep-colored beauty of his manhood. Providence has sent
us a man "to give the whole thing a fillip." ·Lenore has
risen to her feet and is facing him. Their hands are not
touching, neither are they speaking, only they are looking
at one another long and dumbly. Embarrassment at the
recollected hostility of their last parting is tying Lenore's
tongue, as I feel; but what is it that is giving that look of
silent, painful wonder to Scrope's face?

"Why are you looking so hard at me?" she says, at
last, in a low voice, with a tremulous asperity. "Is there
any thing *odd* about me? Do not you know that it is not
good manners to look so hard at any one?"

"I—I—beg your pardon," he says, stammering. "I—
I—did not mean—you see, it is so long since I have seen—"

I have scrambled to my feet and shaken the illicit noonday sleep from my eyes. "Charlie!" I cry a second time, coming forward; and, not being a person with any great command of language, I add nothing to the pertinent brevity of this observation.

He turns, and takes my ready hand in the cool, familiar, brotherly clasp with which, in their day, so many good and handsome men have honored me, and for which I have never felt the least grateful to them. "Did not you know I was coming?" he asks; "did not they tell you?"

"Not they?" reply I, laughing. "To let you into a secret, we are not quite on *confidential* terms—rather *en délicatesse*, as you may say. I dare say they thought we were not good enough to be told such a piece of news— that it would exhilarate us too much."

"They were nearly right there, I think," says Sylvia, to whom, being a little lower down, the answer to her prayer has been first vouchsafed. "It is never my way, as a rule, to make people conceited—men especially; I am sure they are bad enough, without one's helping them; but certainly, if one wishes to know how thoroughly to appreciate a friend, one must come to the Engadine."

"You are glad to see me, then?" he says, stretching out his hand to her, too, with a broad, eager smile. The question seems addressed to Sylvia, but his eyes seek Lenore. "Truly, honestly, without figure of speech? You know I had my doubts."

"A perfectly unjustifiable question," returns Sylvia, giving her head a little, playful jerk. "We totally decline to answer it—do not we, Jemima?"

"And *you!*" he says, impulsively, stooping over Lenore, and lowering his voice a little.

She has sat down again, and, leaning on her elbow, is listlessly picking a bit of daphne to pieces: the little treacherous color that his first sudden coming had sent into her cheeks ebbing quickly out of them again.

"*I!*" (with a little start). "Oh, of course—yes, I think so—I suppose so—why should not I be?"

Her eyes were lifted to his; they mean to be kindly, but they have of late got a settled look of weary *nonchalance*, that they could not, if they would, put away.

"What have you been doing to her?" he says, leading me a little away from the others, on pretence of looking over the slender plank bridge that crosses the fall, grasping my arm, and staring with an angry, painful vehemence into my face. "They told me she was so altered that I should not know her again—*not know her again!*"—(with an accent of scorn)—"she would have to be altered indeed before *that* could come to pass. I thought they only said it to set me against her; that was why I followed you. I could not wait. My God! she *is* changed" (loosing my arm, and clinching his own hands together). "I could not have believed that any one—any young, strong person—*could* be so changed in five months."

I do not answer, for the excellent reason that I cannot. My throat is choked, and my silent tears drop on the bridge-rail and into the emerald pool beneath. One must love something. I have not had many people to love in my time; nobody very good, or that love me much; and, for want of them, I love Lenore. I suppose he thinks that my speechlessness comes from callous indifference.

"You have taken no care of her," he continues, harshly; "you have not looked after her. When did she ever look after herself? You—who are so much older than she, that one would have thought that you would have been like a mother to her."

He stops abruptly. She of whom we speak has risen and followed us.

"You are talking about me," she says, slightly smiling. "Yes, you both look guilty! what are you saying? No, I do not care to hear; nothing very interesting, I dare say."

So saying, she saunters slowly away again.

"You are no wiser than you were; I see that," I remark, smiling away my tears, and trying to smile when we are again alone.

"You are mistaken," he answers, with eager quickness; "I am perfectly cured—perfectly; and, when one is once thoroughly cured of a complaint of this sort, one does not sicken again. If I had not been sure of that, I would not have come near you; I would have put the width of all Europe between us."

I shake my head in a silent skepticism.

"See," he cries, earnestly, "do you remember how I used to tremble all over if my hand touched hers?—how I grew redder than any lobster if she spoke to me? Do I tremble now?" (stretching out his right hand to me)— "am I red?"

Still I am silent.

"Do you hear?" he asks, impatiently.

"Yes," I answer, dryly, "I hear."

CHAPTER VI.

"I feel the daisies growing over me."

WHAT THE AUTHOR SAYS.

THEY are sitting, they two, the lover and the loved one, in the tiny graveyard of the little church upon the hill. They have risen up hastily from the noisy supper, where the fusty German mother had shut the window, where the fusty German daughters had made weak and steaming negus of their *vin ordinaire*, on this sultry summer evening. They two, and Jemima. They have passed through the small, still street, along the silent road, where even the dust lies quiet and white, and does not harry one as in the daytime; up the lane, past cottages and fields, to the little church that stands below the rocky mountain. Lenore has ridden; she could not have walked so far up the hill-side; ridden the fat pony, "a beautiful pony, just like a tea-pot," as Kolb, with doubtful compliment, remarked of him. Now he is tied to the church-porch, and is eating forget-me-nots in the evening gray. Jemima has discreetly strolled away, but her discretion has pleased but one of her companions; the other has hardly noticed it. It is all one to Lenore whether she goes or stays. It is eight o'clock. Pontresina Church is telling the hour sonorously, and the little hill-church beside her is answering with its one grave bell; the church, with its rude stone tower and little extinguisher top, its windows deep set in the wall, like deep-sunk eyes.

"Lenore," says Scrope, presently plucking a great forget-me-not, twice the size of those we see in England, from one of the low graves, "do you think it wicked to tell lies?"

"It depends," she answers, laughing slightly. "I think truth is rather an over-rated virtue."

"I told a gigantic lie yesterday."

"Did you?" she answers; but she does not seem to care to ask what it is.

He waits a moment, but, finding that her curiosity will not come to his aid, volunteers his information.

"I—I—told Jemima that I was perfectly cured" (reddening a little).

" Yes, that was not quite true," she replies, quietly.

" Are you glad or sorry ? " he asks, eagerly.

She has plucked two blades of fine grass, and is carefully measuring them, to see which is the taller. Perhaps that is the reason that her response comes slowly.

" I am glad," she says, " quite glad ! Formerly, when I was strong and well, I did not mind who cared for me or who did not; I cared for myself a great deal—*immensely* —and that was enough ; but now that I am so weak and sickly, and *waughing*, as they say in Staffordshire—is not it a good word ? does not it give a limp, peevish, unstrung idea ?—why, now I like some good, patient person to be near me, and look sorry when I am out of breath and in tiresome pain."

He does not answer, but I do not think she takes his silence ill.

" Care for me," she says, simply, stretching out her hand, with a sort of *naïveté*, to him—" care for me a little —care for me a good deal, but do not care for me too much ; it is silly to care too much for any thing—one misses it so if it goes ! "

He takes the hand she so frankly gives, but he is afraid violently to press or kiss it, lest, with a sudden change of mood, she may snatch it angrily away.

" Do you remember the day we parted ? " he asks, in a hesitating voice.

" Yes," she says, with a rather embarrassed laugh, " to be sure I remember. We both went into heroics, and you, after abusing me in good, nervous English, fell on your knees before me, and, in so doing, gave Pug's nose such a kick that it has never been the same pattern since."

" It is nearly six months since then," he says, in a low voice; " five, at least. If I had taken you at your word—"

"I am so glad you did not !" she interrupts, hastily.
His face falls.

"So glad are you? Why?"

"Do not you know that I like to take all and give nothing?" she says, with a sort of smile. "That was always my way—always—let me have it a little longer. I know that I cause you pain every time that I am with you, but somehow I do not mind—I have no remorse; you are strong, and pain does not kill; sometimes it braces. See, I have suffered a good deal, and I am not dead."

He clasps the slight, cool hand he holds tighter.

"Thank God, no !"

"Have you ever known what it is to be very unhappy?" she says, looking with a sort of pensive curiosity into his face. "If I asked you, you would say 'Yes,' you would swear it; but somehow I doubt it. How clear and blue your eyes are ! They look as if they had always slept all night and smiled all day. You are not *fat*, certainly—far from it—I hate a fat man; but how well and strongly your bones are covered !"

He does not asseverate; he makes no apology for his healthy manhood; but I think, when he next looks in her face, she knows that one may wear a sore heart and yet eat well, and have broad shoulders and a stalwart presence. There is no sound but the wind speaking pensively to the pines—the wind that makes all the meadows one cool shiver.   •

"Why are you so faithful?" she says, presently, with a sort of impatience in her voice. "There is no sense in it; there is something stupid in such fidelity; it is like a dog; it is not like a man, at least not like the men I have known."

A hot flush rises to the young man's face.

"It *is* stupid," he says, humbly. "I have often thought so."

"Why cannot you take a fancy to some one else?"
she continues, sharply; "to one of my sisters, for instance;
not Sylvia—no, I do not think I can conscientiously recommend her—but Jemima; she would worship the ground
you trod on, and she is not so *very* old, either. I have
heard some people say that an Englishwoman is at her
prime, mind and body, at twenty-eight; and she is only
twenty-nine."

Scrope does not seem to jump at the tempting offer
thus made him; he looks down on the flowery grass at his
feet.

"She is not much to look at, certainly," pursues Lenore, coolly, "but neither am I, for that matter, just now;
but, of course, when I grow strong again, I shall get my
looks back, shall I not?"

He is busy, apparently, in trying to make out the Romansch inscription on the small broken pillar beside him;
at least, he does not reply.

"Why do not you answer me?" she cries, angrily.
"You used to be glib enough with your compliments and
fine speeches; if you cannot say 'Yes,' at least have the
honesty to say 'No.'"

"My dear," he says, with a sort of tremor in his voice,
"what should I say either 'Yes' or 'No' to? In my eyes,
you have never lost your looks; how can you get back
what you have not lost?"

She looks at him with a scared discontent in her pale
face.

"You have got out of it very lamely," she says, with a
brusque laugh. "I never heard any thing clumsier in my
life. There—never mind. I suppose you could not help
it."

Her eyes stray thoughtfully away to the hills; a lumin-
ous mist, a dimness, yet a glory—seems spread over the

high mountain amphitheatre that looks down on Pontresina ; great, glorious battlements, lifting high heads against the higher heaven—citadels that a God must be dwelling in : that dim effulgence is the skirt of his trailed robes. Below, the meadows flash in yellow, and the river twists in silver. O heavenly Zion ! O fair City beyond the clouds ! can thy jasper walls and pearly gates be yet fairer ?

" And you find that it is quite as impossible as you did six months ago ? " Scrope asks, with a tremble in his low voice, after they have sat silent some time.

" Quite," she answers, briefly.

" And it is always *he* that is in the way ? " he says, with an accent of bitterness.

" Yes," she answers, softly ; " always he—always he." (Then, with a dreamy smile), " You see that there are other people who can be stupidly, *doggishly* faithful, as well as you; *you*, at least, cannot blame me."

" If he did but know it ! " the young man cries, smiting his hands together, and looking passionately upward to the faint skies above him; " if some one would but tell him— if he did but see you now—he could not keep his senseless resentment any longer. It is against my own interest to say so, but he could not—he *could* not ! "

" He has no resentment against me now," she answers, quickly, " none ; he is no longer angry with me."

" How do you know ? " with a hasty suspicion in his voice ; " has he written to you ? "

" No."

" How, then ? "

" I have seen him," she says, briefly.

For a moment, astonished disappoinment keeps him silent; then the two words, " When, where ? " come, low but hurriedly, from his mouth.

" We had a long talk," she says, with the same un-

mirthful, tender smile, "quite a long talk—on a bridge—
in the moonlight, at Bergun; the accessories sound roman-
tic, do not they? Moonlight always makes one feel sentimental; I am not quite sure that we were not a little so."

A pause. Through the larches in the wood above them,
a long—long sigh passes; then falls—dies—then revives
again; a sound as of infinite yearning.

"When he is coming here, give me warning before-
hand," says Scrope, in a voice that is next door to a whisper. "I suppose he will be coming here soon?"

"Perhaps," she answers, with a little laugh that is
almost malicious. "Who knows? Perhaps he may take
it in his wedding-tour."

" *His wedding-tour!!*"

"Yes," she answers, looking away from his bewildered
face again, on the perfect content, the evening placidness,
of the landscape; "it is *contrariant*, is it not? but he is
going to be married."

"Who told you so?" (very rapidly).

"He told me so himself."

"And *you?* how did you take it? what did you say?"

"I said, 'Oh, are you?' I believe I laughed—I am
not sure."

"And then?"

"And then—no, not quite *then*" (drawing in her breath
slowly)—"a little afterward—he went."

"And you?"

"And I—oh, I lay down on the grass—nice, crisp, dry
grass, by the river, with my head in a clump of trefoil—
what a noisy river it was!" (speaking with a sort of pensive complaint)—"sometimes I hear it now, at night, running through my head."

"And you stayed there all night—*you*—in the damp?"
(with a tone of reproachful solicitude).

"No, not *all* night; about half the night, I think—I forget about the time; talking is very tiring work, and I was tired."

"Yes?"

"And then they grew anxious—Jemima and Sylvia—and came to look for me."

"Well?"

"And then they scolded me, and asked me what had happened to me, and I said I had seen a ghost; so I had."

The wind has no more to say; he has dropped; there is no noise but the swirl of the far water.

"Sylvia was quite interested," pursues Lenore, rousing herself, and even looking rather amused; "she wanted to know what sort of a ghost it was—whether a man's, or a woman's, or a child's, or a dog's—she said she had heard of dogs' ghosts being sometimes seen—and also whether it carried its head under its arm. I said, 'No, it did not;' and—and—and that is all, I think."

On the glacier-mountain there is a white glory that cannot be moonlight, for moon is there none; it must have stolen some of the sunset, and kept it in its bosom; the shadows steal over the lower snow, but the peaks keep that strange shining, such as Moses' face had when he came down from his high talk with God.

"Charlie," says Lenore, suddenly, with an abrupt change of subject, "does not it occur to you that at Pontresina the dead are much better lodged than the living? Would not you rather be here than at the *Croix Blanche?*"

"At the present moment, certainly," he answers, with a smile. "I prefer *you* and the smell of flowers to the German squaws and the smell of negus."

"Look," she says, rising from her grassy seat, "I am going to show you something. If I were old, or had any complaint that was likely to kill me, I will show you the exact spot where I should like to lie—how can you see? you have turned away your face. Pshaw! how absurdly sensitive you are! you are as bad as Jemima. If either of *you* were to point out to me the place that you wished to be your grave, I should listen with the most composed attention, and try to bear it in mind against the time when I should have the misfortune to lose you."

"I quite believe it," he answers, bitterly; "I have no doubt you would."

"See," she says, not heeding the bitterness, hardly hearing it, but pointing, with a smile, to a spot of ground, richer even than its neighbors in manifold-colored flowers and fine green grass, "did you ever see any thing so luxurious?—this wall's shadow to shelter me from the sun at noonday, and all these pink plantains to ripple above one's head. They say one does not hear when one is dead—well, as to that, I have my own opinion; but if one *could* hear, it would be pleasant to listen to the wind softly buffeting their tall heads in the dim summer nights, would not it?"

No answer.

"I would have no gilt tears, however, on my cross," she adds, a few minutes later.

He stoops and plucks a handful of the pink plantains, angrily, and then throws it away again.

"What are you doing?" she asks, turning with a gesture of surprise and remonstrance to him. "Why do you look so cross? Why are you frowning and clinching your hands? You foolish fellow, do you think, if I meant to die *really*, that I should talk about it so lightly—that I should pick and choose my grave? Good God! no!" (with a strong shudder)—"I should keep far enough from the subject!"

CHAPTER VII.

"On pain of death, let no man name death to me; it is a word infinitely terrible."

WHAT THE AUTHOR SAYS.

"Yes, they are certainly coming round," says Sylvia, with a tone of self-gratulation. "I met Mrs. Scrope just now on the stairs, and she said: 'You have been to the Rosegg? I hear there is quite a practicable road there? When once one has the *men* on one's side, one is all right; and, somehow, we always manage to enlist the sympathies of the fathers and husbands and brothers.'"

"I do not agree with you," says Jemima, taking her hat off and laying it on the table. "I think it is just the other way—the *women* to be propitiated, and the *men* follow naturally. Take care of the women, and the men will take care of themselves."

"They certainly dress very well," continues Sylvia, complacently; "nothing *voyant ;* all those pretty mouse-colors, and sad colors, and smoke-colors, that I am so devoted to. Very good taste; and, say what you will, *that* alone is enough to prepossess one in people's favor."

.   .   .   .   .   .

"I have just been falling into the arms of that dreadful little widow," Mrs. Scrope says, reëntering her own apartment at the same time as Sylvia has made her reappearance in hers. "Ambling up the stairs and coquetting with the banisters, as usual. She is *always* on the stairs."

"She reminds me of the women in Isaiah, don't you know?" says Mrs. Lascelles, laughing; "'walking and mincing as they go.' I wonder had they high-heeled shoes and a pannier? If it were the fashion to sew pillows to armholes nowadays, what gigantic *bolsters* she would have!"

"My dear, atrociously as that girl behaved, we never can be too thankful to her for having delivered us from the Prodgers connection. *Prodgers!*—such a name!"

"Do not halloo before you are out of the wood," says Mr. Lascelles, looking up from his novel for a moment, and instantly immersing himself in it again.

"I believe what first set her against him was the awful description I gave her of *our* honeymoon," says his wife, laughing again. "I told her about your being sea-sick all the way to St.-Malo. I remember she looked awe-struck at the time."

"It will be all on again before you can look round," says Mr. Lascelles, again emerging from his romance.

Both women shake their heads.

"Poor soul! it would hardly be worth while her being 'on' as you say, with any one."

"You mean that she is not long for this world?" replies he, dropping his book entirely this time. Mr. Lascelles's voice is never as low as Cordelia's, and the door is ajar.

"Hush!" cry both the women together. "Some one is passing; it may be one of them."

"I wish I could induce you *sometimes* not to speak at the very tip-top of your voice," says his wife. "If you remember, when you proposed to me, at the Inniskillings' ball, you expressed your wishes so loudly that you drowned the band."

CHAPTER VIII.

WHAT JEMIMA SAYS.

THE hotel is fuller than it was. This last week has made a difference. Several more little whitewash rooms are occupied. A member of the Alpine Club, with a harem of three gaunt women, battered and unsexed by much scaling of high mountains; two or three new couples. The last, an elderly clergyman and his wife, occupy the room next mine. Only this morning I was remarking on the thinness of the partition-walls: I can hear him alternately splashing and groaning in his tub.

"They have not been married long," Lenore says. "They say the Lord's Prayer together very loudly every night."

And Scrope asks, laughing, whether that is a proof of being newly wedded.

This was after breakfast. Since then we have been to the Rosegg glacier. Lenore has not been with us: gradually she is slipping out of our excursions. "For the present," she says; "just for the present, I am better at home." Now we are back again, Sylvia and I, in our own little sitting-room—a cheerful little place, whence one can look down on the white houses of the clean, narrow street, see the outgoers and incomers to the hotel, and catch bright glimpses of the mountains.

The door opens and Lenore enters, and at the same moment Sylvia passes out. "Is she gone?" says Lenore, advancing toward me; "*really* gone, do you think? I do not know why I ask; I have nothing particular to say." Her face is disturbed, and her eyes wander uneasily round.

"I—I—I have been *eavesdropping*," she says, beginning to laugh. "What do you think of that? And they say listeners never hear any good of themselves. That, however, is not a case in point, for I heard nothing about myself, of course—*nothing*."

"Eavesdropping!" I repeat, surprised. "That is not very like you. What do you mean? What are you talking about?"

"I was passing by the Scropes' door just now," she says, with a sort of hurry and agitation in her manner—"it was ajar, I wish people would keep their doors shut" (with a tone of irritability)—"and they were talking; the man—the husband—you know what a sweet, low voice he has—was saying, in a tone as loud as all the bulls you ever heard bellowing: 'She is not long for this world.' Whom do you think they were talking about?"

"My dear child," I say, impatiently, "what extraordinary things excite your curiosity! Am I a diviner of dark sayings? Probably some friend of their own that we never heard of."

"And then the woman said, 'Hush, hush!'" pursues she, with her eyes still watching my face. "Why did they say 'Hush?' if it were some friend of theirs; why should they mind being overheard? They were saying no ill of her."

"Pshaw!" say I, pettishly; "how do I know?"

"He said *she*, certainly—not *he*," she continues, as if unable to leave the subject. "*Not long for this world?*" (uttering the words very slowly). "Poor soul, whoever she is, I am sorry for her, are not you, Jemima?"

"Yes, yes, of course—very sorry," I answer, indistinctly, turning to the window.

"And yet it is absurd to be sorry for a person one has never seen—never heard of—is not it?" persists Lenore, again breaking out into a laugh. "Perhaps we are throwing away our compassion—perhaps it was a dog or a cat—who knows?"

"Very likely, very likely!"

"But why did they say 'Hush?'" she says, brooding over the word, and addressing the question rather to herself than to me.

I do not answer.

"Jemima," she says, following me to the window, "look round—I hate not being listened to when I am talking—I am going to make you laugh—you often laugh at my ideas; well, they are sufficiently ridiculous now and then; do you know I took it into my head—one is so egotistical —that perhaps they were talking of—of—me."

I lean out of the window, and try to persuade myself that my voice, as I say "*Nonsense,*" sounds lazily indifferent.

"You are not laughing," she cries, in a tone of alarm. "I thought you would have laughed. Why do not you laugh? Is it possible that you see nothing ridiculous in it —that you think it—it—is—*true!*"

"I think nothing of the kind," I answer, irritably: "do not be so absurdly fanciful."

"If they *did* mean me," she says, with the same restless, strained laugh, "they are alone in their opinion, are not they?—*quite* alone. It does *me* no harm, and it amuses them, I suppose—ha, ha!"

"What disease do they mean to kill me by, I wonder?" she says, after a pause, spent by her in rapidly traversing and retraversing the little room. "Consumption, of course" (shuddering). . . . "They should have seen you last winter," she resumes, by-and-by, standing beside me, and uneasily trying to see my face, "when you had that attack of influenza. How you coughed! Worse, far worse, than I do, and your head ached torturingly—mine seldom aches

—and you were so weak you could scarcely lift a finger, and yet it was only influenza!"

"Only influenza," I echo, mechanically; "influenza is nothing."

"Tell me," she says, a little reassured, and looking into my face as if she would *wring* from me the answer she longs for, "you must have an opinion one way or the other; do you *think* they meant me?"

"My dear," I say, driven into a corner, "did I hear what they said? I only know what you tell me; it—it is very conceited of you to imagine that they must be always talking of you."

"People are so fond of killing their friends, are not they?" she says, with the same wistful, searching look in her great and lovely eyes: "so are doctors, and very often the killed outlive the killers after all."

"Very often."

"Next time that I pass their door I shall run past with my fingers in my ears. Feel how my heart is beating!"

"You are growing as bad as Sylvia," I say, trying to speak gayly; "she is always requesting me to feel how her heart is beating; if you *both* set up nerves, I shall decamp."

"You think I may make my mind quite easy," she says, in a lighter tone, taking my hand in her two hot slender ones.

"Of course—of course."

"That they were talking of some one else—or that, if it *were* me, they were utterly and unaccountably mistaken?"

"To be sure!—to be sure!"

"But florid people often seem to think that those who are not so red and bulky as themselves must be in *articulo mortis.*"

" So they do."

"Jemima!" (still strongly clasping my hand in both hers), " if you believe it so firmly, you will not mind *swearing* it."

" What is the use of oaths and asseverations ? " I ask, uncomfortably. " Will not a simple assertion do as well ? "

" You *won't* swear ! " she cries, in a tone of profound alarm. " Why not ? Jemima, I do not like your face ! Your eyes will not meet mine—your lips are quivering— you are half crying. I know that I am very sick—that I have not much peace, day or night—but you do not think that it means any thing bad ?—that I am—O my God ! I cannot say the word ! "

Her sentence breaks off, smothered in a shuddering sob.

" I think nothing of the kind," I say, hastily, thoroughly frightened at her agitation. " Why *will* you gallop away with an idea ?—O Charlie! *do* come here; she is *so* impracticable—*so* unreasonable—she is talking *such* nonsense."

The door has opened, and Mr. Scrope is looking doubtfully in. At my words he enters hastily.

For the first time in her life she runs to him of her own accord, and throws herself into his arms. "O Charlie ! " she cries, wildly, " you are the only person in the world that is kind to me. They have been so cruel to me—so cruel. They have been saying such things of me—you would not believe it. That man—that Mr. Lascelles—says I am not long for this world, and Jemima quite agrees with him."

" Jemima is a fool ! " says Mr. Scrope, unjustly, looking with a momentary expression of raging hatred at me over her prone head.

" *Not long for this world !* " she repeats, with a sort of

moan, lifting her face, and staring pitifully into his. "Those were his very words: I have not altered one."

"Lout! idiot!" cries Scrope, angrily; "he had not an idea what he was saying!—he never has. My darling" (closely straining her to his heart, as if neither God, nor his fleet angel, Death, should avail to tear her thence), "please God, you are longer for this world than he is— than I—or Jemima—or any of us."

"Do you mean it, *really?*" she says, with an awful anxiety in her tone. "Are you serious? O God! how I wish I could think so!"

"Are you so anxious to outlive us all?" he asks, with a passionate melancholy. "Well, I dare say—it is natural, I suppose. Why should not you? Very likely you will have your wish."

"I want to live to be *quite* old," she says, hurriedly, not heeding his upbraiding eyes or tone. "I want to live a great many years: people are often happier when they are middle-aged than in youth; but it is pleasant to be young, too. It is not *all* pleasure, but there is a great deal. I do not complain—I do not complain." (She is trembling violently.) "Hold me!" she says, hysterically. "Do not let me go. You are the only person in the world to whom it matters much whether I die or live. Promise me that I shall not—oh, that dreadful word!—promise me!"

"I promise, darling," he says, "I promise."

"You speak uncertainly!" she says, wrenching herself out of his arms, and staring at him in a distrustful agony; "you are like Jemima—your face is all quivering. I believe you are telling me falsehoods on such a subject! Great God! can there be any thing wickeder than to deceive one—to tell one lies—in such a case?"

"Oh, my dear, I am not telling lies! Before God, I am not! I confidently trust—I altogether hope, that I shall yet see you strong and well as ever again. If I thought the contrary, do you think I could bear my own life for one minute?"

"What does it matter what you think—what you hope?" she cries, roughly, with one of her old, petulant movements; "will your trusting and hoping keep it off? Will telling lies about it make it any better?" (with an angry flash of her lovely, miserable eyes at us both). "Whatever you say—whatever you do—it is coming!—it is coming!"

She flings herself down on the little sofa, shuddering from head to foot, and buries her face in the pillow, while her whole frame is shaken by the violence of her sobs.

"My dearest child!" I say, half out of my sober wits with fright and pain, advancing to her, and gently touching her on the shoulder; "for Heaven's sake, do not be so excited! You are not very ill now, really, you know; you can go about a little, and walk, and talk, like the rest of us; but, if you behave in this way—"

"Where have my eyes been?" she interrupts, sitting up again, and speaking connectedly, but not calmly, while the great tears pour down her cheeks. "How is it that I have not seen all your looks and signs? If they had not thought me very bad, would the Scropes have spoken to me the other night? Not they! So I excited their *compassion*, did I? I had no idea that I was an object of *pity!* I never used to be. Oh, I am, indeed! They were right! I am, indeed!" (breaking into a fresh tempest of great sobs, and again hiding her face in the cushion).

"You are mistaken!" cries Scrope, beside himself at the sight of her agony, and throwing himself on his knees. "Look up, Lenore! Look up, beloved! Look in my face, and see whether I am telling truth. They talked to you

18

the other night because they knew that, if they were not civil to you, I should never speak to them again—because they *dared* not be impertinent to you. Why *should* they pity you, except for being younger and prettier than themselves?"

"You may save your breath," she answers, looking at him fixedly, with a sort of resentment; "there is no untrue thing that you would not say to me now, to keep me quiet. . . . It is very unjust," she cries out loud, clasping her lifted hands in a frenzy; "it is hard—there is no sense in it—that I, that am the youngest, should go first!—I, that was so pretty, and enjoyed my life so much! Some people only *half* live. Until we went to Dinan I lived every moment of my life. Since then I have been miserable, certainly—very miserable, now and then—but it was not half so bad as this! Oh, how gladly I would have it all over again! At least, I was *alive* then," she says, trembling violently. "Nobody pitied me *then!* After all, what does it matter what happens to one, so long as one is alive?—*that* is the great thing! Sometimes I have said I wished I was dead; but God knows I did not mean it. One says so many things that one does not mean. He *cannot* be so cruel as to take me at my word! Oh, He cannot! He cannot!"

Her voice dies in a wail—a wail of unspeakable fear.

"Good Heavens! what is the matter?" says Sylvia, opening the door and entering, her commonplace voice striking on us with a painful incongruity. "Why are you all pulling such long faces?"

We none of us answer her.

CHAPTER IX.

" Though one were fair as roses,
 His beauty clouds and closes ;
And well though love reposes,
 In the end it is not well."

WHAT JEMIMA SAYS.

LENORE has been very ill. Her very fear has acceler-
ated what she feared. During the night following the
conversation detailed in the last chapter, in a violent fit of
coughing, made more violent than usual by overpowering
emotion, by uncontrolled weeping, she has broken a blood-
vessel. It is in the dead of night ; every soul in the hotel
is asleep. Until they have tried it, no one can realize the
feeling of absolute helpless desperation that assails one
under such a catastrophe, happening in a remote and hard-
ly-accessible corner of Switzerland, utterly without doctors,
and four days' post from England. Since the days of Lenore's childhood, I have been entirely unused to the sight
of sickness. I have not the remotest idea what remedies
to apply ; neither is Sylvia any wiser. In my despair I
turn to the one person from whom I know that I shall get
at least passionate sympathy. Apparently he is not
asleep, for before I knock at his door he has opened it,
and stands before me in the dishevelled dress in which a
person usually appears who has sprung out of sleep into
his clothes, his curled locks tossed in the untidiness of
slumber, and the heavy lids still weighing on his blue
eyes.

"I thought it was your step," he says, hurriedly.
"Good Heavens ! what is it ? Is she—is she—"

"She is much worse; she has broken a blood-vessel," I answer, breathlessly. "What are we to do? what are we to do?" (wringing my hands). "No doctor to send for! One is so utterly helpless. What *is* to become of us?"

For an instant he has clinched his hands, with a movement of despair more absolute even than mine; then, under the urgent need for them, his strayed wits come back.

"There must be a doctor at St. Moritz," he says; "among two or three hundred visitors there always are one or two. I will knock up M. Enderlin, and make him saddle me a horse to go there."

"But what are we to do meanwhile?" I ask, helplessly. "You cannot be back for two hours, at soonest. We know nothing! Perhaps we may be throwing away her life, for want of knowing the right way to keep it."

"I will send my mother," he says.

He is already half-way down the long, chill passage. In twenty minutes more he is gone, and the whole house is astir. Doors are being opened; people of both sexes, evidently so slightly dressed as to avoid rather than court notice, protrude their heads, and ask what is the matter. Mrs. Scrope has come hurrying to us, with the entire self-forgetfulness of a kind-hearted person; come hurrying in a limp and corsetless dishabille, eminently becoming to a young girl, but cruelly trying to the best-looking woman of more advanced age. How many secrets of the prison-house must a fire, an alarm of burglary, or a sudden illness, have revealed before now! She has put something of calm and order into our disordered consternation. We do what little we can—alas! it is but little—and then wait—wait —try to imagine, as we sit in absolute silence and weary stillness in the little bare room, how far up the mountain-road to St. Moritz our messenger is; fancy a hundred times that we hear the hoofs of his back-coming horse long before he can possibly have reached his destination. Sylvia has disappeared. Certainly she was here when first I went to call Charlie, though she entirely declined to accompany me on that mission. Has she actually had the heart to go to bed again? I am not long left in doubt. As we sit, not speaking, in the dawn of the summer morning, that seems to have run half-way to meet the so-lately-gone evening, the door opens softly, and she enters. She has been making a toilet; an embroidered wrapper embraces her form, and a saffron ribbon is twisted in her black hair. The ruling passion strong in death!—not her own death, but that of another person.

"Can I be of any use?" she says, looking in.—"O Mrs. Scrope, how good of you to come to us in our trouble! I had not an idea that you were here."

I make signs to her not to speak, and also that the room is too confined to admit of *three* nurses. She disappears. It is full morning before the joyful sound that for hours we have been straining our ears to catch greets them. The doctor has arrived. He is a dirty-looking little fellow; some paltry apothecary, probably, to whom, were one in England, one would hardly intrust the care of a sick dog; but *now*, with what utter faith, with what intense and believing anxiety, do we listen to his *fiat!*

"He says it is only a small blood-vessel, after all," I say, trying to speak cheerfully, as I rejoin Charlie outside the door, and looking haggardly into his still more haggard face, in the early splendor of the strong young daylight. "Perhaps we have been making ourselves too miserable. She is to be kept absolutely quiet; only one person at a time in the room, and that one not to speak. She is to have all sorts of nourishing things. Good Heavens!" (breaking off in a sort of despair), "where are they to come from—here, where there is nothing but spiced beef as hard as a shoe, and skeleton fowls?"

"Why did you bring her here?" he asks, in a tone of angry misery. "Were you *mad?* It was *murder!*"

"We did it for the best," I answer, humbly; "the doctor recommended it, and she fancied it." . . .

As ill-luck will have it, next day there is a great yearly *fête* celebrated in the village; a stir and festal noise all the long day in the crowded street and through the house; doors banging, loud voices laughing. We have tried so earnestly to keep them quiet, but all in vain. When one is merry with beer, and that one has a holiday only twice or thrice a year, one cannot always, every moment, bear in mind the sufferings of an unknown, unseen stranger. It is drawing toward night again; still the clamor shows no symptom of abating. Now and again I hear Madame Enderlin's low, kind voice, in earnest remonstrance; but even she remonstrates in vain. The weather has grown very hot. Lenore lies on her side, dozing uneasily, moaning now and then. I sit beside her, bathing her hot hands with eau de Cologne and water, and give a fresh start of exasperation and apprehension at every fresh noise that penetrates through the door, left ajar to admit a little air into the close room, where open windows are forbidden, at least in the evening. Presently, a louder noise than any of the former ones reaches my tortured ears—a great and heavy stamping up the stairs—up—up—up. It reaches the passage on which all our doors open. I stretch my neck to see what it is, without moving, and, to my horror, discover that it is an Italian hurdy-gurdy man, with his instrument on his back. He is just stooping his hand to turn the handle, when I see Charlie rush wildly out of his own door, and with furious gestures stop him. The poor man is much surprised. "What! must not he play for the nora?"

. . . .

A month has passed. Lenore is again up; lies on the sofa in the sitting-room, dressed; again talks, sometimes again laughs.

"She wishes to see you," I say to Mr. Scrope, as we went in the passage; "she is quite looking forward to it. Will you go now?" My fingers are on the door-handle; I half turn it.

"Stay!" he cries, hastily, but in a low voice, putting his hand on mine to check it; "I am not ready. Wait a moment—tell me, how do I look?"

"What do you mean?" I say, half-laughing. "Are you taking a leaf out of Sylvia's book?"

"You know what I mean," he answers, impatiently. "Do I look cheerful—in good spirits—as if I had nothing on my mind?"

I scan his face doubtfully; I cannot answer in the affirmative.

"Her eyes looks me through and through," he says, excitedly. "No matter how much I lie, she is not deceived. Tell me, Mima, how can I make my face tell lies?—how can I look content?"

"She will ask you no questions," I answer, sadly; "at least, I think not—she has asked me none."

"Shall I—be—be—very much shocked?" he asks, in a whisper, "it is better to know what to expect—tell me."

"She is pulled down, of course," I answer, sorrowfully; "very much pulled down" (then, after a little pause): "my poor fellow, what is the use of buoying ourselves up with untrue hopes? It is the beginning of the end; the doctor himself said as much to me the other day."

CHAPTER X.

" The light upon her yellow hair,
    But not within her eyes ;
    The light still there upon her hair,
    The death upon her eyes."

WHAT THE AUTHOR SAYS.

" How much better you are looking ! "

In his own mind he has been practising this little speech—practising it with the proper intonation of half-surprised cheerfulness; when he comes to pronounce it really, it is a failure. There is a strained gayety in his tone that would hardly deceive a baby.

"More perjuries," she says, with a languid smile, looking up at him half-compassionately from her couch. "I will dispense you from telling any more stories; you told a great many the other day, but I do not think they will come much against you in the last account—but still—be on the safe side—tell no more of them."

"I—I said nothing but what I thought," he begins, with a stammering haste, but her great clear eyes looking steadily, though not unkindly through him, make his voice decline into silence.

" I have done crying for myself now," she says, with a sort of smile; "do not you think I have had plenty of time to do that in, during these last long, endless nights? I could not have believed a summer night *could* be so long. I have been sorrier for myself than I ever was for anybody else—but—but—I am getting used to it—I kick and scream no longer. Where is the use ? "

What had become of the stiff smile into which he had

so carefully trained his features? He has taken possession
of one of her pale hands; he seems to be very welcome to
it; she does not care whether he has it or has it not; he
has stooped and laid his bronzed cheek upon it to hide his
face.

> " ' As flies to wanton boys, so we to the gods ;
> They kill us for their sport ' "—

she says, dreamily repeating this couplet out of " King
Lear." " I suppose they are killing me for their sport ? "

" You are not to talk. Jemima says so," he says, raising his head, and speaking with a tone of shocked distress.

" Bah ! " she answers, slightingly, " if I am silent *forever*, will it save me? Do you think that, if I thought
there was the remotest chance of *that*, I would once open
my lips ? But what is the use of setting up one's little
bit of life, like an end of candle on a save-all, to make it
burn a few moments longer ? " A little dumb pause.
" You are crying," she says, presently, with one of her old
quick and irritable movements, which contrasts oddly and
painfully with her changed and almost extinguished voice.
" I hate to see a man cry ! It is unnatural—womanish—
it always makes me inclined to laugh."

" For God's sake, laugh, if you feel disposed ! " he
says, fiercely, dashing away his tears, as if ashamed and
angry at them. " I have been your butt always, Lenore !
I am willing to be so still."

" Are *you* going to quarrel with me ? " she asks querulously. " I suppose so ; sooner or later everybody does."

" Do they ? " (speaking softly, and again stooping his
head, to kiss her fingers).

" You blame me for talking," she says, presently, with
a sort of weary pettishness, " and then you do not volunteer a word yourself. Some one must speak ; we cannot
both sit dumb—mumchance."

"You are right," he says, making a great effort to speak easily and lightly. "I am more than ordinarily stupid to-day—headachy, I think—cobwebby."

"At least, do not look so woe-begone," she says, staring at him with discontented, tired eyes; "you make it worse for me—harder. I have been trying to persuade myself that what happens to every one cannot be so very bad— but you—your face upsets me!"

"How can I mend it?" he says, humbly and fondly. "I will try."

"After all, it is no such great catastrophe," she says, with a little bitter laugh; "nobody is much to be pitied but me—nobody cares much except myself, and, perhaps, *you*. Jemima *thinks* she is enormously grieved; she pulls a long face, but it is easy to see that it will not be the death of her—that she will survive many long and happy years to talk about ' poor dear Lenore.' "

He silently caresses her hand, but does not trust himself to embark on any speech.

"How strong you are!" she says, her eyes wandering steadily and coldly, with a sort of envy, over his face and figure.

"Certainly there are hands and hands" (again taking possession of her own, and laying it beside his to compare them). "If you do not play tricks with yourself—if you are moderately steady—what a long life you will probably have, full of action and pleasure and pleasant business! O my God!"—(breaking out into the passionate and so-absolutely-useless upbraidings that we sometimes address to the great Power above us)—"it is not fair—indeed it is not. How have you been so much better than I, that you should live so many happy years after I am gone?"

"O my love!" he cries, in a tone of the acutest pain, "why do you throw my strength in my teeth? Can I help it? Do you think it gives me any pleasure? Do you think that if I could be weak and sinking like you—*now*—this minute—that I should complain much?"

"Of course you would," she answers, feebly but brusquely, "as much as I do. Of course you are glad to be strong; you would be an idiot if you were not; as long as one has good health, one has *every thing!* one can get over every other trouble but that—that—"

He shakes his head dissentingly. More than once the effort of talking has brought on an access of coughing, but Scrope's remonstrances are vain; she is resolute to carry on the conversation.

"Fifty years hence you will probably still be here," she says, in the same faint, envious voice. "You are twenty-eight now—yes—a hale, strong man of seventy-eight—still alive—still enjoying—children and grandchildren all about you."

"Never!" he says, violently starting up, and walking about the room in disordered haste. "I shall never have a child! If you leave me, Lenore, I shall never have a wife."

"Pooh!" she says, contemptuously, "five years hence you will be a respectable *père de famille.* What do I say? *Five* years?—three—two—and, when you are talking about your conquests, you will have to think twice before you can recollect what color my eyes were, or which of the dry, dirty hair-locks in your pocket-book was mine."

"At least you are consistent," he cries, fiercely, stopping suddenly beside her, his face white and disfigured with angry grief; "all your life your object has been to give pain. Well, I congratulate you; weak and changed as you are in other ways, you are still unchanged in that—are still as able as ever to cut to the heart."

"Why should not I?" she says wearily, rolling her

head from side to side on the pillow. "I have been cut to the heart enough in my day; why should not other people go shares with me? . . . . Until we went to Dinan," she resumes, by-and-by, "I had always had my own way; I never remember the time when I had not. I always said that, if ever I not did get my own will in any thing, it would be the death of me. I remember telling Paul so almost the first time I saw him; I thought it rather a fine thing to say; I never dreamed of its coming true, but it has."

"Not yet—not yet!" he remonstrates, passionately.

"Not that I am dying of love," she says, raising herself, and speaking with more energy than she has yet shown. "Never say, or let any one else say, that. Whatever tales one may have heard to that effect, I do not believe any one ever did such a thing in this world. If I had not been sickly to begin with, I *could* not have fretted myself into my grave, however hard I had tried. I should have grown yellow, and pinched, and withered, before my time, but should have *lived*. Yes, if I had not been sickly, radically sickly, to begin with, I should have lived."

"Live now!" he cries wildly, throwing himself down on his knees beside her sofa, and looking up with all the sorrowful madness of his blue eyes into her face. "Why should not you? Perhaps you will never again be very strong, but there is no reason why you may not live—yes, live for many years. This climate is too harsh for you; when you grow a little stronger, let me take you away to a warmer, suaver one—to Italy—the south of France; let me take you, Lenore—take my *wife*—the only wife I shall ever have."

"Your *wife!*" she says, with a smile wholly sorrowful yet touched with a little gratification. "I thought we had heard the last of that old story."

" *Never !* " he answers, vehemently. " *Never !* As long as I am near you, you will *never* hear the last of it."

"If you honestly wish to marry me," she says, looking half-gratefully at him with her large and languid eyes; " yes, you look honest, it is a way you have; but, if you wish it seriously, it must be only as a penance. Even good men, who have loved their wives to begin with, if they fall sick, and remain for a long time ailing invalids, grow tired of them; against their will they grow tired of them. If I lasted long enough, you would grow tired, heartily tired, of me."

"" Should I ? " (with an expressive accent).

Again she shakes her head.

" There are worthier occupations in life for a young and handsome man than carrying cushions and shaking physic-bottles."

"Tastes differ," he says, smiling a little, though not very merrily. " I think not."

" Who *could* love me now ? " she asks, with a movement of disbelieving self-contempt. " *Aimer d'amour*, I mean; they might love me in the sense in which good and tender-hearted people love any thing that is miserable and suffering; but that is not the way in which I used to be loved—not the way in which I care to be loved."

" Neither is it the way in which I love you," he answers, firmly.

" Why do you tantalize me ? " she cries, angrily, pushing her heavy hair irritably away from her blue-veined temples; " talking about what we shall do *if I live*. I shall *not* live—I shall die ! Often—so often—in the past nights, when you have all been comfortably, warmly asleep, I have said over and over to myself, 'Lenore Herrick is dead,' trying how it would sound."

" Hush—hush ! " he says, unutterably pained; then,

after a little silence, "Lenore" (speaking with a shaking voice and quivering features), "even if you are right—even if you are not to live long—why do you make me face this frightful possibility? But even if it is so, let me at least be able to look back out of my desolation, and think, that though God was in a hurry to part us, yet that for a short time—after long and weary waiting—you were my very own—belonging to me—called by my name."

"If I am to die," she says, harshly, "what does it matter what name I am called by?—what name is cut on my gravestone? Shall I lie any the easier because you wear crape and weepers for me?"

Again he says, "Hush! hush!"

"You are unwise to wish that I were well," she says presently, with a sort of pitying smile; "it is against your own interest. I am quite fond of you now—*quite!* I like to feel your hand coolly clasping mine; I like to send you on messages; you are so zealous and so speedy. I like to see your handsome, sorrowful face come in at the door."

Again he bends his head over her hand to hide his dumb agony.

"If you had not been here, I should have sadly felt the want of some one to cry over me," she continues mournfully smiling; "nobody else would have done it, certainly. I do not blame them; I never cried over anybody else, or was at all pitiful or sympathetic in my day. I reap my own sowing, but still it is pleasanter as it is."

He is kissing her hands over and over again, but he makes no rejoinder.

"But yet," she pursues, gravely, "I have a misgiving that, if I grew strong and well again, I should have as little relish for your society as ever; I should shrink from your touch, and fly at the distant sound of your voice, as I did in the old days of our engagement. Do not look mis-

erable; my affection for you will never be put to that test
—only say nothing more about my being your wife; I wish
for that as little as ever. I love you as a child loves its
nurse, not as a woman loves her husband."

Poor Scrope! his last Spanish castle has fallen into
ruin: by her cold and friendly words she has torn into tatters the airy fabric of his last poor dream.

"I was wrong," he says, after a pause, in a strangled
voice, "selfish as I always am. I will be—be—content."

A long, long silence. Outside, the cheery footsteps of
guests in the hotel running down-stairs, in preparation for
some pleasant expedition; loud and happy voices calling
to one another. Lenore lies back, with closed eyes, exhausted by the previous conversation, and yet it is she that
resumes it.

"How long do they give me?" she asks, faintly, but
calmly; "if you are truly my friend, you will tell me.—
No? Well, then, I must remain in my ignorance."

Another pause; the gay picnic-party have packed themselves into their carriage; with a noise of wheels and bells
they are off.

"Before you go," says Lenore, again speaking, "I have
one more thing to say to you; it will pain you sharply,
but that is nothing new, is it? You will writhe and shudder,
as I have already seen you do two or three times to-day—
well—I cannot help it—you are the only person I can
speak to about it; if I were to broach the subject to Jemima, she would put her fingers in her ears, and run out of
the room.

"What is it?" he asks, indistinctly.

"When—it is—all over," she says, very slowly, but
with composure; "when I am—*gone*, do not let them take
me back to England; was not it Châteaubriand who said
that there was something revolting to him in the idea of a

dead person on a journey?—well—I agree with him. Make them bury me here—in the little mountain grave-yard, where you and I sat on that Sunday evening, when first you came—are you listening?—will you promise?"

"I promise," he answers, unsteadily.

"How grand it was!" she says, leaning back, with closed eyes, and smiling dreamily, "I see them now—all those great peaks cutting the pale-green sky with their jagged teeth—now that I am to leave the world so soon, I wish it were uglier; perhaps 'it would be easier to go— O my God!" (opening her eyes, and clasping her hands together in utter bitterness of spirit), "I do love this very world—just as it is—other people find fault with it, but I do not—I love it—I love it—oh, why may not I stay a lit-tle in it?"

.   .   .   .

"Bury me under the west wall," she says, "beneath the catchfly and the blown dandelions!"

CHAPTER XI.

WHAT JEMIMA SAYS.

YET another month has smoothly slidden past, and we are here still. We know not how much longer we may have to bide here; but, alas! we do know that when we go we shall not all go; but that one of us, whether we will it or not, must stay behind. One of us God has called, saying to her, both in the dark night and in the broad blue noon, "Come!" and to that strong bidding there can be said no "Nay." This is an invitation to which we cannot say, "I will not," or "I will." Bidden, one must go.

Thus our Lenore is going. We say so now, and so it is. At first, we did not breathe it even to ourselves; then, after a while, each whispered it low to her own sad heart: *now*, we say it aloud to one another.

We have been here ten weeks; the summer, that we found in its first cool youth, has now assumed the hot gravity of its August ripeness. We have outlived many lovely dynasties of the flowers; have seen them arise and prosper, and then sweetly die. O flowers! give us a lesson; teach us your way of dying, your gentle, unregretting extinction. *Our* Death is a cruel fellow; he is not content to take us with a kindly mildness. Did he but stretch out a friendly hand to us, some among us would not be overloath to put ours in it, and go away with him whither he list. But he comes with his eyeless, ash-gray skull-face; with his racks and his scourges—can he blame us that we shrink and shiver away from him? Lenore has been looking him steadily in the face now, for a long time past, but still she shivers, still she pales, at the sound of his nearing feet. Lenore is among those who go, *knowing* it. Some depart smiling; ignorantly babbling of fond home trifles, with eyes still fixed on earth's dear, sunshiny hills and plains. Overhead in the flood are they plunged, or ever they know that they are within sight of its bank. But Lenore knows. I am uncertain whether we should ever have had the heart to tell her; whether we should not have let her slip into the next world, without being aware of it. For myself, I think it the kinder plan; I think that, to one whom God has summoned, *Himself* will reveal it in meet time, without the intervention of any harsh human voice saying roughly, "You will die." But, as you know, an accident has revealed it to Lenore. Sometimes she forgets it for a moment; sometimes the conquered spirit of youth reasserts itself; sometimes she talks gayly of what

she will do next year; sometimes she rives our hearts by
making plans for the winter, whose snows she will never
feel, for the now-distant spring, whose flowers will open
upon her grave.   But it is only for a little while that the
beautiful illusion lives; always it vanishes, as the cold dew
vanishes from the fine, fresh morning grass.

It is a fearfully hot day, softly overcast; the keen
mountain-air, cool and crisp, which so rarely fails from
these high places, has gone to draw new sharpness from the
snows, and left us gasping.   A silent day, but for the
loud rumblings of the thunder in the great, grand hills.

Sylvia sits in her bedroom, crying over the last volume
of a Tauchnitz novel, benevolently lent her by Mrs. Scrope,
which makes her hotter still.   Lenore lies, with heavy eyelids drooped over sunk eyes, on the sofa in our sitting-
room; it has been transformed, as much as possible, into
the likeness of a couch, and drawn up close to the window,
to catch any stray little travelling breeze.   Breathing is
always difficult to Lenore now, but to-day specially so.   I
am sitting beside her, fanning her.   She expressed a while
ago a sudden longing for lemonade, as a nice, cool drink.
I ask Kolb to make me some, as it is a beverage that does
not grow ready-made in these parts.   Kolb's lemonade is
produced by pouring hot water on lemons; five minutes
ago it entered *boiling*.   I have been pouring the whole
stock of water contained in my bedroom's tiny ewer and
bottle into a wash-hand basin, and causing the lemonade-
jug to stand in it, in the forlorn hope of cooling it through
the agency of this half-pint of tepid water.   Now I have
returned to Lenore, and am fanning her again.   The languid flies come and march about upon her outflung arms,
with their little tickling, maddening legs, and when I
strike out wildly and indignantly at them, with a little
self-conscious buzz they fly away and elude me.   With my

resentful eyes I have followed one to the wall, where he stands twisting his hind-legs together. Then my sad gaze returns to the place where it has dwelt all morning—Lenore's sunken, weary, pained face; the face that might as well be any one else's, for all resemblance that it bears to hers—hers, our beauty! O bad, cruel Death! Why cannot you take us all at once, without first stealing beauty and grace and harmony? Do you care to hold nothing but disfigurement and decay in your frosty arms? I am sorrowfully pondering on the probability of her passing to-day—half wishing it, and yet half grudging—when her eyes slowly unclose, and she speaks.

"You fan me badly," she says, feebly and complainingly; "so irregularly, and intermittently—not half so well as Charlie does. Send him."

"But, my dear," I say, gently remonstrating, "you always *will* talk to him, you know, and you are not up to it."

"I *mean* to talk to him," she says, with a pitiful shadow of her old resolute wilfulness. "I have something to say to him—something I *must* say to him—a favor to ask of him."

"A favor?"

"Yes," she answers, petulantly, "a favor; but it is nothing to you; it is not you that I am going to ask—send him."

So I obey. I find him sitting in his own room, his hands thrust into his tossed bright hair, and his eyes, red with watching and weeping, idly fixed on the cruel color of the unfeeling smiling hills. "She has sent for you," I say, entering listlessly. "She says you fan her so much better than I do. She has also something to say to you, a favor to ask—a *favor*—what can it be?" I end, a little inquisitively. He does not pay any heed to my curiosity;

he is already in the passage when I call him back. "Stay,"
I say; "before you go, bathe your eyes and try to smile;
you know, poor soul, she—she likes us to look cheerful."

CHAPTER XII.

WHAT THE AUTHOR SAYS.

"How long you have been!" she says, querulously.
"I thought you were never coming. You might have
made a little haste."

"I will be quicker next time, darling," he answers,
kneeling down gently beside her, and speaking firmly and
cheerfully.

"Fan me," she says, panting; "fan me strongly and
regularly."

She lies back exhausted, and he hears her mutter:

"At least wherever I go, I shall have breath."

Utter silence for five minutes, save for the gentle noise
made by the winnowing of the fan.

"Lift me," she says, stretching out her arms to him.
"Lying down I gasp."

He lifts her with delicate care, and her dying head
droops in sisterly abandoment on his kind shoulder.

"Dear old fellow," she says, faintly; "kind old
brother."

Yet another pause; no sustained conversation is possible.

"I am going very fast, Charlie."

"Yes, darling."

"I was always one to do things quickly, if I did them at all—I was never a dawdle."

No answer.

"You will get away before the season is over, after all."

"O love, hush!"

"You would do something to oblige me, would not you, Charlie?"

"Any thing possible, beloved."

"But supposing it were impossible?"

"Still I would do it."

"That is right," she answers, with a sigh of relief. "I am glad."

Then she is again silent for a long time. The thunder still grumbles deeply in the hot heart of the hills, and the flies still walk about torpidly upon her white wrapper.

"You know all the old story—about Paul," she says, presently, with a little excitement in her faint and hollow voice.

"Yes, I know it."

"You know the reason why I have borrowed the advertisement sheet of your *Times* every day?"

"I—I have guessed it."

"I have daily looked carefully through the marriages," she says, with a sort of feeble eagerness, "but I have never seen *his*."

"Neither have I."

A long and painful fit of coughing intervenes.

"Tell me the rest to-morrow," he says, gently bending over her.

She smiles slightly.

"It is all very well for *you* to talk—*you*, who are rich in to-morrows. How do I know that I have one?"

Again he fans her, trying to coax the cool little waves of air to her hot and parted lips.

"He said it—was—to be—*immediately*," she murmurs, after a pause; "since it has not been yet—perhaps—it will never be."

"Perhaps."

"Very likely it is broken off," she says, a ray of pleasure lighting up her face. "I never told you so before—but—between ourselves—I do not think—he was very eager about it. No doubt it is broken off."

"No doubt."

She has taken his hand, and is stroking it with a sort of patronizing caressingness.

"Kind, good, patient Charlie!" she says, softly. "Whose errands will you run on—when I am gone?"

No answer.

"I have *one* more errand to send you on," she continues, with feeble eagerness; "longer, disagreeabler, more difficult, than any of the others. Will you run on it, too?"

"O beloved, try me!"

"There is at least one advantage in being in a dying state," she says, by-and-by, gravely and solemnly; "as long as I was well I could not send for him—could not ask him to come back to me—could not move a finger to bring him—all the advances must have come from *him*. But now—*now*—I may send for whom I please, and no one will call me unmaidenly, will they?"

"No one," he answers steadily, though his face is drawn with the pain of finding that still, in those last hours, he is second, always second. She is looking earnestly at him; her large gray eyes—unnaturally, unbecomingly large now—are reading his countenance like an open book.

"It hurts you," she says, calmly; "well, I have always hurt you. I suppose you like it, or you would not have stayed with me, but would have gone, as Paul did. Well,

have I made you understand? I wish to send for him."
For a second he turns away his head, and gathers his
strength together; then he says, kindly and gently:

"Do you wish me to write or telegraph?"

"I wish neither," she answers, with a little impatience;
"do you think that *that* is my errand? That would not
be a very hard one, just to walk down to the post-office; I
might charge even Sylvia with that. Listen: of course
you need not do it unless you wish; of course I cannot
make you. I wish to make sure. I wish you to *go and
fetch him.*"

He gives an involuntary start of utter pain and anguish.

"And leave *you*, O my darling?"

"And leave me," she echoes, pettishly; "what good
do you do me? What good does any one do me? Can
you give me breath or sleep?"

He rises and walks to the window. The evening draws
on, and the thunder is dumb. He looks out on the great
mountains—lilac while the sun is setting, gray when he is
gone—the mountains whose playfellows the swift snow-
storms are, and about whose necks the clouds wreathe
their wet, white arms; looks at the deep torrent courses
that furrow their sides, and at the straight, dark pines,
which the winter strips not, and to whom lavish Spring,
with her gentian-wreath, and her lap full of flowered
grasses, brings no embellishment; looks at them all, without seeing them. Then he comes back to the couch-side,
and says—

"I will go."

"You think he will not come?" she says, looking wistfully at him. "I see it in your face, but I know better; if
you had seen him at Bergun, you would have thought differently. Yes" (with a little, shining smile), "he will
come!"

" There is no doubt of it," he replies, quietly.

" Even if he is married he will come," she says, still smiling; " his wife will spare him for those few days, and, if she hesitates, you may tell her that, whatever I was once, I am not a person to be jealous of now."

Silence.

" You will set off to-morrow morning, *early*," she says, feverishly. " I am afraid it is too late to-day. You know his address? Oh, yes, of course; you have been there?"

" Yes."

" And you will *certainly* bring him—*certainly?* "

" Yes."

She closes her eyes with a long sigh of relief. She lies so still that he is uncertain whether she sleeps; but, after a time, she opens them again.

" You wonder why I wish so much to see him again," she says, slowly, " when he does not wish to see me; you think it is *love*. No, it is not. When one is as sick as I am, one is past love; only all the night through his face *vexes* me. I am worried with it; it never leaves me; I torment myself trying to recall every line of it. I *must* see whether I have remembered it right; it has been with me every moment in this world. I must take it, distinct and clear, with me into the next."

CHAPTER XIII.

"Lilies for a bridal-bed;
Roses for a matron's head;
Violets for a maiden dead."

WHAT JEMIMA SAYS.

CHARLIE is gone. Very early to-day he set off. I stood by him on the steps, in the cool of the young and shining morning, as he prepared to step into the carriage which was to take him up and down the long, steep mountain-passes to Chur.

"Keep her till I come back," he said, wringing my hand with unknowing violence. "If I come back to find her gone, I shall never forgive you—never. Promise!"

"How can I promise?" I said, sorrowfully. "Have I life and death in my hand? How can I hinder her going?"

So he is gone, and we are waiting—waiting with strained ears and hot eyes—to see which will win the race to Lenore's side, Death or Paul. Lenore herself fights with all her strength—alas, how little!—with a strength not her own—on Paul's side. She *refuses* to die. For more than a week past she has turned with loathing from every species of nourishment; now she demands it greedily. She will not speak—will not utter a word—for fear of wasting the little breath that remains to her. People are very kind; every hour of the day solicitous faces meet us on the landing-place, with pitying gestures and expressions of sympathy. Guests in the hotel tread softly, and scold their children when they hear them whooping and noisily tumbling, with the utter unfeelingness of childhood, down the slight stairs, and along the thin-walled passages.

19

. . . .

And now all the days between Scrope's going and his expected back-coming have rolled away. Before he went, we calculated accurately together distances and times; this is the day on which he engaged to return. Lenore is still here—still fighting—disputing her life, inch by inch, hand to hand, with the all-victor.

"He will come to-day," she has said, speaking for the first time for many hours—speaking confidently. "It is my lucky day; something tells me so."

I have drawn the scant window-curtain, and thrown wide the window, and looked out on the unutterable majesty of the morning hills.

"I *will* not die to-day!" she says, clinching her feeble hand. "I have some life left in me yet—more than you think. It would be too cruel to go before he came; he would be so disappointed." I turn and gaze mournfully at her. Her voice is stronger, and the inward excitement of her soul has sent a last little flame of color to her cheeks. "Let us be ready for him," she says, with a tender smile. "Take away all those physic-bottles—every thing that looks like sickness. Make the room pretty; gather plenty of flowers."

So I obey her. All about the room, following her directions, I place the gay, sweet flowers. O wonderful, lovely flowers!—whence do you steal your tender strains? Is it from the brown earth or the colorless wind? Later on, as the day draws toward noon, she expresses a wish to be dressed. I remonstrate gently, fearing the exhaustion consequent on so unwonted an exertion; but she is resolute.

"I shall wish so few things any more," she says, simply and pleadingly; "you may as well let me have my way." Thus I tearfully consent. "The old blue gown," she says, with an eager smile; "Louise will find it among my things. It is the only one among my clothes that he ever praised. He never was one to notice clothes, but he liked that. Only the last time I saw him he was talking of it."

So, with many pauses, slowly and mournfully, with sorrowful faces, as if we were already dressing her for her grave, we dress her in the old blue gown. Alas! it is pitifully large for her. But she is not yet satisfied. In spite of pain, in spite of utter prostration, she must also have her hair dressed—her long, bright hair—the one thing that remains to her.

"Plait it round and round my head," she says, looking with feverish entreaty into my sad face. "Take great pains. Put no *frisettes*—nothing artificial; he does not like it; but yet let it be becoming."

Becoming! at such a time! O God! Amazed I look at her, and a half doubt enters my mind that I have been allotting her too short a space of further life. Her voice sounds certainly stronger, and there is a ray of living animation in her great, sunken eyes. Toward evening she grows very restless, and I hear her murmur to herself, "He must make haste—make haste. The road is long and steep—so many sharp turns and twists. I hope the horses are sure-footed. But it is only for *once;* he might make haste." She is as one running a hard race that is nearing the goal, but hears his rival's feet close upon his track, and strains every tense nerve in the effort and agony of attainment. Will she attain her goal? It is the question that, as day droops into night, makes us all ever more and more breathless. She speaks little with her faint lips, but with her hunted, piteous eyes she *entreats* us to keep her. I cannot bear those eyes.

The light is gone, and the candles are lit. "Let me read to you a little," I say, softly, in a tear-strangled voice.

"Yes," she answers; "yes; if you will—if you like."

But she is not listening. I sit down with the Bible upon my knees. I can hardly see the page for tears. I scarcely know where I turn. I begin at the words of god-like consolation that fit any grief; that come never amiss: "Come unto me all ye that labor and are heavy laden." They open the fount of my own sorrow, that requires but a touch to unclose it. "Are you listening?" I ask, gently, trying to scan her face across the candle's feeble flame.

"Yes," she answers, with a sort of hurry; "yes—to be sure—I am listening!—but read lower; one cannot hear any little noise outside when you read so loud."

Sighing, I lay down the book, and walking to the window look out—look out at the little quarter moon, and the travelling stars—the sky, that speaks of deep and unutterable quietness—the dark mountain-bulks, with flashes of silver on their giant flanks—the narrow street, with the lights from the hotel playing on the little houses opposite —the small, white cross gleaming in the moonlight—the solitary pacer down the tongueless street—the solemn glacier-river that saith nothing light, but singeth ever the plain, hoarse song.

"After all—I shall have to go!" she says, with a low wail. "I cannot wait—I cannot. O Paul! you might have hurried!"

I here thrust my head as far out of the window as it will go. I am listening. At first, nothing but the river— nothing! O river! I hate you; be silent for once. Then a little noise mixes with it—so small and uncertain that one cannot positively say at first that it is not a part of the stream's roar; then it separates itself—grows distinct— nears. I turn to the bed, with an unspeakable weight lifted from my heart. "He is coming!" I say, with a smile; but already she has heard. Could I expect my ears to be keener than hers? Even in death she looks very joyful. As the carriage noisily rolls up toward the hotel, I turn with the intention of going down to meet the travellers; but she stops me.

"Stay!" she says, stretching out her hand eagerly. "Do not go! I forbid you! I will have the first look!"

So we remain in absolute silence for two enormous minutes; then the sound of a step running quickly and lightly up the stairs—*a* step—surely there is only *one!* The door opens, and Charley enters, haggard, travel-stained, and *alone*. She does not even look at him; her eyes are staring, with an awful, eager intentness, at the door behind him; but no one follows, nor does he leave it open, as if expecting to be followed. On the contrary, he closes it behind him.

"Great God!" I say, running up to him, half out of my wits with excitement, "what is this? You have come without him. You have not brought him!"

He does not answer.

Putting me aside, he goes hastily to the couch, kneels down beside it, taking her gently in his arms, and says, in a hoarse voice:

"My darling, I have broken my promise—but I could not help it—it was not my fault. He—he—has not come, because—because it was his wedding-day when I got there. O beloved, speak to me! Say you forgive me—you are not going without *one* word—speak—speak!"

But Lenore will never speak to him any more: her head has sunk back, with all its pretty, careful plaits, on his shoulder—Lenore has

"Gone through the straight and dreadful pass of death."

THE END.

COOPER'S
LEATHER-STOCKING NOVELS.

"THE ENDURING MONUMENTS OF FENIMORE COOPER ARE HIS WORKS. WHILE THE LOVE OF COUNTRY CONTINUES TO PREVAIL, HIS MEMORY WILL EXIST IN THE HEARTS OF THE PEOPLE. SO TRULY PATRIOTIC AND AMERICAN THROUGHOUT, THEY SHOULD FIND A PLACE IN EVERY AMERICAN'S LIBRARY."—*Daniel Webster.*

A NEW AND
SPLENDIDLY-ILLUSTRATED POPULAR EDITION
OF
FENIMORE COOPER'S
WORLD-FAMOUS
LEATHER-STOCKING ROMANCES.

D. APPLETON & Co. announce that they have commenced the publication of J. Fenimore Cooper's Novels, in a form designed for general popular circulation. The series begins with the famous "Leather-Stocking Tales," five in number, and will be published in the following order, at intervals of about a month:

I. The Last of the Mohicans.
II. The Deerslayer. **IV. The Pioneers.**
III. The Pathfinder. **V. The Prairie.**

This edition of the "Leather-Stocking Tales" will be printed in handsome octavo volumes, from new stereotype plates, each volume superbly and fully illustrated with entirely new designs by the distinguished artist, F. O. C. Darley, and bound in an attractive paper cover. *Price, 75 cents per volume.*

Heretofore there has been no edition of the acknowledged head of American romancists suitable for general popular circulation, and hence the new issue of these famous novels will be welcomed by the generation of readers that have sprung up since Cooper departed from us. As time progresses, the character, genius, and value of the Cooper Romances become more widely recognized; he is now accepted as the great classic of our American literature, and his books as the prose epics of our early history.

D. APPLETON & CO., Publishers, New York.

GRACE AGUILAR'S WORKS.

HOME INFLUENCE. A Tale for Mothers and Daughters. Cloth, $1.

THE MOTHER'S RECOMPENSE. A Sequel to Home Influence. Cloth, $1.

WOMAN'S FRIENDSHIP. A Story of Domestic Life. Cloth, $1..

THE VALE OF CEDARS; or, the Martyr. Cloth, $1.

THE DAYS OF BRUCE. A Story from Scottish History. 2 vols. Cloth, $2.00.

HOME SCENES AND HEART STUDIES. Tales. Cloth, $1.

THE WOMEN OF ISRAEL. Characters and Sketches from the Holy Scriptures. Two vols. Cloth, $2.00.

CRITICISMS ON GRACE AGUILAR'S WORKS.

HOME INFLUENCE.—" Grace Aguilar wrote and spoke as one inspired ; she condensed and spiritualized, and all her thoughts and feelings were steeped in the essence of celestial love and truth. To those who really knew Grace Aguilar, all eulogium falls short of her deserts, and she has left a blank in her particular walk of literature, which we never expect to see filled up."—*Pilgrimages to English Shrines, by Mrs. Hall.*

MOTHER'S RECOMPENSE.—" ' The Mother's Recompense ' forms a fitting close to its predecessor, 'Home Influence.' The results of maternal care are fully developed, its rich rewards are set forth, and its lesson and its moral are powerfully enforced."—*Morning Post.*

WOMAN'S FRIENDSHIP.—" We congratulate Miss Aguilar on the spirit, motive, and composition of this story. Her aims are eminently moral, and her cause comes recommended by the most beautiful associations. These, connected with the skill here evinced in their development, insure the success of her labors."—*Illustrated News.*

VALE OF CEDARS.—" The authoress of this most fascinating volume has selected for her field one of the most remarkable eras in modern history—the reigns of Ferdinand and Isabella. The tale turns on the extraordinary extent to which concealed Judaism had gained footing at that period in Spain. It is marked by much power of description, and by a woman's delicacy of touch, and it will add to its writer's well-earned reputation."—*Eclectic Rev.*

DAYS OF BRUCE.—" The tale is well told, the interest warmly sustained throughout, and the delineation of female character is marked by a delicate sense of moral beauty. It is a work that may be confided to the hands of a daughter by her parent."—*Court Journal.*

HOME SCENES.—" Grace Aguilar knew the female heart better than any writer of our day, and in every fiction from her pen we trace the same masterly analysis and development of the motives and feelings of woman's nature."—*Critic.*

WOMEN OF ISRAEL.—" A work that is sufficient of itself to create and crown a reputation."—*Mrs. S. C. Hall.*

D. APPLETON & CO., Publishers.